A GOOD
NEIGHBORHOOD

ALSO BY THERESE ANNE FOWLER

A Well-Behaved Woman

Z: A Novel of Zelda Fitzgerald

A GOOD
NEIGHBORHOOD

THERESE ANNE FOWLER

ST. MARTIN'S PRESS ⚏ NEW YORK

First published in the United States by St. Martin's Press, an imprint of St. Martin's Publishing Group

A GOOD NEIGHBORHOOD. Copyright © 2020 by Therese Anne Fowler. All rights reserved. Printed in the United States of America. For information, address St. Martin's Press, 120 Broadway, New York, NY 10271.

www.stmartins.com

Designed by Omar Chapa

The Library of Congress Cataloging-in-Publication Data is available upon request.

ISBN 978-1-250-23727-9 (hardcover)
ISBN 978-1-250-27053-5 (international, sold outside the U.S.,
subject to rights availability)
ISBN 978-1-250-23728-6 (ebook)

Our books may be purchased in bulk for promotional, educational, or business use. Please contact your local bookseller or the Macmillan Corporate and Premium Sales Department at 1-800-221-7945, extension 5442, or by email at MacmillanSpecialMarkets@macmillan.com.

First Edition: February 2020

10 9 8 7 6 5 4 3 2 1

For Wendy and John, who always see me through

ACKNOWLEDGMENTS

This story formed itself in my mind long before I felt ready to write a word of it. *A Good Neighborhood* is very different from the historical novels I'm known for, and to change course could be a career risk. Yet these characters and their intertwined fates, the story of their conflicts and the fallout that ensues, felt urgent to me. To write their story felt necessary, a kind of activism in our troubled and troubling times.

But there was also the matter of me, a white author, needing to create points of view for two African American characters who are integral to the story. I approached the project with respect, aiming for accurate representations, mindful of the ways white authors have gotten things wrong. Around that time I saw Zadie Smith give a talk. Responding to a writer in the audience who asked whether white authors should ever write from black characters' points of view, Smith said, in essence, an author can and should write whatever she wants to. She said if you're going to have characters who aren't like you, just do your homework. This echoed my belief. I did extensive homework (on that issue and all the other relevant ones) and with everything I'd learned in mind, I wrote this novel.

I see my friends and neighbors in these pages, the faces of my community and of my country and of our interconnected world. It's a story that I hope will provoke readers to consider how easy it is for good people to make poor choices, not through deliberate malice but more often due to habit or convention, to inattention or fear. And it's a story that says malice is at work, too, and we have to become the bulwark that refuses to let it win.

I want to extend my gratitude to the following folks whose guidance, aid, oversight, vetting, faith in me, assistance, support, and/or friendship helped make this book and its publication possible: Wendy Sherman, Sarah Cantin, Sally Richardson, Jen Enderlin, Lisa Senz, George Witte, Dori Weintraub, Rachel Diebel, Jessica Zimmerman, Lucy Stille, Jenny Meyer, Cherise Fisher, Trina Allen. Special thanks to Olga Grlic for another stunning cover design, and to the entire St. Martin's Press sales and marketing team, and to the booksellers and authors who read *very* early and offered enthusiastic endorsements.

On the home front, I'm ever grateful to Sharon Kurtzman, who hears all and tells none. Also to our fellow local writer-gals, whose camaraderie enriches my writing life in myriad ways. Ditto my long-distance cohorts. You all rock, and are my rocks.

Shout-out to my sons; parenting them gave me so much insight for this novel—and also, they're just excellent fellows. And last but not least, to the other excellent fellow in my life, uber-talented author John Kessel, who offers unending support, valuable suggestions, commiseration, sustenance of all kinds, and who never minds if I'm working in my bathrobe all day because often he is, too.

PART I

1

An upscale new house in a simple old neighborhood. A girl on a chaise beside a swimming pool, who wants to be left alone. We begin our story here, in the minutes before the small event that will change everything. A Sunday afternoon in May when our neighborhood is still maintaining its tenuous peace, a loose balance between *old* and *new, us* and *them.* Later this summer when the funeral takes place, the media will speculate boldly about who's to blame. They'll challenge attendees to say on-camera whose side they're on.

For the record: we never *wanted* to take sides.

———————

Juniper Whitman, the poolside girl, was seventeen. A difficult age, no question, even if you have everything going for you—which it seemed to us she did. It's trite to say appearances can be deceiving, so we won't say that. We'll say no one can be known by only what's visible. We'll say most of us hide what troubles and confuses us, displaying instead the facets we hope others will approve of, the parts we hope others will like. Juniper was hiding something, and she didn't know whether to be ashamed or angry or just exactly what.

This new home's yard was much smaller than Juniper's old one—not even a third of an acre, when before she'd had three. Where was she supposed to go when she needed to get away but wasn't allowed to leave? There was hardly any space here that was not taken up by the house and the pool, and what space there was had no cover. There was no privacy at all. At her previous address, Juniper had liked to sit among the tall longleaf pines at the back of the property, far enough from the house that she felt like she could breathe and think. She liked to be amid the *biota,* as the scientists call it. It made her feel better. Always had.

But the builder of this big, gleaming white house had cleared the lot of the stately hardwoods that shaded the little house that had been here, the house that had been demolished without ceremony and removed like so much storm or earthquake debris. Except there had been no storm, no earthquake. There was just this desirable neighborhood in the middle of a desirable North Carolina city, and buyers with ready money to spend. Just that, and now this great big house with its small but expensive naked yard and its pool and its chaise and its girl and her book.

Juniper thought the rustling noises she heard in the yard behind hers, a yard that still contained a small forest of dogwood, hickory, pecan, chestnut, pine, and a tremendous oak that had been there for longer than anyone in the neighborhood had been alive, came from squirrels. She wasn't fond of squirrels. They were cute, sure, but you couldn't trust them not to run straight under the wheels of your car when they saw you coming. And they were forever getting into people's bird feeders and stealing all the seed. Juniper had a novel in her lap and steered her attention back to that. The story was good, and she'd become skillful at escaping into stories.

"Hey," said a voice that was not a squirrel's. Juniper looked up, saw a teenage boy standing at the edge of her backyard with a rake in one hand, the other hand raised in greeting. He said, "You must be our new neighbor. I'm about to clear out some leaves and saw you there, so, you know, I figured I'd say hey."

His appearance was a surprise in two ways. Juniper hadn't

known anyone was nearby, so there was that. But even if she had suspected there was a person, a boy, a teen like herself, she would have expected him to look like her—that is, white. Everyone in her old neighborhood was white. Instead, he was black, she was pretty sure. Light-skinned, with corkscrew hair the darkest possible shade of gold.

"Hey," she said. "Yeah. We moved in yesterday—my little sister and my parents and me."

"You all from out of town?"

"No, just farther out in this town."

He smiled. "Cool. Well, I didn't mean to bother you. Just, you know, welcome."

"No bother. Thanks."

If this had been the extent of it, if they'd been able to greet each other and then leave it at that—well, everything would have been a lot simpler for everyone. To say the least.

2

North Carolina has a temperate climate. That's a big part of its draw. Winter is mild. Spring arrives early. Yes, summers are hot, but fall brings relief and lasts a long time. The oaks keep their leaves well into December, and sometimes, when winter is especially gentle, some of the varieties—the live oak being one, with its slim, feather-shaped, delicate-seeming leaves—stay leafed throughout winter as well.

The boy who greeted Juniper that first day, Xavier Alston-Holt, knew a lot about trees. They weren't a special interest of his; he was far more interested in music, and in particular, music made using acoustic guitars. Guitars, though, are made from wood, so when his mother talked to him in endless detail about various trees, their habitats, their residents, their qualities, their vulnerabilities (greedy homebuilders topping that list), he mostly paid attention. When his mother stood in their backyard taking video and crying the day the lot behind theirs was cleared, the day men with chainsaws and grinders started at dawn and continued until dusk and his ears rang for the rest of the night, he stayed there in the yard with his arm around her shoulders because that was what he could do for her. She'd done so much for him.

And so Xavier was not surprised, nor were any of us, that his mother was not eager to meet the new neighbors who'd bought the freshly built house behind theirs. Valerie Alston-Holt was not sure how to be friendly with the kind of people who would put up the money to tear down the old house and cut down the trees. *All* of the trees. "People like that," she'd said more than once—for this kind of thing was happening throughout Oak Knoll now in varying degrees—"people like that have no conscience. It's like they're raping the landscape. Murdering it. Trees are life. Not just *my* life," she would add, since her fields were forestry and ecology, "but life, period. They literally make oxygen. We need to keep at least seven trees for every human on the planet, or else people are going to start suffocating. Think of that."

Xavier walked around to the wooded front yard where his mother was clipping peonies for display on a sick neighbor's bedside table. The plant beds around their modest brick ranch, a house that had been built in 1952 and had hardly been updated since, were Valerie's favorite things, second only to her son, and one tree, the massive old eighty-foot oak that dominated their backyard. You might not think a tree could mean so much to a person. This tree, though, was more than a magnificent piece of arboreal history; for Valerie Alston-Holt, it was a witness and companion. Its wide trunk was the first thing she noticed each time she looked out the windows into the backyard. It recalled to her many moments from the years they'd lived here, not the least of which was the summer night she had stood and pressed her forehead against its nubby gray-brown bark and cried while Xavier slept in his crib, the boy too young to know that God had just robbed them blind.

Six varieties of irises. Peonies in four different colors. Azalea, phlox, snowdrop, camellia, rhododendron, clematis, honeysuckle, jasmine—you name the plant, if it grew in this state, Valerie Holt had installed it somewhere on their plot. Tending her plants was her therapy, she liked to say, her way of shutting out the stresses that came with teaching undergraduates at the university—or more often, the stresses that came from dealing with the department head or the dean. The kids were actually pretty great. Curious. Smart. Political in ways she approved of—useful ways, ways that helped protect natural habitats, or tried to, anyway, and that was worth a lot. Young people were going to save the world from itself, and she was going to encourage them in every way she could.

Now Xavier said to her, "The time has come."

"What time is that? Are you going somewhere?" She laid the flowers and clippers in her basket and then stood upright. "I thought you were going to clear out those dead leaves for me."

"I am. We have new neighbors."

"Oh, that. I know. It was inevitable. Like death," Valerie added with a rueful smile.

Xavier said, "I met one of them just now. She says it's her and one sister and their parents."

"Only four people in that huge house?"

Xavier shrugged. "Guess so."

"How old?"

"The girl? My age, I think, give or take. And a little sister, she said. I didn't ask about her."

His mother nodded. "Okay. Thanks for the intel."

"Do you want me to find you if the parents come outside?"

"No. Yes. Of course. I am going to be a good neighbor."

"You always are."

"Thanks, Zay."

"Just telling it like it is."

"That's what we have to do, as much as we can."

Xavier returned to the backyard and got to work raking the leaves from an area where his mother intended to put a koi pond. With him going off to the San Francisco Conservatory of Music for school in the fall, she'd said she needed new beings to keep her occupied so that she didn't call him every day to make sure he could survive on the opposite side of the country without her. He knew she was joking; she wouldn't call daily regardless. She'd want to, but she wouldn't. He understood. They'd been a pretty exclusive duo for a long time.

He'd said, "Make the pond, and maybe date someone *local.*"

"Oh, look who's talking about dating."

He gave her that crooked smile of his that had made him so popular with all the older ladies here in Oak Knoll, as well as with, we were sure, the girls at his school. He said, "I'm too busy to have a girlfriend."

"Too picky, it seems to me."

"I know you are, but what am I?" he said.

The fact is, Xavier was both picky and busy—but mostly picky. He hadn't met anyone who made him feel like he ought to change any of his priorities. He had plenty of female friends and, among them, girls who would have dated him if he'd pursued their interest. He hadn't pursued it, though, because he knew himself well enough to understand he was an all-or-nothing kind of guy. Always had been. He'd hooked up with a couple of girls in the past year mainly due to lust and opportunity, but a relationship was not workable for him right now. His music was his love.

Now he glanced at the poolside girl, the new neighbor, the girl he'd sort of met. *What's her name?* he thought. *Why do you care?* he also thought. *Just do your work.*

Xavier had been six years old when he first strummed a guitar, at a birthday party for the daughter of one of his mom's colleagues. Several of the adults had brought instruments—guitars, mandolins, bongos, a harmonica—and after the cake and presents, everyone gathered on the uneven brick patio in plastic lawn chairs to play and sing. First it was Raffi songs, for the kids, then a lot of Neil Young and the Beatles and some James Taylor. Xavier thought the music was fine, but it was one particular guitar that snagged his curiosity. He liked the look of it, and its clear, bright tone. He'd asked its owner, a history professor named Sean, if he could try it. Sean sat him down and put the guitar on Xavier's lap. The instrument was huge in comparison to the boy's skinny little self. Xavier held the neck and reached over the top and strummed, and that was it, he was gone. A week later he took his first lesson. By ten, he was fixed on classical music exclusively; of all the genres, classical was the one that made him *feel* beauty, and he needed that feeling to help him get through all the emotional noise in his world. Then early this year, now eighteen years old, he'd auditioned for a coveted spot at SFCM and got it.

Xavier raked the leaves into a pile and began stuffing them into the biodegradable bags Valerie bought from a shop where every item cost four times as much as its cheaper but usually toxic (in one way or another) alternative. Most of their cleaning, bathing, storage, and clothing products came from there. Between this expense and the gardening and Xavier's music lessons, it was little wonder there wasn't much money for updating the house, had Valerie been inclined to bother. We made fun of her sometimes—the way we did with our friend who'd gone so far with the Paleo Diet that he wouldn't even eat food made with grains unless that grain had been milled by hand with a stone. Valerie took our ribbing in the spirit with which it was given: affection, since we couldn't help but love a woman as caring as she was, and respect the way she stuck to her guns.

The new neighbor was still on the chaise by the glittering blue in-ground pool, still reading. Xavier liked the sight (of the girl, mainly, though the pool looked really nice). Though he hadn't yet had a chance to study her features, his initial impression was favorable. White girl. Really long brown hair. Pretty face. Plaid shirt tied at the waist, sleeves rolled up. Cutoff denim shorts. No shoes. Dark toenail polish—green, maybe? He kept an eye on her as he worked, and had the odd but pleasing sense that she stayed deliberately aware of him as she read.

"Sunscreen, Juniper," a woman's voice said. Xavier looked up from his work to see a woman coming outside through tall French doors to the covered porch, a bottle of sunscreen in hand.

Juniper.

The woman's hair was blond and long, but not as long as Juniper's. She wore it in a high ponytail above gold hoop earrings, which did not, in Xavier's opinion, go with the tight fitness tank top and shorts and tennis shoes, all of it in trendy patterns and colors that, if he had known about fitness fashion, he'd have recognized came from Ultracor's spring collection. She looked like a catalogue ad.

Watching the woman, Xavier thought *well-kept,* the term he'd heard some of the women use when his mother had her friends over for book club. While they always did eventually get around to discussing the book, whatever it might be, first they had the "graze and gossip" part of the evening. Lately that term, *well-kept,* was in the gossip part of the evening a lot, in correspondence with the increasing number of high-end houses being built nearby. The women tried to make it simply an observation, but Xavier could tell that it was a judgment, too. These women were all professionals: some were teachers or professors, like his mother; some were in public health or social work or ran a small business. None of them were kept.

Xavier liked to hang out with them, not to gossip (their business was their business) but to avail himself of the appetizers and salads they brought. They brought wine, too. Plenty of wine. He was eighteen now, old enough to die for his country and therefore old enough to have a glass of wine with his hummus and olives, his chèvre-stuffed figs, his lentil-arugula salad, et cetera, that's what they all liked to say. Xavier wasn't much for wine, but he would never say no to the so-called crack dip, a hot cream cheese, Ro-Tel, spicy crumbled sausage *extravaganza,* as far as he was concerned. He planned to buy a Crock-Pot for his dorm room so that he could make the dip himself and basically live on the stuff.

"*Juniper,*" the well-kept woman said again, this time with annoyance.

"Juniper," Xavier said to himself softly, trying it out. Then he thought, *Idiot. You got no time for this.*

"Seriously, Mom?" said Juniper.

"On your face? Absolutely. Arms and legs, too. You have to take care of your skin now, or you'll end up spending way too much money treating sun damage later. Do you want to end up looking like Grandma Lottie? I wish *I'd* had a mom as smart as I am."

"If you do say so yourself," said Juniper, taking the sunscreen.

"By the way, do *not* tell Grandma I said that."

Next came a shirtless man with a golf tan, wearing coral-colored flowered shorts below the protruding belly common to so many middle-aged men. He left the tall door open behind him. "Is this the life or what?" he said. He carried a bottle of beer in one hand and a pitcher of something pink in the other. Setting the pitcher on a teak dining table, he added, "Who's ready for a swim?"

"I am!" said a little girl, skipping outside behind him.

The woman said, "Are you sure the water's warm enough? They just filled it yesterday."

The little girl, maybe seven years old, fuchsia bikini, big yellow sunglasses, put her hands on her hips and answered, "Mommy, are you a man or a mouse?"

Xavier, realizing that he was staring, finished stuffing a bag and then put down his rake and turned to go find his mother. Might as well get the introductions over with. Before he got more than a few steps, though, the man called to him.

"Hey there, son."

Xavier turned around. The man was waving and walking toward him.

"Listen," he said, coming into the yard, "I'm wondering if I might hire you to do some work for *me* when you're done here. We just moved in and I've got boxes to haul out and break down, some furniture to move around—my wife, she couldn't make up her mind with the movers, so . . ." He chuckled. "Fifty bucks sound fair? I don't need you for but an hour or so—pretty good pay, right?"

"Oh, I . . . That is, I'm just helping out my mom." Xavier pointed toward the house. "I'm Xavier Alston-Holt. Most people call me Zay," he said, extending his hand.

"Ah," the man said, and shook Xavier's hand. "Brad Whitman, Whitman HVAC. You've probably seen my commercials, right?"

"Maybe?" Xavier said. "We don't have TV."

"I'm on the internet, and radio, too."

"Okay, sure."

Brad Whitman leaned in and tapped Xavier's shoulder with his fist, saying, "Heh, I thought you were *hired* by the old lady who lives here."

Xavier smiled politely. "I don't think my mom would appreciate being called 'the old lady.'"

"No, right? What woman would?"

"She's only forty-eight."

"That so? Guess my Realtor got it wrong," Brad Whitman said. "But there *are* lots of old ladies in the neighborhood, isn't that a fact?"

Xavier nodded. "And some old men. Everything, really."

"Sure," Brad said. "That's what we want, right?"

Xavier nodded. "So, I was just about to get my mom. She wants to say hello."

"Sure, good. Bring her over." Brad pointed toward his house. "Julia just made some pink lemonade. The girls love it. I'll offer you a beer if you've got ID saying you're twenty-one."

"Not yet, but thanks. Be right back."

Xavier was almost to the house when Brad Whitman called, "Bring your dad, too, if he's home. I've got a cold one for him, at least."

Xavier raised his hand to acknowledge he'd heard.

Bring his father? He wished he could. He had always wished he could.

3

Before we depict the first encounter between our story's other central players, we need to show the wider setting in which this slow tragedy unfolded. As our resident English professor would remind us, *place*, especially in stories of the South, is as much a character as any human, and inseparable from—in this case even necessary to—the plot.

———

Valerie Alston-Holt had fallen in love with our neighborhood, Oak Knoll, the first time she stood on one of its sidewalks. She was a Michigan native two years out of her Ph.D. program, twenty months into her new job at the university, one year married, and seven months pregnant. She and her husband, Tom Holt-Alston, who was a young sociology professor, had been renting a cozy apartment near campus. Now, though, it was time to buy a house—and this was the neighborhood their colleagues loved most. Tom and Val couldn't go wrong here, everyone said so.

As with a lot of American suburban neighborhoods of a certain character, Oak Knoll had been conceived in the boom years after the Second World War. Wide streets, sidewalks, and—because this is North Carolina, which is rich in both trees and *clay*—brick-clad ranch homes, the basic three-bedroom, one-bath design, small but functional, set on spacious tree-filled lots.

Spring was Oak Knoll's showy season: white and pink dogwoods in bloom along with chestnuts and pears and viburnums and camellias, cherry trees, persimmon trees, hawthorn shrubs, hollies. Also tulip magnolias, those heralds who now and then made their eager pink appearance only to be punished by a late frost. The neighborhood was known particularly for the dogwoods, delicate, slow-growing trees that need two decades to achieve the size of a six-year maple. Valerie brought Tom to walk around and see for himself how lovely it was here, how perfect for them and their child-to-be. Some of us still remember seeing the two of them that day, Valerie so pregnant, so dark-skinned, such a contrast to her tall, blond husband. We won't pretend that no one paid attention to this contrast. Of course we did. Mostly we felt it gave them an exotic appeal, a kind of celebrity status in a neighborhood that had come to think of itself as progressive yet was not doing much to demonstrate that character. The most that could be said was that some residents were white and some were nonwhite, some were on fixed incomes and some were young professionals in low-paying fields, and we treated one another with kindness and respect. To be fair, what more was there to do?

Oak Knoll was never, at least until recently, thought to be a prestigious part of town. People with serious money lived in nearby Hillside. Hillside had the blue bloods, the politicians, the surgeons, the founders of industry and big retail chains, many of them living in enormous homes made of stone and brick, fairy-tale homes with gates and ivy and long driveways and porticoes and sculpted shrubbery and, of course, towering oaks. Valerie admired these mansions and also the slightly lesser versions of them tucked into the smaller lots there—also beautiful, the yards also verdant. Who wouldn't? But there was no way, not in any life that might be available to her (short of winning a multimillion-dollar lottery jackpot), that she could ever call Hillside home. And even if she did have millions, many of the Hillside residents would say a black woman with a white husband had less legitimacy there than the black hired help, because *she* obviously didn't know her place.

As time passed and the city grew, the type of people who were then known as yuppies bought big graceless houses in new outlying subdivisions on acre-plus lots, where the properties were dubbed "estates" and many families kept a golf cart in their three- or four-car garage. The Whitmans had lived in one of those neighborhoods because, let's face it, you get a lot more house for your money out there and your neighbors aren't close enough to know your business. Also, Whitman HVAC was a growing company, not a mature one, and to get the kind of house he wanted for a mortgage he could afford while still driving his BMW and giving Julia a new Lexus SUV and paying for the girls' private schooling, Brad Whitman, who secretly yearned for the prestige of Hillside, had to settle.

Then he invented some gadget or part of an HVAC system (we're not clear on what exactly it was), patented it, and sold it to a big manufacturer, netting something like two million dollars. This meant he could afford to move Julia and the girls to a house in Hillside. To one of the lesser houses, true; four thousand square feet instead of six or eight. But Brad was fine with that plan; his property taxes would be lower than with the true mansions and he'd still have that enviable Hillside address.

Moving there would have been the Whitmans' plan, except that their best friends, the Jamisons (Jimmy was in pharmaceuticals and doing well these days), had discovered Oak Knoll, with its aging houses and, in many cases, aging residents. Aging residents who were one by one selling off and moving into assisted living. Or they were dying off and their kids had no interest in returning to live in the cramped one-bathroom houses they'd grown up in, houses that now smelled of mothballs and Preparation H and had nicotine stains on the ceilings and walls. And so the kids were clearing out the tchotchkes and selling the places as is.

Unlike in Hillside, where the houses were at least as old or older (if better smelling—sometimes—and better kept), in Oak Knoll you didn't have to pay through the nose to get the house and then pay again to modernize everything. Oak Knoll homes were cheap enough that you could raze them and build a brand-new showplace, put in the best materials, best technology, great insulation and low-e glass, have lower utilities and maintenance and tax bills and a larger return on investment if you sold—Oak Knoll was where it was happening, Jimmy Jamison told Brad. He'd already picked his builder, and Brad was not going to *believe* the media system he'd designed. Jimmy took Brad to see one of the builder's just-done houses (Mark and Lisa Wertheimer's, now). The men stood in the kitchen with its ten-foot ceilings, its marble countertops, its Sub-Zero refrigerator and Wolf range, and Brad said, "Damn. I reckon I ought to build one of these for Julia and me."

———————————

From the far more basic Alston-Holt kitchen, where Valerie was arranging her peonies in vases, she watched Xavier speak with the new neighbor. Visually, the man fulfilled every expectation she'd had for who was going to live in that house: white, late forties, trendy on-brand swim trunks to go with the swimming pool and the enormous stainless-steel gas grill on the flagstone patio nearby. He wore flip-flops and a backward-facing ball cap. A man-child with money.

There were a lot of them around these days. She'd had dates with a couple such men, fix-ups by a friend in the engineering college who had regular dealings with men in local industry. More like pre-dates: meet someplace during happy hour, see if there's any chemistry, try to gauge whether or not the guy's interest in dating a black woman arose from an honorable place in his soul. Valerie Alston-Holt was not some exotic oversexed chick waiting to satisfy some white man's slave-sex fantasy—and yes, there really were men who entertained themselves with that idea and thought she'd be entertained by it, too.

Valerie didn't mention any of that to Xavier. Even when she dated a man for real, she kept it very low-key. To wit: her current gentleman, a man she'd connected with at a conference in Virginia almost three years ago but whom Xavier had met only twice. His name was Chris Johnson—the most nondescript of names, we thought. He had great credentials, though, being tenured faculty at the University of Virginia in the Frank Batten School of Leadership and Public Policy. Also, he sang baritone in a prizewinning quartet. Their "dating" so far amounted to regular FaceTime conversations and the occasional weekend getaway, now that Xavier could stay home on his own.

Valerie didn't invite Chris down here, save for the two times we mentioned, and didn't talk about him much. As all single parents know, dating while raising a child or children is no simple endeavor. Valerie didn't want to make Xavier anxious about a thing that might happen, might not. Once that boy got fixed on something, he had a hard time letting go. She'd seen that about him early: a favorite blankie, a favorite food, a toy, a book, an author—one summer he'd read nothing but the Brian Jacques *Redwall* novels, all twenty-two of them. He had two close friends, who'd been his friends since preschool. And of course there was his music and his guitars.

Here's another example of the boy's intensity: The possibility that Xavier's first-choice college might not take him had kept him awake nights, though he was as skilled and talented as anyone he'd competed with over the years. To the delight of those of us who lived nearest and could hear him play when the weather was mild and the windows open, Xavier increased his practice schedule to an hour before school every day and two hours at night after he got home from his job stocking groceries. Then he did his homework. For two days before and a day after his SFCM audition in January, he could barely eat, which is saying something. And although he did get himself back into a more normal routine after they returned from San Francisco, he stayed keyed up until his acceptance letter came in mid-March. This was just the sort of young man he was. Valerie had done her best to teach him to make that intensity work for him. Good grades, good work ethic, good recommendations from his teachers and his boss—and it had paid off.

But it might have as easily worked against him, and still might; how many nights in the past few years had Valerie waited up for her son, praying that he and his friends not be stopped by the police? Praying that he never got put in a position where he felt wronged and defensive and turned that intensity of his on the cops? He was tall. He was black. Valerie had told him *so many times,* "If they get scared of you, they'll shoot," hating that she needed to say it at all, hating that the progress toward that post-racial future she and her husband and others like them had fervently fostered was now being reversed. Why couldn't we see one another as simply human and pull together, for goodness' sake? The planet was dying while people fought over things like who was most American—or who was American at all.

Now she watched Xavier leave the man-child-with-money and come inside the house. "They're all out there," he said, joining her in the kitchen.

"I saw. Let me just finish this and wash up."

Xavier leaned against the counter, took an apple from a bowl and polished it against his T-shirt. Then he put it back and did the same with another, saying, "He thought I was your hired help."

"Are we surprised?"

"He also thought you were an old lady. Well, not you specifically. He thought an old lady lived here. Said his Realtor told him that."

"Well, that is a fair mistake." She dried her hands on a dish towel. "Did you get his name?"

"Brad something. HVAC. That's his line of work. He said he has TV commercials, like I should know him."

"Oh, right, right. I remember Ellen said a local celebrity was buying here. She just couldn't remember which one or which house. Clearly there's a good buck in HVAC."

Valerie considered and then rejected changing out of her sweaty T-shirt and fraying cargo shorts. Let them take her—or not—as she was. She put on sunglasses and a hat, and then she and Xavier walked over to the Whitmans' together, moving from their wooded paradise to the Whitmans' sculpted strips of mulch and sod that surrounded the patio and pool.

"Greetings," she called as she stepped onto the flagstone. At least the Whitmans had chosen natural stone and not poured concrete. The stone wasn't a great choice in terms of the environmental effects of excessive hardscape coverage, and Valerie suspected the builder had gotten a variance for the pool and patio and possibly the house, too, or how could he get away with covering so much of the land? But flagstone did have slightly better permeability than concrete and looked much more natural.

The real problem was the risk to the nearby trees. Large ones, like the old oak in Valerie's backyard, had shallow root structures that spread laterally and might extend hundreds of feet from the trunk. Valerie, who taught classes on recreational forest management (among other subjects), knew this better than any of us. She'd been watching that oak for signs of stress since the day the Whitmans' lot was cleared.

That tree meant a great deal to her. She couldn't look at it without seeing baby Xavier in the bright red canvas swing they'd hung from one of the lower branches; little Xavier, age four, on the wooden "big boy" swing that came next, moving his legs back and forth in his first attempts to pump; ten-year-old Zay and his uncle Kyle building a tree house, in which Zay and his best friends, Dashawn and Joseph, would spend untold hours in the years ahead with their comic books and video games and great quantities of snacks. Both the tree house and swing were still there. Xavier and his friends still sometimes used them, as if they were as reluctant to break these tethers to childhood as Valerie was to see them broken.

Julia Whitman was the first to return Valerie's greeting. She stood up from where she'd been sitting in a cushioned teak chair on the covered porch. "Hi, join us. I'm Julia. Let me pour you both some lemonade."

"Hi. Valerie Alston-Holt." She directed her words at Julia but went straight for Brad Whitman, her hand extended. She knew from experience that it was necessary to set the tone right away. "You must be Brad."

"Brad Whitman, Whitman HVAC. Good to meet you. Thanks for coming by."

Then Valerie shook Julia's hand and accepted a filled glass before taking the seat nearest Brad's. She said, "We've been waiting forever for this house to be finished."

"Us, too," said Julia, as bright in attitude as the orange block print on her shorts.

"*Eight months* of noise and commotion," said Valerie, not really meaning to go there but also kind of wanting to. "The air compressors and nail guns and saws, the drywall guys blasting their music all day long . . . Honestly, every day off I've had since September was spoiled by the noise."

"Oh," Julia said. "I'm so sorry."

"Done now, though," said Brad. "All's well that ends well."

Valerie said, "Until one goes up next door or across the street from you. Then you'll see for yourselves. You met my son, Xavier?"

"Brad did. Hi," said Julia. "Pink lemonade?"

Xavier sat down in a chair next to his mother's. "No, I'm good, thanks."

"That's Lily in the pool," Julia said, "and that's Juniper." She pointed to her older daughter, who had set her book aside and was getting up to join the group on the porch.

Hanging on to the pool's edge, Lily said, "Hi, Mrs. Neighbor. I'm sorry, I forgot to hear your name."

"She's Mrs. Alston-Holt," said Julia. "Did I get that right?"

"*Ms.* Alston-Holt," Valerie amended. She did not personally mind if the kids used her first name, but a lot of parents in the South insisted on the formality of titles. If that was how these people were, they should at least get the title right.

"I like the girls' names," she added. "Plants are my thing." Then she said, "Brad, you say you do HVAC work? Maybe you could have a look at my compressor. It's making a strange noise."

She glanced at Xavier. He was holding back a laugh. He knew

that this was not a sincere request, that there was no troubling noise; Valerie was razzing Brad Whitman in return for his assumption that Xavier was her yard boy.

"Glad to," Brad said. He set his beer on the table. "Let me just get a shirt and shoes, and—"

"Oh. I didn't mean this minute." She had not expected him to be willing to do it himself. "Thanks, though. And, you know, it doesn't even make the noise all the time. I don't think I heard it today. Zay, did you hear it?"

"Not today," Xavier said.

"It can keep. Besides, I wouldn't think to bother you about it on a Sunday."

"God's day," said Juniper, who'd sat down beside Julia. "Except we don't go to church anymore."

"We go sometimes," Julia said.

Lily said, "God is everywhere, even right here in the pool."

"Yes indeed, sugar pie," said her father. He told Valerie, "I confess: I like to golf on Sunday mornings. Better tee times."

"He *likes* to golf *every* day," Julia said. "But he only goes on Saturdays and Sundays."

Valerie said, "We're not regulars at church, either. Especially this time of year. I like Sunday mornings for working in the yard." This, too, was a little bit of a dig. These people barely had a yard, and what there was of it was professionally landscaped to within an inch of its life. There would be no yard work for them, Valerie was sure, only yard workers.

Brad said, "You're going to think, 'What a pushy guy,' but I'm just one of those people who likes to know things, so here's my question: Is there a Mr. Alston-Holt?"

Valerie said, "No. It's just us."

"Sure," said Brad. "No problem."

"I'm a widow," she clarified.

Both Brad and Julia reacted as new acquaintances always did: the quick look of surprise that preceded *Oh, I'm so sorry,* and then the lingering curiosity that they were too polite to voice.

Julia said, "Juniper's about to be a rising senior at the Blakely Academy. Are you in school, Xavier?"

"I'll graduate from Franklin Magnet in a few weeks."

"Oh, high school. I thought you might be older. Congratulations!" Julia told him. "I bet that feels good. Will you go to college this fall?"

Valerie answered. "He got a scholarship to the San Francisco Conservatory of Music. I'm very proud of him."

"Partial scholarship," Xavier said. "But, yeah. I play guitar."

Brad said, "Hey, like Jimi Hendrix!"

Xavier shook his head. "Acoustic. Classical. Don't worry, nobody even knows it's a thing."

Juniper turned to him. "Is it true that kids at Franklin bring guns to school for gang fights, and the only reason there hasn't been a shooting is because security guards confiscate the guns?"

"What?" said Xavier. "No. Where did you hear that?"

Juniper looked at Brad. "Isn't that what you said?"

Brad glanced at her sharply, Valerie thought. This reaction (if she read him right) suggested that his cheerful man-child exterior might be a veneer. If so, she would not be surprised. In her experience, some men—well-off white men in particular—were so accustomed to their authority and privilege that they perceived it as a right.

Juniper's botanical name notwithstanding, to Valerie she seemed an ordinary teenager. A tiny bit hostile maybe, nothing unexpected there, given that her parents had moved her to a new house just weeks before the end of school when she probably had papers and projects due. Fortunately, she wouldn't to have to change schools for her senior year. Private education did have that advantage.

Now Brad was saying to Juniper in a kind tone, "You got something mixed up, honey," and Valerie decided she had misheard and misjudged him. She did have some prejudice, because of the clearcutting. *Lighten up,* she told herself. *Give the man a chance.*

Brad went on, "I might have said something about some other school. Or maybe you heard it from one of your friends."

Juniper said, "Maybe. I guess."

"For the record," said Valerie, "Franklin is one of the highest-performing public schools in the state."

"Well, sure," Brad said. "Just look at Zay here. Classical guitar. I don't know what that is, exactly, but if you got a scholarship to do it, you must be good. Juniper takes piano—though I don't believe she'll win any scholarships with her playing."

Julia said, "She needs to practice more. But she's very at good cross-country running. She ran varsity as a freshman."

"Nice," Xavier said to Juniper. "Will that be your thing in college?"

"Like a sports major?" Juniper replied. "No, I think I want to study zoology or botany. I'm hoping to get into a program in Washington State."

"Since when?" said Julia.

"I've been thinking about it."

"We'll see," Brad said. "I'm sure your mother's not crazy about the idea of you going to school so far away."

"Or at all," Julia said, shrugging. "What can I say? She's my first baby; I don't want her to grow up."

Valerie was about to empathize with Julia when a half-dozen Latino men in matching bright yellow T-shirts came around the side of the Whitmans' house to the back property boundary. One man had a spade. Another had a gas-powered posthole digger.

"*There* they are," Brad said, rising. "Fence guys. They were supposed to have this done before we closed—got backed up because of last week's rain, they said. We got the C.O.—certificate of occupancy—anyway; I know a guy in the permits office. He was useful in a lot of ways," he said with a wink. Then he went to speak with the crew.

"You're putting in a fence," Valerie said to Julia. "Of course. I'd forgotten about that regulation. Used to be no one in Oak Knoll could afford a pool."

Julia said, "A nice wooden fence, don't worry. Not chain link."

It wasn't the fence material that worried Valerie. It was the further disruption of her trees' root systems that would arise from the digging. And what could she do about it? Nothing. The pool was in. A fence was required.

Brad returned to the porch. "It'll only take them a couple of days for the install," he said. "Apologies in advance for the noise. It'll be nice, though, right? More privacy for everyone."

"Sure," said Valerie.

She sincerely wanted the noise to be the worst of the trouble. And root disruption aside, she approved of there being a fence between her yard and theirs. She had no desire to forever be looking out her windows at this pool and patio, which alone must have cost as much as she and Tom had paid for their house. Nor had she been crazy about the prospect of seeing young, beautiful Julia Whitman lying around the pool all summer—in a bikini, probably—showing off her five-day-a-week-workout-fit body when she, Valerie, had ten extra pounds she'd been failing to lose for about as many years.

She said, "You know what Frost says: 'Good fences make good neighbors.'"

"Frost who?" said Lily.

Juniper said, "Robert Frost. He was a poet."

Valerie nodded approvingly. Yes, the youth were going to save them all.

And so the Whitmans and the Alston-Holts sat a little longer in the shade of the covered porch and talked of inconsequential matters, parting after another twenty minutes as the fence crew got under way, Brad and Valerie satisfied that they all were as well acquainted as they needed to be. This was as auspicious a beginning to the relationship as any of us could have hoped for. None of us were giving the trees or the kids a second thought.

4

Two days later, Xavier was standing at the kitchen counter making himself a grilled ham-and-cheese sandwich for an early supper when his mother joined him.

"How was school?" she said, coming over and putting her arm around his waist. He was a good ten inches taller than she was, which still felt weird to him. He'd spent most of his life wishing he were bigger, taller, grown—and now he looked down at most adults, not up. Now he could see the top of his mom's head. Now he was six-three, an inch taller than his dad had been. He wished he had a dollar—no, make it ten—for every time someone assumed he played basketball.

He told Valerie, "Review for exams. Pretty dull." He lit a burner and set a griddle over the flame.

"Finish line's in sight." She gave him a squeeze, then let go. "Hey, so I've been thinking of this and I wanted to ask you: What's your read on our famous new neighbor, Brad Whitman?"

"How do you mean?"

"I found him . . . opaque. I couldn't tell if he's as good as he seems."

"I thought he was all right," Xavier said. He'd buttered the outer sides of two sandwiches and was about to put them on the griddle. "Want me to make one for you? Then I have to go to work."

"Sure, thanks." She got a tomato, a knife, and a cutting board, and sat down at the kitchen table. "Maybe I'm being too sensitive. I don't want to think the worst about these people when I don't even know them. Prejudice is ugly. I don't like to think I'm capable of it."

"I hate to break it to you, but you're human," Xavier said, assembling a sandwich for her. "Besides, it's not prejudging if you're doing it after you meet someone, right?"

"I basically judged them from the second the chainsaws started, and that bothers me. I try to give everyone a chance, or how can I complain when people prejudge me?"

Xavier placed three sandwiches onto the griddle. They sizzled, sending the hot butter's lipid molecules into the air. Scent was chemistry. Breathing was chemistry. Digestion was chemistry. Plant growth and oxygen production from those plants was chemistry, too. His mom had taught him all about the plant stuff especially, hoping, maybe, that he'd come to share her passion for ecology. He'd gotten deep into it for a couple of months, and then his interest was sated.

That happened a lot. Xavier had learned that while he was interested in many different subjects, there were few he loved. Every time he'd latched onto something new, though, his mom let him indulge himself, encouraging him to take it as far as he wanted to go. She said this was one of the benefits derived from the civil rights battles. That is, he was the child of a white man and a college-educated black woman, being raised in a middle-class household in a country where, she said, "you can pursue anything you want. *Anything*. And you get to be just a kid, not a *black* kid. We have to give credit where it's due, Zay, and not take any of this for granted."

He knew it wasn't wholly true, though, this *just a kid, not a black kid* assertion. He knew she didn't believe it, either. There were a lot more folks nowadays who tried not to differentiate their treatment of others based on skin color, yes. Then there were the ones—mostly older white folks—who scowled at him or avoided him or watched him, hawklike, when he was in a store, as if he was going to stuff his pockets or pull a gun. Once he'd asked his mom, "Why doesn't half white equal white the way half black equals black?" Her answer, i.e., the history of the one-drop rule, etc., made sense but didn't satisfy him. Factually he was just as white as he was black.

He said now, "Your issue is with the things the Whitmans did, not who they are. Every complaint should be evaluated on its merits, period." She'd taught him that, too. Use logic. Be fair. Demonstrate your humanity and integrity the way Dr. and Mrs. King had always done, the way John Lewis still did.

"Yes, but I have to tell you, Zay, this kind of antipathy is new for me. I've had preconceptions of people and things lots of times—it's impossible not to, right? But I can't think of a time when I've been so predisposed to *despise* something or someone this way." She shook her head. "It's the situation, I guess—the fact that it's so personal to me."

He looked over at her and said, "Don't be too hard on my mom. She's a good person."

This brought a smile. "Thank you, sweetie," she said. "How about you?"

"How about me what?"

"What do you think of them? The Whitmans."

"If you don't count them being fine with the clear-cutting and all, then, like I said, they seemed okay to me. Neighborly, for sure. Can't say I've really thought about it since the other day."

"No, of course. You've got plenty of more important things on your mind."

"I do," he said. He'd been thinking—too much, he already knew that—about just the one Whitman. Juniper.

5

Though there were other big new homes and new residents in Oak
Knoll, we were especially curious about the Whitmans. Their house
was the largest, had cost the most, and had upscale details that most
of us hadn't seen except on homes in Hillside or in the movies or on
TV. For example: copper gutters and downspouts; landscape lighting; a double-sided fireplace between the family room and screened
porch. A butler's pantry. A steam shower. It also had Brad Whitman,
who, as he'd indicated to Xavier, was a minor celebrity in the region.
He did his own commercials for Whitman HVAC, so a lot of us had
seen him on our screens. We'd heard him on the radio. There wasn't
a more charming man in the region. Warm. Affable. In every TV
spot, he looked right into the camera and said, "*You* are my favorite
customer and that's a fact."

We'd used his company to service and repair and replace our
aging heating and cooling systems. We felt privileged—some of us
did—that he'd chosen to make our neighborhood his new home. We
wanted to get to know him and his beautiful family, see up close how
the other half really lived. We were keenly interested in the wife,
Julia. She seemed so lovely, so young, so fortunate.

"What's on your schedule today?" Julia Whitman asked her husband as he left their bed and headed for the shower.

"The usual," he said. He reached into the shower to turn on the water, then stepped out of the silk shorts he slept in. "You?"

"Same. Except tonight."

Her evening promised a change of pace: she'd been invited to attend Oak Knoll's neighborhood book club. Tonight she'd be just a visitor, since she hadn't read this month's book, a historical novel. Usually she read contemporary fiction—legal thrillers and woman-in-peril stories and British cozy mysteries. But if the group liked her and the discussion was good, she might pick up tonight's book along with the one for next month's meeting, "a beach read," neighbor Kelli Hanes had told her when she'd invited Julia to come. They always did a beach book for the June meeting and everyone was supposed to dress accordingly. That would be fun.

Julia said, "I'm going to Valerie's—the neighbor behind us?—for a book club meeting. You'll be home, right?"

"Yep," he said, entering the shower. "Got a Chutes and Ladders date with Lily."

Julia watched him for a moment. He was still a handsome man, everyone said so. That sandy hair and impish grin, those startlingly blue eyes. But he'd gained at least fifteen pounds since the first time she'd seen him naked. He was doughy and pale every place the sun didn't reach. His hair had thinned atop his head, though he combed it in such a way that it was hard to tell. Middle age was settling onto him, even if he wasn't settling into middle age—his newest car being a vivid example of his resistance. Did men never stop being teenaged boys?

She went to her closet. "Omelet?" she called to him.

"Scrambled. Throw in a couple of sausage links, too. Thanks."

The Whitmans' weekday morning routine was systematized: Julia and Brad got up at six; he showered while she dressed in the appropriate clothing for her morning fitness activity, be it tennis or

Pilates or barre or spinning; she had a hot breakfast for Brad on the table at 6:20 and woke the girls right afterward; then the girls came down and she ate with them—something light for her, yogurt or a hard-boiled egg, and she encouraged Juniper to eat light, too; she cleaned up the kitchen while the girls got dressed (uniforms made that easy); Brad left for work at 6:35, and she had the girls in the car by seven. Being in the new house wouldn't alter this routine, since they lived as near to the school as they had before, just in another direction. Though she thought she might need to nudge their departure time up a little, depending on the in-town traffic. An unremarkable routine? Yes, which was why it pleased her so much.

It was now 7:05 on this, their first Monday morning here, and Julia was still waiting on Juniper. "Come on, we're late," she called from the mudroom at the bottom of the back stairway, where Lily was joining her now. The house smelled of wood stain and fresh paint and putty, but she loved it, loved every spotless, solid inch of the place. Reclaimed oak floors. Six-inch baseboards. Marble countertops, marble backsplash tile. A pantry as large as Juniper's first bedroom had been. Heated bathroom floors. A bathtub in the master so deep you could almost swim in it. Their previous house had been large, and nicer than any place she'd lived before, but in terms of quality and luxury it had nothing on this one. *If I've dreamed this, no one pinch me,* she thought, not for the first time.

To Lily she said, "What's taking your sister so long?"

"Teenagers are slow like old turtles. Except at cross-country. Juniper is fast at that. Maybe that's why she's slow now. She used up all her fastness in her races."

Julia smiled at Lily, then yelled, "Juniper, come on!"

"I *am*," Juniper called.

The sound of footsteps assured Julia that her daughter was in fact on her way—and slow. Juniper took her time coming to the stairs and then down the stairs. Julia assessed her: tired for sure, and something else she'd been seeing these past several months. Sadness? Anger? Whatever it was, it pained Julia to see that it still had a hold on her here. Their life was so good!

Much as she wanted to get some answers from Juniper (who'd been less than forthcoming so far), now was not the time. And maybe she shouldn't bother her about it more than she already had. Maybe she should just continue to let her have some space and trust that it would sort itself out. Julia remembered being a teenager. She'd hated her mother's bugging her all the time about every little thing. Her mother still bugged her all the time about every little thing.

When they were in the car, Julia asked Juniper, "What was the holdup?" She kept her tone deliberately casual.

Juniper said, "I couldn't find my shoes."

"All your shoes were in the same box."

"These weren't."

"I had the movers pack them that way deliberately."

"Well, they didn't," Juniper said.

"Where were they, then?"

"In a different box."

Julia tried to recalibrate. She said, "All right. Well. I'll finish organizing your room today, so we won't have any more problems finding things."

This would be as much for herself as for Juniper. The activity would give a focus to her afternoon, and the sooner the house was fully in order, the better. Disorder bothered Julia a lot more now than it had used to. It felt like backsliding.

Pre-Brad, disorder had been a fixture of her often-frantic existence, when order, desirable as it might be, was an out-of-reach luxury. And since she couldn't have it, she didn't think about it—that was how you managed when you lived paycheck to paycheck, how you survived from one day to the next without making yourself crazy. She might *want* a spacious, spotless apartment in a well-managed community, a unit where the interior doors latched when you shut them, where you had enough cupboard space, where the toilets flushed correctly and didn't run all the time, where those enormous ugly camel crickets weren't lurking in the closets. For that matter, she might want a whole weekend free to wash *and* put away the laundry and shop for groceries and vacuum and haul out the recycling and take her daughter to the playground or to a movie. She might want a lot of things she couldn't have because she worked two jobs just to buy food and pay the rent and day care and a babysitter, but what good would longing for all of that have done for her? It would only make her feel more inadequate than she did already, and she'd hated that feeling. Despised it, in fact.

—We should interject here that once we'd learned about her past, we felt Julia had not been inadequate; she had been unlucky. That was the truth she needed to make herself remember as well. Some people were born into privilege and had everything handed to them; some were born white trash and had to hustle to get even a thousandth of what the privileged had. Some people had sex without protection and never got pregnant; some got knocked up before they knew the guy's surname. Some pregnant women had abortions to resolve their bad luck, and some decided that a child would be a salve for their painful existence, a person all their own who had to love them no matter what.

Did Juniper still love her? Julia glanced at her daughter in the seat beside hers. Maybe this was a stupid thing to wonder. Some days, though, it was hard for her to tell. She was so thankful to also have Lily, "silly Lily," who was not just a ray of sunshine in their lives but a whole entire sun. The child had practically been born giggling.

Julia felt guilty about the stark differences in her daughters' early lives. But as Reverend Matthews at New Hope had reminded her when, freshly married and pregnant with Lily, she'd shared her anxieties with him: she'd done the best she could with Juniper. Emphasis on *best* and *could*.

"Knock knock," Lily said now, from the backseat.

"Who's there?" said Julia.

"No—Juniper. Knock knock, Juniper."

"Who's there?" Juniper said, lowering the math book she was studying.

"Hatch."

"Hatch who?"

"Bless you!" Lily said. "Get it?"

Julia smiled at her in the rearview mirror. "A sneeze."

"Knock knock."

"Who's there?" said Julia.

"No, *Juniper.*"

"Who's there?" said Juniper. "I'm trying to study. I have a test in second period."

"You didn't study last night?" Julia said.

"Hey, Mommy," Lily cried. "You interrupted. Start over. Knock knock, Juniper."

"Who's there?"

"Avenue."

"Avenue who?"

"Avenue answered this door before? Ha!"

"You're a riot," Juniper said, smiling.

"You tell one."

"I can't think of any."

Lily said, "I can think of a hundred."

"Yeah, but can you do trigonometry?"

"I might be able to if you teach me."

Juniper said, "Ask me to in ten years, when you're a junior."

"You'll be way far away in a rain forest or something."

"I might. I'll teach you by FaceTime."

"Deal!" said Lily. "Pinkie-swear it."

Juniper reached back and the girls linked their pinkies. "I swear," said Juniper.

Seeing the girls being playful this way heartened Julia. Juniper had become moody and at times withdrawn, even from Lily. She had not wanted to move, didn't care in the least that they'd have a gorgeous house in an increasingly prestigious area closer to the center of town, making the commute to many of her and Lily's extracurriculars more convenient for Julia, who felt she spent most of her waking hours behind the wheel.

"She's so temperamental," Julia had said to Brad one night a while back, after they'd taken the girls to see the house, still a shell but far enough along to picture what it would become. Juniper had walked around inside with them but hadn't said a word.

"Don't be too tough on her," Brad said. "She's a teenage girl. They're hormonal."

"I just don't want her to be ungrateful for everything you've done for us—*are* doing for us, for *her*. She needs to remember how things used to be, before."

<hr>

We'll just say it: Julia's history was nothing like we'd imagined—which goes to show that even experienced, well-meaning people can get things wrong. In her *before*, she had just been fired from the job that was supposed to make everything easier, an administrative position with a national mattress store chain, after she'd refused—four times—to sleep with her supervisor, a short, wiry, splotchy man who kept his fingernails almost as long as hers—which was not very long, but still, something about this trait put Julia off. Well, she was put off anyway. Plus, she was not in the practice of mixing her personal and work lives, having already learned that doing so could make things awkward and messy. She didn't tell the supervisor any of this. When he came on to her, she said simply, "I really think I'd better not," and "I'm flattered, but it's not a good idea," and two other answers along those lines. Then she'd arrived late to work one especially difficult morning when nine-year-old Juniper had been up sick all night with what looked like strep throat and the babysitter agreed to take her but charged double and Julia was exhausted and frazzled from rushing around making rearrangements—and now here was an envelope in her time card slot announcing, in generic corporate language, her dismissal.

After sitting in her car crying for maybe ten minutes, Julia blew her nose, freshened her makeup in the mirror, and drove to the county employment office that had helped her find the job. Her intention was to file a complaint. By the time she arrived, though, and took a number, and waited, waited, waited, she thought what she'd better do was let it go and use this session to find other work. She didn't have the time or the energy to fight some asshole mattress store manager just to, what, get the same job back? Probably.

The job counselor made a note that Julia had been let go for tardiness, then suggested she apply for a similar position that had opened the day before with Whitman HVAC. Julia dutifully drove across town to the company's location, a low, square building in a remote industrial park. She saw a pair of brightly painted service vans with the not-yet-familiar blue-and-yellow logo, parked alongside a glossy red BMW sedan. If this was the boss's car, she thought, she might as well turn around and go pick up Juniper. The last thing she needed was another thinks-he's-a-hotshot man in authority trying to put the moves on her.

No way to know, though, without going in.

The car did belong to the boss. The boss, though, was nothing like she feared. He was, in fact, possibly the loveliest man she'd ever met.

Brad Whitman took the time to meet her personally and thank her for her interest in the job. At her callback for an interview, he accepted without further questioning her explanation of why she'd been tardy and fired. After she got the job, he took time to say hello each morning and to ask how her day was going. He praised her work ethic. He hung out with her during slow times and talked about his upbringing, asked her about hers. Sometimes he ordered in lunch for her and the other employees. He often inquired about Juniper. When Julia brought Juniper to the company picnic a few months later, he played tag with her and the other kids, he brought both Juniper and Julia ice cream sandwiches, he carried Juniper on his back for a relay race, and he asked—respectfully—if he might take Julia out for dinner the next weekend. Charmed by this and all that had preceded it, she decided to put aside her rule and say yes.

At dinner that next weekend, in a trendy downtown restaurant, he said, "I don't really want to be your boss. I want to be your husband," and presented her with a princess-cut solitaire diamond ring that must have set him back six or eight thousand dollars. It was crazily romantic. Julia's mother, on the phone later that night, cautioned her to slow down, make him wait for her answer, see if he really was as good as he seemed. Julia was already wearing the ring.

———

At the curb now, in the Blakely Academy drop-off lane, Julia said, "Have a great day, girls. Juniper, good luck on the trig test. After school maybe we'll squeeze in time for frozen yogurt before running and dance, okay?"

Lily, having unbuckled herself, reached her arms around Julia's seat and hugged her from behind. "Great plan, Mommy!" she said. "I want sprinkles *and* a cherry, please."

"Naturally." Julia looked over at Juniper. "Sound good?"

"You know I don't like to eat right before I run," Juniper said, and got out of the car.

Julia told Lily, "Your sister is a grump."

"That's what Daddy said after *he* tried to cheer her up, too. I don't want to be a teenager," Lily said, slipping into her backpack's straps. "Way too much drama. I'm going to skip it."

"Good plan."

Julia waited for Lily to climb out and then pulled away from the curb, thinking of Juniper—the tension in Juniper's tone when speaking to her compared with the warmth she'd shown Lily. Something was just not right. Never mind giving her boundless time and space; this needed to be dealt with. She'd wait another week or two, see if things improved, and if they didn't, it might be time to suggest that, although their church attendance had fallen off, they might see Reverend Matthews for counseling as a family, so that Juniper wouldn't feel singled out.

As quickly as Julia decided this, though, she vacillated: Brad wouldn't like her taking their business "outside." He believed in self-discipline, in solving one's own problems, so there was that. He also believed in keeping personal matters quiet. It was a privacy thing. He was a public figure of a kind, and while she trusted Reverend Matthews absolutely, Brad regarded him as being "a little too in love with his own opinions and with sharing them widely. Perfect for a preacher, sure," he'd once said, "but don't go telling the man every little thing about yourself or the girls or me."

Maybe Juniper would come around on her own and Julia would be able to avoid a difficult conversation with Brad. He was so good to her, but he was also set in his thinking. He'd be reluctant to admit that Juniper could possibly have an actual problem, that everything wasn't in perfect order, that he wasn't in complete control of his domain.

And, well, Juniper *was* resilient, thought Julia, pulling into the tennis center's parking lot. Probably she, Julia, was worrying too much. They'd been through a lot worse than this. *Worse?* For heaven's sake, what was she thinking? This, their move, was a marvelous gift, not a problem! She needed to relax. Juniper was just being a normal teenager, and Julia was just being a normal overprotective mom. Everything was going to be fine.

6

Juniper waited near the Blakely Academy entrance doors for Lily to catch up, then walked with her inside.

"Knock knock," Juniper said as they went toward the Lower School corridor.

"Who's there?"

"Spell."

"Spell who?"

"Easy: W-H-O," Juniper said, and Lily burst out laughing in that whole-body, unabashed way she had. Juniper envied her. Everything was so straightforward for Lily, so clean and easy.

"You *got* me," Lily said, grinning at Juniper. "I can hardly believe it."

"I've been saving that one up. See you later, flower girl," said Juniper, and watched while Lily continued on toward her classroom.

Back in the main corridor, a pair of teenaged girls, seniors, saw Juniper coming and stepped into her way.

"Well, if it isn't Juni*pure* Whitman," said the first, a girl named Meghan who'd been deviling Juniper more or less the whole time she'd been a student at Blakely, and had ramped it up three years ago when word got around that Juniper had made a purity vow at church. "How's your day so far, Princess Junipure?"

"Look at her expression," said the other girl, Kathi, Meghan's usual sidekick. "She's totally like, *Go fuck yourself*."

"But she'll never actually say it because she's so pure."

"I wish *I* could be so pure," said Kathi. "Wait, no, I don't."

"So dull," said Meghan. "You should be at the Christian Academy with the other Jesus freaks."

Kathi said, "Seriously, why aren't you *there*?"

"Balance" was why she wasn't there. When Julia married Brad and turned her life around, she wanted Juniper in private school away from the kinds of bad influences that had led to so much of her own trouble. New Hope had a small K–12 program, but Julia felt that secular education on weekdays and religious education on Sundays was the best formula for making sure Juniper's influences were as well balanced as the meals she could now afford to feed her.

Blakely was supposed to be the best possible school environment your money could get you—in this part of North Carolina, at least. The best kids from the best families. The best teachers and best technology. The best hot lunch menu, curated by culinary goddesses—that's basically how the school sold it to the parents, anyway, and the parents loved it. Boutique education, like boutique hotels. There was talk of raising funds for an on-site spa.

As far as Juniper could see, Julia was all in for all of it. Between Blakely and New Hope, she was making certain her daughters were groomed into angels on earth. She made sure they did the "right" extracurricular activities, too, and she encouraged them to have the "right" kinds of kids as friends. Julia wasn't a helicopter parent; no, she was worse. She was an entire atmosphere surrounding her daughters' bodies, controlling their lives.

Juniper hadn't always seen Julia in such a negative light. In the first years after they joined up with Brad, Juniper was relieved to have so much order imposed on her life. Overjoyed, in fact. Lately, though, she'd begun to feel smothered and critical—of Julia, mainly;

Brad was another story altogether. Appearances were all that mattered to her mom: more than ever they had to have the perfect house, and Juniper had to be the perfect model child, visible proof that all the misfortunes and mistakes of their earlier lives had been remedied, with no lingering effects. Juniper resented that, and she resented this, these girls with their actually ideal lives and superior attitudes. She couldn't wait to be done with all of it, to be in charge of her own fate.

Juniper gave the girls no reply.

Meghan said, "She might be too big a freak even for the Christian Academy."

"That *is* possible," said Kathi. "You could be right."

"I *am* right. She doesn't even *want* to be normal, even Christian normal."

"Are you done?" Juniper said.

"Are we?" said Kathi.

Meghan cocked her head. "I suppose so. I need to go practice up on how to be so holy."

Kathi said, "Me, too."

"I'm sure it takes a lot of time and effort—which is why we never see Junipure at any of the good parties. Either that or she's never invited. Have *the* most wonderful day, princess," said Meghan. Then the two girls went around Juniper and on to their first period classes.

Sotto voce, Juniper said, "Go fuck yourselves," then continued down the hall. *Junipure.* Meghan thought she was so clever. Well, let her. Let her think it was better to get shitfaced every weekend. Let her think it was better to be a person who would drop her panties for any boy at any time than to be one who exercised discretion. Girls who behaved like Meghan ended up having abortions or babies; who knew that better than Juniper, who had herself been one such baby?

A young woman's virginity, her purity, was her superpower—Brad had said so, and the church had more or less taught the same, and right this minute Juniper could feel that it was true, as evidenced by how Meghan's and Kathi's bullying barely even made a dent.

Also, Juniper had the respect and admiration of many adults whose opinions mattered to her. Whereas girls like Meghan and Kathi couldn't know if even their own boyfriends respected them or were only on board for the easy access.

This was what she told herself, anyway, to help stay dent-free.

Being a chaste Christian girl didn't mean she was totally naive. It didn't mean she didn't have urges or temptations, or that she didn't get confused by things that would trouble any girl. Being "pure" hadn't made her magically able to solve all of her problems. *Would that it could,* she thought, walking into her English classroom, where they'd been reading classic British literature. Everything sounded better in British.

Her friend Pepper waved her over. "I've *got* to tell you something *big*," Pepper said, and Juniper smiled.

"Spill it," she said.

7

The Oak Knoll book club met at Valerie Alston-Holt's house on the third Thursday of every month. In the early years, the club members had taken turns hosting. Assigning the schedule, though, was always a hassle, and Valerie, as part of her adjustment to widowhood, yearned for the commotion of having her house full, so she'd offered to host perpetually and no one objected. Getting away from their domestic duties for an evening appealed to the other members, and this way no one's husband would complain about the cackling laughter (Belinda) or the hooting laughter (Lisa) or the number of empty wine bottles lining the table at evening's end. Also, the members enjoyed hearing Xavier playing guitar in the background if he was home and practicing.

For this May meeting, most of the club was in attendance. The others wished they could be; it was the first *public* connecting of Valerie and Julia, and we all were curious to see how Valerie would behave. We didn't expect trouble—Valerie wasn't the type to deliberately make someone feel uncomfortable. She was, as Xavier had said, always a good neighbor, quick to check on a sick friend or new parents, a great organizer of birthday parties and bereavement committees. Even so, everyone knew she was in actual psychic pain over last summer's clear-cutting and that Julia Whitman was a representative of the offense that pained her.

"Hello? Am I late? I cut through the yard," Julia said, knocking on the doorframe as she arrived at Valerie's back door. Valerie waved her in. Valerie and two other women were standing at the kitchen table loading their plates with food. Julia said, "I hope that was okay."

"That's what gates are for," Valerie told her, taking the basket Julia held out as an offering.

Inside the basket was a tin of foie gras and assorted gourmet crackers, along with a bottle of pinot noir that had been recommended by the wine guy at the market. Julia hadn't wanted to go cheap, but now that she was standing in Valerie's kitchen, she felt like she'd overdone it. —Which was no criticism of Valerie's home; the house was tiny but charming and a lot nicer than Julia's childhood home (a trailer). Nicer, too, than pretty much all of the places she'd lived as an adult before marrying Brad. Rather, Julia suddenly felt she was going to seem pretentious. Foie gras? Jesus. She'd been too eager for these women's approval and now they were going to think she was an ass.

As Valerie unpacked the basket and added its contents to the other foods laid out on the kitchen table, Julia said, "Honestly, I didn't see the point of having a gate there, but the fence company said we'd be glad we gave ourselves easy access to the rear of the property, for maintenance—"

"Meaning when my honeysuckle and pyracantha start taking over," Valerie joked.

"I love honeysuckle," Julia said.

"As if you'd allow any of your plantings to get out of control," said one of the other women, who then introduced herself. "You must be Julia. I'm Lisa Orlean. I live on Mimosa Court. Kelli says you all just moved in?"

Valerie said to Lisa, "Right over there," while pointing with the knife she'd been using to slice herself a piece of cheese.

Lisa nodded. "Impressive house. I was in it while it was under construction. I think pretty much everyone was."

"Thanks," Julia said. "We're very happy with it."

"Not I," said Valerie. "I mean, I wasn't in it during construction."

"Of course not you," said Lisa. She asked Julia, "What do you do?"

"Do . . . ?"

"Professionally."

"Oh, right." It had been a while since anyone asked Julia that. Her friends from the old neighborhood and the women she knew from tennis and the gym were all at-home moms. She said, "Well, I used to be an administrator," a bald overstatement of her prior work history. "Now I do a lot of volunteering at my daughters' school."

"Great," said Lisa. She was a petite black woman who looked to be about thirty years old.

Julia said, "You?"

"I founded and run a nonprofit that provides medical and health supplies to, mostly, Central American communities, though we try to also step in elsewhere when there's a temporary crisis—hurricanes, earthquakes, like that. We coordinate with the local Red Cross, Doctors Without Borders, et cetera."

"Wow," Julia said. A social aid nonprofit. Lisa had *founded* it. Julia felt equally surprised and diminished.

Lisa said, "If you're looking for new volunteer opportunities, give me a shout. We can use your help."

Julia listened for any note of judgment or criticism and heard none. She said, "I will. Thanks."

Xavier appeared in the kitchen and grabbed a plate. "Oh, hey, Ms. Whitman."

"Hi, Xavier," Julia said. She hadn't expected to see him. "Are you in the book club, too?"

"No," he said, filling his plate but avoiding the foie gras. "Food thief is all."

Valerie said, "He ate right after school, and now he's eating again, and he'll have a snack after his homework, too."

"No more homework this year, though," he said. "Exam prep is all. Which will also require snacks. Nice to see you again," he said to Julia before exiting through a door off the kitchen.

Julia said to Valerie, "He's so . . . I'm not sure what to call it. Grown-up?"

"Self-possessed," Lisa said.

"That's it. It's impressive. You've done a good job with him, Valerie."

"Thank you," Valerie said. "I really appreciate you saying so."

The trio joined the eight other women who'd gathered in the living room and were seated with plates on their laps and drinks in hand, apprising one another of the latest goings-on in their lives. It was a mixed group in every aspect: race, ethnicity, age, education level, and now that Julia was among them, class (if only by marriage and luck). What a wild turn of events, Julia thought, that she, who'd lived in a ramshackle trailer half her life and had dropped out of high school, was probably being perceived as the snooty one.

Valerie had added six metal folding chairs to the furniture layout, which consisted of a long gray couch and a green striped loveseat, one end table, one coffee table, a tall, narrow bookshelf, and a three-tier wrought-iron plant stand that was more or less hidden under an array of lush houseplants. There was no television. This more than anything else made an impression on Julia; her new house had . . . (she stopped to count) . . . six TVs, each one of them "smart" devices hardwired to super-high-speed internet. Further, Brad had directed the installation of whole-house audio and security systems, both of which he could control remotely with apps on his phone. They had automated landscape lighting and an irrigation system, too. Brad loved technology. He had suggested that Julia do her grocery shopping online and have everything delivered—leaving more time in her day for . . . what? She *enjoyed* pushing the cart up and down the aisles, taking her time, perusing the varieties of produce and proteins, the soups and spices, coffees, pastas, pastries . . . If anything made her feel like a queen in this, her reconstituted life, it was having the time and ability to shop for any food she liked. She still sometimes bought SpaghettiOs just because, and ate them in secret when no one was home.

Kelli Hanes, the white OR nurse who lived across the street from Julia and who'd invited her here, said, "Everyone, this is Julia Whitman, newest Oak Knoll resident. She told me she's an avid reader, and I said, 'I've got the group for you!' This is her first-ever book club meeting, so be nice."

"When are we ever not nice?" said Belinda Johnson, and then she cackled with laughter.

Kelli said, "We all remember last month, when you and Esther fought about whether Lolita was complicit in Humbert's treatment of her."

"Well, that was a *ludicrous* judgment."

"Where *is* Esther?" said Lisa.

Valerie answered, "Probably home sticking pins in an effigy of Belinda. No, I'm kidding. She called me; Hank's not well. She said she hoped to be here, but only if he'd improved, so . . ."

"Hank's sick? What's the matter?"

Valerie said, "Cough, weakness—they're doing tests. Esther says probably heart failure. He's almost eighty," she told Julia. "His health's been poor for a while now."

Julia listened to the women as they made a plan to visit and aid the couple, Esther and Hank. *This,* she thought, *is what it is like to be a part of a community.* These women all knew one another, they cared actively—it made her happy just to be in the room with them. Though she was sorry for ailing Hank, whoever he was.

It wasn't like this in their old neighborhood. The families were loosely familiar with one another, but everyone minded their own business. The only women Julia had been even a little bit close to were the three who also sent their kids to Blakely and one who played tennis in the same league she was in. Oh, sure, everyone waved to everyone in passing. But no one made a schedule to bring food and check in on the sick old neighbor. Possibly because there hadn't been any sick old neighbors—everyone was youngish. If any of the youngish residents had been sick, no one had said so. If there was a book club, she hadn't heard about it.

Eventually the women here in Valerie's living room got around to the book of the evening. There was a lively discussion, with some debate but no fights. Julia loved how even something as personal as the experience of reading a novel could be made into a community activity. She loved hearing these intelligent women speak thoughtfully about what they'd read. She noticed, however, that although people had gotten up throughout the discussion to get seconds and even thirds of some of the dishes, the foie gras remained untouched except for the portion she'd taken herself.

Later, when the others had gone and Julia was helping Valerie clean up, Julia slid the tin into a waxed paper bag and said with attempted levity, "I guess this wasn't as much of a hit as the book."

"Don't worry about it. People have different tastes."

"It makes me look snooty, right? You can tell me."

"Yeah?" Valerie said, looking closely at Julia to see if she meant what she'd said. "Okay. So it isn't exactly about *snooty*, although maybe a couple of people think that. Marta—the one sitting at the left end of the sofa? She is one hundred percent against the bourgeoisie, so she's never going to love you, but don't worry because it isn't personal. Most everybody else? It's about how foie gras is made. How they force-feed the birds in order to create a fatty liver. They put tubes down their throats. It's pretty awful."

Julia imagined this and was horrified. "I . . . God, I had no idea. How do you—how is it that you all know this?"

"There was a story about it on NPR a while back. We talked about it at the time."

"I sort of wish you hadn't told me," Julia said. "Brad loves the stuff." She put the tin into the trash—then just as quickly wished she hadn't, because it seemed doubly a waste that way and Brad *would* eat it if she brought it home. But then she'd have to say why no one here had eaten it, and he'd probably call the women *bleeding hearts* and maybe even bring it up at the housewarming party they were going to throw . . .

She left the tin in the trash.

Valerie extracted the tin and scraped its contents into her countertop compost bin, saying, "Ignorance is bliss for sure, but it won't help the ducks and geese. Maybe knowing doesn't help much, either, though. I mean, lots of people are still going to buy foie gras and every other offensive or dangerous thing I boycott. Don't even get me started on plastics! I do what I can, though, so that I can at least face myself in the mirror. *Anyway*," she said, "tonight was good, right? You enjoyed it?"

Julia nodded. "Is it like this with every book?"

"Some invite more contention. As you heard about *Lolita*. Ever read it?"

Julia shook her head. "I've heard of it, of course. It's the one about that teenage . . . what, temptress? She seduces—"

"*Not* a teen, and *not* a temptress, and no seduction," Valerie said. "She's twelve when she's kidnapped and corrupted. Raped, basically."

"Oh. I didn't realize. And Esther—the one you were talking about, she thinks the girl is complicit?"

Valerie said, "Esther's eighty-one and comes from a very traditional upbringing. She feels that if a girl has sex before marriage, even if she's forced, it's because she was asking for it one way or another. The girl shouldn't have dressed a certain way, or looked at a man, or been alone with him or alone at all—you name it, she's got her justifications. It made Belinda really angry. Made me angry, too, to tell the truth. Too many young women have been traumatized by men and then also by attitudes like Esther's! It's no wonder most of them never report the crime—to anyone."

"True." Julia nodded. She hesitated a moment, then said, "That was me, once upon a time. I was thirteen and it was my mom's boss. Well, one of her bosses."

She glanced at Valerie and saw, what? Acceptance? Yes. Women did this—not so much in Julia's experience, but she knew it did happen, knew there was a sisterhood she might be welcomed into if she was able to open up about her past. The wine had loosened her tongue and she wasn't sorry at all. She wanted to be in the sister-hood. She wanted a new friend, *this* friend, Valerie, who Kelli had said was the connector here in Oak Knoll. Glowing dark skin, eyes that snapped with intelligence and humor, a smile that welcomed everyone. "She's an earth mother," Kelli said. "She likes to tend everyone, but she also doesn't overdo it." Unlike Julia's mother, who made *overdone* her special art.

Julia went on, "My mom cleaned houses for a few different families and sometimes she made me come with her to help. I was doing the upstairs bathroom while she did the kitchen, and this man, he just came in and locked the door and . . ." She paused, recalling the terrible, painful few minutes that would have an outsize effect on the years that followed. "He said, 'You're *hot*. I just need a min-ute or two.' I was so ashamed, and so afraid that if I fought him or made a scene my mom would get fired. We had *no* money," she said. "I mean, as it was, we could barely afford to pay the rent for the shitty trailer we lived in."

"I'm sorry," Valerie said, squeezing Julia's hand.

"Thanks," said Julia. She shrugged. "It was a long time ago."

"You're, what? Thirty . . . ?"

"Thirty-four. I had Juniper at seventeen."

Valerie gave her hand another squeeze, then set to washing the wineglasses. "Nothing so bad as that happened to me," she said, "but there was this guy—we called him Uncle Ray—who lived up-stairs from my family when I was a kid in Michigan. Uncle Ray was a creep. Had a thing for coming down to get his newspaper in nothing but a robe, and if my folks were away and he knew I was around, he'd leave his robe open, give me a good look at him. He might have done it to my little sisters, too. I never said anything about it to any-one, and they never mentioned it to me. We all just get through the bullshit, right? And we raise our sons, if we have sons, to be decent men."

"And protect our daughters from those kinds of situations," Julia said. "I'm trying to, anyway. Brad's a great dad—a lot stricter than mine was before he left. He's bighearted, you know? Our rules are kind of old-fashioned, but they're fair and good for the girls. I admit, it was a relief to marry him and have someone else to share the parenting load. Juniper was never a difficult kid, but when you're the only parent—"

"So Brad isn't Juniper's father?"

"No. She was ten when I married him. Lily's his. He loves Juniper like she's his own, though. There *are* some good guys in the world."

Valerie nodded. "I used to be married to one myself."

"Maybe you will be again."

"We'll see. I'm dating someone," Valerie said. "He's pretty great."

"Our house?" Julia said, pointing toward it. "It was all Brad's idea. He had some really good luck with something he invented, and he wanted the girls and me to benefit."

"That's generous."

"It is," Julia said, electing not to mention the beach house he'd bought, too. There was sharing, and then there was showing off—that's how it might come across, and she didn't want to ruin this promising start.

"Anyway," she said, "I better get back. Lily likes me to read to her at bedtime. It was *really* nice to talk with you. I'm so glad we're neighbors."

"Will you come to next month's meeting?" Valerie asked, turning on the light outside the back door.

"I'd like to."

"Good. I'm sure I'll see you before then—I'll be out there in the yard a lot, putting in a koi pond. Zay jokes that I'm going to replace him with fish."

"Well, the gate's always open, so to speak," Julia said. "If you hear splashing, come on over."

"Maybe I will."

Julia said good night and walked through Valerie's woodsy yard, glancing upward at the big oak's extensive branches as she went. It was a remarkable tree, and she was glad to have a view of it from her own kitchen windows.

She arrived home feeling warm and buzzy and pleased with the evening, especially the conversation she'd had with Valerie—but a bit chagrined about the foie gras. It was so hard to navigate the world these days. Ignorance *was* bliss, particularly when you found yourself amid a group of informed people who were disgusted by what you'd inadvertently done but too polite to call you out for it.

⸺

Julia also couldn't have known how tentative Valerie's *maybe I will* was, which was good because she'd have taken it personally when in fact it wasn't a judgment against her at all. Now that Valerie had gotten to know Julia a little, she liked her just fine. It was Brad who was the problem, Brad who made Valerie prefer to stay on her side of the fence.

Julia seemed to be merely an unwitting accomplice to (or we might even say a cooperative victim of) her husband's ambitions and desires.

8

Though the time would come when we'd all know why Juniper Whitman sometimes felt such a keen need to be alone, on this night nearly two weeks after her family's move to Oak Knoll, we knew only what Xavier Alston-Holt knew: She was attractive. She seemed quiet. We might have called her *bookish* and meant it as a compliment.

Twilight, the end of May. A time when lots of folks went outside to look for fireflies and enjoy the cacophony of birdsong, finches and cardinals and chickadees and mockingbirds singing the sun down. For Juniper, twilight promised a kind of cover. She could walk along the sidewalks and not feel exposed the way she did in daytime. *Junipure, the freak.* Though not for the reasons her classmates thought.

"You're not going running at this hour," Brad said, startling her as she sat down on a bench in the foyer to put on her shoes. He was in the front room, or "parlor," as Julia and the decorator had been referring to it. The room had four big upholstered armchairs and lighted wall art and a faux zebra-skin rug. And Brad, who'd been sitting there alone, possibly watching the sunset. Juniper hadn't seen him before he spoke.

She told him, "No, just a walk."

Track season was over, so she'd cut back her running schedule from six to four times a week, getting Julia to drop her off at the state park where she could run on the multi-use trails. She enjoyed being out in the forest, where the air was cooler, where she was away from traffic, away from school, from home, from her life. She also liked seeing the birds and deer, liked the way the sunshine made the forest into a lush green wonderland. She liked the tree trunks standing like thousands of sentinels along the trails, upright and protective. She liked the variety of undergrowth—plants whose names she hadn't learned yet but whose shapes and structures invited her to meander while she cooled down after a run, invited a closer look, a photo—which a normal teen might share on Instagram, say, but Juniper, forbidden to use social media, would save to an album on her phone, then print the images later and tack them up in her room. Julia did phone spot checks to keep her honest.

Brad said, "I want you back here by nine."

"Okay," said Juniper, standing up. "But you know, I'm going on eighteen. It's okay for me to be out after dark."

"Sorry. What I meant is, this is a good neighborhood, but we don't know everybody here. I just want you to be safe."

He never worried about her running at the park, but he was worried here? She said, "I'm sure I'll be fine."

"You have your phone?"

"Yes." She took it from her pocket and showed it to him.

"Go on, then. Enjoy your walk."

Juniper closed the front door behind her and went down their short flagstone path toward the public sidewalk. The warm air was heavy, humid, the sky blood-orange at the horizon, cobalt overhead. A couple of stars were visible.

What, she wondered, made a neighborhood *good*? To her parents, *good* seemed to mean there were mainly other people like themselves. So: white, privileged, *very* concerned with appearances (her mom) or perceptions (Brad). Though to be fair, this new neighborhood was mixed, and also, both Brad and her mom had worked like dogs to get their privilege. Nothing got handed to them—unless Brad's marrying her mom was a kind of handout. It was a hand *up*, that was for sure. And Juniper would be lying if she said she hadn't been just as happy as Julia at the time, just as relieved to be pulled out of the chaotic morass of those earlier years. Brad was ten-year-old Juniper's hero, her savior, her most favorite person in the world.

So much had changed since then, some of it in ways she didn't like to think about—but how could she control those thoughts? Her brain wouldn't always cooperate, and now she was stuck here in this neighborhood where the houses were so close together and there were people around all the time and there was Brad, just sitting in the dark—

Juniper stopped at the sidewalk, drew a heavy breath. *Leave it alone,* she thought, exhaling, and then she set off on her walk.

The Whitmans' house was now completely in order and Julia was turning it into a showplace, using a decorator to help her choose every piece of furniture, every pillow and lamp and rug. Each room in the house was painted according to a "complementary palette" of pale grays and pale blues with "pops" of color, those pops coming from local artists' wall art and from throw pillows that were absurdly expensive. Juniper had seen the interior designer's itemized bill: $94 for one pillow. For $94 they could adopt a piece of rain forest, help the Earth keep breathing a while longer.

Or they could adopt a dog from the local shelter. Lily had been angling for this, for them to get a dog after they moved—"Just a little one, it can sleep with me, I'll walk it and feed it, I *promise*," and Julia had made noises like she might give in. But now that there was a $3,000 rug and pure white furniture in the living room, and 100 percent wool carpet imported from New Zealand in their bedrooms, Juniper knew there would be no dog—or cat or rabbit or hamster even, because they'd done the hamster thing when Juniper was ten, a present to go with Julia's marriage and their temporary move from the latest crappy apartment to Brad's "starter house," he'd called it. And then the animal gave birth to six pups and ate four of them, traumatizing Juniper, who hadn't known such behavior was possible.

Now, though, Juniper was seventeen. She understood a lot more about life. That said, she'd been relatively sheltered these past seven years, and so by no means did she understand everything. Maybe not even enough, because if she had understood enough, then after she'd rounded the corner of her street and walked along the connecting street and onto the one where Xavier lived and seen him and two friends sitting on the trunk of a car beneath a streetlight that had just come on, she would not have stopped to talk.

No, a wiser, more cautious Juniper would have said, "Hey," and kept going, up the long street and around the next corner and the next, and returned home in more or less the same mood she'd been in when she left the house. Okay, maybe she would have felt a little more upbeat for having been outside and away for a while. That, though, would have been the whole scenario start to finish.

But rather than blame Juniper for trouble she could not have foreseen, we should credit her for being friendly, for not having that knee-jerk fear of brown-skinned males that so many white girls have, in the South especially.

We, with our collective wisdom but imperfect knowledge, did not foresee the trouble, either.

———

Xavier waved at her when he saw her approaching. "Juniper, right? How's it going?"

"Okay, I guess. How about you?"

"All good," he said, and then he gestured toward one of his companions. "This is my friend Joseph."

"Hey," Joseph said. He was Xavier's opposite in terms of height and coloring: short, pale, towheaded. He wore his hair in dreadlocks. Juniper couldn't recall ever seeing a white kid with dreads.

"And this is Dashawn," Xavier said, pointing to the other boy, who was darker skinned than he. Dashawn's hair was puffy—*an Afro*, Juniper thought. She wanted to touch it, press it to see how springy it might be. Probably he wouldn't like that, though (as if she'd even dare to do it), the same way she didn't like random people touching the birthmark on her forearm.

"Hey, Juniper," Dashawn said.

"Hey. Nice to meet you."

"Juniper lives behind me." Xavier pointed in that direction.

Joseph gave a low whistle. "I've seen that house. Nice digs you all have."

"She goes to Blakely," Xavier added. "Junior, right?"

"Unfortunately."

He said, "Next year will go a lot faster than you think. So, we were about to go inside and play some music. Me on guitar, no surprise. Joseph here plays sax—alto and tenor."

"And baritone."

"And baritone," Xavier echoed. The two boys tapped knuckles. "Dashawn is an awesome drummer. I've been messing around with jazz just for fun, and they're putting up with my mediocrity. Want to hang out?"

When in Juniper's life had any boy come across so cool? Never, that's when. Xavier Alston-Holt didn't just look good (and to Juniper, he looked pretty close to perfect), he had talent and an outgoing personality she admired. At her house that first day, when he and his mother had come over to meet her parents, he'd sat there as if he was one of the adults, comfortable, tuned in, polite in a way that didn't seem at all put on. Most of the boys she went to school with acted fake and smarmy around the adults, as if they thought themselves superior but knew they had to pretend it was the other way around. Xavier had . . . well, she would have to say he had a *presence*. And she was responding to it. It wasn't that she wanted to, but how could it be helped? It couldn't be. She didn't really *want* to help it, either, and that surprised her.

Juniper told him, "Thanks, but I have to get back. Brad thinks I might be attacked by vampires or something if I'm out past nine."

"That your brother?" said Dashawn.

"Stepdad."

Xavier said, "He's the Whitman HVAC guy."

"I know him," Joseph said. "Not, you know, *know* him—"

"The ads," said Juniper, and Joseph nodded.

"He get along with your real dad?" said Joseph. "My two act like they're ready to throw down over stupid shit *all* the time."

"I don't know my real dad. He's not . . . I mean, he's never been part of my life. I . . ." She paused. "I don't even know who he is."

"It happens," said Joseph, and the other two nodded, and Juniper felt proud of herself for telling them something she didn't usually volunteer.

"But that shit ain't happenin' to me," Dashawn said. "I keep it covered."

"Thanks for sharing," Xavier said. He told Juniper, "Maybe call and see if Brad'll let you come inside, away from the vampires. Well, except this one," he joked, nudging Joseph. "My mom's home, if that makes a difference."

Juniper thought of it: calling Brad, telling him that Xavier had invited her in.

"Okay, I'll check." She took her phone from her pocket and called her mom's cell instead.

"Hey, it's me. I'm around the block and Xavier—the boy behind us?—is here with a couple of friends and they want to know if I can hang out with them for a while. Ms. Alston-Holt is home."

"Friends meaning boys, or girls, or what?"

"Boys."

"Not a good idea," said Julia. "You know that. Time to come on home. It's almost nine anyway."

"Seriously? It's Friday."

"You know the rules. You should've made plans with your girlfriends. Come home. Lily and I are watching *Frozen*, if you want to join us."

"Fine."

Juniper hung up, then told the boys, "Can't, sorry."

"Next time," Xavier said, and Juniper felt herself flush with pleasure.

Joseph said, "Are they always strict like that?"

She shrugged. "They're pretty protective—"

"Brad seems nice on TV," Dashawn said.

"No, right, he is. It's just . . . they're old-fashioned about stuff like this. I didn't think I'd get a yes, but I wanted to try."

This last part Juniper directed at Xavier. She was rewarded with the crooked smile all the Oak Knoll ladies adored. She began to think she might adore him if she got the chance. Or took it.

9

We can't say that even after a few weeks of casual acquaintance we knew Brad Whitman all that well, despite his gregarious behavior with the neighbors and the information about him available on the internet. His style was to ask people about themselves, to draw them out, make them feel important, seen. He didn't offer them much about himself beyond the surface-level facts. He was, however, every bit as charming as he seemed on TV, that much we knew.

Local and regional newspapers and business journals liked to write about him, this North Carolina–born boy who'd come from nothing and pulled himself up by the proverbial bootstraps, building a company that had become familiar to most of us, those blue-and-gold service trucks and vans seeming to be everywhere you looked. Hot weather meant trouble with air conditioners. Cold weather meant trouble with furnaces and heat pumps. For Brad (in this), trouble was money in the bank.

The Whitman HVAC technicians were all clean-cut, polite, honest men, every one of them white because, we surmised, Brad understood a truth about his fellow Southern citizens: a great many of them would not open their door to a man of color—especially a black man, no matter how clean-cut or polite. And Brad couldn't afford to have customers refuse to do business with him owing to their unreasonable fears. He was, we agreed, practical—possibly to a fault, though we couldn't know yet one way or the other.

That said, we were making what we thought were pretty fair guesses about who he was and what motivated him each day when he set his feet on the hand-loomed Himalayan Snowmass Alpaca rug the interior decorator had selected to go underneath his and Julia's bed. Real understanding (though perhaps *understanding* is an overstatement) is something we arrived at later; we hardly saw him in the neighborhood as summer got under way, given that he had a thriving business to run.

"Whitman HVAC is solid," said Mark Lewis, Brad's accountant and friend since way back. Mark had just presented his biannual assessment, and "solid" was the bottom line. He said, "You've never been in better shape."

They were in Brad's office at what they called the Hub, the company's headquarters, the center now of a wheel that had seven satellites in four cities. The office, small and tidy, was painted gray and had little character. A utilitarian desk. A single tall file cabinet. An old couch—Brad's first, from back when he'd had a studio apartment and survived on microwaved lasagna and burritos, living off his credit cards while he got the business (such as it was at the time) up and running. Mark sat in a plastic IKEA chair, while Brad sat behind the desk in the room's single indulgence: a leather Eames Executive Chair, possibly the most comfortable piece of furniture ever made and no question the best Brad had ever owned.

Brad patted his belly. "Good shape? Eh, I might do with a few more hours at the gym."

"Maybe now's the time for that," Mark said. Like Brad, he wore a designer-brand golf shirt. Unlike Brad's, his didn't strain in the front. "Scale back a little here, spend more time in the gym, more time in the great outdoors. You keep saying you're going to buy a boat."

"I do keep saying that."

"Usually when you say a thing, you do a thing."

Brad said, "That's a fact."

"Well, I mean it. You're in great shape, Bud. You've already got the beach house; now you should buy that fishing boat and get to work angling for swordfish."

"I might could," Brad said. "Though a sailboat appeals to me, too."

Mark closed the files on his tablet and tucked it into his briefcase. "Any boat'll get you on the water. You just need to pick one and buy it. Boat ownership is the natural progression of things. Oh, and of course you'll need a first mate."

Brad laughed. "Well, I guess I know who to call. Meantime, you and Carrie are coming to our little soiree, right?"

"The housewarming? Definitely. And let me know if you want me to connect you with Ed Levinson—he's the boat broker some of my other clients use."

"The way you're pushing this boat thing, I suspect you get a commission."

Mark shook his head. "Nah, I just like having friends with boats. That way I'll never have to bother with owning one myself."

"I'm not sure if that makes you lazy or smart."

"Proudly both where boats are concerned." Mark stood and Brad walked him out. "You think on it—and the rest of it, too, all right?"

"I'm not getting any younger, that's what you're saying."

"None of us is. Carpe fucking diem while you can."

"You are a fine poet, my friend. But don't give up accounting."

When Mark was gone, Brad went back to his office and put his feet on his desk in a rare display of ease. Getting Mark's latest assessment of the business confirmed what he'd thought was true, and now Mark's advice—which had always been solid and had in part led to these great results—was worth thinking about.

Should he stop here, with eight Whitman HVAC locations running smoothly, just about minting money now that the expansion costs were behind him? Was he content with the little kingdom he'd built, no need or desire to expand further? Growth always had to be managed closely, which took time, and time was one commodity he wasn't going to be able to buy himself more of. *Twenty years* of hustle, and a lot to show for it, sure, but now he was itching for fresh challenges and new experiences. He'd never meant for HVAC to be his *life*.

He'd started the company with less than nothing: four thousand dollars of debt, which he'd accumulated by taking a bunch of college courses he had little use for. Philosophy. Psychology. Sociology. English. *Very* basic science and math. What was he meant to do with the stuff they were teaching in these classes? Sure, some of it was interesting, but he was there for a degree in electrical engineering, and yet his entire first year's schedule was made up of these so-called core classes.

In the middle of his second semester he'd walked out of an excruciatingly dull composition class, went to the registration office, and dropped out. Then he'd enrolled in a HVAC certification course that would let him get straight to work in a field that, in this state, was almost as essential as undertaking. Smartest thing he ever did— that's what he told everyone anytime the subject came up. "I was too smart for college" was the other thing he always said. He'd said it to Juniper last night, in fact.

"I was too smart for college, and honestly, honey, I think you're too smart, too. There's no reason for you to go off to Washington or wherever. Nothing you learn there is going to be practical for your future."

They'd been in the bonus room while Julia was in reading to Lily before bed. Brad was channel surfing. Juniper had her laptop out and was looking up college programs she thought might suit her. She said, "That depends on what my future is, doesn't it?"

"It does, it does. If you're lucky, you'll have a great life with a man who loves and takes care of you so you don't need to work at all. You can go to Seattle on vacation."

"I guess."

"Work is . . . well, it's *work*. One of the great pleasures of my life is being able to take care of you girls so that you have it easier. Who wouldn't want that, if they could get it? Your mom sure did."

Juniper said, "I want to get a job. I mean, right now I do. I need something for summer so I don't die of boredom."

"Well, I can understand that for sure," he said, and then he had an idea. "Come to work for me. We're just getting ready to hire someone to help with dispatch at the Hub."

"Work for *you*?" Juniper said. "I don't know if . . . I mean, maybe. I think I'm going to apply to some places first, though, and see what happens."

"I'll need someone to take the reins one day," he said, the idea blooming just ahead of his words as they emerged. "I could train you from the ground up."

She looked at him in surprise. "I thought you were with Reverend Matthews on the 'women should aspire to be wives and mothers' thing. Like you just said."

"Well, sure, but if you *want* to work, I can't think of a better opportunity for you. Keep it all in the family. Nothing not to like about making Whitman HVAC a family thing."

Juniper tilted her head, seeming to consider it. "I never thought you'd go for something like that. I mean, not that I necessarily even want to work there. No offense."

"I'm capable of surprises," he said. "You just have to give old Brad a chance."

She glanced at him, then back at her screen. "You're not *so* old."

"Forty-seven next month—so yeah, not *so* old. Not *too* old." He sure wasn't going to let his age or anything else keep him from pursuing what he wanted. Never had, never would. He said, "You think about it, all right? That's all I'm saying. Think about it. I'll pay you ten percent over the best offer you might get."

"Okay, I'll think about it."

For his part, he could hardly imagine a better scenario than having her come on board with him. Later, after their conversation, he'd lain in bed considering how he might go about setting it up, grooming her to take on a management role, work with him side by side. Then she wouldn't go off to college at all. Then she would be right there where he could see her every day. Julia would like that, too.

It used to be that when Brad sat here at his desk and looked out into the lobby, he saw Julia at the reception desk. Usually she was on the telephone managing one thing or another, but sometimes a customer would come in with a question or, rarely, a complaint. Julia was good with people, and good with him. He hadn't minded a bit those times when, after they'd gotten engaged, she had come into his office and closed the shades, given him a little workday release. She knew how much he appreciated her talents.

He'd appreciated everything about his wife, that was a fact. They'd met at a time when he'd grown bored with the dating scene and the sorts of women he met in the clubs and bars. They all seemed to be trying too hard. He was in favor of appealing presentations, sure he was—the artfully dyed and styled hair, the long, painted nails, the short dresses and high heels, a touch of makeup and false eyelashes, too, why not? And he had taken his share of the offerings. For him, however, these women lacked something, though until he met Julia he couldn't have said what that something was. Then he understood. Underneath Julia's appealing exterior (admittedly not as refined as some back then, given her meager funds) was a kind of grittiness and fortitude, and something else: genuine need.

What was also a fact, though, was that their sex life nowadays was barely a notch above perfunctory. She had so much going on with the girls—piano, track, dance, soccer, plus school stuff with Lily's class especially, since she was the grade mom. Her daughters were her life. She might seem mild-mannered, but where the girls were concerned, she could be fierce. The whole thing with his joining New Hope—that had been her deal, 100 percent. He'd gone along, since it didn't hurt his public image to warm a pew every Sunday morning, and he agreed that Juniper was already benefiting from "belonging to a community of faith and love" as she approached puberty. Julia had been grateful to God and Brad in equal measures back then. Juniper had outright worshiped him.

He could trace his sex-life energy drain to the later part of Julia's pregnancy with Lily. He'd understood how she might not feel sexy when her belly was swollen and round as a basketball. He'd understood how in the months after Lily's birth she'd felt like her body was still colonized, only now by a nursing infant instead of a growing fetus. Fact was, most of that turned him off, too.

From there, though, she hadn't returned to the level of interest and attention she'd paid him before. She never said anything and she never turned him down, but he could tell the difference. He felt the slight remoteness when they were in the act, the diminished enthusiasm. And frankly, it had the effect of making him less interested in her. A man liked to feel desired, liked to feel as if his woman wanted it as much as he did—or was at least eager when the chance arose. Julia was not eager.

If he thought about it too much, he could persuade himself that maybe she hadn't ever been all that eager, that maybe she had put on an act in order to get what she *did* want. He didn't like thinking this way; not only did it diminish Julia, but it made him out to be less desirable than he believed he was. It made him look as if he could be fooled.

He needed to feel *vibrant*. To feel wanted. He needed—as we all do—to feel secure.

A lot of men in Brad's shoes didn't think twice about finding alternative outlets for their needs. Titty bars, gentlemen's clubs, a coworker, the hot young childless wife down the block—if a man wanted to step out, it was simple enough to do. Most such men would settle for an easy lay, no strings attached. None of that was Brad Whitman's style. He didn't want a whore or a dalliance, he wanted total devotion, same as he was willing to give. He wasn't like most men—never had been, never would be.

Brad Whitman was an all-or-nothing kind of guy. In this way, he and Xavier Alston-Holt were alike.

10

A striking and, to some, controversial photograph—a portrait—sat on the Whitmans' new credenza alongside other family photos. In the photo, Brad Whitman is dressed in a navy blue tuxedo. He stands behind Juniper, who wears a long white gown. Though the gown is an off-the-shoulder design, it's simple in its style. Silk organdy, no ruffles or lace or trim. Modest. Brad's hands rest on Juniper's waist. His eyes are closed, as are hers. Behind them is a high mantel decorated with white flowers and white ribbons.

"This must be from Juniper's Purity Ball," said Sheila Jamison, wife of Jimmy, the friend who'd built a house one street over from the Whitmans in Oak Knoll. This conversation took place at the Whitmans' housewarming party as the Jamisons were admiring both the credenza, a handcrafted piece done in light and dark maple woods, and the photo.

Sheila told Brad, "I don't think I've seen it before."

"Julia had it on our dresser at the old house."

"Interesting portrait," said Jimmy.

"It was an interesting night," Brad said.

Those of us who were also at the housewarming and within

earshot—for the Whitmans had invited everyone on the block—
noted the hesitation in Brad's remark, his emphasis on *interesting*.

"What," said Jimmy, elbowing him, "you aren't a true believer?"

"It's a good program, no question. I'll probably do it again with
Lily when she's a teen." Brad leaned toward the pair and lowered his
voice. "I needed a couple of drinks that night, though, to get through
the ceremony straight-faced—it goes a *little* bit further than might
be necessary, seems to me. That picture was taken when I was sufficiently greased."

Jimmy said, "So those New Hope folks aren't against liquor,
then."

"Officially? It's discouraged. The good reverend and I got to be
pals, though, so he managed to turn a blind eye to my flask. And I
was discreet, of course."

Belinda, our cackling friend, had been standing near enough
to catch all of this. She eased herself over to the three of them and
said, "I thought I overheard something about a Purity Ball?"

"I was admiring this photograph," said Sheila. "It's from the
ball."

Belinda studied the photo. "So it's a father-daughter thing?"

Brad said, "That's right."

Belinda lived catty-corner from the Whitmans and had developed a fascination with Brad. She wanted to hear him, watch him
speak, get up close to those too-blue eyes. "Fill me in," she said.

"Sure," Brad replied. "Well, the ball culminates a ceremony
wherein the dads promise to protect and support the girls, and the
girls promise to stay virgins until after the dads hand them off at
their wedding."

"How old is she, there?" Belinda said, pointing at the portrait.

"I guess she was fourteen?" said Brad. He paused, thinking,
then said, "Yep, three years ago."

Jimmy said, "Lily's, what, seven now? Still a ways off for her,
then. Though maybe starting early is the way to go."

"At birth, if you can," Belinda said, nodding. "I raised a wild child myself. Turned out all right, though. She's a dental hygienist in Atlanta."

Brad said, "Julia's thinking Lily won't need the program. Different influences, you know."

"We really admire you, Brad," cooed Sheila. "Raising a teenage girl these days is no easy feat."

"Right?" said Jimmy. "That's why we had boys."

"And you took it on voluntarily," Sheila added, laying her hand on Brad's arm. "You really made all the difference in Julia's life—and Juniper's."

Brad smiled. "I joke with Julia that she's a rescue wife. Things *were* pretty rough for her before we got together."

"Well, you have a beautiful family now," Sheila said.

Jimmy patted Brad's back. "You could still have a son. Get the full range of experiences."

"It's not impossible," Brad said, though he sounded as if he was not at all interested in having a son. "To your point about raising girls: it is a challenge for sure. And I do like challenges, as you know. In this area, though, Julia and I felt the purity thing was a smart approach to making adolescence easier on her—and us."

Juniper wasn't in the room during this conversation, but when Belinda related the exchange to a few of us in the next room afterward, we wondered whether Juniper thought pledging her virginity to her stepfather in a ritualistic ceremony did in fact make things easier on her.

None of us knew she was harassed about it in school; certainly *that* was a disadvantage. Were there benefits, though, that we weren't seeing? Was it somehow easier to handle your sexual maturation by effectively denying it until marriage, whenever that might take place?

Some of us wondered what Juniper might think about there being no equivalent pledge or ceremony or standard for young men.

Some of us thought, Why should having sex be regarded as an act of impurity? What did *impure* even mean? What was *pure*, and why was it so desirable for a girl to be that, while boys could be however they liked? And where was Juniper just then, as Brad went

on to describe how proud of her he was for always being well behaved, for never drinking alcohol, for being willing to put off dating
until after graduating high school? We'd noticed her earlier, nicely
turned out in a modest green dress and shoes with low heels—not
those stilettos we'd been seeing on some people's teens in prom pictures on Facebook, where the girls often resembled lounge singers or
worse. Juniper looked just as attractive as any of those girls, and
also age-appropriate. Whatever we might think of purity promises,
we could see the sense of discouraging overt sexuality and injurious
"fuck me" footwear.

Just then, Juniper was outside in the far corner of the backyard—
away from the glow of the light strings that crisscrossed above the
patio; away from the pool lights, the security camera; away from
the fawning remarks by her parents' friends over how absolutely perfect and gorgeous this new house was, what an accomplishment,
what a pleasure it must be to live so well. Those gorgeous countertops! That luscious rug! Away from her inquisitive little sister, who
had a half-dozen other kids around to play with; they had all of Lily's
Barbies out and were enacting the dance scene from *Beauty and the
Beast*. There were a couple of teens inside as well: the Jamisons' oldest son was Juniper's age, and he had a brother who was fourteen.
She'd managed to set them up in the bonus room with the Xbox and
then gave them the slip.

Juniper was grateful for the party, and would return to it before she could be missed. Because now she was sitting on a cushion
on the mulch, talking quietly with Xavier Alston-Holt.

She was holding his hand.

In a few minutes she would be kissing him for the first but not
(she hoped) the last time.

11

See Xavier, though, in the aftermath:

"I'm not doing that again," he told Dashawn from where he was lying on his bedroom floor, having just related what had happened with Juniper at the party a few nights earlier. "*Complete* mistake."

"You're too hard on yourself," Dashawn said.

He was at Xavier's desk, doodling. As good a drummer as he was, art was his passion. He'd been admitted to the graphic arts program at the state university and had big plans for doing a wall mural downtown for his senior project, even though that was years away. Like Xavier, he was ambitious. These two were young men with goals. But they were also simply young men.

He told Xavier, "It's almost summer break, dude, have some fun. You kissed her. It's not like you two have to get married."

Xavier's bedroom still featured much of its original décor. The walls were the same pale aqua Valerie and Tom had painted it, their first task after moving in a week ahead of Valerie's due date. The lamp on his bedside table had a ceramic lamb as its base—a gift for newborn Xavier from Valerie's father, who'd been a sweetheart with Xavier if not with Valerie, at least until Alzheimer's claimed him; now he was in a special home in Lansing and didn't recognize any of the family any-more. The rug upon which Xavier lay was the same braided rug Valerie and Tom had hauled home from a local craft fair on a day when Tom had carried the infant Xavier in a sling against his chest while he and Valerie held hands, drawing hostile stares from some of the folks they passed and approving smiles from others. Xavier didn't remember this day, but he remembered the story of it—him in the sling, his mom see-ing the rug, the Cambodian refugee craftswoman who'd made it de-claring, upon seeing Xavier, that he would grow up to *matter*. He was taking the rug with him to SFCM for his dorm room. On his bookshelf he had several books that had been Tom's, volumes by James Baldwin, W.E.B. Du Bois, James Weldon Johnson, Angela Y. Davis, among others—books Tom had relied on to help him understand what it was to be black in America. Valerie had saved these especially for Xavier. He'd read bits of most of them, not so much to learn black history as to help him understand what it was to be Tom.

Gazing up at the equally old songbirds mobile that hung in front of his window, he said to Dashawn, "If I don't see Juniper again, she'll think I'm a player."

"So see her."

Xavier stood up. "I just told you, it was a mistake. And anyway, she's not supposed to date. Her parents made her do one of those creepy purity-promise things."

"So *don't* see her," Dashawn said. "See someone else. I know like five girls who'd hang with you if you say the word."

"I don't want to hang with any girls. I mean, I do, but right now what's the point?"

"This is why you're still a virgin."

"I am not a virgin."

"Well, you act like one."

"What, because I don't try to jump every girl I know?" Xavier said.

"Anyway," said Dashawn, "I bet her dad—"

"Stepdad."

"*Stepdad* wouldn't be good with his pretty virginal white prop-

erty going off the reservation. You're black, in case you haven't noticed. Sure thing he has."

"I'm white, too."

"You know this isn't even a debate."

"Whatever. It's the twenty-first century. Even white girls can
choose their own boyfriends. I mean, she's almost eighteen, so—"

"*This* white girl? Dream on."

"I don't need to dream. Her stepdad likes me."

Dashawn gave him a sideways look. "Yeah? Then it's only 'cause
you're so white-*like*. Classical guitar, you know. And let's see, what
else? No grill. Pants up at your waist. Straight-A student—" Dashawn
turned to look at him. "Man, you *are* white."

"Oh, so now if I'm not a caricature of a thug, then I'm not
black?"

"Pretty much," said Dashawn, turning back to his drawing. "I
don't make the rules."

Xavier looked over Dashawn's shoulder at the sketch of a leap-
ing panther. "Pretty good," he said. He took a snow globe from the
desk, shook it, held it up between himself and the window and
watched the flakes swirl. "The thing about Juniper . . . I don't know.
I should back off. I kind of love her name, though. I mean, mine's
not common, but have you ever met anyone else with hers?"

Dashawn shook his head and started to sketch a bear balancing
on a tennis ball. "A juniper is a tree, right?"

"A genus of trees, actually." Xavier shook the snow globe again.
"Remember how she said she doesn't know who her dad is?"

"Yeah—what's up with that? Does her mom not even *know,* or
is it, like, a secret she's keeping? Maybe he's a criminal. Or one of
the X-Men."

"She told me her name has to do with him, or the lack of him,
more like."

Xavier and Juniper had been sitting outside in the dark, in a
far corner of the yard, leaning against the new fence. His mom was
inside with the rest of the party guests. He'd been inside, too, and
after having some food and talking with Juniper and the neighbors,

he told Valerie he was heading home—which he did, but then he and Juniper met again at the gate.

He knew he shouldn't have suggested they meet outside to talk where it was quieter and, yes, private. But they'd hit it off, and he didn't want to resist how good that felt, how right. She had this captivating quality of being both shy and bold at the same time, and, well, he just wanted . . . more.

She was intelligent, that was already obvious to him. And so pretty. High forehead, wide eyes, a nose that had some character to it, lips that were fixed in a slight smile, *Mona Lisa*–like . . . He'd studied her while they stood talking in the Whitmans' insanely perfect kitchen. Her neck was long. Her lime-green dress made her eyes look almost as green.

Outside, she'd grabbed a couple of cushions and brought them over for them to sit on. In this corner, they could be seen by her next-door neighbors only if those neighbors happened to be outside and the kids caught their attention before settling onto the cushions. Not likely. Rosa and Lyle Morton, whom Xavier had known his whole life, were in their eighties and were sure to be asleep by this time of night, nine-thirty, party notwithstanding. Rosa was an early riser who was up and at the senior center by six o'clock most days. She played mah-jongg and did water aerobics. Lyle was up and out early, too, walking the one-mile loop around this Oak Knoll block before the sun got too high. He'd had a run-in with melanoma a decade earlier and wasn't taking any more chances.

The teens each sat down on a cushion, close enough that his left knee and arm nearly touched her right knee and arm. The moon had risen over the house and was casting its reflected light onto Juniper's face. Xavier liked how Juniper's eyelashes made shadows on the crests of her cheeks. He liked that she wore her hair in braids. The smell of her—faintly soapy and, underneath that, the musk of perspiration, an earthy, pleasant, sexual scent. He wanted to know everything about her. Was green her favorite color? Did she play any musical instruments? Was she as content with her life as it seemed she ought to be? How long had Brad and Julia been married? Did

Brad treat her the same way he treated Lily? What did she like to eat, watch, read, do? Questions about her crowded his brain, leaving no room for him to question himself.

He had to start somewhere, so he said, "I've been wondering, do you not know who your real dad is at all?"

"Nope."

"Like, not even a story about him?" His mom had told him all kinds of stories about his dad.

"Nothing," she said. "All my mom's ever told me is that he was just a guy she shouldn't have bothered with. She says he's not worth knowing and don't waste my time even thinking about him."

"Do you, though? I mean, how could you not?"

"I sometimes wonder how much I might be like him, but . . ." She shrugged.

Xavier could feel her body's heat radiating off of her. He supposed she could feel his.

"So Brad adopted you?"

Juniper shook her head. "Mom had my name changed, is all, so that everyone's matched."

"You're cool with that? Not being his legal kid, I mean."

"I guess I was just too old when they got married to think of him as my actual dad. I remember Mom asking me about it—did I want to be adopted?—and me saying something like 'He can't be my dad because he's not.' So they didn't force it."

"That's decent," Xavier said. "So, okay, here's my next question—"

"Hold on," Juniper said, laughing. "You have to answer some questions, too."

"Way less interesting for me."

"Too bad. Here, I'll start with something easy. I've been wondering why your hair's not black. Or is that a really weird thing to ask?"

"My dad was white, that's how. Okay, my turn: Is Juniper a family name, or what?"

She laughed again. "Hold *on*. It's still my turn. Your dad was white? But . . . President Obama had a white mom and his hair is like regular black guy's hair."

Xavier said, "Just how it goes. We aren't a predictable blend of our parents' genes. It's not like, you know, mixing ingredients for a cake and every time it comes out the same."

"I guess not. I like cake, though. And I like your hair."

"Some white people are one hundred percent sure it's dyed. I don't even argue it anymore. Okay, so, you. Name. Why."

"Fine," she said, "but then I get another turn."

He nodded, happy with this game, this moment, the way being close to her made his blood rush, all of it.

She said, "Junipers are supposedly some of the most resilient plants there are, and Mom says she figured that since she was single and young and not very well off, I'd need a strong name to live up to, or a name that would inspire me, something like that."

"I like it."

"I like it, too, I guess. Except people mess it up all the time. They hear *Jennifer* or—how about this: *Jupiter.*"

"Out of this world."

"That is so incredibly clever."

"Right?" He said, "I get *Ex*-avier a lot. Think I might change my spelling, put a Z on the front, make it easier for everyone."

"The X is cool. Unique," she said. "Now tell me about *your* dad."

"Nah, that's a depressing story. You don't want to hear it." This wasn't a false demurral intended to get her to encourage him to say more. He really did not like to talk about it.

"When did he die?"

"When I was still a baby."

She reached for his hand. "That sucks."

"Thanks."

The whole time they'd been sitting there, Xavier had been dying to touch her, and now by some small miracle his hand was in her small, warm, dry one. The sensation of skin to skin sent a thrum of electricity straight to his belly.

Idiot, he told himself even as he'd leaned over and put his face close to hers, looking for a sign from her that he should stop or not stop. She leaned closer, and then he pressed his mouth to hers. It was a sweet kiss. Might even have been her first, he thought. The idea pleased him—more, probably, than it should have.

"Kissing her was *stupid,*" he told Dashawn now. He picked up his old Epiphone—the first of the guitars he'd bought with his own money—and sat down on his bed, started running through some scales. "I'm *not* getting into a relationship now, when I'm leaving for school in August."

"Fine, don't," said Dashawn.

"Should I tell her that? Or just leave it alone?" He ran up and down a D major scale, then an F major. "I don't know. Maybe I'm overthinking it. Maybe we could go out, if she wants to. If her parents won't freak about her breaking the do-not-date vow or whatever. It's not like we have to get married."

Dashawn turned around to face him. "Are you going to be like this all summer?"

Xavier set his guitar in its stand and flopped backward onto the bed. "Just shoot me now," he said.

12

"I do *not* like what I'm seeing," Valerie Alston-Holt said to Ellen Davies, president of the Oak Knoll HOA and Valerie's good friend and neighbor of nearly twenty years. They stood outside in Valerie's backyard looking up at her beloved oak tree.

It was an otherwise perfect day. Not too hot. Not too humid. Valerie and Xavier had been out early that morning with string and stakes to delineate where the koi pond would go. Then, as had become her habit, at midmorning Valerie got her binoculars and made a close study of the tree's branches. What she saw made her feel the way you might upon hearing of a dear friend's cancer diagnosis: weak and sad and angry and helpless. She'd called Ellen for a sympathetic ear.

While Valerie's attachment to the tree had everything to do with Xavier, that tree was beloved by most of us. Its diameter had to be nearly six feet. It had seen scores of ice storms and hurricanes and droughts, and had witnessed more than just Valerie's grief during its long life. Almost a century before there'd been a proper neighborhood, a small band of former slaves squatted here on land that officially belonged to some white man who evidently had no use for it. The newly freed Negroes, as they were called back then, built two-room planed-log cabins on the kind of stone foundations you can still find in the state's parks and along the greenways. Those folks certainly knew grief, and surely told their tales within earshot of this oak when it was little more than an acorn's upshoot straining toward the sky.

One such tale was that of a young woman—almost a girl, really—whose owner had reluctantly complied with the Thirteenth Amendment by hiring (for a pittance) slaves who would stay on to keep his house and work his land. He was an old man for his time, close to sixty, and had managed to keep the Yankees out of his cotton and his home. War be damned, he'd been determined to carry on independently—that carrying on not limited to farming: he'd gotten his mind fixed on this girl, a laundress, and in time coerced her such that she was pregnant with his child. Her daddy, unhappy with his daughter being ill used by a man who no longer possessed that "right," persuaded most of the other slaves who'd stayed on that it was time they take their chances elsewhere.

This band of "goddamned ungrateful defectors" went by foot across the wide state, aiming for Kentucky, where one of the women believed she had kin. The travel wasn't such a hardship for people who were used to being on their feet all day. The pregnant young woman, though, came into her eighth month during this time and began to have difficulty keeping up. She'd always been scrawny; that was why she'd been made a laundress and not a field slave. Now it seemed that the baby inside her was drawing her down further as it grew. No way she was going to make it to Kentucky.

As the story goes, that pregnant young woman collapsed in a small clearing near the young tree that became Valerie's great oak. For three days it was touch and go for both her and the baby inside her. On the fourth day, the baby (a boy) emerged hearty and loud, taking all of its mother's life with it. He lived only a few weeks before he, too, was called home. They buried him just a few paces from the tree where he had been birthed, next to the woman who bore him.

The tale, while sad at this juncture, takes a somewhat heart-warming turn—or it did for a time. The keeper of stories tends to be the oldest among us (Esther, in our case), and in her telling, mother and child became benevolent haints, protecting the tree and the land around it. We have no explanation for why that protection didn't last.

Valerie's voice wavered as she looked at the tree and fought back tears. "This is so bad. It's exactly what I was afraid of."

The tree stood about thirty feet away from the back of her house and shaded both the yard and the structure. Other, younger trees grew in its proximity, mostly on the fringes of the canopy perimeter, where there was more available sunlight. This tree was the reason Valerie and Tom had chosen this house, which was smaller and had been more expensive than the other one for sale in Oak Knoll at the time.

"See there?" Valerie pointed. "Those limbs are in distress. They've been dropping leaves all day and are at maybe thirty percent of the leaf density they had last summer. *Thirty percent*. You can see the damage there, too." She pointed again. "That's seventy percent or so."

"Maybe it will recover," Ellen said. She was an optimist—which was part of the reason we liked having her head the HOA. We appreciated her positive approach to problem-solving, her preference for inclusiveness. We liked having a black woman in a leadership position. It seemed like proof that even as the character of the neighborhood at large was changing, our ideals for what Oak Knoll should and could be (inclusive, color-blind, progressive) were holding fast.

"Recover?" Valerie shook her head. "I want to hope for that, but . . . I think this is a death knell. Not only for those limbs—for the entire tree." Tears welled again. "Goddamn that builder. I knew when I saw the foundation go in—and then when they were digging that pool . . . It's too much damage to the root system."

Ellen said, "How can you know that's the reason and not, I don't know, disease?"

Valerie turned toward her. "Seven years of college is how. A Ph.D. is how. Experience is how! I can't believe you would even ask me that question."

"Okay," said Ellen. "Sorry. I'm just—"

"The city never should have given them a permit. And the builder—he knows what he's doing to the trees, that's why none of them even try to leave the big ones in place. They'd have to build smaller and therefore less profitable houses to accommodate the trees. They'd have to avoid severing or covering or compacting roots— they'd have to be *careful*. Careful costs money. Profit is everything."

"Okay, yes, but—"

"I'm going to sue those heartless bastards," Valerie said. "The builder, the pool company, the—"

"Hold on," said Ellen. "What if you get those limbs pruned first and see if that does the trick? You don't want to go stirring up trouble if you don't have to."

Valerie sat down at the base of the tree and leaned back against it. She tilted her head and looked upward. Two blue jays were hopping from branch to branch to branch and making their screechy dinosaur calls. A mating ritual? A territorial debate? Chickadees squeaked and chattered as they flew from the tree to the feeder and back.

Valerie said, "I wish you could be right, about pruning." Her voice was thick. "God knows I do. But you're not."

Ellen was quiet for a minute. Then she said, in as kind a voice as anyone could muster, "Valerie, hon, it's just a tree. No one is dying."

"You think I'm overreacting," Valerie said. "You think I sound like some crazy woman."

"Not crazy . . . just, well, we all need to keep our sense of proportion. It's a great tree, maybe even an historic tree, but like I said, it's just a *tree*."

"It's . . . it's a part of my life here, and Zay's. It's a *friend,* El. And all right, not everyone has plants as friends. Some of you have cats or dogs that you tend like children—and, I remind you, you mourn their loss the same as if they're members of the family. For me it's plants, but this tree especially." Valerie pressed her palms against the thick roots. "Look, a lawsuit would be me standing up for a principle. I'm an ecologist. If I don't take a stand for environmental protection this way, who will? You have got to stand with me on this, Ellen, or before you know it, there won't be one tree left in Oak Knoll."

"Okay, sure. But . . . maybe you want to talk to the Whitmans first. Try to work it out that way."

"Work what out? How would a conversation help this situation? The damage is done and can't be repaired. They might say they're sorry, but I'm not looking for an apology from them or their builder. I want to force a change to policy and practice."

"We used to have harmony here," said Ellen.

"You are not blaming me for this."

"There's already so much conflict in the world. I'm *tired,* Val."

Valerie stood up. "Who isn't? Come on inside and I'll revive you with some pimiento cheese so good that it will change your life. Cold beer, too, if you want it."

"*Now* you're talking," Ellen said.

"And I won't stop—you know that, and you love me, right?"

Just the same, before Valerie took action toward bringing a lawsuit, she waited and watched a while longer, observing the tree closely, checking again for signs of disease or infestation. She very much wanted her initial assessment to be wrong. Or even just less dire. Anything to prevent her from antagonizing the Whitmans. She wanted to keep the peace and continue to be everyone's favorite neighbor (our words, not hers). She wanted to see whether Julia Whitman might become a friend. The tree, however, insisted on its own agenda, dropping leaves ever more rapidly as if to challenge Valerie's integrity and test her commitment. *Don't ignore the bigger picture, Val,* it seemed to say. *Do right by me, or what is all your work for?*

She sought counsel from a white lawyer named Wilson Everly. Though she would have preferred to hire a person of color, this choice was strategic. Not only was Everly white, he was Southern-born, with a family that had been rooted in this state since before the Civil War. A family with numerous members who'd become ardent environmentalists. Everly was a Southern white card-carrying member of numerous conservation agencies and a prominent attorney in a respected firm. Valerie could not have a better combination for her purposes.

Wilson Everly, who we'd have to describe as upright in appearance as well as in reputation, met her in the law firm's austere lobby and ushered her into his office. The month being May, he wore a pearl-gray suit. His shirt was crisp and white, with collar stays, not buttons; no preppy oxfords for this gentleman. His narrow tie, apple green with thin violet stripes, was the only visible clue that he was something other than a traditional Southern gentleman. *We hide in plain sight,* Tom (a Southerner) used to say about men like himself and Everly, men who when taken out of their usual context were assumed to be the stereotypical conservative Christians of Southern tradition and power. And in reply, Ellen would say how nice it must be to pass in a way that conferred an advantage—because for her, a Haitian émigré, being presumed African American (as happened often) was of no benefit at all.

Everly said, "Please, have a seat. May I offer you something? Iced tea? Water?"

With that Old South accent, his was the voice of innumerable plantation owners long past, the voice many blacks associate with oppression and cruelty, even if only on a subconscious level.

Valerie remembered how she'd fretted about moving from Michigan to the South, though she'd been excited about taking the teaching position and eager to live in a place where snow was considered a rare treat. Her *rational* brain told her that there were many, many white folks in the South who did not wave the Confederate flag, who in fact were ashamed of that heritage. *Irrationally* she expected every white person here to try to diminish her whenever the opportunity might arise. She'd said this to Tom the first time they met, at a university mixer for incoming faculty, then waited for him to defend himself and the state and the South the way other white people had done. Waited for him to say she was overly sensitive. To insist that racism was a thing of the past. But he'd said with full sincerity, "I'm

sorry. That can't feel good. I admire you for coming here anyway."
When he'd gone on to tell her he was a W. E. B. Du Bois acolyte,
well, they were off to the races.

Now Everly said, "I want to know all about what's going on
with you and that wonderful tree."

"Formerly wonderful. But thank you. So, as I told you when
we spoke on the phone, its root system has been fatally disrupted.
The tree is dying."

"This, because of the construction in the lot that adjoins
yours"—he checked his notes—"at the back."

"Yes—but more specifically, because the house and pool and
patio cover too much of that lot. I looked up the permits: KDC Homes
got a variance without revealing that there was a tree of this size
within seventy-five feet of the proposed structure. And I have to guess
that either the inspector who granted the permit never visited the lot
to see for himself, or signed off on it anyway."

Everly nodded. "Either of those could be true. I've seen both."

"KDC knew what the effect was going to be—that's why they
took every tree off of that lot before they built. Every single tree.
That way there's none left to die later, and therefore no homeowner
complaint and request for the builder to pay for removal," Valerie
said. "It's all about money. Laverne Michaels, the woman who'd
lived there since 1961, had a pair of ancient dogwoods in the front
yard that some folks made a special point to come see each spring.
Do you know what's there now? Boxwoods. Boxwoods! They're . . .
they're Disney World shrubs. They aren't going to shade a thing."

"No," said Everly, nodding in that patient manner some older
gentlemen have. "That they are not. Now, you said you think the
homeowner, too, was aware that what he wanted to build was not to
code. What makes you think so?"

"He basically said it." She recounted the conversation she and
Brad Whitman had on his patio that first day, when the fence crew
arrived. "He said he had a friend on the inside and then he *winked*,"
she said. "None of them believe in regulations. They don't care what

the effects of breaking them might be. Rules are for losers and cowards and poor people!"

"I understand your frustration, Ms. Alston-Holt. But I believe you'll feel better if we keep our focus on action rather than emotion. I do share your view—please don't mistake me. But I have found that not only am I more effective when I set aside the emotional aspects of a situation, I sleep better, too."

"I can't sleep well knowing that sooner or later I'm going to have a tree service in my yard using chainsaws to . . ." Her voice thickened and she paused for a moment to collect herself, remind herself to stay focused on the goal, to pursue not retribution but justice. Justice was a force she believed in. Justice would be enough.

She said, "Taking down that tree will cost me several thousand dollars that I don't have to spare. My son's going to a private college this fall, and though he did win a substantial scholarship, it's not even close to covering the full expense. I've saved some," she said, wishing for the thousandth time that Tom had taken out a life insurance policy (something they'd both intended to do but hadn't gotten around to). "But I'm borrowing a lot more. How am I going to come up with the money for tree removal? That's partly why I'm here. That expense shouldn't be on me."

Everly said, "Indeed—I've seen this kind of thing run into five, seven thousand, depending on whether they've got to bring in a crane and so forth. And beyond that is the alteration to your property that will result once the stump and roots are out."

Valerie winced. "God, I hate even *hearing* this."

"I guess I don't have to tell *you* that when you take out a tree of that size, you alter the ecosystem in its proximity. Which means incurring additional expense to restore the landscape."

"It does," Valerie said. "My backyard will have to be reforested. It's . . . I . . ." She cleared her throat and wiped her eyes. "Sorry. I can't seem to help myself."

"We should talk about this," Everly said, gesturing toward her. "The emotional damage this situation has caused and will cause."

"You just said I should leave emotion out of it."

"Yes, I did. And you should when we're making decisions and pursuing a course of action. There is no denying, however, the distress you're suffering. For that, we'll want to include a request for those damages. It's important to make folks like this feel the consequences of their actions materially. It's a matter of justice and also, one hopes, a deterrent against future such acts. I want to start a damages claim at five hundred thousand and see where we get."

Valerie blinked twice and leaned forward. "I'm sorry, did I hear you right? Five hundred thousand dollars?" Had she been asked to put a figure on it, she'd have said ten thousand. Fifteen, tops.

Everly said, "It's a large sum, yes. It needs to be large to be effective. I think the apportionment would be fairly put at four hundred from KDC and one hundred from Mr. Whitman. Plus, of course, a reimbursement of your total expenses including my fees. If I start digging—forgive the pun—and discover evidence that the city was willfully involved, we may want to include them in the suit as well."

"I . . ." Valerie began. Her first impulse was to protest the amount, to say that while she was absolutely wrecked by the impending loss of that tree, a half-million dollars in compensation was absurd.

Then she thought of how, if they prevailed, she'd be able to pay all Xavier's college expenses not covered by his scholarship. Neither she nor Xavier would have to borrow a penny. She could pay off the balance of her mortgage. She could make donations to the NAACP and the ACLU and the Southern Poverty Law Center along with a whole list of organizations that made environmental protection their mainstay.

She said, "Wow. If you really can do that, a lot of people will benefit."

"Doing is not as easy as saying. But we'll set our course and get under way, and I have no doubt that you'll come out of it better than how you're going in."

"Really, that's all I want. If we can stop these soulless bastards— Sorry, I'm supposed to put aside my anger, I know. Let me try that again: If in the end we can encourage—no, *require*—better future behavior, everyone wins."

"There you go," Everly said.

––––––

We've said this before: no one who'd known Valerie before Oak Knoll's gentrification began had ever thought of her as any kind of troublemaker. No one saw her as a difficult person. Just the opposite, in fact. She sought consensus, was respectful of diverse points of view. She volunteered her time and expertise. She wasn't much of a cook, but you could count on her to organize a bereavement committee or retirement party or birthday celebration and have it go off beautifully.

We did know her as a tree hugger, as a guardian of what made Oak Knoll such a lovely place to live. The HOA had adopted her suggestions to require application and approval any time a resident wanted to remove a tree with a diameter greater than four inches—which was as much as we could regulate; the city had its own codes that superseded ours. Some trees did need to go—Valerie was expert on this. Selective culling and intelligent habitat management benefited not only the trees but the human residents and the animals, too. Possums, foxes, raccoons, squirrels, deer, chipmunks, lizards, hawks, every kind of songbird, five varieties of woodpecker, including the yellow-bellied sapsucker and the pileated . . . all these creatures coexisted here with us—or had, before the infill began; by now no one had seen a pileated woodpecker in better than a year. And we won't even get into the detrimental effects that might occur on the less obvious categories of insect life and soil health and the complicated equations of carbon dioxide and oxygenation, which we can't speak to except in the most general terms.

Maintaining the visual character of Oak Knoll and keeping an ecosystem in balance was, we all felt, a worthy endeavor. We liked having a local authority who was motivated to serve the community in ways it hadn't known it needed serving. Hardly a day went by between February and November when one or another of us didn't stop by or call to ask Valerie a question about planting or pruning, fertilizing our grass or killing our weeds in bug-, bird-, and pet-friendly ways. And in truth, we were sometimes also checking in on her, especially in the first year or so after Tom was gone. In sum, Valerie was like a turtle: tough shell, tender underside, easy to have around.

We had reservations, though, about including the Whitmans in this lawsuit-to-be. Equal to ecological harmony, we valued social harmony. Valerie did, too—we all knew that. So then, what about the effect this suit was certain to have on her developing friendship with Julia Whitman? What about our friendships with both the Whitmans and Valerie? What about the kids' friendship—friendship being all we thought (if we thought of it at all) was going on at the time? Might a less visible, less contentious, less financially injurious process be a better way to go, even if, as some of us would remark, it wasn't like Brad Whitman was going to be bankrupted if he was made to pay?

We wondered, had Tom lived to see what was going on now, would he have cautioned Valerie against filing a lawsuit? Or at least cautioned her against naming Brad Whitman in the suit?

Those of us who'd known Tom best said nope, absolutely not. He'd loved her *because* she was both tender and fierce.

13

The scene at the Whitmans' dining table on the evening Juniper asked for a car was one we would have liked to witness. Because as much as any of us could stand on the sidewalk and gaze at their picture-perfect house, seeing the warm glow of costly light fixtures inside, noting the way the copper gutters caught the dying western sun as the crickets began their night song among the boxwood shrubs . . . as much as we envied the ability to live as well as the Whitmans did even while disapproving of the size of the house and the process by which it had come to stand here towering over its near neighbors, we wondered how they treated one another when no one was watching. We were curious to know whether their family life was as enviable as their home.

For example, Juniper might be a fuel source for drama just by being seventeen and impatient for adulthood, as most of us are at that age. Then there was the impending visit of Julia's mother, which Julia had mentioned to Kelli Hanes as the two women chatted by their mailboxes on a recent afternoon when Kelli was about to leave for second shift in the OR. Apparently the mother, Lottie Corbett, was having financial and health troubles and would be bunking with her daughter's family for a while. Capping all of that: Brad Whitman didn't know yet that he was about to be sued—an event that was certain to cause Sturm und Drang between the Whitmans and Alston-Holts.

For the moment, however, the issue was a car and, even more to the point, a job.

———————————

Supper had concluded, and while the girls cleared the plates, Julia brought a strawberry-rhubarb pie to the table. "Who wants a scoop of ice cream, too?" she asked.

"Me!" said Lily, raising her arm and waving it.

"Clean plate club members welcome," Julia said.

Juniper said, "I'll have some."

"How about half a scoop?" Julia said, recalling how she had gotten plump at Juniper's age. A diet of nothing but sugary garbage would do that to you: Twinkies and soda and candy bars and Pop-Tarts . . . she'd eaten whatever she could persuade a boy to buy for her at the convenience store up the road from the high school, or whatever she could slip into her waistband or pocket when the clerk's attention was elsewhere. Both habits had led to trouble of similar kinds: boys expected certain favors in return; clerks who caught her blackmailed her for those same kinds of favors. It had been a terrible time, but Julia didn't shy away from the memories. They gave her the power to hold the line when the girls protested rules stricter than what their friends' parents set.

Juniper said about the ice cream, "I'm still running thirty miles a week; can't I have a whole scoop?"

"Sure," Brad said. "That's reasonable." He gave Julia a look that seemed to say, *Lay off.* Julia bristled for a moment, then gave a nod. He was right. She was over-parenting again.

As Juniper took the plate Julia held out to her, she said, "Also . . . I was wondering if you guys could help me buy a car. I'll pay you back."

"A car? For what?" asked Julia.

Most teens these days—or at least the ones at Blakely—were in

no rush to drive. They were so accustomed to using their mothers or
a service to get around that the idea of having a car seemed not to
occur to them. Julia and Brad had made Juniper take a driver's training course so that she could, if need be, safely and legally get behind
the wheel. They made sure she took her test and got her license. They
did not, however, intend to let her go off driving on her own for no
good reason—which was fine, since Juniper had not been inclined
to ask.

She answered Julia, "For work. Fresh Market offered me a job
stocking shelves and I don't want you to have to always drive me
back and forth."

"You got a *job*?" said Julia.

Brad said, "Now, why'd you go and do that?"

"I told you I was applying," Juniper said to Brad. "Remember?"

Julia said, "Why didn't you tell me?"

Brad replied to Juniper, "I remember we said you'd come to
work for me."

"No," she said, frowning. "I said *maybe* I would—"

"When was this?" said Julia. It was all news to her.

"Like, two weeks ago? I told him I wanted to get a job so I
won't be bored all summer."

"And *I* said I had a position opening up in dispatch—which I
would've advertised," Brad said, directing his gaze at Juniper, "if
I'd known you weren't serious about my offer."

Juniper looked miserable. "I only said maybe. I'm still thinking about what I want to do."

"*I* want to have some pie and ice cream, please," Lily said, looking up at Julia, who, so prompted, went back to her task of slicing
and serving.

"Do?" Brad said to Juniper. "With what? Your summer or your
life or what?"

Lily said, "Juniper's going to college, she told me so."

"She might," said Julia. "She should, if she's going to have a
career, but we know there are other equally good choices for women,
right?"

Lily said, "Right! I'm going to marry Daddy and make him build me a house just like this one, except orange."

"You can't marry your own dad," said Juniper, not unkindly.

Even so, Lily's face threatened to crumple. "Why not?"

"Honey, Daddy's married to Mommy," Julia told her. "You'll marry someone else."

"*Who?*"

"Someone you'll meet later, when you're grown up."

"But . . . but I already know Daddy and he loves me and I love him."

"I do, sugar pie," Brad said. "But Juniper and Mommy are right. When you're older you'll meet somebody who knocks your socks off and he'll build you your own big, pretty house and I'll come and visit you there. How's that sound?"

"Terrible. I don't even know him. This is dumb," Lily said, digging into her pie. "There's too many rules."

Brad said to Juniper, "So you didn't already accept the job?"

"No, I did—but . . . I could do both. How about that?"

Julia said, "I don't know. You've got *a lot* of reading to do this summer, plus piano—"

"I want to quit piano."

"Me, too," said Lily. "What day does Grandma get here?"

"We'll pick her up from Miss Mabel's on Thursday," Julia said. "You're not quitting piano."

"Is Juniper?"

"Juniper is old enough to decide for herself."

Brad was rubbing his chin. "Okay," he said. "Sure. Sure, I'll buy you a car—no paying me back—and you go ahead and take that grocery store job, as long as you can give me four hours three days a week. Deal?"

Juniper lit up. She said, "Deal." Brad held his hand out and she shook it.

"You get a car?" said Lily.

Juniper looked both relieved and surprised. "I guess so."

Brad said, "We'll go car shopping tomorrow after school."

"She runs tomorrow," Julia said, feeling as though the whole situation had gotten away from her.

"I don't have to," Juniper said. "Tomorrow's great."

Lily said, "Me, too? Can I shop for Juniper's car?"

"Dance lessons," said Julia.

Brad told Lily, "You and me, we'll have a date of our own the next day, how's that?"

"That'll do, I guess," Lily said. She returned to her pie.

Juniper went to Brad and hugged him. "This is so awesome, thanks."

He kissed her forehead. "You bet, honey. Don't let anyone ever say that Brad Whitman doesn't take the best care of *all* of his girls."

⸻

Later, when Lily was in bed and Juniper was in the bonus room talking on the phone to one of her friends—presumably about this automotive windfall that was about to come her way—Julia joined Brad on the patio by the pool. The night was not as hot as nights would get when full summer took hold. That's when she'd appreciate the pool most—when she could slip in after dark, the pool lighted and inviting like something at the resorts she used to see in the movies or on TV, like the pools owned by millionaires in Miami and L.A. and Hawaii. She and Brad were millionaires now—or Brad was, which made her one by extension. They didn't live at the level of the truly rich, with mansions and apartments all over the world, say, and yachts and private jets and all of that. Nor did Julia want that kind of lifestyle. She wanted exactly what she had right this minute: a perfect home, perfect safety and security, and a perfect husband (or close enough) whose stated goal was to provide to her and her daughters this perfect life.

She sat down in a chair to Brad's right. "I was surprised to hear you wanted to hire Juniper."

"I meant to tell you," he said. "Sorry about that."

"And, a car? That's awfully generous."

He was looking at the pool. Its light threw pale ripples onto his face and shirt and across the rear of the house. On the table at his elbow was a bottle of a locally brewed beer, provided to him for free in the hope that he'd give it a public endorsement. He did that sometimes, in his commercials. Always casually—Brad was not a salesman. And that's why his product placements had become a matter of popular interest and speculation, if only in the region. A sport, almost. What would he be eating or drinking or wearing or holding in his next ad? For vendors who wanted to curry favor, it was now a competition. Brad enjoyed this—a lot of free local products came his way. Julia enjoyed it as well, and she liked how Brad had grown so popular. He was always gracious when people recognized him and wanted to stop him for a minute to talk. If you're on television, you are de facto famous, even if what you do every day is run a heating and cooling company. Big fish, small pond: it suited Brad, and it suited Julia.

He said, "It's time for her to have wheels, don't you think?"

"Maybe, but I don't have to like it. One more thing to worry about."

"We'll install a tracker on the car, how's that? There's all kinds of technology now that'll let us see how she's driving and where she goes. Makes kids more conscientious and therefore safer. That's the pitch, anyway."

Julia said, "All right, good," because as a mother she was all for it, though teenaged Julia would have been appalled if her mother had been able to track where she went.

She continued, "I'm surprised by Juniper, too; running dispatch doesn't seem like the kind of work she'd like."

"I guess we'll see. She might take to it. She's not going to like stocking grocery shelves, I'll guarantee you that. Once I have her in the shop and she gets the lay of the land, I'm betting she'll develop an appreciation for the whole works—I told her I'd train her up and bring her on in upper management later, if that's what she wants."

"Management? She says she wants to go to college."

"I don't see any point in that, do you?"

Julia said, "If she's going to have a career—"

"I'm offering her one."

"And it's really generous of you," Julia said carefully. "But maybe she'll have other interests."

Brad turned to look at her. "You're singing a very different song lately than the one you sang three years ago when you signed us up for the Promise program."

"What, because I'm being supportive of alternatives to marriage and motherhood? I'm being realistic. The Purity Promise has been exactly what she needed—but do we really expect her to honor the vows once she's over eighteen? Do you think she really intends that?"

"I want to be clear on what *you* intend."

"Me?"

"You send her mixed messages. 'Save yourself for marriage—but don't get married too soon. Go to college first and have a career. But please don't go to college if college is far away. Or at all—just marry well and let your husband take care of you.' It's no wonder she's confused and moody. Me, I'm giving her a real, concrete, unambiguous option for her future."

Irked by his accusation, Julia said, "Have you also told her she doesn't have to stick to the pledge?"

"No, I've reminded her she should take herself seriously, that chastity is a young woman's superpower."

A superpower that Julia hadn't possessed—couldn't, it had seemed to her back then, since she'd already been ruined. *Raped.* The word was hard but accurate. She wouldn't have kept herself chaste anyway; she lacked the wisdom, the strength, the support—all the things that, through New Hope's program and through the ways she and Brad parented, she was ensuring her daughters got.

Brad said, "You do realize that if she decides Whitman HVAC suits her, you'll have a lot more time with her at home, or at least close by."

"That'd be all right with me."

"I knew it would. You see? I'm always looking out for my girls, all of 'em."

Julia had a swig of his beer and thought about whether her

messages to Juniper were so mixed. To start: Yes, she did encourage Juniper to take seriously everything that was part of the Purity Promise. She wanted her daughter to value herself more than she, Julia, had done as a teen, wanted her to see chastity as the thing that made her the boss of her fate.

Also, Julia believed wholeheartedly that even with its drawbacks, marriage combined with full-time motherhood was a far better existence than having to juggle work and child care along with marriage to a man who was never going to see parenting and housework as equally his job. She'd told Juniper she honestly did not know one working woman (or any woman) whose husband was a true partner in that area.

At the same time, Juniper was bright and inquisitive and might love having some kind of career, at least for a while; Julia hadn't wanted to discourage that—so long as Juniper didn't go away for school.

Guilty as charged.

She said, "You're right about all you say. I'm wishy-washy, but only because I love her so much. I want her to be happy. If running the business with you is what she decides she wants, then great, I'm all for it. Especially since then she likely won't marry someone who'd try to move her out of state."

"No, indeed," Brad said.

Julia watched the rippling light on the water's surface. Even now, sitting here, she felt everything was always in motion. She was harried all the time, ever working to maintain or improve her life, their lives . . . If she wasn't driving carpool or volunteering at Blakely, she was exercising to keep her pudge from returning, or she was planning their meals or managing the cleaning service or working with the decorator or running endless errands or handling her mother's troubles—hours on the telephone with doctors and home health services and Lottie herself. Where was the ease she'd imagined would come with this marriage? She'd missed most of Juniper's first nine years, and although she was much more available now to both the girls than she'd ever been for Juniper alone, she often still felt as if she was the proverbial hitched horse chasing the carrot—and that she'd hung the carrot herself. Her girls, meantime, were growing up, getting further away from her with each passing day.

She said, "I wish I could stop time. Am I ridiculous for wanting to hold on to her, to both of them, for as long as I can?"

"After how you grew up? Not a bit."

"I don't want to seem like some desperate mom who won't let her kids have lives of their own."

"You are not turning into your mother, I promise you."

"Ugh. Lottie. Having her here is going to be a trial. I'm sorry. I wish she could just stay there with Mabel while her new trailer's on order."

Recently, Julia's mother had created a conflagration that destroyed much of her trailer and landed her in outpatient rehab, due to the smoke; Lottie's best friend, Mabel, had been happy to have Lottie stay with her, but only until next week, when Mabel was having a knee replaced and would herself need tending. Mabel was going to her son's house in Pittsboro and Lottie was coming here.

Brad said, "I reckon we'll need to find things for her to do. Didn't you say your pal Valerie there"—he pointed toward Valerie's house—"is about to dig a little fishpond?"

"That's right."

"She seems like the sort who wouldn't turn away a bored, sick old lady with time on her hands who wants to watch the progress, even if—when—that old lady gets to be a nuisance. We don't have to warn her in advance."

Julia smiled. She was fairly sure Brad was joking.

14

"Ready to do some ultimate shopping?" Brad asked Juniper, having picked her up from Blakely at the end of the school day as promised.

"I guess," she said.

"You guess," he said, imitating her tentative tone and making a long face. "Sure, take the wind right out of my sails."

She buckled her seat belt. "Sorry. I am ready. But . . . it's weird. I mean, a *car*."

"You *asked* for a car," he said, pulling away from the curb with a wave to the vice-principal, who was on duty in the pickup line.

"What if I ask for a giraffe?" Juniper said, making an effort to lighten her mood. She didn't want him to be sorry he'd made this bargain, rethink it, change his mind.

He said, "We'd need a bigger yard, too bad. But a car we have room for."

"Okay then, just the car. For now."

"Oh, 'for now,' is it?"

She smiled and nodded. "Yeah, I saw this website where you can buy basically any kind of tree frog. The red-eyed is my favorite, but I like the clown and tiger-leg, too, so . . ."

"Your mom would have opinions on that," Brad said, laughing.

"I know. That's why I haven't ordered any. Yet."

Juniper was enjoying this lighthearted exchange with Brad more than she expected to. It felt like old times, gave her some hope that her anxieties about working for and with him might turn out to be unwarranted, that everything was going to sort itself out properly. She didn't want to always have Brad on her mind. Better—*way* better—to think about Xavier.

Touching Xavier.

Kissing Xavier.

She gave herself a mental shake. Car shopping: focus.

Juniper hadn't had much occasion to ride in this, Brad's car, his "toy," he called it, a sleek and glossy black Maserati Gran-Turismo convertible, a 4.7-liter V8 with a price tag Juniper knew was $160,000 because Brad had tacked the window sticker to his bulletin board. This car was *not* the type she'd ask for, even if given carte blanche—if, say, instead of Brad making two million dollars from the gizmo he'd invented, he'd made ten or a hundred. This kind of luxury made Juniper nervous. One tiny wrong move, either inside the car or with the car, and you had a stain or a rip or a scratch or a dent that itself would cost a fortune to fix. Also, it wasn't at all her style. She was into rugged, earthy stuff. Brad liked to take this car out to the interstate late at night when there wasn't much traffic and "open it up." Juniper would rather drive a Jeep or truck up into the mountains, take it off-road at, like, ten miles an hour until she found an idyllic waterfall and campsite. She and Xavier could go together— not now, but someday, maybe. Lie on a blanket and stare up at the stars. And do some other things, too.

For now there would be no taking the vehicle anywhere except to work and back unless she got special permission, that's what her parents had said. The other rule was that she would have to pay for gas herself. Also: no boys alone with her in the car (which was supposed to go without saying). No passengers at all without prior approval. She was fine with that; what mattered is that she'd have a car to take her to a job, where she would see her favorite soon-to-be co-worker, Xavier. She hadn't mentioned that part of the scenario to anyone but Pepper, who'd messaged him for her with the news but so far had gotten no reply.

Damn, she was doing it again; it was like every mental pathway wanted to lead her to Xavier. *Focus, girl,* she thought, smiling inwardly. It was a nice problem to have.

As she and Brad made their way across town, he asked, "How was school today?"

"All we're doing is reviewing for end of grade. It's so boring."

She didn't say that Meghan had followed her into the girls' bathroom and taunted her about missing a classmate's birthday party the previous weekend, a party that was *the most fun ever.* No parents, plenty of booze, some recreational drugs, dancing "like I'm sure you're not allowed to do."

Juniper had replied, "Jealous I got an A on the English test, are we?" and Meghan frowned. "All of that's a waste of time."

Brad said, "Can't wait to be out of there, huh?"

Juniper nodded. "Yep."

"I remember that feeling."

"And there's still another whole year to go. I wish I could just test out of senior year and get my diploma early."

"Can't you?"

"I don't know," she said. "I never heard of anyone doing that."

"Well, sweet cakes, here's adulthood lesson number one: You want something, ask for it. Simple. Now, when I say *ask,* I don't mean that you can literally say the words *Hey, can I have x?* and it'll be handed to you—today's little outing being an exception," he said, smiling over at her. "You did ask, and you did get—or will—pretty directly. But I mean as a general life lesson: Find out how to get whatever it is you want, and then do whatever it takes to get it."

Juniper considered his words. This was *not* the message she'd gotten from Reverend Matthews at New Hope. When her mother had started taking her to Sunday school and church and, later, youth group and the Purity Promise program, all Juniper heard from Reverend Matthews and most of the adults she knew (outside of school) was the Bible's direction for women—that is, to aspire to be obedient and submissive to her future husband and to see motherhood as the ultimate achievement, eschewing work outside the home. A woman was supposed to be modest and undemanding, unambitious, grateful to her husband and supportive of *his* ambitions and needs.

As best Juniper could tell at the time, Julia had happily embraced that model and appeared to still be doing so. As the family had gotten out of the habit of regular church attendance, though, Juniper heard less of the dogma—but little contradiction, until recently. Now her mother was acting like college and a career might be an okay choice. And Brad wanted her to work for him and his company. So . . . had they changed their minds, Juniper wondered, or had they ever held the beliefs to begin with?

We wondered, too. Possibly Julia's motivation for following the dutiful-wife model had been purely pragmatic. After all, she'd been pinballing from job to job to job since she'd started babysitting at age eleven, so what was not to like about a belief system that basically *required* her man (whoever that man might be) to let her stay home and do nothing but raise Juniper and keep house? She'd begun going to New Hope in the first place only at the suggestion of another Whitman HVAC employee, Cindy in accounts receivable. Julia liked the church environment, the caring and support, the concept of renewal and inclusion (through baptism, yes, and why not?). That Brad seemed to approve only motivated her further. We suspect Jesus had little to do with any of it.

And it was evident to anyone who'd known Brad pre-Julia that he didn't hold those strict traditional beliefs and possibly never had. Juniper was beginning to see this, too. She didn't think it was necessarily *bad,* all things considered, just disconcerting.

Juniper said, "So then . . . if I really could graduate from Blakely early like that, you and Mom would be okay with it?"

"You'll be eighteen years old in December. It's your life to do with as you choose."

"Okay," she said, seeing doors opening ahead of her where before she'd seen walls. "Cool. I'll look into it."

"But here's the thing," said Brad. "Let's say you get to skip out on some or all of senior year—which is never everything it's cracked up to be, and that's the truth. If you do, I recommend you not rush into any plan for early *college,* if that's what you're thinking. In fact, I'll be straight with you, Juniper, and say I don't want you to go to college at all. Big waste of time and money for someone in your shoes. Give me a year, all right, before you make up your mind. We'll start you in dispatch, but I'll show you all the ropes and then you decide what you want."

"Okay," she said, since that was the only answer under the current circumstances. "But I don't even know if I can skip."

"Right, sure. Either way."

Either way, she thought, *I'm not staying at Whitman HVAC.*

Brad pulled into the CarMax parking lot. "Okay, ground rules. One: nothing with more than thirty thousand miles on it. Two: big pickup trucks are out—their gas mileage is shit, pardon my French, no need for you to waste your money filling the tank. Three: no tiny car—I want you to be safe. Last: stay under forty thousand."

"You just said thirty."

"Dollars," he said.

We think it's worth pointing out here that although Juniper was living in a house that according to the county's tax records sold for $1.7 million, and although she had arrived at CarMax in an imported sports car that her stepfather paid more for than any of the long-term Oak Knoll residents had paid for their homes, and although she'd long ago grown accustomed to wearing trendy clothes that fit well and to sleeping in her very own bedroom, Juniper was stunned by the budget Brad had just prescribed. Speechless. She stood there for a moment looking at him with her mouth open.

"And as I told your mama, we'll have a monitor installed, to make sure you're driving responsibly and we know where you are if you ever need help."

"Sure, okay," Juniper said readily, since she had no intention to try to fool them about that kind of thing.

Brad bowed and ushered her onto the lot. From the smorgasbord of offerings, the rows and rows and rows of clean, shiny cars with decent gas mileage and good safety ratings and window sticker prices that read less than forty thousand, Juniper selected and test-drove three different vehicles and then chose a three-year-old white Land Rover Range Rover Evoque with 22,000 miles on it. Brad wrote the saleswoman a check for just north of $30,000 and then, a short time later, when the SUV had been washed and filled with gas and brought around for delivery, handed Juniper the key and said, "All right, honey, she's all yours."

Juniper took a picture of the car to share with Pepper, and then she put her arms around Brad the way she always used to, the way he surely expected her to do now. "Thank you. Thank you *so* much."

"You're welcome. I mean that. Now, don't make me sorry, you hear?" The look he gave her brought all of her anxieties back.

15

Extenuating circumstances, when you know them, have a marked influence on the way you see a thing or a person. We liked Juniper fine, inasmuch as we knew her at this point. But it sure was hard to see a girl her age in a luxury SUV that most of us couldn't responsibly afford.

However, had the story of Juniper's third birthday been known to us at the time, we'd have been a lot less inclined to raise our eyebrows at the vehicle she drove home that day. We wouldn't have remarked to one another that she was spoiled. We'd have admired that polished white status symbol without envy—or with less envy, anyway—because we'd understand better the kinds of things she'd been through in her early life. The fact was, in taking advantage of Brad's offer, she'd done the same thing any of us would've done under the same circumstances.

(Our judgment of her parents, though, for actions present and past would be something else altogether.)

What happened was this: Julia and Juniper were living out in eastern North Carolina where Julia had grown up. Lottie, Julia's mother, lived in the trailer we've heard about, but Julia, nineteen years old and fed up with being subject to Lottie full time, had gotten her own apartment—a room is all it was, really, above the barbershop right in town—the word *town* being an overstatement of the place, which was more accurately a crossroads hung with a flashing amber caution signal at its center. A few commercial buildings held down the intersection's four corners. Residents were distributed around those corners in a scattershot pattern of shacks and trailer houses and small farms, stretching out for two miles or so.

Juniper's third birthday had a bumpy start. The furnace had been stuck on all night, so the apartment was sweltering, despite the one window near the bed being kept wide open. Neither daughter nor mother had slept very well, sweaty and cranky the entire night through. And now Lottie had Julia on the telephone while Julia was trying to get herself and Juniper fed, dressed, and ready to leave for the day.

Bear in mind that Julia, who'd be twenty in two weeks, was a single mother who hadn't yet found time to get her GED—a girl, really, trying to find her way into adulthood with a little more integrity than she'd managed in her teenage years.

She was on the phone with her mother—a corded phone, because a mobile was too expensive on top of her rent and her car payment (at 24 percent interest) and what she paid the babysitter who watched Juniper while Julia worked. There was no way she would leave her with Lottie, who was still earning her income by cleaning houses for well-off folks in the nearest town of size. Even a landline cost more money than Julia wanted to spend, but how could anyone get by without a phone?

This morning, Lottie was having a problem with a dog and had called to tell Julia all about it.

Julia listened for a minute, then said, "Mama, I don't have time for this, I have to get Juniper to the babysitter and get to work. Just tell Barney to tie up that dog or you'll call the county, it's not that hard."

"I don't have the county's number. What is it?"

"Look up the number. I sure don't know it."

"You think I have a phone directory? They don't bring 'em out here, if they even make 'em anymore."

"Well, go to the branch library and look it up there."

"I don't want you bringing Juniper out here later if that dog's still around."

"All right, then come here. We're making cupcakes."

"You aren't going to feed her a hot meal?"

"I *am*," said Julia, though in all probability it would be a hot dog. "Come or don't. I have to go now, Mama."

Without waiting for a reply, Julia hung up and turned to Juniper, who was seated at a card table eating peanut butter from the jar with a spoon. "All right, Juni, my little birthday girl, let's get your coat on."

"I want boots, too," said Juniper, scooting off the chair.

"It's not raining."

"Boots!" she declared, already on her way over to the futon that doubled as their bed, under which their footwear was stored along with plastic bins of socks and panties and Juniper's collection of Beanie Babies, all bought secondhand at the thrift shop one town over, near the branch library Julia mentioned to Lottie and up the road from where Julia worked.

"Fine, boots," Julia said. "But we have to hurry."

They were nearly out the door when the telephone rang again. Julia hesitated, but hoping it might be her manager at the Dance-n-Dine telling her there was a water main break or maybe the health department had shut them down temporarily and she could take the day off, she answered. It was Lottie again. Her car wouldn't start and she wanted Julia to come pick her up.

She said, "Now, Julia, you know I can't get through this day if that dog is hanging around my door, growling at me. I'll be a prisoner."

"Is the dog there now?"

"Yes."

"And you made it to your car fine, right?"

"With my life in my hands! Don't tell me I should walk over to Shay's—that woman's white trash and I won't have nothing to do with her."

"Come *on*, Mama. You'll make me late."

"Patty will understand."

"Patty will fire me. I can't lose my job."

"I don't like you working there anyway. Those men all watching you like you're . . . I don't know what. Fresh meat. Let her fire you. You can move back home."

"No."

"Well, that's a choice, ain't it?"

"Yes, it is. Be ready when I get there—and you'll have to get your own way home, hear?"

"How—"

"I don't care. You figure that out."

Juniper remembered being hurried out the door and down the stairs and into her car seat. She was sweaty inside her jacket. The car smelled like stale cigarettes, having been saturated with smoke by its previous owner, or owners. The AMC Gremlin was older than Julia and had seen a fair amount of unhealthy and possibly unsavory behavior over the years.

After retrieving Lottie and dropping her off at the library, Julia drove at what felt to Juniper like an unsafe speed to the babysitter's place, a little ramshackle house on a rural road about four miles outside of town. The house was square and faded mint green, with a tar-paper roof. A chain link fence had been set in a complementary square around the house, to corral whatever dogs and kids were being kept there at a given moment. Currently, Juniper was the babysitter's only human charge.

"Karen, we're here," Julia called, hurrying Juniper inside the gate and up the wooden steps. The door to the house stood open.

There was no answer.

Julia ushered Juniper inside. "Where is she? Karen!"

The house—all four rooms of it—appeared to be empty, save for Karen's old hound, Doofus, who lay in front of the TV and wagged his tail but didn't otherwise trouble himself to greet them. On the TV screen, a morning talk show was in the middle of a cooking segment.

Julia stood with Juniper in the living room and thought for a moment. Then she knelt down and said, "Mommy has to go, Juni. Sit there on the couch, okay, and don't move. Karen will be back in a minute."

"I don't want to."

"Honey, Mommy has to be at work or she can't buy you another Beanie Baby next time we're at the shop."

Juniper said, "Don't go."

Julia picked her up and touched her nose to Juniper's. "Karen's coming right back. You be my big girl—keep an eye on Doofus, okay? He needs somebody to take care of him." She set Juniper on the couch. "I'll see you right after nap time, and then we'll make birthday cupcakes. Yay!"

Juniper replied, "Yay," tonelessly, as if it was an answer to a question.

Julia left. For a time, Juniper sat where Julia had placed her, her feet with their rubber Dora the Explorer boots sticking straight out. She was careful not to let them touch the couch's fabric. She kept her jacket on, though she still felt sweaty inside of it. She watched the cooking segment. The people on the show were talking about making a roux, which Juniper translated as Roo, the tiny kangaroo character in Winnie the Pooh stories, and so she watched carefully, waiting for Pooh's little friend to somehow emerge from the stockpot.

When it became apparent that Roo was not going to appear, Juniper felt close to tears. They'd *said* they were making a beautiful Roo. Nothing was going right today.

Doofus was asleep now. Karen still had not appeared. Juniper wanted to change the channel, but she had been told to stay on the couch and she didn't want to get in trouble if Karen returned and found her off of it.

Can you see this child on this blue plaid couch, her light brown hair in pigtails, her pink flowered boots sticking out above a worn braided rug—this one a vintage seventies design in orange and brown and tan? Her jacket was bright green and had a small bloodstain on the front, probably from the previous owner's having had a bloody nose, but who could say for sure? Juniper's cheeks were flushed. She blinked away tears.

Her rainbow-striped leggings peeked from between the boots and her pink ballerina skirt. While she waited, she pinched the fabric over her knees and pulled it up, then let it go. This she did four or five times. She picked her nose. She scratched a spider bite on her neck.

Her tummy growled, saying it must be snack time. She hoped Karen remembered that today was her birthday. Maybe her snack would be gummy worms.

Also, she needed to go potty.

It was this last that gave Juniper the courage to move from her seat. She was certain Karen would be angrier with her for peeing on the couch than for leaving it.

The windowless bathroom was a small, humid, dark cave. Juniper disliked it even at the best of times. Today it seemed sinister. Something could be hiding behind the shower curtain, waiting to jump out and grab her. She approached with trepidation.

In order to reach the light switch, Juniper had to pull the step stool out from beneath the sink and climb onto it. Her little bird's heart pounded as she did these things, then pushed the switch upward. The light flashed and popped loudly, startling her, then went dark. She started crying and at the same time she wet herself.

And still Karen didn't come.

Beyond running out of the bathroom, Juniper didn't know what to do. She stood in the living room, her soiled clothes growing clammy and cool against her skin, her face streaked with tears. No one was ever coming back. She was alone here with Doofus and would be alone forever and there would be no birthday snack or cupcakes or a present from her grandma. No one would change her into dry clothes. No one would put a movie in the player or read her a story before nap.

She was three years old to the day; she didn't have an intellectual sense of what love was, but love as she knew it meant someone who wrapped their arms around you and someone you hugged tight. And now she had no one.

How much time passed with Juniper alone like this, convinced she'd been abandoned and would never be saved? It's hard to say. What Karen told Julia later was that she'd been next door tending to her father, who had MS and had needed a little extra assistance with his morning routine. She'd arrived back at her house to find Juniper sitting under the kitchen table pantless, with a bagged loaf of bread beside her. The bag was open and Juniper was eating a slice. Her rain boots were propped upside down in the sink.

Neither Karen nor Julia was especially troubled by the situation. As far as they were concerned, nothing serious had gone wrong. Yes, Juniper had a little bit of difficulty with the potty while she was waiting, but she'd handled the situation admirably. What a smart little girl! Happy Birthday.

16

Xavier's last day of high school:

"I am not going to miss this," said Joseph, the sax-playing white boy with dreads, in response to the 7:20 homeroom bell. He looked rough, as if he'd been up all night or had rolled out of bed ten minutes earlier and run across the school's ball diamond, which bordered his backyard, in order to make it here on time.

"I kind of am," Xavier said from the seat beside him.

The classroom was two-thirds full; some of their classmates had decided to skip. There wasn't much on the agenda for seniors today—an awards assembly being the main event. So it was likely that the missing kids weren't expecting any awards. Joseph would be getting one, for concert band. Xavier would be getting three: for concert band, Citizenship, and Scholarship. He'd finished the year with a 4.2 GPA.

Overachiever, his uncle Kyle had called him recently, with a mixture of admiration and something like spite; Valerie had managed to leave their working-class life behind her, while he, Kyle, never had. Kyle's life was blue-collar car-building factory work, paycheck to paycheck, same as their father's had been. Kyle's son had graduated from high school three years earlier, but only by the skin of his teeth, and was currently ankle-cuffed for buying weed. "Bet you think you can be the next black president," Kyle had said to Xavier during the phone conversation, and Xavier had replied, "Um, no. Who'd want that job?" He admired President Obama, as you might expect; he did not have any desire to live with a target on his back or to be subject to the sort of vitriol that was leveled at anyone in politics. Bad enough to be subject to assessment from music teachers, competition judges, and, one day, critics.

He worried that this aversion to the political meant he was weak. His dad had been both a professor and an activist, teaching undergraduates and speaking to organizations and even Congress about racial discrimination and profiling. In one of Tom's talks, now hosted on YouTube, he'd addressed his audience, saying, "Why am I doing this? Well, for one thing, white men listen better to other white men. And white men bear the responsibility for undoing the damage their forbears have done. But every person who cares about justice for him- or herself—and that's all of us, I'm pretty sure— ought to stand for group justice, too. Do you see?"

Xavier could see. He'd watched that video and others that featured his dad over and over again. He could see; of course he could, but he didn't want to put himself in any crosshairs and he didn't want to let anything supplant his own passion. Not now, at least, not when he was just getting started on the road to a career in music, music full time, music as his livelihood, days spent in practice studios, evenings in performance venues, a world populated by people who valued the arts. What was the point of all the progress toward equal rights if a guy like him—i.e., not white—had to keep agitating rather than live in the results?

So no, he didn't want anything but a life of music.

Exception: Juniper. Juniper, he thought, might be able to exist side by side with music. The feelings he had when thinking about her were not all that different from the ones he had when he played a guitar (the sexual desire part notwithstanding).

Would his dad understand this? Xavier wondered. Would he be proud?

Now Joseph said to Xavier, "You are a freak. I bet you were up at six practicing."

"Five-thirty, actually."

"Like I said."

Xavier might have replied that if Joseph practiced more, he, too, could have gotten a music scholarship at a school out of state, or at least elsewhere in the state, someplace new and interesting, someplace where every single landmark, every street and strip mall, every big church and big mansion and big oak tree wasn't as familiar as your own face in the mirror. He might have said that getting up early gave a person a sense (false though it might be) of having control over his life, of being a part of the action that powered the world. Also, Xavier didn't *like* to sleep late. He didn't like the way he felt on the few occasions when he'd slept past, say, nine o'clock; it was as if the day was half gone, like he was behind on everything, like he'd lost time he couldn't ever get back.

His mom was an early riser, too, and they'd gotten so that they sat in the kitchen in the mornings as the sky lightened, drinking coffee and just talking about whatever came to mind. Lately the subject was the big oak tree and how long it might hang on and how much she was dreading the day when it would have to go.

This morning being his last day of public school forever, she'd said, "I know I say this a lot, but today especially I wish your dad could've been a part of your life."

Xavier said, "Yeah, me, too," though until she'd said it, his dad hadn't been on his mind at all.

Fact is, he tried not to let his brain go in that direction too often—because what was the point of indulging the pain of loss? Focus on what truly matters: that's the practice that had gotten him through all these years successfully. Did he sometimes lose that focus? Sure he did (viz., *Juniper Whitman*). It had gotten easier over the years, though, maybe because he was closer and closer to being in charge of his own destiny—inasmuch as anyone ever is.

He wished he'd had his dad all along. He hadn't had his dad all along. *Life's a bitch,* his uncle Kyle had said the other day. *If you don't know that already, you will. Mamas can't protect their precious angels forever.*

Xavier knew. Sort of.

He didn't relate any of this to Joseph. He said, "Well, I got to see four deer in my yard at sunrise. What did you see when you got your sorry ass up?"

"I saw this place—but not for much longer!"

Their homeroom being seniors only, and this being the last time this group of students would gather in this room, Mr. Hopkins, whose teaching duty was English, including a whole course just on F. Scott Fitzgerald and his wife, Zelda, didn't bother with his standard effort to quiet the class while the day's announcements were being broadcasted over the PA. Instead, he went around the room with a plastic bin full of packaged breakfast bars and muffins and offered them to the students.

Xavier took an orange-cranberry muffin. "Thanks," he said, and Mr. Hopkins—a black man, we should add, because no white teacher would do this for any number of reasons—reached over and mussed Xavier's hair. Joseph took a breakfast bar. Mr. Hopkins did not muss *his* hair.

When Mr. Hopkins was past, Joseph said, "Suck-up."

"I love you, too, bro."

"Hey," Joseph said, "there's a thing tonight at Marco's. We should go."

"Okay, sure—but I gotta work tomorrow morning."

"Meaning?"

"Meaning," Xavier said, unwrapping the muffin, "I'm not staying over."

"Dude, what's the point if you don't stay over?"

"The point is I'm looking at a thirty-G bill for school next year. I can't afford to miss work."

Joseph said, "What, you lost your scholarship?"

"No, man, that's *after* my scholarship and financial aid."

"Damn. You should just go to State."

It wasn't as if Xavier hadn't considered it. Both Dashawn and

Joseph were going—Joseph (a C student at best) by virtue of choosing communications as his major and by having a mother who worked in the Office of Admissions. Xavier loved him like a brother despite his slacker ways; Joseph, whose saxophone was very nearly a fifth limb, understood and shared Xavier's compulsion for playing music, the same compulsion that has driven musicians since the time of the first bone flutes and skin drums.

Xavier said to him, "And major in what? Nobody's doing classical guitar at State."

"Anything. Who cares? It's not like there are any jobs for grads now anyway. We could get an apartment together and party as much as we want."

"Freshmen live in the dorms, not in apartments."

"Whatever. At least you'd be around. Wouldn't he?" Joseph said to Andrea, the girl sitting to his left, nudging her leg with his foot.

She turned. "Keep your nasty feet off of me."

"Wouldn't it be good to have Zay at State next year so we could all hang together?"

"I wouldn't mind," Andrea said. She smiled at Xavier.

Xavier said, "Well, it's not happening."

He didn't smile back or even look at her. Andrea was one of the girls he'd hooked up with last fall and who since then had texted him every week or so with what were more or less invitations for repeat encounters. He knew he was supposed to want to jump if and when any girl asked. What normal cis male wouldn't? Sex without obligations, without expectations—that's what hookup culture was supposed to be. Well, fine, if that's what worked for her and for some of his friends, but he'd figured out fast that he wasn't built for that.

He'd wanted to have sex, sure. He'd been glad, even grateful, to do it. At the same time, though, he'd felt weird getting naked with a girl he didn't know very well and wasn't interested in knowing much better. There'd been a few minutes of intense physical desire and release, and then she said as she got dressed, "I'm supposed to meet my friends downtown in, like, twenty minutes, so I'll see you at school, okay?" And he said, "Sure." And then it was just him alone

in his bedroom with his lamb lamp and his mobile and a used condom he'd quickly wrapped up with notebook paper and stuffed in
his trash can. He'd felt empty and strange. It wasn't like he wanted
more of anything with *Andrea,* he just wanted . . . more. Of something. Connection, maybe. Emotion. Was it lame and old-fashioned
to think sex and love should be linked?

Then he'd done it again with a different girl, as much to see if
the results would be the same as to take advantage of a sure-thing offer. That girl, Rachel, hadn't been as abrupt as Andrea. Even so, the
encounter was nothing more than a few recreational minutes spent
matching up parts that fit together. It felt good, and then it also kind
of felt bad. He wasn't doing it again.

Andrea said, "You guys going to Marco's tonight?"

"We are," said Joseph as the bell rang, ending homeroom.

"See you there," she said.

"See her there," Joseph said to Xavier, watching her leave.

Xavier slung his book bag over his shoulder and got up. "You
see her."

"You're not backing out."

"If all the party's gonna be is—"

"Chill. It'll be a lot of things," said Joseph. They went into the
hallway and entered the stream of teenagers moving along to first
period. "Is this about that girl?"

"Which girl?"

"The neighbor, the Blakely chick we talked to that night out
front of your house. Dashawn told me."

"What? No, it's not about that. And her name is Juniper."

17

"So, listen," Valerie said that evening as she and Xavier walked together from her lab at the university toward the parking lot. "I didn't want to say anything about this until the details were set, but now they are, so here's what's up: I've hired a lawyer and I'm suing the Whitmans' builder and the city and Brad Whitman for killing our tree."

"You can do that?" Xavier asked. He was carrying a tray of seedlings, as she was.

"I can. A civil suit, not a criminal one. Nobody will go to jail. The penalty is financial. It's meant to disincentivize these people from continuing harmful and deceptive building practices."

Xavier said, "You said Brad. Not his wife, too?"

"No. Our assertion is that he and the builder made the relevant decisions."

"Do they know? Do the Whitmans, I mean?" Xavier sounded mildly alarmed.

"Not yet. The first step, service of process, will happen by registered mail after my lawyer gets all the paperwork in place—in a couple of weeks, I believe. You've heard the expression 'being served,' right? This is that. Sometimes the sheriff does it in person, but that's not how this will go."

Xavier stopped in place. "I don't see why you had to take it this far."

She gaped at him. "Are you serious? Have you not lived with me every single day for eighteen years and, what, seven weeks? Did you not sit in my summer-semester classes for, like, five years straight so that I wouldn't have to send you to day care? We have to fight for what's right or nothing ever changes."

"You said you were going to be a good neighbor."

"This isn't personal."

Xavier smirked. "Oh, what, you think Brad Whitman's not going to take this personally?"

"I don't see why you're getting worked up about it—you're not even going to be here while it gets sorted out. It could take six months, maybe longer."

"*Sorted out?*" he said, and now he was clearly agitated. "Mom, it's a *lawsuit*. If you wanted to 'sort it out,' you could've just gone over there and talked to the guy."

"Oh, you think so? Just *ask* him to pay a hundred-grand penalty and swear never to do it again? Ask him to get his builder and the city to cough up four hundred?"

"What—five hundred grand? Is that how much you're suing for?"

"I know," she said. "It sounds excessive. My lawyer came up with the figures, and when he explained his logic, I agreed. Need I remind you that the college you chose costs almost seventy thousand dollars a *year*?"

"Wait—you encouraged me to pick my dream school and now you're, like, blaming me for the cost?"

"I didn't mean it like that."

"Besides, my scholarship—"

"Pays half. I know. But if something gets screwed up or if you don't sustain the required GPA—"

"I will."

"I expect so. But things happen. Maybe you'll have a really tough semester along the way, and . . . All I'm saying is that while I wouldn't have pursued this just for the money, the money can make all the difference in what the next four years will look like for you. Think how much more time you'll have for your music if you don't have to hold down a job along with everything else. You could earn your degree without either of us taking on any debt at all. You could think about grad school."

Xavier was quiet, but he looked upset. She could see his mind working. "What is it?" she said. "Why is this so troubling to you?"

"Nothing," he said. He started walking again. She did, too, and he went on, "It's fine. Probably better this way—that the Whitmans become our enemies."

"Enemies? Don't be so dramatic. We won't have to be enemies. When Brad Whitman understands how much damage his choices caused—"

"Then, what, he'll have you over for a barbecue? *Hey, my bad, here's a check. Let's let bygones be bygones,*" Xavier said in an imitation of Brad.

"No, but if and when we run into each other—"

"You aren't going to tell them?"

"That's not how it's done," she said. Truer was that she didn't want to confront Brad directly; he was, no question, the kind who'd try to charm her into changing her course, and she wasn't having it. As for Julia, she didn't want to offend her personally, which was what would happen if she tried to explain. Better to let that situation lie. It would speak for itself.

"If and when we run into each other," Valerie repeated, "I'm sure he'll be civil and I'll be civil, and that'll be good enough for me. I've had a lot of practice coexisting with people who've got nothing but disdain for who I am and what I've done with my life, the choices I've made, the issues I've supported. I don't care if Brad Whitman likes me, I care about what's right."

"I thought you and Julia were getting to be friends."

Valerie said tightly, "I have all the friends I need."

They'd reached the car and now loaded their seed trays in silence. They drove in silence. When they got home, Xavier retreated to his bedroom, where Valerie heard him take up one of his guitars—the José Marín Plazuelo, it was—she could tell from the sound—a $6,000 spruce instrument he'd paid for himself. He played a piece he'd been working on for a while now, *Asturias,* a nineteenth-century Spanish composition. It was complex and expressive, full of both melancholy and passion. Appropriate, she thought, for where he was in his life right now. And so true to who he was as a person.

Listening, Valerie felt equal parts pride and fear and sadness. In too few weeks he was going to launch himself out of her immediate reach and into the world. How had he gotten so tall, so grown-up, so past the place where she could pull him onto her lap and wrap her arms around him and assure him that everything was going to work out all right? When she'd held him, she, too, could believe it, for a little while anyway. How would anything possibly be all right, though, when she wouldn't be able to hear or see him daily?

Ah, the curse of motherhood.

A little later, when Xavier was about to leave for a party at his friend Marco's, something occurred to Valerie. She said, "Hold on, we got off track earlier. What did you mean when you said it's probably better to be enemies the Whitmans? Why probably better?"

"Nothing."

She put her hands on her hips. "Try again."

"*Nothing.* I like Juniper, is all. We were—I don't know. I thought we might go out, you know, if her parents were willing to let her."

"You want to *date* Juniper Whitman? She's . . . I mean, did you not see that picture of her with Brad, the purity thing, when we were at the housewarming? Xavier Alston-Holt, that is not a girl you should spend two seconds thinking about."

"That picture's from when she was fourteen. She isn't buying into that crap anymore."

"It's a worldview. She was raised up with that. You think she can just take it off like an old sweatshirt?"

"You don't know her. But it doesn't matter anyway. It doesn't make sense for me to date anybody here."

"Especially not her."

"She's *fine*," he said.

"No doubt. I like her, too. But—how do I put it? She's very, very white."

He rolled his eyes. "Seriously? That's all you got? Nobody cares about that anymore."

"Some don't. But some do care. A lot. Think about what happened to your dad."

"A long time ago. It's different now."

She shook her head. "Not as much as it seems from where you stand. This country's only partway integrated. In bubbles, pockets of populations where tribalism isn't so strong. You're inside, so you can't see it—and maybe that's on me, raising you so middle class, thinking that if I lived my own life like I was in *The Cosby Show* and race didn't matter, the whole world would come along for the ride." She put her hand on his forearm. "Really, Zay, it'd be better for you if you didn't date anyone who's white."

"That's some hypocritical bullshit, coming from you. You *married* a white man."

And look where it got us, she thought. Look where it got *him.* She didn't say this, though. She said, "All right, I'm probably being overcautious. But not where Juniper's concerned—not where her family is concerned, I should say, specifically Brad. Making her do a virginity pledge? Come on. Those kinds of people are all about keeping their girls *and their bloodlines* 'pure.' Forty, fifty years ago his kind would lynch you just for looking at her. Maybe they're not stringing boys up anymore, but the attitudes haven't gone away."

Xavier said, "Whatever."

"You're resorting to *whatever* with me?" She shook her head in wonder. "You must *really* like this girl."

"Even if I did, so what? You're going to ruin it with that lawsuit before it could even be a thing." He opened the front door, saying, "I'll be home by midnight," and left Valerie standing there nonplussed. Half an hour ago, she'd lamented there being so little time before he left for college. Now she felt like it couldn't happen soon enough.

18

And now we have come nearly to a turning point in this story. Here are some things to bear in mind:

The stories we as a culture love best almost always have a villain.

If we were to ask Valerie Alston-Holt who in this story that villain might be, she would name Brad Whitman. She wouldn't say he was your typical TV villain, a metaphorically black-hatted, black-hearted egotist or psychopath. If anyone understood the fine gradations of what could be considered villainous, Valerie surely did. Just the same, had the question been put to her, she'd have pointed at Brad as the architect of her current troubles, and she wouldn't be wrong.

Who would Brad Whitman name as this story's villain? At the current stage in the goings-on, when he's soon to be hit with a six-figure lawsuit, that answer seems obvious.

The obvious, however, isn't always the answer.

Who would we have named? Would we have named anyone at all? Or would we have said something like, "These things happen," as if there were nothing anyone could do?

PART II

19

On this, Juniper's fifth day at her grocery store job, a hot June day in the week after school let out, she and Xavier stood in the Fresh Market parking lot between her new car and his old one—a twelve-year-old silver Honda with faded, flaking paint on its hood, roof, and trunk, the flakes held in place by pine sap, a result of its being parked at home and school beneath North Carolina's ubiquitous longleaf pines. The contrast between the two vehicles was stark. The kids didn't care.

They'd been dismissed early from their respective work shifts because a delivery truck had broken down, failing to deliver what would otherwise have needed to be stocked. So now, together, they were free of both obligations and supervision.

Today was the first time their shifts had aligned and the first chance they'd had to speak in person and in private since their tête-à-tête in the corner of Juniper's backyard. Both were dressed in the khaki-pants-and-green-shirt uniform all the employees wore. Juniper had plaited her hair into two French braids. Her mother had told her she looked tidy and efficient. And cute. Juniper hated the word *cute*. She wasn't so keen on her mother, either, for that matter; Julia seemed unable to stop herself from remarking repeatedly on how surprising it was that Juniper got that Land Rover, and in the process she was making Juniper feel increasingly bad about it and herself. While we doubt this was Julia's intention, the effect was the same.

Julia had been completely taken aback. Some said this was because her own SUV, though it had cost more than twice the price of this Land Rover, was the same year as Juniper's, and shouldn't she have a car newer than her daughter's? Admittedly this assertion was unsubstantiated. Some of us were willing to give Julia more credit than that. She might have been taken aback simply because the vehicle went well beyond a teenager's need for reliable transportation and she worried about Juniper's being spoiled. Whatever the case, Juniper, who'd been annoyed when leaving the house today, was not concerned with any of that now—because, Zay.

He was a word Juniper preferred over cute: *winsome,* a word she'd learned from a book. She knew it meant *attractive or appealing in character,* but she also liked how it was a (not literal) opposite to *lose some.* She'd watched him at work. He'd been stocking in aisles four through seven while she was in two and three, and she'd made every excuse to walk past his aisles to get a glimpse. He was no slacker, which came as no surprise to Juniper or to any of us— how does a teenaged boy earn enough money to buy himself a $6,000 guitar unless he's willing to work hard with practically no days off?

So yes, Juniper had been admiring Xavier while he worked. She'd also been thinking about how they'd started off really well, but then for these past couple of weeks, while they were both swamped with school stuff and, for Xavier, graduation, everything had stalled. Until right now, or so she hoped: as they'd been clocking out, he said, "Hey, do you have a minute? I was hoping we could talk." And she'd said, "Yeah, me, too." And they'd walked out here together.

As they did, she could hear her heartbeat inside her eardrums the same way she had that night when he'd kissed her, and she felt suddenly warm all over. This fascinated her; it was as if some unconscious and primal part of her knew things her conscious self was far less certain about. She and Xavier had something real going on, that's what these reactions were telling her. They told her that she was, *finally,* being given the guidance she'd prayed for.

Xavier said, "I've been wanting to tell you how bad I feel about that night, you know, at your housewarming party."

"What? Why?"

"I owe you an apology." He was holding his phone, turning it end over end over end as he spoke.

Juniper said, "No, you don't. You didn't do anything wrong."

"I appreciate you saying that, but . . . For one thing, you said you aren't supposed to date, or whatever, so what was I thinking, basically making you break the rules?"

"You didn't *make* me. I do have a mind of my own."

"Yeah, no, I didn't mean that. Obviously you have a . . . I'm not saying this right. Man . . . I knew I was going to mess this up and now you think I'm an ass—"

"I don't," she said. "At all."

"I wanted to do this sooner, but since I don't have your phone number . . ."

Juniper waited. He'd wanted to do *what* sooner? Apologize? Or was there more? Because he was acting like there was more.

Xavier leaned against his car and stuffed his phone and hands in his pockets. He said, "Maybe it wasn't *wrong,* but also maybe not the smartest thing—for me. I mean, I like you. A lot. It'd be cool if we could hang out and, you know, go out. Assuming you wanted to, and could. But we'd just be making things hard on ourselves since I'm gone in August. You get that, right?"

Juniper had been watching him while he spoke. Now she looked down at her shoes and shrugged. "I guess, sure."

"It'd be hard for *me,* anyway. But we can be friends. I mean, since you aren't supposed to date anyway—"

"No, right, I'm not supposed to." She glanced up at him. "But I figured if we—that is, if I decided that there was someone I wanted to go out with, well, I'd just talk to my parents about it. They actually seem like they're loosening up. But it's academic, I guess, since like you say, you don't want to start anything when you're leaving. Which is smart, I guess."

He was staring at her intently. "Yeah," he said, "but . . . maybe stupid, too."

Her pulse jumped. "Stupid how?"

"Well, I might be seeing it all wrong. I mean, I'm just thinking about it some more, and is it actually stupid to deny ourselves a chance to make it work?"

"Stupid not to give ourselves any credit for being, like, intelligent and mature?"

"Yeah. Exactly."

There was an awkward silence while they both smiled at their shoes, and then Xavier said, "So, this ride." He pointed to her SUV. "It's pretty sweet."

She said, "I don't know. It *is*, but I'm kind of embarrassed by it."

"Nah. Count yourself lucky."

"I just . . . I was excited about getting to pick what I wanted."

"Of course. I would be, too."

"But now I think I should've gotten a Corolla or something."

"What? No, take what you can get."

Or as Brad had said, *Find out how to get whatever it is you want, and then do whatever it takes to get it.*

Juniper looked straight at Xavier. "Do you want to go get a milk shake and test out our intelligence and maturity? No one expects me home for at least two hours."

"Yeah," he said. "I do."

Oh, Xavier. He had just stepped onto a tightrope and didn't even know it.

═══════════

As the teens drove to the restaurant where they would get their milk shakes, Xavier tailing Juniper as they went, Juniper felt both bold and nervous. Bold and nervous were, in fact, the two emotions she'd been feeling most acutely of late.

The boldness had everything to do with her feelings about

Xavier. The nervousness arose from her taking the dispatch job, from working with Brad (only one week, so far; three shifts) and seeing his enthusiasm as he'd brought her around the Hub to speak to everyone who worked for him there, letting them all know that Whitman HVAC had become, if only in this small way, a family concern. Everything about Brad these days made her feel nervous—and for a very good reason, which we're going to get to shortly.

The teens met up inside JJ's, where some of the best milk shakes in town were to be had. Juniper ordered mint chocolate chip. Xavier opted for chocolate peanut butter.

"We'll call this an un-date," Juniper said as they took their selections to a table beside the window.

"Un-date?"

"Like a non-date, except *non-date* sounds like people trying not to date, whereas an un-date sounds like people hanging out and getting to know each other better to evaluate whether they *should* date."

Xavier laughed. "If you say so."

"I do. So, okay, tell me two things about yourself that I don't know yet."

"Hmm." He thought for a minute, and then he laughed again. "I don't know. This shouldn't be hard, right?"

"I'll go first, if you want."

Xavier said, "What if I ask you something I already know I want to know?"

"That'll work."

"Okay, so, I'm curious about the Purity Promise thing. I read up on it a little, and it seems, well, kind of bizarre. I was wondering, did you *want* to do it, or did you *have* to do it, or . . . ?"

Ah: the question so many of us would have asked in his place.

"I wanted to," Juniper said. "Surprising, right? But at the time, I really did."

What she hadn't wanted, initially, was to attend church at all. This was earlier, when she was nine and Julia, newly employed by Whitman HVAC and trying to remake their lives, was turning over every new leaf she could think of.

Thanks to having a regular Monday through Friday schedule, their weekends now were completely free and could be filled with any and all kinds of family enrichment activities that Julia might want to plunge them into. Juniper had long been accustomed to weekends of being sat in front of cartoons and videos while Julia was at work. She didn't want to get dressed up on Sunday mornings to go to a new place and meet new people who might not be nice to her. But Julia had latched onto the idea that Jesus or God (Juniper wasn't clear, then, on which one Julia credited, or maybe it was both, or maybe they were one and the same?) had entered their life as demonstrated by Brad's hiring her. And what could be better than to show their gratitude by making worship a regular feature of their week? Juniper didn't share Julia's conviction. Too bad. TV was out, Jesus was in. Juniper had better learn to like it.

And as it happened, she did. The church was huge and clean and full of light. There was music and singing. The people were calm and unhurried. They seemed to always be smiling. *Welcome!* they said every time. *We're so glad you're here to join us in giving thanks for this glorious day, this gift from our Lord.* Everyone was grateful. Everyone was cheerful. There were special classes for kids, with lots of treats and crafts and music. No one was crabby or stressed out. Kids didn't fight with one another or yell at the teachers or call one another names or offer to sell her drugs. It was a place—really, the first place she'd ever spent time—where the atmosphere was one of harmony and peace.

We're *so* glad you're here.

At church, everyone loved her. And, she soon learned, the Lord loved her, too.

New Hope's mission was to see that all the girls felt themselves *worthy*—of God's love, of Jesus's admiration, of respect from each and every man they'd be encountering as they got a little older and began to receive the attentions of young (and less young) men. Love, admiration, respect: Who doesn't want all of that?

To have it, they said, a girl needed to understand and embody the behaviors and traits that would engender it: Modesty. Obedience. Chastity.

They said (and we agree) that there are so many pressures on young women to be and to do things that will lose them the *love*, *admiration*, and *respect* they deserve. They also said (and here we are less persuaded) that every girl should rely on her father as her best guide during the most dangerous years, those years when she's physically mature and therefore attractive to men, but not ready yet to be released from her father's care.

Xavier was not the only one who thought that purity vows were bizarre. Others used terms like *gross*, *perverse*, *damaging*, *wrong*, and *reprehensible*. But few of those people have participated in the program or the ritual. Few have been the girl involved. We want to give Juniper the benefit of context.

Juniper told Xavier, "My mom and me, we had some really hard times before she met Brad—and then everything changed *so* much, it was basically a miracle, that's what she says. Which is why she had us join a church. Also, she wanted me and then Lily, too, to be better grounded than she was as a kid. She and Brad figured church and the Purity Promise thing would counteract the unhealthy pressures I'd get everywhere else. Which I think worked, to be honest."

"You seem fine to me," he said. "I mean, it still seems extreme, but . . ."

"I don't necessarily believe all of it anymore."

"Either way, everything is good now. Obviously."

"Yeah, it's great," Juniper said, and in that moment it felt almost true.

"So are you planning to stick to it? Virginity until marriage?"

He said this casually, as if out of curiosity rather than personal interest. Even so, Juniper felt the color rise in her cheeks. "Well, I'm not planning to, like, rush into marriage or anything, so . . . I guess it'll be something I decide when it comes up."

Xavier nodded. "Everybody should decide what's good for themselves."

"It's not a one-size-fits-all world."

"Exactly."

"I mean, I wanted mint chocolate chip today," she said.

"And I wanted chocolate peanut butter."

"Tomorrow I might want . . . a hot Krispy Kreme doughnut."

"I might want poutine."

"Poutine? For dessert?"

"Yeah, why not?"

"Yeah," Juniper echoed, grinning at him. "Why not?"

They finished their milk shakes in this happy mode, impressed with their combined intelligence and maturity. Maybe this dating thing was worth a try, they agreed. Maybe it could work.

When they were on their way out to their cars, Juniper said, "We need to keep this between us for the time being, okay? Just until I figure out how to handle my parents."

"Okay, sure."

"Radio silence until I tell you."

"Got it."

They'd reached their cars and stood between them once again, facing each other. Juniper glanced around to make sure no one who knew her was watching them, and then she reached for his hand. "I like the calluses," she said, touching his left-hand fingertips. She'd noticed the calluses the night of the party. All the pads were hardened from pressing guitar strings. "Makes you seem tough."

"If a tough guy is what you want, you're going to have to keep looking."

"No, you're tough. Just like I'm tough. Because we've been through things that most kids haven't had to deal with and probably never will."

A brief but tender kiss. A reluctant but happy parting.

―――――――――――――

Juniper's declaration about fortitude and experience had more behind it than has been revealed up to now. She'd been keeping a secret for five months, a secret that even the person involved in it didn't know she knew. A troubling and unsavory secret, as we're sure you'll agree once you know the details.

Her declaration was also an example of an occasion where the Fates, observing, laugh and shake their heads as if to say, "You ain't seen nothin' yet."

20

Among Oak Knoll's longtime residents is a husband-wife pair of cultural anthropologists to whom we would later turn for help in putting some of the more upsetting things we witnessed or heard about into context. As with extenuating circumstances, context matters when it comes to understanding how and why our fellow human beings behave in the ways they do.

Humans, as we all know, are complicated creatures. Even the simplest of us isn't simple. We are, every one of us, shaped by who raises us and where we're raised and how. Do we have two parents? One? None? Do we live in luxury's lap, or perhaps abject poverty, or solidly in the middle class? The differences make differences. Changes in circumstance from better to worse or worse to better matter, too.

Are we well tended? Are we loved? Are we the awkward kid, the mean kid, the violent kid, the shy kid, the popular, the celebrated, the disabled (either emotionally or intellectually or physically)? What traits do we have built into us in terms of talents and interests? Juniper had a connection to nature, a love of frogs and bugs and flowers. She was not so different from Valerie, in that way. Xavier loved music he could make with guitars, and had a preternatural ability not only to play that music but also to laser his attention and devotion on whatever captivated him. Everyone has something. And that something has a lot to do with what we want, who we are, what we do.

And then there is the power of that odd and ineffable thing called attraction.

Even more mysterious: love.

Juniper's secret, part one:

When it happened, Julia Whitman was away with Lily at Lottie's place. This was in early January this past winter, and Juniper sensibly had refused to accompany her mother and sister to that miserable trailer with its sagging floors and cockroach-ridden cupboards. It wasn't that Juniper didn't have sympathy for Lottie, who'd been diagnosed with COPD generally and emphysema in particular, and was in the process of figuring out how to manage an oxygen canister without setting herself and the trailer on fire (that would come later). It was that Juniper couldn't stand being there for more than a few minutes; when she was inside at Lottie's, her early childhood was there with her—every too hot or too cold or too hungry lonely scary painful hour, or so it felt to her.

Outside was a bit of a different story; outside were memories of wandering the loamy, pine-studded land upon which the trailer was anchored, poking about through the wildflowers and weeds to discover the great wonders of what seemed to her the wilderness. Beetles and butterflies and toads and tree frogs, and sparkly slivers of pyrite that she collected and saved in a Pringles canister. Outdoor playtime, for little Juniper, had been a suspension of all the bad.

Now she was seventeen, though, and it was wintertime, and when Julia asked if Juniper wanted to go with her and Lily out to Lottie's place, where they'd be staying over for one, maybe two nights, Juniper said no. She said she had reading to do before school started up again on Monday. She'd stay home with Brad.

Let us backtrack here—for context—to when Juniper was fourteen and the New Hope Purity Promise program was under way.

This was the rehearsal for the ceremony and ball. In the church's Great Hall, fifteen dads and daughters were standing in pairs facing each other, her right hand in his left, each person's free hand clutching the page on which their respective vows had been printed.

Juniper watched Brad's face as he and the other men took their turn reading aloud: "I choose before God to cover my daughter as her authority and protection, to be pure in my own life as a man, father, and husband, to be a man of integrity as I lead and guide my daughter to a future in which she will find a worthy husband to take my place."

She watched him and was filled with gratitude and warmth. But, too, in a cascade of thoughts that were at once flattering and shameful, she had an odd sense that the expression she was seeing was a different kind of love than she felt for him.

And if it was? He was not her father. They had no blood relation. She'd known him for only a few years. It would not technically be wrong.

Suppose she'd invited it—though not deliberately—in the way she'd been crushing on him all along? What to her had been hero worship might have come to seem like something else to him, something laced with desire and intent.

Did he desire her?

What if he did?

Juniper said nothing to her mother or anyone about it. Maybe she'd been mistaken. What did she know about men and . . . whatever it was she thought she was seeing in his eyes? It could've been nothing more than some mixture of pride and happiness and anticipation, right?

So Juniper studied him at the ball the next night: the way he smiled at her as she made her vows and he made his; the pride in his expression as they held hands and walked to the dance floor; the admiration in his eyes as he gazed down at her during the waltz. Totally paternal. Nothing inappropriate at all, she was sure. She relaxed, then, and let herself be fully in the moment as it was intended— which is to say, filled with certainty that the Lord had brought them together for only this kind of pairing, protector and protected, no different than the other men and daughters here. He was impressed by her commitment and devotion. He loved her like a daughter, and she loved him like a father. He would help her become the best young woman she could be.

═══════════

This explains the look of bliss on Juniper's face in that portrait from the ball. But what about Brad's also blissful expression?

═══════════

The secret, part two:

January, this year. With Julia and Lily gone to Lottie's place, Juniper had taken on the role of cook for the evening. When Brad got home from work that day, the house—their previous house, not the one here in Oak Knoll—smelled like onions and garlic and roasting beef. He found Juniper in the kitchen at the stove wearing an apron. Her hair was up in a loose knot. She had her earbuds in and was singing along to a song he didn't know. She sang in a half-audible way, as if the action was unconscious. As if she was happy and engrossed.

Something was cooking in a pot, and she was tending it, and the whole scene struck a chord in Brad—or more like a single low, clear tone. It affected him the way a firm strike on a temple gong does when the sound rings out and surrounds and moves straight into the gut of all who hear it.

Look at her, so thoughtful. She didn't have to make dinner. They'd talked, the day before, about going out for sushi, which neither Julia nor Lily would eat. Yet here she was, dressed up and playing house on Brad's behalf, and he was delighted.

She'd already set the table. Noticing he'd come in, she now took a beer from the refrigerator and poured it into a pilsner glass for him. She asked him how his day had gone. While they ate a surprisingly good beef roast—better than Julia ever managed to make—she talked about the book she was reading. She was upbeat. Funny.

Lively. Lovely. There was no question in Brad's mind: Juniper had made this effort solely to please him.

He went to his den after dinner, bemused by the demonstration. What, exactly, was she up to? Was she up to anything at all? Did he want her to be?

He did not.

No, he did. Sort of.

Why not admit it? He was attracted to his stepdaughter and had been for a while now, God help him—which was why he'd made an effort to shut that down, keep it out of his head the way he kept a lot of his youth out of his head, no benefit to him or anyone to let that stuff clutter his brain, affect his actions. He'd fronted his feelings with demonstrations of fatherly affection and pride, as in that portrait. He had plenty of other things to think about—a business to run, projects to work on. He had a daughter of his own who was one of the lights of his life. The most he'd allowed himself to do was watch Juniper and appreciate what he saw, not so different from the ways he sometimes watched porn. Consider: a man could admire and lust after a woman without ever even meeting her, let alone knowing her. He could soap himself in the privacy of his shower and close his eyes and think about her while he satisfied some of that lust, and no harm to anyone. If Brad sometimes had Juniper in mind, so what? No one was the wiser, and if no one was the wiser, there was no problem at all.

But . . . supposing she wanted him, too?

No.

No. For all intents and purposes, she was his daughter, same as Lily, and he would treat her interest 100 percent paternally. He should never have indulged his inappropriate thoughts in the first place.

Not that there was any harm in that.

Leave it, Whitman, he thought.

He stayed in the den, watched a movie.

He went to the dining room liquor cabinet, poured himself a scotch.

He read the local news, then the sports news.

He thought about taking a shower.

He got another two fingers of scotch.

Julia called; he told her everything was fine, that Juniper was upstairs reading, that yes, he would enforce a reasonable bedtime. Had he been drinking? A little, sure. Why did she ask? His speech was a little fuzzy? Well, he was tired. Off to bed soon.

The house was quiet when he went upstairs. Juniper's bedroom door was open, the light still on. She'd fallen asleep reading. He stood in the hallway remembering how sweet she'd looked in sleep when she was younger, how when they'd traveled she sometimes fell asleep in the car or in the airport or on a beach towel after a full morning of romping in the surf. He hardly ever had a chance to see her asleep nowadays.

He went into the room to turn the light off. She lay on her back. So pretty in sleep. So pretty all the time. A smart girl. Sweet. She'd been obedient just the way the church taught—a surprise to him and Julia both, given their own capacities for getting into trouble in their youths. But then everything had been different for Juniper, a rescue child who had always wanted to please people, to do right, to be loved.

At her bedside, Brad leaned over, intending to kiss her on the forehead. The kiss, though, almost of its own accord, landed on her mouth.

Juniper stirred and Brad pulled back half in a panic, but she didn't wake.

For a long moment he watched her and warred with himself over what to do next.

Her lips . . . So soft, so virginal. That young, firm body . . . God, the temptation! He hated and loved it both.

She'd be scared, but eager, too, definitely eager. He sensed it. He knew it.

But.

No, *damn it,* he thought, and he turned and left the room.

It would be wrong, *was* wrong, was not even something he ought to be considering.

But.

He wanted to have her, *could* have her, he believed. Under the right circumstances.

Which would never come to pass. He wouldn't allow it, even if she threw herself at him. That's not the kind of man he was. He had a wife and a daughter to consider.

But, Jesus, it was painful to know she was absolutely in reach if he wanted to pursue her, if he was willing to accept what she was offering.

And it galled him to know that something he wanted was not in fact gettable. There had been very little in his life so far that wasn't.

21

The secret, part three:
    Juniper had not actually been asleep.

22

Chris Johnson, Valerie's beau, frowned at her from across the table at the restaurant where they were having dinner. She didn't like his severe expression. This expression was not what she'd driven three hours to see.

She said, "I take it you disapprove."

"You don't need my approval—but no, I don't disapprove of your taking action against the builder. The homeowner part of this worries me, is all. You've dramatically increased your burden of proof in requiring a jury to hold him jointly accountable."

Valerie shook her head. "I don't think so. I've got plenty on him to prove his complicity. *If* it even goes to trial, which my attorney thinks isn't likely. The negative press would be bad for all of them."

Chris said, "I wish you had talked to me about it before you—"

"Please don't try to pull some kind of mansplaining thing on me," Valerie said, not letting him finish. "I hired an eminently qualified attorney to advise and represent me in a jurisdiction he knows all about."

"My, you're prickly. I wasn't going to mansplain anything. I was going to say, I wish you had talked to me at the time so that I could've lent my support from the start."

"Oh," Valerie said. "Okay, I'm sorry. This has been really stress-ful, and I'm . . ." She swallowed hard. "Let's start over, okay?" She picked up the cocktail menu.

"You don't have to go through all of these things alone, Val. I know you're tough and capable, but, you know, sharing a burden can be a good thing—for a relationship but, more importantly, for a stressed-out individual who's already dealing with an impending major event."

"You mean Zay leaving."

"Yes. I've been there; who can relate better?"

He meant he'd seen a fledgling of his own leave the nest: his daughter Talia, who was now twenty-six and was getting married at the end of June. One of the reasons Chris was so appealing to Valerie was that he'd raised a child to adulthood largely on his own, as she had. "And he's black," her mother had said when Valerie told her about him. "I guess now you've learned your lesson." "That's inci-dental," Valerie had replied, and her mother had said, "Humph."

To Chris, Valerie said, "Sure, you launched Talia. I don't know that you can relate to the tree situation, though."

"Not directly, but so what?" He reached across the table for her hand and said, enunciating each word slowly, "I am on your side."

Valerie drew and expelled a heavy breath. Her shoulders were practically up around her ears; she relaxed them, took another cleans-ing breath, and then said, "I am going to order a cocktail."

Chris squeezed her hand and let it go. "I want to be . . . It's hard to do this long distance."

"We've talked about that."

The waiter arrived at their table. Chris and Valerie each ordered a drink, and then Chris said, "Let's talk about it again."

"And draw the same conclusions. So maybe we should just flip a coin to see which of us gives up two decades of connections to their school and colleagues."

"That might be the only way to resolve it."

"What we're already doing works fine."

"It does not work fine," Chris said. "It works barely."

He wasn't wrong. What kept it functional was that they had excellent chemistry, had felt it the minute they met, continued to feel it whenever they were together, and felt it sustaining them when they were apart. Further, they had a strong intellectual connection, both of them idealists, activists, committed and experienced educators. Everything about the relationship worked gorgeously, except the geography.

They'd talked about it a lot, and the issue Valerie had so far managed to avoid addressing (because she knew her answer was in some ways lame) was why she was so reluctant to consider relocating. UVA was a good school—she'd be pleased to teach there. And central Virginia was beautiful. The summers were cooler than here.

The answer to why was this: her house and her friends and her outdoor plants. She was entrenched. To say so, though, would make it sound like she valued those things over Chris. Which she didn't. But still.

Xavier was going to college. Their oak tree was going to die. Maybe she should be going to some kind of new situation, too.

She said, "Here's something else I haven't told you yet: Xavier likes the girl whose father I'm suing."

"Well, that's . . . untidy. Did you know? Before you filed suit?"

"He never breathed a word of it—and probably never would have except that he got pissy with me about the lawsuit and it came out that that was why."

"So it's going to mess things up for him."

"It would, except that she's forbidden to date."

"Date *him*?" Chris said.

"Date anyone. That is, she made a purity pledge when she was fourteen, which we can only call blatant coercion. Though even if she could date, I'm sure Brad wouldn't be wild about her seeing a black boy. Julia, the mother, is genuinely friendly toward us—or she has been; I think that'll change once the suit's served. I know I *should* give Brad the benefit of the doubt, but—"

"Except where your tree is concerned."

"Except there," she said.

"Would *you* be okay with them dating—tree notwithstanding?"

"Truth? I did not react to the idea favorably. I *like* the girl. I'm absolutely in favor of people getting together in whatever combinations work for them, color or gender or class or whatever. But I don't have to tell you, racism is getting uglier and more overt all the time." She took a roll to butter and went on, "I told Xavier she's too white."

"Oh?"

"I know—Tom was white, I'm a hypocrite. But here's the thing. Her parents are willfully cultivating that young lady's ignorance. Education and access to birth control are what works. It's *proven*."

Chris said, "Yes, well, if safe sex was the goal, that'd be a whole different story. The goal is 'purity,' remember."

"Yes, exactly. Purity, which might as well be a synonym for whiteness, in this case. Not to mention female disempowerment, a 'marry them off and keep them barefoot and pregnant' effort. Let's just all go back to the Dark Ages together," Valerie said, her voice rising. "Those good old days, when life expectancy was thirty and lynching Negroes was all the rage. Why *wouldn't* I want Xavier to get himself mixed up with folks like that? I'm getting all wound up, sorry."

Chris smiled. "You're trying to protect Zay, that's all."

"That's my job. Or it was my job."

"And you've done it well."

"Have I? After our little chat, he left for a party and I haven't seen him for more than maybe three minutes since. It's like he's punishing me."

"Probably is."

"He *said* he'd decided not to pursue her, but he still got mad when I agreed he shouldn't."

"Sure, he *said* it."

"You think he didn't mean it."

"What do *you* think? I don't know him well enough to say."

"I think . . . he *wanted* to mean it. But I have a feeling he's caught." She sighed. "Damn. I *do* like her, though. Just yesterday she came over while I was working in the yard. We had a nice little visit."

Valerie had been turning the compost when she heard Juniper and a friend come outdoors, the other girl doing most of the talking. It seemed a mutual friend of theirs was maybe bulimic, maybe anorexic, how to be sure without asking? Also: how to ask? One thing was clear: Hailey was getting way, way too skinny, *absolutely skin and bones, don't you think?* and Juniper's friend wondered if they should make plans for an intervention.

While the girls discussed it, they batted a beach ball from one side of the pool to the other. Valerie heard the soft bumps of hand against plastic (those things would last centuries in a landfill), saw the ball at the top of each arc. She listened keenly, as she often did to the students milling in the hallways on campus. These girls were, what, seventeen? And no mention by either of them of involving adults in this possible intervention or of getting adults involved at all. Not surprising, really—Valerie remembered being that age, her total lack of confidence in adults at the time. Adults *caused* the problems, they didn't solve them. And wasn't that still generally true? Yes, it was.

The ball came sailing over the fence and bounced into Valerie's yard, followed moments later by Juniper coming through the gate, her friend following. Both of the girls were in bikinis that made middle-aged Valerie almost blush for them but in which seventeen-year-old Valerie would have strutted proudly.

Youth. Would she go back to her own if she could? She'd be tempted, sure. Imagine getting to regain the excitement of her first serious romance—with ecology, not with any boy from that time; ecology was the love that had lasted.

She could recall the day it happened. She was ten years old, sitting with her family in church and waiting for her grandmother's funeral to begin. While the adults murmured to one another, Valerie observed the display in front of them. There was a coffin, its top half open to reveal Gram from the waist up, its lower lid closed and covered with a casket spray of peach and lavender and cream-colored roses—Gram's favorite colors, the lavender especially, which she had often remarked matched her hair. An overstatement, but then Gram had been prone to hyperbole. To hear her tell it, her whole life before moving to Michigan from Beaufort, North Carolina, at age twenty was a series of Depression-era trials and tribulations that rivaled Job's tests.

So: casket flowers, and two urns of similar floral bouquets set on pedestals, and three more big arrangements on easels. Valerie turned to look around her. The first four rows of pews had smaller floral sprays at their ends. Flowers and funerals: Why did they go together? Not until she researched it later would she know that the original purpose was to mask the smell of death—that is, decomposition. No matter; the connection she was making as she sat there that morning was that flowers and plants *made folks feel better.* That's why people also sent them to hospital patients. Flowers and plants made folks feel *good,* happy—why?

That was the question that got her going. What was behind the interrelationship between humans and flora? Between one plant and another? Plants and animals, plants and insects, plants and the atmosphere? Why did one seed turn into a flower and another into a shrub and another into a tree?

That feeling: curiosity, excitement, love. Love was the root of all of it, no pun intended. Love came so easily in youth.

Now Juniper saw Valerie and said, "Oh—hi, Ms. Alston-Holt. Sorry, the ball got away from us."

"No trouble," Valerie said. "Beach balls do that."

The friend said, "Hi! I'm Pepper. You must be Zay's mom."

"I am. Nice to meet you, Pepper. Are you girls having a good summer?"

"So far, so good," Pepper said. "Looking forward to going to Juniper's beach house. Her parents are *so* nice to let me come. I *hate* being stuck here in summer, and my parents are *always* working—they own a restaurant. I work there, too. Not as much as them. As they. I love the beach. Do you?"

Valerie watched Pepper with amusement—and gratitude that

her own child didn't operate at this speed. The girl could wear a person out fast. She was a real contrast to quiet, watchful Juniper. Valerie said, "I do enjoy the beach, but maybe for different reasons than you-all. I like to go to the marshes and muck around there. Ecology is one of my specialties. I'm no expert on the coastal region, though, so it's always a treat to go and learn something new. Also, my gram was from out that way, in Beaufort. I heard lots of stories, growing up."

"I want to study ecology," Juniper said. "And botany, and maybe zoology, too."

Valerie said, "That's ambitious. Do it."

"You don't think it's too much?"

"As I tell my students, nothing is too much unless you decide it is. And you can't make an informed decision if you don't try first."

Pepper said, "*I* want to do textiles and fashion design."

"I could use some fashion design myself," Valerie said, indicating her faded Prince T-shirt and cutoff sweat pants.

Juniper pointed at the compost bin. "I think you're dressed just right for the occasion."

The girl had a sense of humor. Valerie could appreciate that. And she approved heartily of Juniper's interests. And she'd enjoyed the conversation that ensued from here, a discussion of how composting worked and why to do it and what to do with the material when it was "done." Juniper was inquisitive, bright, sociable enough, open—though neither she nor Valerie spoke of Xavier even once.

None of this, however, meant Valerie was any less reluctant to endorse Zay's interest in Juniper than she'd been before.

She said to Chris, "I understand why he likes her. I just don't want him to."

"As the great bard sayeth, 'Love looks not with the eyes but with the mind, and therefore is winged Cupid painted blind.' That's been my experience, anyway."

"It's true. Sadly. Happily. Why does everything have to be so complicated?"

Chris said, "It doesn't. What do you say we flip that coin?"

She stared in surprise. He looked serious. "Do *you* want to?"

They gazed at each other. Chris waggled his eyebrows. Valerie laughed and said, "Maybe wait until after I get a second cocktail in me."

<hr>

Chris had called Valerie prickly, and we would agree that this was a fair descriptor for how she'd been behaving in recent days. She'd agree, too, and she didn't like feeling that way. She hoped the lawsuit would be resolved in short order so that everything and everyone would more or less go back to normal. What she'd said to Xavier bears repeating: she knew the Whitmans would never be her friends and she was all right with that. She was okay with being seen by some as too passionate about her issues—surely there'd been people around Rosa Parks who wanted her to let well enough alone. Surely some of the Reverend Dr. King's friends had told him he might be going too far. Not that environmental protection was quite the same thing as civil rights, and not that she was on par with any of the real warriors. But she had to do what she could, that was just how she was built.

See Valerie when she'd left home for college, high on winning a full-ride scholarship to nearby Michigan State University. Having nourished herself for years on Nina Simone's sixties hit "To Be Young, Gifted, and Black," she was now eighteen years old, a petite dynamo with chin-length Janet Jackson hair, oversized tees, baggy jeans, high-top sneakers, and a can-do attitude about saving the planet. She'd just spent four years with her head down, nose in her books, aiming for the grades that would carry her out of that duplex where "Uncle" Ray lived upstairs—with his mother now, probably thinking about his good old days of flashing Valerie and hoping for Mama to pass soon so that he could pick up where he'd left off; there was a new family of girls next door.

Learning, for Valerie, was like eating for most of us. It energized and sustained her. It gave her power on a lot of levels. It gave her purpose. Had she been born a decade or two earlier, her energies might have been put to the ongoing civil rights movement. As it was, she believed the cause that now needed people like her was the environment. She believed she could contribute more there. She was not prickly back then, she was *sharp*. Well—not sharp like fashionable. She'd never been that. Sharp like intelligent, energetic, ambitious.

During holiday breaks and summer vacation, she volunteered her time any and every place she could get to that needed kids who'd clear trash and pull weeds, who'd build and plant community gardens, who'd lead grade-school children on educational hikes, who'd count birds or deer, who'd sample water from creeks and streams, who'd chart data and write proposals that organizations could then take to politicians (back in the days when climate change wasn't a partisan issue).

She'd been as terrified to be in college as she was excited to get there. Suppose she failed? Suppose she sat in those classrooms with their white professors and white students and made a poor showing? Suppose everyone was smarter than she was, and all she'd prove was that black girls didn't deserve a spot, didn't deserve a chance?

But no. She'd excelled there, too. A B.S. in forestry. Then a dual Ph.D. in ag and ecology. When she finished her education, she'd been as hopeful as a black woman could be in America, or maybe anywhere. Job offers came from several solid universities and a couple of prestigious ones. She had her pick of five different states, so she picked the one with the climate and biodiversity she liked best: North Carolina, a state with an incredible array of plant and animal life due to its wide variety of ecosystems. Appalachian highlands on one end, coastal estuaries on the other, and in between, hills and rivers, forests and plains, protected parklands and huge swaths of farms. Cotton. Peanuts. Tobacco. Hogs. Horses. Strawberries! Valerie loved strawberries. North Carolina was the home she'd always wanted, thanks in part to Gram and her stories. And before long, she met the man she'd always wanted—though she hadn't known who that man was until she met Tom Holt.

Tom was eight years older than Valerie; she didn't care.

23

Having avoided visits home to Jackson, Mississippi, for more than a year since Xavier's birth, Tom Holt-Alston agreed to take his wife and now-toddling son to visit his mother and the extended family for Thanksgiving. They'd flown into the recently renamed Jackson–Medgar Wiley Evers International Airport, a grand-sounding moniker that overstates the actual experience of travelers there.

In size, Jackson-Evers is on the lesser end of small—though not tiny. The main thing to emphasize here is that the state of Mississippi's largest airport bears the name of a black hero of the civil rights movement, while the state itself continues to fly a flag that has as a significant part of its design the entire flag of the Confederacy. This kind of dichotomy is the South in a nutshell.

As so many family holiday gatherings are, this one, which was now concluding, had been pleasant in some aspects, an ordeal in others. The food was excellent, so there was that. And little Xavier was a trouper, sociable and willing to go from stranger to stranger (as they were to him) to have his gorgeous baby-smooth light brown skin and wild-curly gold-toned hair remarked upon again and again, mostly by the younger women who, like Tom, had rejected the prejudice they'd been suckled on.

Tom was Southern and white; Valerie didn't care. (Her family did, but she didn't care about that, either.)

Tom had, in his youth, tried on communism—in its idealized state, he always said, defending himself from those who imagined him buddying up to Stalin or Mao Zedong (who were dead, but still). Valerie did not care. Or rather, she thought all of these things were the facets of his character and life that made him interesting. Mainly he was an intelligent, freethinking, passionate young professor whose pet cause was social justice. Tom wanted to do with society what Valerie wanted to do with the environment, and what was not to like about that? Also? He was six-three and handsome. Blond. Violet eyes. Valerie's colleague Michelle called him Ken, after the doll. Grinning, Tom remarked, "Barbie should be so lucky."

We might digress and tell you, here, all about Tom's family and their struggle to accept Valerie as his chosen mate. We might describe how Valerie's family—her mother, especially—had the same struggle in reverse. Neither family could say they were *surprised*; they knew better. Why, though, would anyone choose to take on the challenges of interracial marriage (especially in the South) when there were so many good reasons not to? Well, said Valerie and Tom, even if the *problems* they'd face weren't simple, the *answer* was: love.

But getting into all the particulars here would be telling you something we're sure you can more or less imagine for yourself, so instead, we'll tell you what happened to Tom.

Valerie, too, was a good sport. Some of the family had met her at the wedding, so she was not so exotic to them as she'd seemed at first. (As if none of Tom's parents' generation had ever spoken with a black woman who wasn't serving them in some way or other.) No one exclaimed over her skin or hair. However, some of them did ask her questions that rode the margin of offense. Such as, Was her daddy employed? Did she sing in her church's gospel choir? Did she hate her hair? Valerie fielded the questions with outward grace, the way she'd been taught to do.

Xavier and Valerie: managing well. Tom: not as well, in part because he could see how put-on the sweet behavior of some of the family was, same as it'd been at the wedding. But mainly because on Friday morning after breakfast, while Valerie was upstairs in the Holt homestead changing Xavier's diaper and getting him ready for their trip home, Tom's great-uncle Brooks started in on Tom.

Brooks, Tom, and Tom's mother were in the dining room with their coffee. Brooks, a tall man like Tom but with another forty years and forty pounds on him, had been talking about Tom's father and grandfather (Brooks's older brother) and how poetic it was that the two men had died together doing a thing they'd loved: crop-dusting. Brooks was oddly enamored with this story (possibly because the event had made him the Holt patriarch) and could be counted on to wax nostalgic over it whenever he had a captive audience. But then apropos of nothing more than the fact that Tom was at the table with him, he changed course and said to Tom, "Well, son, I guess this is too late to fix now—legally anyway—but that child of yours, well, you've made an abomination. If you were *my* boy bringing it and that woman home, I wouldn't have you in the house."

"Brooks!" said Tom's mother. "Stop it now. I told you, I won't tolerate you causing trouble."

"I've tried to keep quiet like you asked, but a man's got to speak up when he sees wrong being done."

"You spoke up before the wedding," Tom said. "And you see how much I cared about your opinions then."

"That's right. You, being stupid and corrupted, went ahead

and married a girl you should've been content to just fuck, and then you bastardized your name, too. *Holt-Alston?* Pathetic, all of it." He spat on the floor.

"Brooks, really!" said Mrs. Holt, presumably due to *fuck* more than the spitting.

Tom pointed at Brooks. "You're the abomination. Ignorant, racist sons of bitches like you are what's wrong with this state—with this country."

"See here," said Brooks, standing up from the table and going to the opposite side where Tom sat. He towered over Tom and put his finger in his face. "What's wrong with this country is boys like you disrespecting men like me who know God's word and follow it, same as you ought to do."

Tom pushed Brooks's hand away. "Sit down, old man," he said calmly. "This is none of your business, anyway. I'm leaving in a half hour and you can go right back to being a bigot, but for now, kindly show some respect for my mother, at least, and shut your filthy mouth."

"Shut my mouth?" Brooks said. He put his finger in Tom's face again. "You'd better—"

Tom stood up. "I'd better what?"

"Tommy," his mother said, "don't give him the satisfaction."

Brooks, eyes narrowed, said, "You never did belong in this family. Why, if it wasn't a slanderous insult to your mother to say so, I might suppose you'd been sired by some traveling . . . *communist.*" He spat again. "Highfalutin nigger-loving socialist that you are."

Tom said, "*Sociologist.* Get out of my face."

"That's enough!" Mrs. Holt said.

The men glared at each other. When Brooks wouldn't move, Tom turned around, seething with anger but unwilling to give the son of a bitch one more moment of his attention. You could never win with these kinds of people, and he was sorry he'd let Brooks get him this riled up.

As he turned and started to leave the dining room, he caught his foot on his chair and stumbled, losing his balance and falling against the china hutch before landing on the floor. Brooks started laughing. Several pieces of dishware toppled along with Tom, breaking as they hit.

The noise brought Valerie hurrying down the stairs, with Xavier in her arms. Tom was getting up, but slowly, with one hand pressed to his head. Mrs. Holt was beside him.

"Are you all right?" Valerie asked Tom. "What happened?"

"Your meal ticket tripped on his big fancy ideals," said Brooks, who'd moved back to the other side of the table and taken his seat. Valerie refused to acknowledge him.

Tom said, "Sorry, Mama, I'll pay for what broke."

"Don't bother yourself about that."

Valerie said, "Are you hurt?"

"I'm fine. Except that asshole is still my relative."

"Please quit it," Mrs. Holt said. "This doesn't do anybody any good."

Tom nodded. "I know, I'm sorry to upset you. Can I help you clean this up?"

"No, you have a plane. We'll manage it."

Tom said, "All right, then," and turned to Valerie and Xavier. "You ready? Let's get him into the car. I'll grab the luggage."

While Tom went upstairs, Valerie said good-bye to Mrs. Holt, ignoring Brooks, while Xavier, who was alert and wide-eyed and quiet, allowed his grandmother to hug him once more. "Come see us at Christmas," Valerie said, trying to keep her voice level, wishing she could add, *Because you'll never see my son or me in this house again*. Not until Brooks was dead, anyway.

Tom spoke little during the drive to the airport. Valerie didn't find this concerning. She'd overheard enough of the argument between him and Brooks to know why Tom would be fuming, turning the thing around in his mind, thinking of how he might have handled it differently.

On the flight to Atlanta, with Xavier napping in the seat between them, Tom asked Valerie, "Do you have some Tylenol in your purse?"

"I think so—why? Headache?"

He nodded. "I hit my head on the dining hutch."

She dug around in her purse and found the bottle of pills. "I wish the two of you hadn't provoked each other like that."

"I wish Brooks would crawl into a hole and never come out."

"Cosign," she said. "Do you have a lump?"

Tom reached up to the spot where he'd hit. "I do. A real goose egg."

"You should have said something earlier. We could've iced it. Want to ring for the flight attendant to bring some ice? They probably have first-aid packs—"

"I'll be fine."

In the Atlanta airport, Tom asked again for Tylenol.

"The first ones didn't help?"

"Not really."

"You shouldn't take them too close together—"

"Another two won't make me OD."

"No, I guess not," Valerie said, and gave him the pills.

He waited for the connecting flight with his eyes closed, head resting back against his seat, while Valerie walked Xavier around and around the gate area. She was thinking about the work she had ahead of her—finals to administer and grade, papers to read and grade, grades to figure and post . . . She was thinking about Xavier and snacks, Xavier and the runny nose he'd developed, Xavier and all this luggage he and she had to navigate as they went around and around the gate area. She was thinking about what a bigoted asshole Brooks was, and wondering how she'd handle Tom's mother's future invitations to visit. Therefore, she wasn't thinking much at all about Tom, who appeared to be uncomfortable but otherwise all right.

Sometime mid-flight he said, "I think I might have a concussion. What are the symptoms, do you know?"

"Headache?" she said, trying to recall anything she might have heard about it. "Mental fuzziness? Blurred vision, maybe?"

"My vision is a little bit blurry."

Valerie, in the window seat, said, "Look this way, let me see your eyes." He did, and she leaned toward him over Xavier's head for a close look. "Huh. Your pupil—the right one—is dilated. Just the right one."

Tom put his hand over his left eye. "Yep. That's the blurry one. Well, shit. I guess I should see somebody about it in the morning."

"You think you should wait?"

"I'm not going to spend the whole night waiting in the ER with all the other pathetic, unwashed fools who didn't have the sense not to get sick or injured on a holiday weekend instead of during regular office hours."

"You do smell kind of ripe," Valerie said—a nervous attempt at a joke. "Still—"

"Let's see how it goes," Tom told her. "I just want this headache to let up so I can think straight."

"According to Uncle Brooks, it's already way too late for you." She smiled and reached for his hand, gave it a sympathetic squeeze.

Tom attempted a smile in return, then closed his eyes again.

You can probably see where this is going. However, Tom did not die on the flight. He did not die at home later, or in the emergency room. He got a walk-in appointment to see his doctor midmorning the next day; the doctor confirmed a concussion, advised painkillers and rest, and sent him home. At home, though, his headache refused to respond to the meds, and in fact grew so severe that Tom didn't put up a fuss when Valerie insisted he go to the hospital. Not only that: he told her to call 911.

In the short time between when the paramedics took Tom by ambulance and when Valerie, having first arranged for Ellen to come stay with Xavier, joined him at the hospital, he lost consciousness.

Tests, scans, emergency surgery to relieve the uncommon-but-not-unheard-of-in-these-kinds-of-situations epidural hematoma—a brain bleed—and, as the sun was coming up over the trees that rimmed the hospital's parking lot and shining through its chapel's stained glass, "That's all we can do for now, Mrs. Holt. You should go home and get some rest."

A long day, then, of waiting for updates, of talking to relatives,

of paying a short visit to this good man, this wonderful father, this
excellent partner who now lay in a bed with tubes and monitors and
remained in some netherworld where Valerie couldn't reach him.
"When will he come around?" she asked his doctors. She asked the
nurses, too—they often know as much or more about the ground
game. In this case, everyone said the same thing: "Brain injuries are
unpredictable. We have to just wait and see."

At 11:45 P.M., while Valerie paced the house and Xavier was in
his crib lost in the bliss of innocent sleep, the phone rang.

Tom was gone.

Gone. Stupidly, perversely gone. Permanently gone.

24

We had to assume that the bulk of Julia's DNA had been inherited from her father, who'd run off with Lottie's cousin when Julia was fourteen. Because her mother, Lottie Corbett, was just about as unattractive—no, we'll cop to our real opinion: ugly—as a human, male or female, could be. Those of us who'd seen the *Lord of the Rings* movies compared her to Gollum. She was short; she was essentially bald; she had protruding eyes and ears; and what teeth she had were yellowed. She did at least clothe herself completely, so there was that.

Just as Julia's good looks were not fully to her own credit, Lottie's ugliness was not her fault. It was bad luck, bad genes. And yes, a lifetime of bad situations that also were not necessarily her fault, like never having sunscreen when she was working in the tobacco fields as a kid, so her skin was now leathery and spotted. Like being too poor to eat right or have time to exercise, so her body was now an uneven composition of squishy lumps.

What was her fault, or at least what had probably been avoidable, was her lung disease. She'd been a two-pack-a-day gal since she was fourteen or fifteen—around the time she'd started tending bar at the hole-in-the-wall her future father-in-law owned. Smoking

made her look older, she thought. It made her feel older for sure.
Everybody did it; tobacco was grown and dried right across the
road, for crying out loud.

This ugly, ill woman was now installed in the Whitmans' guest
suite with her oxygen tank and line and cannula, her caftans, and
her cigarettes. "What point is there in quitting now?" she'd said, but
promised to adhere to Julia's absolute no-smoking-indoors-or-under-
any-covered-surface policy.

Cigarette in one hand, "co-cola" in the other, Lottie sat in the
sunshine beside the Whitmans' pool watching Lily and Juniper race
each other end to end. Juniper, being so much bigger and a more expert swimmer, handicapped herself by being a dolphin—that is, she
kept her arms pinned to her sides as she swam while also giving Lily
a head start.

At the conclusion of one such race, Juniper got out and dried
herself off while Lily went to the pool's edge near where Lottie
lounged. "Grandma, can you swim? Do you want to race me?"

"Used to be I could," Lottie said. "Not with this, though." She
gestured to the cannula where it lay on a side table, temporarily; Julia had insisted that she not use the oxygen at the same time she
smoked—a not-unreasonable request, given that she'd burned down
her trailer doing just that.

Lily said, "Are you dying?"

"More or less."

"Which one?"

"What?"

"Is it more, or less?"

"Everybody's dying," Lottie told her. "It just takes some longer
than others, is all."

"Do you know how long for you?"

"Whenever God makes up his mind," Lottie said.

Lily asked her, "Is my grandpa already in heaven? I wanted to
meet him."

"I doubt they'd let him in," said Lottie. Then she called to Juniper, who sat at the far end of the pool with a notebook and pen in hand, "What are you up to over there? School's out."

"Nothing," Juniper said.

Lily climbed out of the pool and went to sit on the end of Lottie's chaise. "Are you going to live with us until you more or less die?"

Lottie snorted with laughter, which then made her cough and cough. Lily waited, picking at a now-soggy scab on her knee.

Finally Lottie said, "Your daddy offered to get me a new trailer, and your mama finally decided to let him. If she'da just let him do it right after he got all that money, I expect I wouldn't be sitting here today."

"You'd already be dead?"

"No, I'd be in my trailer, because it wouldn'ta caught fire, because it'd have all the new fire-resistant whatevers they use now. Lucky I didn't blow myself up—which woulda been your mama's fault if I did, and don't think I haven't told her that to her face. The way she acts so stingy and bossy, you'd think she made all that money herself."

Juniper had gotten up while Lottie ranted, and was going inside. "Hey there," Lottie called. "Where you off to? Bring old Lottie another co-cola, won't you?"

"Ask Lily," Juniper said. "I'm going to the park for a run."

Lily said to Juniper, "But Mommy's not home."

"I get to drive myself now," Juniper replied, and went into the house.

"Well?" said Lottie, looking at the child.

"Can I have one? Mommy never lets me."

"All the better," said Lottie. "Bring two."

25

About to go to his weekly guitar lesson, Xavier was in his car, ignition on, seat belt buckled, Sanel Redžić starting on his car stereo, when he noticed a piece of paper tucked underneath the windshield wiper on the driver's side.

He unbuckled his seat belt, opened the door, retrieved it. It read:

Today I'm in the mood for blueberry cornbread. You?
Meet in our corner at 9:30 P.M. I'll share, or BYO poutine.

"Finally," Xavier said. He'd heard nothing from Juniper and the radio silence was killing him. "But damn, I hate cornbread." He was smiling.

———————————

At nine-thirty, she was there waiting when he arrived. The sky had darkened to deep violet. Crickets chirped and tree frogs sang from his yard behind the fence. The scent of gardenias from his yard sweetened the night air.

Xavier hadn't brought food; he was too nervous to eat. Juniper had been at the front of his thoughts full time since their un-date at

JJ's. He'd scoured the internet for photos of her, needing some part of her, no matter how small, with which to ground his feelings while he waited. He found almost nothing. One photo of her in a news article from two years earlier, where she was in a group of several New Hope kids serving food at a shelter after a hurricane. It was her, though, and now here in front of him was the real her, the current her, shorts, T-shirt, ponytail, and a smile that reflected both welcome and relief.

"You got my note," she said, standing up.

"Low-tech communication. I like it." His hands were clenched. He felt hyper. Happy. Scared. "My guitar teacher is big on low tech. He won't even pick up an electric guitar. I don't like them much, either. There's something great about scaling back, you know? It's, like, good for the soul."

She had a quizzical expression. "Scaling back?"

"Nothing. Never mind," he said, feeling stupid for going on that way, for being nervous when he should be calm. Girls didn't want hyper guys. Guys were supposed to be chill and in control.

Juniper said, "No, tell me." She looked up at him, and there was a moment—a cue?—that made him think maybe he should kiss her. He wanted to. His heart thumped hard. Crazy. He'd never had this kind of response to a girl before, this kind of anxiety, this hesitation. Why was it harder now than it had been that first night?

He continued to look at her, unsure, and then said, "You want to sit down?"

"Okay."

He didn't kiss her. Should he have kissed her?

They sat so that they faced each other. She said, "By the way, I already ate the cornbread. I'm sorry."

"By the way, I don't even like it, so . . ."

"Oh! Perfect, then."

"Good thing it wasn't—"

"Poutine," she finished, and they laughed. His pulse slowed a little.

She said, "So I really want to know: What do you mean by *scaling back*?"

"Less . . . mental noise. Everything is high tech, right? Laptops, gaming, streaming. We all go around with our screens and headphones like they're umbilical cords to Life. But with a classical guitar, which is pretty much just wood and strings, you can produce music that'll rip people's hearts out or make them feel happy or calm them down . . . Like, a guitar can tell a story. Its tech is so *basic,* but its effect can be profound. And you never have to charge it." He smiled.

Juniper said, "Same as books. Paper and ink's all a book is, but when I was little, books made me feel hopeful. Like I had friends. Like maybe there were good things to look forward to someday."

Xavier pointed toward the pool and house. "Pretty good result, I'd say."

"Who cares about that? I like *this,*" she said, pointing at the two of them.

"I do, too."

She watched him, bottom lip between her teeth. Then she said, "Do you . . . Do you want to kiss me?"

He moved closer, put his hands on her shoulders. She put hers on his waist. They looked at each other, their faces shadowed. She smelled like flowers. Her hands were hot through his T-shirt. He glanced at her lips, closed his eyes, pressed his mouth to hers. His heart sped again. Other parts responded, too.

After a minute, she said, "Am I doing this right? I haven't really—"

"You're great," he told her.

"*You're* great," she said.

"You smell good."

"So do you."

They were turning this into a game. He said, "I like the sound of your voice."

"Yeah? Well, I like yours, too. Plus, your earrings."

He touched the two small hoops on his right earlobe. "Joseph thinks I should wear diamonds. As if, right?"

"Well, diamonds *are* low tech," Juniper said, and then she kissed him there, on his ear. "Though not as low tech as metal hoops," she said, and kissed his jaw. "And this . . ." she added, kissing him lightly on his mouth, "is even lower tech."

"Like I said, scaling back is great."

Basic.

Profound.

The simplest of pleasures. These two, kissing in the dark under the stars.

26

One of the still-true-but-for-how-long? facts about North Carolina's coast is that it's relatively undeveloped. Vacationing there—whether it be on the Outer Banks or a little farther down the coastline at Topsail Beach or Wrightsville Beach or on the soigné, car-free Bald Head Island—means you've got few hotels to choose from. But there are campgrounds and lots of rental homes and long swaths of beach. Or you might be able to do as Brad Whitman did and buy a place of your own.

A great deal of wildlife can still be found along the Atlantic and the Intracostal: oystercatchers and terns and herons and sharks and dolphins—even wild horses on the Shackleford Banks. Sand dollars. Sea turtles. Whales, during migration. Brad was not what we'd call an outdoorsman, but he enjoyed using the outdoors—and the beach especially—the way most of us do: in small doses, with plenty of sunscreen and insect repellent on hand.

Brad being an up-by-the-bootstraps self-made man, as soon as he came into money, he'd bought a cedar-sided, metal-roofed ocean-front house that was three stories tall and had a widow's walk at the top. Five bedrooms, four baths, and an elevator. Decks on every level. An outdoor shower and fish-cleaning station. A six-person hot tub. Weatherproof stereo speakers on the main deck that worked wirelessly with the state-of-the-art audio system he'd had installed inside. A gas grill, naturally. Weatherproof furniture, including a dining table that could seat eight. It was as good as anything you could get for under three million and he'd gotten it for a song—the previous owner had gone underwater with it, no pun intended, and filed for bankruptcy, letting the bank foreclose. A savvy guy could and, Brad believed, should see another man's misfortune as his great luck; after all, *someone* was going to get the deal, so why not him? Such was the circle of life.

As he'd done with the Maserati and the just-built house, he'd leveraged his money here, taking advantage of low mortgage interest rates while investing the bulk of his windfall in funds that paid three, four, twelve, even twenty times (in one case) the rate he was paying out. Every time he was able to do this—that is, buy a big-ticket item for his personal use or for Whitman HVAC—he felt like he'd accomplished something profound. He—a guy who'd started life as nothing, a nobody, a scrawny kid who'd lived for a time in a World War II surplus canvas tent when his dad was between jobs and therefore houses that they could afford to rent, a kid who had gotten beaten up defending his low circumstances, a guy who'd dropped out of college (*by choice*, he always emphasized)—now had no trouble whatsoever walking into a bank with a request for money and walking out with a Maserati, walking out with a small mansion, walking out with a beach house. Maybe now he'd do as his accountant had suggested and get himself a boat—a yacht, it would have to be. He didn't want something he could just write a check for; that was something that would have excited the old Brad. The newer Brad saw how large a guy could live using *other* people's money and wanted in on *that*.

Today, though, he was not thinking about money or leverage. He wasn't really even thinking about yachts, although being here at the beach meant seeing some pretty ones now and then. Prettier still, to his mind, was the sight before him as he sat in his chair on the wide oceanfront deck: Juniper.

Juniper in cutoff denim shorts and a bikini top.

Just looking, he told himself. No way to avoid seeing her or any attractive female who was around. It was the beach, after all.

Such was Brad's rationale.

Juniper was playing Frisbee out on the beach with Pepper, whose given name was Penny. Penny had come to be called Pepper *not* due to having a spicy personality but rather because, as we've seen, she had a great amount of pep. Excessive pep, some might say; they'd been here less than forty-eight hours so far and already Brad was tired of her constant chattiness. The girl talked and talked about everything: school, cross-country training (starting up again in July), her mother's broken leg, her parents' business (a French restaurant), her brother who was currently at camp and had contracted lice . . . Earlier this morning Brad had sent the girls off to the bakeshop for cinnamon rolls and bear claws just so he could sit on the deck and drink his coffee in peace.

Julia, on the other hand, was a fan of Pepper's. She said now, "Pepper has such good energy—that's what Juniper needs."

Brad, behind his sunglasses, watched Juniper and admired the lithe shape of her arms and legs, the grace in her motion as she pulled the Frisbee close and then sent it flying. He said, "I think Juniper's doing fine. I've kept my eye on her at work and it's nothing but good energy there."

This wasn't wholly true. Her approach to the work itself was strong, and she got along great with the rest of the employees, but when it was just the two of them, she seemed cautious, tentative. Like she was worried about saying or doing something wrong. Displeasing him.

Julia said, "She'll hardly talk to me."

"You need to give her some space, is all."

"When did you become the expert on teen girls?"

"Who says I am? Maybe it's just easier for me to treat her like a person than like a daughter, a child."

"What, because she isn't yours?"

He shrugged. "Could be."

"Well, then, just wait until Lily's a teen and you'll see how hard it is." Julia got up and went inside, where Lottie was still "pulling herself together" and Lily was playing iPad games.

Brad thought Julia should try loosening up, not only with Juniper but with him. That'd go a long way toward helping to keep his mind where it ought to be. With Lottie around, though, Julia had not given Brad even the slightest I'm-tired-but-let's-go signal. So he hadn't pursued her; he decided to let this play out a while, see how long the dry spell would last if he didn't make the first move.

Now Lottie inched her way out onto the deck, tank in tow. She was dressed in a pair of garish patterned culottes and a neon pink T-shirt that, with its off-the-shoulder style, recalled the eighties dance club scene. Julia had said her mother was spending much of the allowance Brad gave her at the online equivalents of Florida dollar stores.

"Ah, to be young again," Lottie said, gesturing toward the teens on the beach.

Brad said, "You ask me, age is a state of mind."

"Easy for you to say."

Brad helped her get settled into a chair. "Comfy? What can I get you?"

"I could eat some Cheetos."

"For breakfast?"

"Lunch and supper, too," said Lottie. "And a Pop-Tart, if you've still got some. Julia's trying to ration me with the junk food, you know, but I say, what's the point?"

"Sure thing. I'm going to change into my trunks and then I'll bring out some snacks and drinks so you can just enjoy yourself here."

"Good boy. Maybe you don't know this, but way back when, I told Julia I was worried about her jumping into things so fast with you. I don't mind telling you now, since I know that you and me, we tend to think alike. I believe you turned out all right."

"Thanks, Lottie. Sit tight now, I'll be back in a flash."

Inside, Julia was just done covering Lily with sunscreen. Brad said to his daughter, "You set? Give me two minutes and we'll go down and see if we can't catch a shark or two."

Lily picked up her net. "Ready and waiting!"

"Want to be a big help for me? Grandma asked could we bring her some Cheetos."

"And a co-cola?"

"Let's fill a cooler for her," Brad said, directing this at Julia. "Make it easier on her."

"And the rest of us," Julia said.

The Whitmans had come to the beach for a week, sometimes two, every summer since Brad and Julia were married. They'd rented a condo when it was just the two of them and Juniper, usually taking a second one adjacent to theirs for Brad's brother, Jeff, and his wife and baby. Then came Lily, and Jeff's next one, so Brad found a vacation rental house big enough for all of them. He discovered that he loved the chaos of having everybody in one place, all the kids underfoot, the adults relaxed and sociable, everybody gritty with sand, faces and shoulders reddened, bellies happy with crab and shrimp and lobster they cooked themselves.

This summer Jeff would be here in a couple of days, and this time he was coming with just the kids: He and his wife had split up right after Christmas, after she'd found him in a bar with another woman on his lap. Jeff was a fool, Brad thought, always had been. Undisciplined. He no sooner thought a thing than he did it, without considering whether it was wise or might have consequences.

Brad told Lily, "Got your fishing net? All right, let's hit the waves!"

He and Lily raced down to the sand, past where Juniper and Pepper now lay on brightly colored beach towels.

"Come on," Lily called to them when she reached the surf's edge. "We're going to catch a shark and we might need help. Sharks can be big."

Pepper sat up and said, "Do you actually plan to catch a shark?"

Brad answered, "If she could, she would. Come on in the water, girls. Look at this surf." The water was as calm as it ever got. "It's a bath!"

"Later," Juniper said, not even opening her eyes.

When Lily tired of not catching a shark or any fish, she put the net aside and asked Brad to flip her. Again and again he cupped one of her feet in his hands while she held on to his shoulders and counted to three, and then he launched her up high into a backflip and she splashed down, shrieking every time.

Finally Lily wanted a break. Brad said, "Who's next? Pepper?"

"I always get water up my nose."

"Juniper? Come on, Juni, you always loved to do this."

"I'm too big now."

"Since last summer? I don't think you've grown that much. Or are you saying I'm too weak? That's it, isn't it? You think old Brad's gotten too weak."

"Maybe she's saying she's gotten too heavy," Pepper said.

"Thanks for that," said Juniper.

"There's nothing to either one of you girls, even soaking wet. Now, you don't want to insult me, do you, Juniper? Come on, test me. I think I can do it."

"Okay, but just a sec," Juniper said, and she reached up to the back of her neck to retie more securely her bikini top's strings.

Brad admired her smooth belly, the skin pulling taut against her ribs. He considered the swell of each small but perfect breast. His own body's response was automatic: a hard-on that, given his standing in water up to his own belly, thankfully couldn't be seen. It strained against his swim trunks, and he thought he might as well be sixteen years old again, wishing that the girl in sight would take pity on his desperate state and help him "detonate and deflate"—that's how some of the guys he'd known referred to orgasm and it was apt, for sure. At sixteen, though, what with his acne and scrawny as he'd been, he couldn't get a pretty girl to look at him, let alone touch him.

When Juniper waded over and put her hands on his shoulders, when she put her foot into his interlaced hands, when she looked into his face and said, "Okay, one, two . . . ," he let himself have the brief fantasy of an empty beach save for him and her, where he'd push her down onto that bright green beach towel and pull down that little slip of fabric—

"Three!"

Up and over and splash. She came up laughing.

"Again?" Brad said.

She pushed her wet hair off her face and nodded.

This time when she put her hands on his shoulders, he put his on her waist—just for a moment, to help steady her. She was already lifting her leg to step into his hands. Her knee, or maybe it was her shin, brushed his crotch and it was all he could do not to groan aloud. He let go of her waist and laced his fingers, catching her foot.

This time she didn't look at him as she counted. Embarrassed, probably. *Good girl,* he thought.

As Juniper left him and went to play with the other girls, he glanced over at where Lily and Pepper were trying to net minnows. Juni hadn't been that much older than Lily when he'd first met her. He felt ashamed that he'd once again let his libido get the better of him. He wasn't a teenager, and Juniper wasn't just some girl he wished would put out or at least help out. So what if he desired her? *Get hold of yourself,* he thought. She's your stepdaughter. You aren't a king. You don't get to have every damned thing you want.

But it wasn't as if he'd be forcing himself on her. She wanted him, too. He knew she was struggling with it, same as he was.

27

How many times had Brad fit in eighteen holes under heavy skies and distant thunder? Golf, summertime, South: Iffy weather is unavoidable.

Teeing off early made that equation a little less likely, storms being more common in the late afternoon. Some days, though, as June cruised toward July and the convection began earlier in the day—reorganized, often, from the previous night's thunderstorm—the sky piled itself with fat cumulonimbus clouds throughout the morning and threatened to send the guys racing back to the clubhouse at any time.

Such was Brad's situation on this Saturday. Late morning, sixteenth fairway. Thunder. A few fat raindrops. While Tony Evans, the county district attorney and Brad's sole companion today, teed up, Brad tilted his face toward the sky.

"I think we'll luck out," he said.

"That'd be me," said Tony. "Since you're trailing by four."

Tony was a short, stout man, fond of Kentucky bourbon and Cuban cigars, an Old South type who would never have paid Brad the young nobody any attention but who was pleased to know and cultivate a friendship with Brad the successful entrepreneur. Friendships like this equaled support for campaigns such as Tony's reelection to the office of district attorney. And in turn Brad got support and connections to all kinds of other men in Tony Evans's orbit. This, too, was a kind of circle of life—if you happened to be white and entitled, as they were.

In golf, Brad had lost to Tony just once before, and then only by one stroke. Today, though, he'd been vacillating every time he went to choose a club. He'd misjudged several shots, missed putts that should have been easy . . . At work, too, he was off his game, slow to make decisions. Hell, yesterday afternoon he'd spent five minutes in his closet trying to decide between a blue shirt and a black one. Why? Distraction. Every time he saw Juniper, he wished he could have her. Not just fuck her; *possess* her. It was like being an addict in a crack house, surrounded by drugs but with no money to score. Or something. He was thinking of her all the time. And though he hated himself for his weakness, he also loved the fantasies of running off with her and living the good life someplace exotic, loved the way those fantasies made him feel—young, strong, hypersexual, desired all the time by some beautiful woman. Basically a teenage boy's version of what adulthood would be like if his acne cleared up and he worked out enough and he found a way to make a lot of money.

Brad knew it ought to be Julia he was hot for. What was he supposed to do? He couldn't help what he couldn't help. So he had to just keep doing right, even if he couldn't keep thinking right.

But it was damned distracting.

Thunder sounded. Closer now.

Less determined men than Brad and Tony would have already left the course. If their usual companions had been with them, these two would have given in sooner; the two men who completed their foursome were both insurance execs who'd risen in the ranks more through cronyism than grit. A little distant thunder and those guys got nervous. Actual raindrops and they were done.

Brad stood back near the cart and watched while Tony set his feet, settled the driver in his hands, pulled it back—

The flash and boom were nearly simultaneous. Next thing Brad knew, he was on the ground, blinking, ears ringing.

"Holy mother of God," said a faint voice—Tony's. Brad turned his head, saw his friend standing in the tee box. Tony dropped his club and ran toward Brad. "You okay?" To Brad, it sounded like Tony was speaking from far away, or through a press of pillows against his ears. His eardrums throbbed. Tony said, "Christ, that was close!" He pointed to the singed and smoking top of a pine twenty yards off.

Brad sat up, put his hands to his ears and rubbed, shook his head. Nothing helped. "Am I gonna be deaf?" he said. His own voice sounded far away.

"My ears are ringing, too. We'll be all right. Give it some time." His words were more certain than his tone.

Brad got himself up and into the cart, saying, "Best to call it a day."

Bit by bit, his hearing improved, and Brad and Tony sat at the clubhouse bar for an hour or better recounting their experience to a growing crowd of fellow golfers. They joked. They laughed. They drank. All the while in the back of Brad's mind ran a looping thought—no, less a thought than a feeling, a sensation, a message.

That lightning strike was for him. It was a sign. His life had been examined, tested, and reset, in the way he used to do with an HVAC system when he was still a technician with a one-man shop. Oftentimes that was all that needed done. Circuits got glitchy. They misbehaved, produced actions that ran counter to what ought to be happening.

Brad had been second-guessing himself about a number of things, his desire for Juniper among them, and second-guessing was not Brad Whitman's style. He'd lost his focus. And now look: He'd nearly been struck by lightning—but only nearly, and that had to mean something.

Some men would see it as a come-to-Jesus moment. Brad, though, felt no closer to Jesus than he had before. The lightning had reset him, that's what this meant to him. Restored him to his best full operating mode. He didn't doubt it, and he was going to behave accordingly.

He understood now, *really* understood, that he and Juniper

weren't ever going to run away together. And if she had any such fantasies herself—which likely she did, sweet girl—it was his job to set her straight. It might be that they both just needed to scratch the itch one time, *once*, that's all, just get it done and out of the way and out of their systems, and then they'd be able to get over it. It was, he believed, a sensitive and sensible approach, all things considered.

28

Let's briefly go back to that night in January when Brad and Juniper had been at home together alone. The night Juniper made a beef roast for their dinner. The night Brad came into her bedroom and kissed her.

With Julia away, Juniper had been curious to try on Julia's role, that of the devoted housewife, the role for which she had in some ways been trained by the New Hope pastors, though by this time the Whitmans weren't regulars at church. Their attendance had fallen off in the preceding year, maybe because Brad had made all that money and bought a membership to the country club he hadn't been able to get into before. With that membership came an excellent golf course—finest in the state—and therefore fierce competition for tee times. Until Tony Evans had brought him in as a new fourth for his preexisting Saturday group, Sunday mornings had been where Brad found his best luck, what with so many of the other gentlemen being truer members of the flock. Their faith was his opportunity. Just like Julia's absence was Juniper's. She could run the kitchen, make an entire meal on her own without her mother's constant oversight and input, see how it would feel to be in charge of her

own domain. It would be like taking the training wheels off her bi-
cycle to ride unaided and free.

While Brad was at work, Juniper planned the menu from what
she found in the refrigerator. The chuck roast was surely meant to be
their dinner on the night Julia returned; well, they'd all go out that
night instead, Juniper decided. Cookbook on the counter, she went
to work slicing mushrooms, chopping onions, mincing garlic, mea-
suring out oil and red wine.

While she worked, she envisioned Brad's surprise and pleasure
when he got home. He'd be impressed with her and proud of her ini-
tiative. He'd recognize that she was maturing, which might lead to a
loosening of the strict rules that had so far prevented her from going
to any of the parties thrown by the kids at her school. Girls like
Meghan and Kathi might never change their opinion of her, but there
were others who, seeing her participating in things like a normal
kid, might.

She wanted Brad to admire her. She didn't want to provoke a
sleeping wolf, didn't even know that wolf was there.

Later that night, she'd fallen asleep reading but roused slightly
when she heard Brad come into her room. Even an innocent teenaged
girl can sense when a situation might take a turn away from innocence. Not knowing what all he might be after and not ready to confront him, she kept her eyes closed and pretended to still be asleep.

The kiss horrified her.

———————————

Had Juniper known all that was going on in Brad's mind now, she'd
have been even more upset. Had he known what was going on in
hers—how she was appeasing him so that she could get more time
with the black boy he'd mistaken as a day laborer—well, who can
say what might have been? We're only here to tell you what was.

Another summer morning working dispatch for Whitman HVAC.

This was not a taxing job. It could be a dull one, though, when
the phones weren't ringing, as they often weren't before nine A.M.

Juniper might hear from two or three early birds with finicky A/C systems. Once the day's heat raced upward and compressors or fans failed to respond, the calls would start coming in.

Juniper sat at her desk in the small office next to Brad's, working on a haiku for Xavier.

Sunrise: a guitar
Sings a melancholy song
The girl hears and smiles

Now that they'd returned from the beach, Juniper was back in the routine: Three mornings a week, she drove to work when Brad did, put in her four hours of answering the service line and coordinating those calls with the technicians in the field. She was good at the work. She listened well, made clear notes, asked the pertinent questions, and then scheduled the techs. And all the while, she felt Brad's presence—not only his presence, his interest. She hadn't forgotten that singular moment when they'd been in the water together. His hands on her waist. His . . . arousal.

A tap on her door, then Brad opened it and leaned in. "How's your day going? Can I bring you some coffee?"

"No, I'm good, thanks. Slow so far."

"That's what coffee's for!"

"I mean the phones."

"It'll pick up. What's your afternoon like? I've got Jason coming at one to wash and wax the Maserati; want to stay and have him do the Land Rover?"

Juniper shook her head. "Pepper and I are going to a pop-up art thing down at the city park at noon."

"Pop-up art?"

"Arts and crafts for sale in booths. There's always cool stuff. Earrings and bracelets, some clothes, you know."

He took his wallet from his pocket and gave her fifty dollars. "Get something pretty."

"You don't need to do that."

"That's a fact," he said, and closed her door.

"Thanks!" she called.

The kiss had been in January—more than five months ago. When it first happened, she'd known that she wouldn't tell anyone. No way. The reaction would surely be outsize to the event (it was only a quick kiss, after all), and she didn't want to face that.

But then she'd thought, shouldn't her mom be made aware of the truth about the kind of guy she was married to?

Or would that just blow up everything for all of them?

Because, really, it was only a simple kiss. He'd smelled like bourbon. He might have just been drunk. A momentary lapse, not a criminal offense.

She could ignore it and the whole thing would just go away. No harm done.

Then she'd thought, what if it wasn't a momentary lapse, and if she didn't tell on him he might go after Lily one day?

No; she shouldn't confuse his interest in her with an ability to commit incest. Right?

The question of what, if anything, to do had messed her up for a while. Talking it through with her mother would've been natural if the two of them were close in that way (and the guy in question wasn't Brad). As it was, long experience had taught her that Julia was just about the last person she could count on to put her interests first. Given how devoted her mother was to Brad (or was *beholden* the word?), Julia might well blame *her.*

Then she'd met Xavier, and for the first time she understood what sexual desire felt like. How hard it was to control the urge to want to touch someone and be touched by someone. How that desire lit you up inside, created what felt like actual heat in your groin.

And so she could excuse Brad somewhat, knowing that, as she'd been taught at New Hope, men had even more trouble controlling their desires than women did. By this standard, Brad was just being male. To him, a pretty girl asleep upstairs when he was otherwise alone in the house equaled an attractive nuisance. Put a couple of bikini-clad teenagers in front of him and he was no better than a horny classmate of theirs. Sure, it'd be great if a girl's own stepdad never thought of her that way, but maybe that was asking too much.

Still, it was gross.

She'd chosen not to mention the erection thing, or any of it, to Pepper. Why derail their fun with that kind of distraction? It was easy enough to avoid Brad for the rest of the trip, with Uncle Jeff and the cousins there. Now she just had to avoid him a little longer—until December. She and Pepper had a plan.

They'd figured everything out while they were at the beach. They'd petition Blakely for early graduation, and then in December move out of their homes and share an apartment they'd pay for out of the money they'd saved from birthdays and Christmas over the years and from their jobs. In the meantime, Juniper would apply to every college in or near San Francisco plus the others she'd been considering. Pepper planned to stay local, with an eye on running a new branch of her parents' restaurant and maybe also diversifying into retail—a French grocery, maybe, with family-branded shirts and aprons and towels, etcetera, she'd design herself.

Juniper's current task was to get her parents' consent to date Xavier. She planned to take Brad's advice and simply ask for what she wanted. Or maybe the thing to do was to leave Brad out of the loop and tell her mother about Xavier in private. Work it through, get Julia's consent first, and then let Julia deal with Brad on her own.

Yes, okay. That seemed like the best way to go about it. Now, timing . . .

As Juniper mused, the postal carrier arrived. Juniper saw her through a window that, like Brad's, looked out onto the lobby.

Brenda, the receptionist who'd been hired after Julia married the boss, handed over the day's outgoing mail and then, in response to something the postal carrier said, stood up and went to Brad's office door. "Registered mail," Brenda said. "You have to sign."

Brad emerged and followed her into the lobby, where he signed for a fat envelope. He went back into his office and closed the door.

Juniper was on the telephone with a woman whose air-conditioning fan wouldn't run when she heard Brad say, "Valerie Alston . . . *What?* You have got to be fucking kidding me!" Then, a minute later, once he'd had time to read the details, "Un*fucking*believable. It's a goddamn *tree*!"

29

Xavier sat in his car in the shade of a towering magnolia tree, waiting for Juniper. It was 12:25; they had been supposed to meet at this city park at noon.

Communicating outside of work had been a challenge. Except for when she'd been at the beach and they'd used Pepper's phone, there could be no phone calls or texts. No social media. They swapped notes by placing them under his windshield wiper—not exactly efficient. Even so, Xavier liked the novelty of it, and the simplicity. He liked the romance. He liked that he had these little pieces of paper with her handwriting on them. She wrote with precision, small bird-like marks made with a fine-point pen, messages that were always warm and sometimes funny. Xavier was in the habit now of keeping the latest one folded into a little square he stowed on his wrist beneath his watch face.

Mid-June meant heat and humidity and a regular chance of pop-up thunderstorms. Xavier sat with his windows rolled down. He could smell mimosa blooms, those fairylike feathery pink bursts of gossamer that grew among delicate leaves—*pinnae,* they're called—that closed with the sunset.

Thunder rumbled well off in the distance. When he was a boy, maybe three years old or so, he'd said the thunder *grumbled,* his imagination conjuring a giant named Thunder who stomped around somewhere in the forest outside of town. Thunder the giant was grumpy that the sky was cloudy, that rain threatened or was falling already; Thunder liked to be able to play outside.

Here in the park's open field, five young Latinx children chased and kicked a soccer ball while their mothers stayed close by, music playing from a portable device. The women sat on a blanket. Plastic containers of food were outspread around them. Xavier eyed the food with envy. He was hungry. Juniper was supposed to be bringing lunch—her idea; she'd said a food truck that came every day to the industrial park had unbelievable empanadas that she wanted him to try.

Farther across the park were two rows of canopied carts: a pop-up art show in progress. Maybe he'd wander over after their date, find a little something to buy for Juniper.

If she showed up in the first place.

.

.

Two thirty-five.

"Where is she?" Xavier said aloud.

"Maybe she changed her mind," he answered himself.

"Doubtful. Why would she?"

He continued the conversation silently:

If she did, you're gonna wonder why you ignored your own good sense.

Maybe it's because I like empanadas, he thought, a joke to ease his anxiety. *Plus, we have amazing chemistry.*

Chemistry, bro? Does anybody say that anymore?

Retro is in, he thought.

Chemistry. A universal thing. Timeless. If you have it with someone, nothing feels better. If you don't, well, forget it, because that's going nowhere.

Next I bet you're going to write an essay about it.

For composition class this fall, why not?

.

You are a nerd.
Takes one to know one.

===============

Xavier's rumination on chemistry merits some examination here (if not an actual essay), particularly where it applied to Juniper and him.

Two people are in each other's company and feel the pull of attraction: We call that pull *chemistry,* but what is its actual substance? What's the biology of sexual attraction, and is that biology the same as romantic love, and did this pair of teenagers have it, whatever it is? Or were the feelings they were experiencing when they were in each other's company (and even more acutely sometimes when they were apart) what many would call puppy love?

When you're as old as some of us are, it can be easy to dismiss young people's feelings (intense as they may be) as nothing but raging hormones. We remember how it feels to be young. We are as familiar with lust as we are with hunger. Look at this hookup thing Xavier got himself involved with for a time: lust, leading to sex. That's what hooking up is all about. But look, too, at how Xavier responded to his experiences: He didn't want to pursue those two young women. He didn't wish they'd keep texting him with new offers to have sex. Had one of them left him a sweet note beneath his windshield wiper, he would not have shaped it into a square small enough to fit underneath his watch face, where he could keep it against his skin as if the sentiment behind the words inside might leach in, making him that much more intimate with the note's author.

Why not?

Chemistry. That's the difference. Therefore, we assert that chemistry does not equal lust—though we acknowledge that lust arises naturally from it.

We talk about how, when two people are especially attracted to each other, there are sparks between them. Not visible sparks, and yet we perceive them as such. So, then, is the chemistry of love a kind of electricity?

Electrochemical change is a reaction that involves electrons moving between electrodes and an electrolyte. This in essence is physics, and without former Oak Knoll resident Jack Martindale, who took a job with NASA, none of us knows very much about physics. What we do know is this: Some force that for all practical purposes is as real as those that can be observed and measured by science draws people together even when they rationally understand that this kind of together is not in their apparent best interests. They are helpless before it. Oh, sure, they can resist acting on it, but they can't prevent themselves from feeling what's true.

Dostoyevsky said, *What is hell? I maintain that it is the suffering of being unable to love.* Unable, meaning being *denied,* being *thwarted.* Those of us who've had love denied—real love, not a passing lusty whim, not a false infatuation based on some imagined connection that in most cases is unrequited—we fellow travelers through hell know Dostoyevsky told it true.

=====

The noise of tires on gravel interrupted Xavier—*there* she was. Juniper, in her glossy white Land Rover. He got out of his car and walked over to her door, smiling wide until he saw the expression on her face.

"Are you okay?" he asked when she opened her door. "What's going on?"

She handed him a heavy paper bag of food that smelled heavenly. "I'm okay. But Brad? Not so much."

Xavier frowned. "Doesn't sound like you mean he's sick or injured."

Juniper got out and shut the door. "Did you know your mom was suing him?"

"Oh," he said. "That."

"So you did know."

He nodded. "I told her I thought it was stupid."

Juniper said nothing.

He said, "I should've warned you, I know. It's just . . . I was afraid that if I did, you'd be pissed at me—well, not me personally, but my mom and therefore me by association. Which maybe now you are."

She was silent for what was the longest minute of his life so far, during which she leaned down to pick up an old magnolia pod and began to pull it apart. "I'm . . . It's not *your* fault," she said. "And I guess if it was the other way around, I might have been afraid to tell you. So . . ."

Xavier breathed easier. "What did Brad say about it?"

"That your mom is—I don't even want to repeat it."

"Crazy?" he said, hoping that was the worst of it.

She shook her head.

"Tell me."

"'An opportunistic bitch' was one thing."

Xavier bristled. "Well, that's harsh." He pointed toward a bench where they could sit and eat. They walked in that direction as thunder sounded again in the distance—farther away now, so that was good at least. He said, "What else did Brad say?"

"He said this kind of thing was 'typical of her type,' and then . . . I don't even want to say this . . ." She paused.

"I want to know."

"So he started talking about how she probably slept around with white guys hoping to get ahead and got dumped by your dad when she tried to entrap him. He said he doesn't believe your dad is dead."

"That is some real bullshit right there," Xavier said, taking it in. "Jesus. Not dead? Anybody can look it up."

"He is an ass. I mean, even if that was true, *his own wife* slept around—probably hoping to get ahead. Maybe I shouldn't say that about my mom, but that's basically what she told me. And then she *did* get ahead, by marrying him."

Xavier was surprised by the revelation and her vehemence, both.

He said, "I know he's pissed off, but this—"

"There's no excuse," she said. Xavier sat down on the bench and she continued, "While he was ranting, I was thinking about how in English class this past semester we studied Shakespeare and Homer and Euripides, you know. All these characters who only showed their true natures when things got intense—which can be good or bad, depending on what 'true' happens to be." She sat down next to Xavier. "I'm really . . . sad. I used to think Brad was wonderful."

"Seems like he's good at making everyone think so."

"Yeah," she said, then began, "And this isn't the first time . . ." but didn't finish.

"The first time what?" he asked.

"Nothing. Never mind. Want to eat?"

"Yes! I'm starving."

"Sorry. I couldn't leave while he was going on about everything."

Xavier unpacked the food: beef, chicken, and chicken-cheese empanadas, along with a bottle of orange soda for each of them. For a time, neither of them spoke while they ate, except for when Xavier said, "I can see why you like these empanadas better than other ones."

"Right?"

When Juniper finished hers, she wadded up the wrapper and said, "So . . . I was pretty much ready to talk to my mom about getting permission to date. Now, though—"

"Not even gonna happen," he said.

"No way. Sneaking around, though, feels kind of . . . I just want to say, well, I'll understand if you don't want to stick with it . . . or me."

Xavier stopped chewing, then quickly swallowed what was in his mouth and said, "No. I do want to. Screw all of them. Their issues've got nothing to do with us."

Juniper looked relieved. "Good. That's what I think, too."

They watched the children playing soccer. Xavier reached for Juniper's hand and clasped it. Even this little bit of skin-to-skin contact felt reassuring.

She said, "I really envy you getting to leave for school. I wish I could disappear from my house and not come back, ever. Well, except I'd miss my sister. But still."

Xavier wanted nothing less at this moment than to go anyplace where she wouldn't be.

He said, "My mom said she thinks once Brad sees the merit of the lawsuit, he'll basically want to settle and pay up without complaint—having learned his lesson or something. Do we believe it could be that easy?"

"Ha. No. He couldn't care less about that tree, or any tree."

"Whereas my mom couldn't care more."

"He really thinks she's just trying to rip him off. I heard him on the phone with a lawyer, I think, saying how he'll fight dirty if he needs to, and she'll be sorry. He said 'start digging for dirt on her,' in case she won't back down."

"They can dig; they won't find anything."

"I figured," Juniper said. "So, enough about all of that, okay? I want to know what San Francisco's like."

Reluctant as he was to think about the time when he'd be separated from her, Xavier was glad to talk about something else. He said, "It's . . . well, it's a lot of things. There's so much going on. So many different kinds of people from all over the world. It's expensive there. But inspirational—like, this neighborhood called the Castro used to be one of the only places in the country where it was safe to be openly gay. Also, the place has insane hills. And weed is legal—you can smell it everywhere. And there's the bay on one side and the ocean on the other, so you can get to water basically anytime. I had Chinese food that's *nothing* like it's made here."

"You sound like you love it already."

"It was *great*. But truthfully I haven't been thinking as much about it lately. I like how things are right here right now." He scooted closer to her on the bench so that their legs touched from hip to knee.

Juniper said, "We have to face reality eventually, though."

"Buzzkill," he said, and nudged her with his elbow. "Where's the pause button for reality?"

"I want fast-forward," she said, her face clouding again. "I'm not going to tell Brad, but I'm on your mom's side. That tree is amazing. It seriously breaks my heart that it's dying just because our house got built. I don't want to live there anymore. I never did in the first place."

"The good thing, though, is that we met."

"True."

"Because, those empanadas . . ."

She smiled. "I know! Two Argentinian guys run the truck."

"I might forget college and see if they'll hire me."

"I like to cook. We could get a food truck of our own."

"What would our specialty be? I make an awesome grilled cheese."

"Yeah? I think the grilled cheese food truck market's already covered, though."

"Creative nachos? I'm pretty good there, too."

"I like that idea. Lots of variety. Savory. Sweet."

"Sweet nachos?"

"Made from tortillas. Cinnamon, sugar—you top them with ice cream."

He said, "We could drive all across the country."

"Even to Mexico."

"South America."

"I've always wanted to see Machu Picchu," she said.

"Our parents can fight it out for years and we won't care. We'll be sitting on top of our truck, enjoying the views, eating poutine—"

"Poutine nachos?"

"Poutine, period. French fries and cheese and gravy. Lots of gravy."

"And you can serenade me—and our customers, too."

He said, "Probably you should finish school first, though."

"Before I try poutine?"

Xavier laughed.

She said, "I'm actually planning to graduate early, assuming I can get Blakely to work with me on it."

He looked at her. "Yeah? Then what?"

"Then . . . I might see what San Francisco's all about."

"What about our food truck?" he said with mock seriousness. That she might come to San Francisco was a hope almost too sharp to indulge.

"No, really. I've been thinking about it. There are great schools out there. I could apply, see who'll take me. My SATs were really good."

What a pretty scene Juniper was spinning, this turning of words into a golden future in which the two of them could have a normal relationship—not that Xavier thought what was going on with the two of them was or ever would qualify for such a meager tag as *normal*. No, this was stellar. This was his being unable to stop thinking about her, his lying awake in his bed knowing she was two hundred feet away lying in *her* bed thinking about him. He knew he never should have allowed himself to get into this.

He was incredibly happy he had allowed himself to get into this.

If this golden future came to pass, they'd be so far away from here that they might as well be in a different country. In San Francisco he could kiss her in public, the way he wanted to do right now.

"I'd be good with that plan," he said. "If you're serious."

"I am. And, you know, if things didn't work out for us, we could still be great friends, right?"

"Sure—but as my mom would say, 'Expect success.'"

"It's good advice."

"She can be intense . . . but I wish I had the kind of conviction she has. My dad had it, too."

"You do have it—you're just directing it toward academics and playing guitar."

"I guess. Conflict is not my thing."

Juniper said, "Yeah, I want everybody to get along. *Love thy neighbor as thyself.*"

"Lawsuits aren't exactly loving. Even if they're right."

"Your mom shouldn't have to be a saint just so she doesn't offend my parents."

"This will sound funny," Xavier said, "but you're really *nice*."

"Yeah?"

"Yeah."

"You are, too," she said, smiling at him.

Love thy neighbor.

30

Julia observed Brad throughout supper that evening. He'd phoned her in the afternoon, livid about the lawsuit. Now, though, he seemed to be his usual sunny self. No mention of the matter while Lottie and the girls were in earshot. No snide remarks about opportunistic leeches or tree huggers or madwomen. Maybe he'd gotten over his initial surprise and anger and taken a more balanced view. Maybe it was the shock of it that had made him nasty. Had to be, she thought. She'd never heard him act that way before.

Her own initial response had been less than generous, she had to admit, even if she was the only one who knew it. She felt betrayed by Valerie, who had been so open with her, so apparently genuine. After hanging up the phone with Brad, Julia went to the master bathroom and ran the shower so that Lottie wouldn't bother her. Then she sat on the floor looking out the window at the dying oak (which to her looked fine) and wondered what Valerie's game might be.

When she concluded that there probably was no game—that based on all she'd seen and heard, Valerie was simply the kind of person who'd sue under these circumstances—she reset her expectations to match this altered reality in which she and Valerie Alston-Holt (and likely a lot of other Oak Knoll women) were not going to be friends after all. There was some self-pity in her disappointment; she'd tried *so hard* to be what she thought she ought to be, and where had it gotten her?

"Terrific meatballs," Brad said, taking his napkin from his lap and setting it on the table. "Lily-girl, thanks for helping your mama make supper. You did good."

"Grandma said I could get meatballs in a can if you let me. Quicker and cheaper, she says."

"Grandma's right," Julia said. "But those don't taste good, so I don't buy them."

Juniper said, "I like them."

"How do you know?" Lily said, turning to Juniper in amazement. "Do you eat them at your grocery store work?"

"Mom used to buy them when I was your age."

"Not fair," Lily said.

"Sometimes I got Cap'n Crunch, too. The generic kind, but it was still good."

Julia said, "Really, Juniper? How is this helpful?"

"She's telling the truth," Lottie said. "A fine trait, truth-telling."

"Lying is bad," said Lily.

Juniper said, "Can I be excused?"

"Go," Julia told her. "But help clear the table first."

Brad sat watching the scene but, as far as Julia could tell, not seeing it. His mind was elsewhere, as it often seemed to be lately. Not that she blamed him; with Lottie around, life in their household was an ongoing mild disaster, and if she, Julia, had been able to get away with tuning out a lot of it, she would have as well.

She told Lily, "You're right, lying is bad. So here's the truth about why Juniper got to eat things I don't buy anymore, things that aren't good for you: I didn't know better back then. Sometimes even grown-ups don't know everything they ought to."

"Why didn't you know? Didn't Grandma tell you?"

Lottie said, "Grandma really likes all that stuff."

"But it made you not healthy," Lily replied, nodding her head sagely, as if she'd just gained a great realization. "Also, cigarettes are bad for you."

Julia enjoyed watching Lily work things out this way.

While Lily and Lottie continued to discuss health matters, Brad told Julia, "I'm going to have a swim."

"Do that," she said. "Want a beer?"

He rattled the ice cubes in his glass. "Another bourbon and Coke, thanks."

"Maybe I'll join you for a swim."

"Sure, sure," Brad said. He was already on his way out of the dining room.

The last time Julia had seen him truly anxious was when he was waiting for his lawyer to nail down the sale of his invention. He'd done what he was doing now: worn a cheerful facade to hide how worried he was that the deal would fall apart.

Julia fixed Brad's drink and handed it off to him on his way outside. By the time she'd cleaned the kitchen and gotten Lottie settled in front of her TV in the guest suite, then gone upstairs to put on her swimsuit and finally gotten out to the pool, Brad was done with his swim and was sitting on the covered porch draped in a towel, staring—or maybe the better word was *glaring*—at Valerie's oak tree.

"I'm sorry you got caught up in this thing," Julia said. "It really should be on KDC completely."

"Trees die all the time. So what? This is a bullshit lawsuit." He said this loudly enough that any of the near neighbors, if they had windows open or were outside, could hear him.

"Honey—"

"What?"

"Let's not bring the whole neighborhood into this. It'll get resolved."

"I know it will: We're going to find a way to persuade her to drop it."

Julia didn't like the way he emphasized *persuade*. "How so?"

she said as if only mildly curious, while she slipped into the water. What a marvel to have her own in-ground pool. She might never get over the pleasure of it, of having come so far in her life.

Brad said, "Lawyers have ways of doing these things. I don't really care how it's done, so long as it gets done. I'm not handing over a hundred grand to an extortionist who for all I know could have poisoned that tree herself."

"You'd get experts to evaluate it before anybody paid anything, though, right? She has to prove her case."

"It's not going to get that far, not if she's got any sense."

Julia boosted herself onto a pool float and lay back, looking out at the tree. "Well, that *is* an exceptional oak. I can see why she's upset about losing it."

"Don't tell me you're taking her side in this."

"No, I didn't say that. I'm just talking about the tree. It's a great tree, that's all."

"I don't need my own wife being disloyal."

"Brad—"

"Did you marry me just for my money?"

"What?"

"You heard me."

"Where is this coming from? You didn't even have that much money back then."

"I damn sure had a lot more than you did, though."

Julia paddled to the ladder and got out of the pool. Before she replied, she wrapped herself in a towel and came to sit beside Brad.

"I married you because I loved you."

"The money didn't hurt, though, did it?"

Lying is bad.

Lying can be necessary.

"I never gave the money a thought," Julia said. A lie. Of course she'd thought of it—and he'd wanted her to. All those fancy restaurants. Drives in his BMW. Weekend trips to the beach where they stayed in luxury oceanfront condos. The engagement ring! He'd displayed his money like a peacock displays its tail feathers, asking the peahens to be more impressed with his than with the others'.

Brad said, "Ever notice how all you women are trained to go after whichever man will set you up best? And the men are taught that it's not just their job but their *privilege* to work their asses off to support a wife and kids. The whole burden is on the man. And what do we get for it? A world full of women who think they've got the right to take a man's hard-earned money however they can figure to do it. Valerie, there, couldn't find herself a husband to get her out of that dump, so she's coming after me."

Julia had to think for a moment to decide which part of this to respond to first.

She began, "You've been teaching the girls to aim for a husband to support them—"

"Well, it was a mistake."

"And what you said about Valerie, it's not true. She loves her house. It's actually a nice place."

Brad said, "Anybody actually see her supposed husband before he supposedly died?"

"Yes. Why would you even question it? Valerie's not a bad person. Maybe overzealous, sure. But . . . I mean, honey, don't take this the wrong way, I know you're mad and all, but you're not being reasonable."

"Here's reason for you," Brad said. "That woman wants to take a hundred thousand dollars that I earned right out of my pocket. She wants *four* hundred thousand from Kevin—who also works his ass off and has for years to get to where he is. There's no tree in history worth five hundred thousand dollars. I'm telling you: She wants to take that money and get herself some upgrades. Shiny Cadillac. Big TV. Diamond earrings. Go on a cruise . . . She wants what all you ladies wish you could get without working for it yourselves."

"Now you're being obnoxious," Julia said. "I don't appreciate this at all. I took any job somebody would hire me to do so that I could stand on my own two feet—"

"Right up until the second you could get it from lying on your back. Maybe look at your daughter's example if you want to see some integrity: Juniper doesn't have to work at all, but she's got two jobs by choice."

Julia got up, fuming. "Are you drunk? Take that back. It was *your* idea for me to quit."

"I said you could if you wanted to."

"And then I had Lily—"

"Who's in school now."

"I'd be glad to work again!" Another lie. She wouldn't be glad. But she'd do it if she had to.

Brad said, "Then what's stopping you?"

"You didn't want me to work! I don't understand where all of this is coming from, Brad. Really I don't."

Brad pointed at Valerie's house. "Your new friend, over there."

"I'm starting to wish we'd never bought this house," Julia muttered.

"We can sell it. Just say the word."

She squatted down in front of Brad's knees and looked up at him. "You don't mean that. Can we stop sniping at each other? This isn't doing anybody any good. Be straight with me: Are you so mad because you think she has a real chance with this?"

Brad glanced at her and shrugged. "Some rules got bent, and the trail's not hard to see for anyone who goes looking real close."

"So then why not offer to settle? Pay—I don't know—half and be done with it."

"Shell out fifty grand without a fight? You kidding me? I've never backed down if I had any kind of choice—you ought to know that about me by now. We'll give her a chance to drop it, and if she won't, we're going to the mat. It's a good bet we'd get a sympathetic jury that also doesn't give a shit about some black woman's tree."

31

This Sunday morning found Valerie in her front yard dividing irises before sunrise. She was a little premature with the effort; irises preferred the drier heat of late summer. So be it. She'd already done her lilies, and the sedge and muscari. The beds were weeded. The roses were fed. She couldn't just sit inside on a morning like this, a day of rare low humidity and cool breeze, so the irises were it.

Much of the neighborhood was still asleep, or still inside at any rate. No cars driving past. No joggers. A few minutes earlier Ellen had come by walking Pritzy, her Labradoodle, but she hadn't stopped to talk for long; she already knew Valerie's happy news. Two cocktails and a coin toss (yes, they really did decide it that way) and now Valerie was looking at her future in an entirely new light.

Even as she'd gotten more steadily involved with Chris, she'd seen herself as single. And she would still technically be single once Chris was living here—here meaning in this *city,* not in this house. Not yet, if ever. If their agreed-upon six months of close habitation went according to what they intended and hoped, however, her marital status—and his—would change.

Possibly her address would change, too.

Dividing a rhizome with gloved hands and a spade, Valerie tried to push her imagination in the direction of that change. Leave this house and Oak Knoll, after more than eighteen years. Find a new home with a new man. Two middle-class black people whose combined salaries would be decent: Where in this city might they go that would feel as right as Oak Knoll had felt that day she'd brought Tom to look around?

She didn't want to move, but how could she put Chris in Tom's house, Tom's bed, on a permanent basis?

Now, to be sure, all of that was a long time ago, and she wasn't going around mooning over her dead husband. Tom was (she hated to admit) more a memory than a man. Which was natural. She didn't "see" him here anymore, not the way she'd done for the first few years after his death. She didn't think of him daily. All physical evidence of him was gone except for the few things in Xavier's room, which she'd left alone, allowing him to keep or not keep what was there as he liked. Really, Tom wasn't here at all.

She'd offered to let Xavier "update" his room—that lamp, for example: Did thirteen-year-old Xavier really still want a lamb on his bedside table? Yes, he did. He wanted the mobile. He wanted the rug. He thought the wall color was just fine, why bother to change it? He'd stuck posters and programs up all over his walls, and consented to letting her replace sheet sets and comforters a few times. Otherwise, the room was as it had been the day she, Xavier, and Tom arrived home from that Thanksgiving trip, Tom leaving in an ambulance that night and not coming back.

Valerie laughed ruefully, chiding herself. Tom wasn't here? Tom was here; all she had to do was open that bittersweet door in her brain and there he stood, looking apologetic and a little bit scared just before he let the paramedics lead him out to the ambulance.

How unfair that the past was irretrievable and yet impossible to leave behind. "Forward," she said, and made herself conjure Chris's face.

The subdivided group of irises had been intended for transplant in a sunny spot alongside the pond-to-be. The pond project, though, was on hold until the situation with the oak got resolved and she had a better sense of what she was doing with the yard and with her life. Next spring, maybe; nothing was happening anytime soon, that was already apparent.

Her phone rang: Chris. She tucked her earbuds into her ears and answered, "Hey, you're up early."

"Trying to recalibrate my sleep schedule so that we're matched."

"Isn't that just a *bit* precipitate? You don't even have a position here yet."

"My mother says I've always been overeager. Never slept through a Christmas Eve in my life."

"Duly noted."

They talked for a minute or two about the lawsuit's status. She said, "Both the builder and Brad Whitman were served this past week, and we got the initial response we expected: calls from both men's attorneys to mine insisting that the suit is specious and that I would do well to think again and drop it, if I'm a sensible woman. Thugs. Now we wait for their *official* response. They've got thirty days."

Chris said, "Anything directly?"

"You mean did Brad come charging over here with his hair on fire? No. I haven't seen or heard a thing from him or his wife. But never mind all of that," she said. "Let's talk more about us. I'm glad to see you really aren't a sore loser."

"Loser? What are you talking about? I won."

"Flatterer."

"What are you wearing right now?"

Valerie laughed. "I'm in my yard, digging irises."

"I dig irises, too, baby," Chris said, his voice low and sultry.

"Why don't you drive down here and see for yourself what I have on."

"Is this a real invitation?"

Valerie hesitated. Was it? She hadn't yet given Xavier the news of Chris's impending move and their plans for what would follow. "Yes," she said decisively. No time like the present.

"Let me just brush my teeth and I'm on the road."

"I'll try to have showered by the time you arrive. You don't want some sweaty—"

"Val," Chris said, interrupting her.

"What?"

"I want you in whatever way you are. All the time. Every day. That's what this is now. Get used to it."

"Okay," she said, her voice thick. "You drive carefully. I'll have lunch waiting."

They hung up and she took the earbuds from her ears, tucked them back into her T-shirt's collar. The sun had broken the horizon and pierced through the heavy foliage, working with the breeze to make a kaleidoscope of light and shade on the ground.

From here she could see the upper half of her old oak, its entire thinning crown. The untrained eye wouldn't yet be able to tell it was starving to death. The tree might live another summer, even two, its leaf density diminishing each season, its limbs and trunk increasingly vulnerable to parasitic invasion by mistletoe (already in evidence), by oak gall and scales and worms. She wasn't sure she could stand to watch it fail, much the way it was torturous to witness, during her infrequent visits home to Michigan, her father's terrible slow decline.

Which is not to say she loved this tree more than she loved her father, necessarily—they were different kinds of love, and where her father was concerned, her feelings were complicated, compromised by what sometimes was anger, other times pain. Why hadn't he seen "Uncle" Ray for the creep he was? Ray's attitudes weren't hidden. Ray, sitting with her father at the kitchen table, the two men swapping stories and drinking Schlitz from the can: *Hey, Val, come here, sweet thing, sit on old Uncle Ray's lap,* the two men laughing, Ray reaching out when Valerie passed, trying—and sometimes succeeding—to give whatever part of her body he could reach a quick feel.

A person might ask why *she* hadn't she ever spoken up—if not to her father, then to her mother or a teacher or a friend? Well, that was complicated, too.

And long done, she reminded herself while a pair of cardinals flitted up to the gutter above her front door and called out to announce their territory. Down the line from these birds, near the corner of the house, a wren was at work digging through debris piled in the gutter, pitching bits overboard. Now would be a good time to get Xavier out here with a ladder and have him clean the gutters out.

Brushing the dirt from her hands, she went in through the front door.

"Zay, you busy?"

No reply.

Stepping out of her clogs, she went down the hallway to look for him. Empty bathroom. Empty bedrooms. Up the hallway, through the living room into the kitchen. No Xavier.

"Where has that boy gotten to?" she said, moving for the back door—and then, glancing out the window, getting her answer: At the rear of the yard, partly hidden between the new fence and an old stand of rhododendron, were two obviously besotted teenagers standing torso to torso with their arms wrapped around each other's waists.

"Oh, Zay," Valerie said. "Really? Now?"

What would you have done if you were Valerie? This is one of the questions we asked ourselves later. Would you have marched outside and separated them? She considered it. Eighteen years old or not, Xavier was still her son, still her responsibility, if only for a little while longer. In her view, there were a lot more reasons why he and Juniper shouldn't pursue their attraction than reasons why they should. And usually she was a person who, in forming plans for action, studied the data and followed the facts to the best, most reasoned conclusions.

Love, however, isn't a hard science. As most parents know, it's difficult to be tough on a kid when they've invested their own hearts in a thing. You don't take a child to an animal shelter unless you intend—that day—to adopt a pet. You don't let them overtake the kitchen with an elaborate stained-glass kit and then insist there's no window in the house where the finished project, ugly as it might be, can be displayed. You don't observe your factually adult son in an embrace with a young woman who clearly adores him and then charge over and embarrass and shame the two of them—or if you do, you've got a much harder heart than Valerie had, particularly where Xavier was involved.

He had never been an easy child in the ways she'd wished he could be. Oh, sure, he'd slept through the night at four months of age, and he'd been as happy to eat vegetables as she was, and he hadn't stopped loving books in favor of video games, and he'd earned excellent grades and he'd practiced his music and he'd worked minimum-wage jobs to earn college money without a lot of complaint. But as we've learned, he did not have an easy time letting go.

Valerie watched the kids and thought about how in a few hours Chris would be there. How she and Chris would be telling Xavier about the plan now under way that could lead to her remarriage. How, after having shared that news, sometime later, at the end of the night, she and Chris would go together into her bedroom and shut the door. If she continued her campaign to discourage Xavier from seeing Juniper just because it might (who could say for sure?) cause trouble of varying kinds, she would be telling him that her right to happiness was more legitimate than his, that she didn't trust him to know what he was doing.

He was an adult now. Hard as it was for her not to "mom" him at this moment, she needed to let him make his own choices and make mistakes and get messy and get his heart broken and lose money and be hungry and miss a bus and be betrayed by a friend and have whatever else that we all know is simply *life* come his way.

Valerie watched the two of them, Juniper's face tipped up looking into Xavier's. Valerie *wanted* a girl (or a guy, if that's how it had gone) to look at her son that way. Not one of us knows what's in our future with any certainty. This, with Juniper, might be only a passing thing. Or it might be the event upon which his whole life would turn. Either (and neither) was possible. Who was she to assert that in matters of his heart, she knew best? Valerie understood that while her son did and always would hold *her* heart in *his* hands, the fact of being a parent was that her son's heart was and must be reserved for someone else.

32

The new Whitman HVAC commercial was being shot at Brad Whitman's own home. A lot of us were at work that day, but those who weren't came out to stand on the sidewalk in front of the house so we could watch the film crew set up what seemed to be a lot of equipment for what we'd been led by ads to believe could just as easily be done with a smartphone. Evidently there was a little more to it.

Right at the curb in the Whitmans' front yard, taking over much of the sidewalk, a square portable canopy was erected so that the crew could gather to keep out of the sun in between takes. The day was clear and hot, the sky that saturated blue we North Carolinians try to claim is "Carolina blue" but is in fact the very same blue you see in every clear sky everywhere. Besides that, the original association of "Carolina" and "blue" has nothing at all to do with the sky.

Brad Whitman's video crew included a cameraman, an equipment technician, a director/producer, a makeup and hair artist, and three other people whose purpose was not apparent. There were microphones and lights and shades and cables and various odd boxes for who knew what.

We couldn't tell yet what the Brad Whitman–endorsed product for this ad was going to be; no product was in sight, and neither was

Brad. For fun, we'd started a betting pool: Odds were good for its being a trendy-ingredient-infused water or maybe iced tea. Also popular and seemingly probable was a plug for Asa's B-B-Q, the new "food stand" that had opened not three blocks away on a corner where Oak Knoll abutted Hillside; we'd seen Asa himself making deliveries here to the Whitmans' house twice in the past week. Maybe it was Lottie who'd been ordering it, maybe not.

Brad's decision to shoot the commercial here was surely a practical one: He didn't have to pay anyone for use of the location. Also, where would he find a more appealing example of the kinds of homes Whitman HVAC was eager and ready to service? In this commercial he intended to highlight the company's great relationships with the area's top new-home builders, in an effort to expand that segment of his business (there was a lot more upfront profit in new installations than in service and repairs) and, yes, a way to put his thumb in Valerie Alston-Holt's eye.

Inside the efficiently cooled house, the parlor had been temporarily remade into a dressing room. Brad and Juniper sat back to back on tall stools while the makeup artist and her assistant put the finishing touches on their subjects' faces and hair. As we'd learn later, this commercial would have no featured product. This commercial would have a featured *person*: Juniper, Whitman HVAC's newest addition and future owner, that's what Brad was going to say. Time to introduce her to the public, make her face familiar, give her a taste of the celebrity experience he was convinced all young women desired.

"Ready to become a star?" Brad said to Juniper while Julia, Lily, and Lottie looked on.

"I want to be a star," said Lily.

"Sugar bear, you're already a star."

"Then so's Juniper. When can I be on TV?"

"Maybe next time," said Julia.

"Sure," Brad said; there was an angle in letting the public see his adorable little girl—a different angle than what he was up to here, but an angle nonetheless.

Marina, the makeup artist he'd used for every commercial he'd made, gave his face a once-over with powder and a brush, then removed the cape she'd put over him to protect his clothes. "You're all set," she said.

He stood and moved so that he could see Juniper. She wore a royal blue golf shirt with the Whitman HVAC logo, same as he did. The color was flattering on her even if the style was nothing special. They both wore white linen-blend pants—though hers were a slim cut that showed off her figure in a way every man who saw the ad would respond to, while also looking sufficiently modest to all women viewers. *A fine start,* Brad thought. What made her outstanding, though, was what the gals had done with her makeup and hair.

Again, the goal had been to balance sex appeal with modesty, so the makeup was subtle in its tones yet made every fine feature stand out. Her eyes looked large and intelligent. Her lips full but not slutty. She looked not so much older as better defined.

Her hair was long and full and wavy—a blowout, Marina called what they'd done to it. Julia told him there were shops now where that was the only service offered. Women's services were a mysterious thing to him, but this was one he liked a lot. The effect on Juniper, in Brad's view at least, was that she appeared *ready*.

"Ready?" he said, reaching for her hand to help her off the stool.

She took it and stood up. "It feels weird to have all this makeup on. Can I see myself?"

From her ringside chair, Lottie said, "Better you don't."

Juniper looked alarmed. "Why?"

"You are *beautiful*," Marina told her.

Julia said, "You are. But . . . I think your grandma's right about this. You don't want to get all self-conscious about it. Just be yourself."

Juniper looked at Lily, who was staring openly. "What? Say it."

"Do you want to borrow my tiara?"

Juniper smiled. "Maybe later on, when this is done. We can play princess; do you want to?"

Lily nodded. "You be the princess and I'll be the star."

"Okay. Start picking out your wardrobe and I'll meet you upstairs in a little while."

The commercial's director/producer, Evan, came in the front door. "We're ready for you on the front porch."

There would be three brief scenes edited into a single sixty-second spot. One scene out front, with both Brad and Juniper; one on the side of the house that would be just Brad and the compressors (temporarily turned off); and one out back beside the pool, where the plan was for Juniper to be solo in the shot, seated at the pool's edge with her pant legs turned up, feet in the pool, while Brad, in a voice-over, would affirm to the viewing audience what a good life awaited them when they didn't need to give their newly installed or freshly serviced HVAC systems a single thought.

Brad answered Evan, "All right, then, let's get to work."

—If you're wondering, as we later would, whether Juniper resisted any of this—the plan to put her in the commercial, the public positioning of her as a future co-owner, the "star turn" there beside the pool—the answer is no. She had an agenda of her own.

When the shoot concluded, Julia treated the crew and any neighbors who'd stuck around for the whole three hours in the heat to a delicious spread in her kitchen, all the food arrayed atop that gorgeous Carrara marble island: shrimp salad; gourmet cold cuts and cheeses; sliced mangoes, pineapple, and kiwi; artisan breads; a watermelon-feta-mint salad with balsamic vinegar; bottles of fizzy waters in fruit flavors and plain. Lottie (predictably) had suggested there also be bowls of potato chips and Doritos, getting an also-predictable enthusiastic second from Lily.

Brad cared not in the least about any of that. He wasn't hungry just now (though he did hold a plate of food in his hand). He was standing at the door to the back porch watching Juniper record a video of a dressed-up Lily marching around in a pair of Julia's high heels. He was thinking about what his next steps toward scratching his itch might be. There had to be a way for them to take care of it with no one else the wiser. It would be like any other once-in-a-lifetime experience: something to remember and savor—if only secretly, just between them. He loved the idea of being her first, of being the center of the special story she would treasure just for herself.

Here's what we wonder: How does a man like Brad become a man like Brad—that is, so assured of his authority and viewpoint that he never bothers to interrogate himself? Maybe it's a question for the ages. We do what we can to find answers, though, which in this case means looking into how he spent his early years. Here's what we know:

Brad and his younger brother, Jeff, lived hand-to-mouth with their parents in an Appalachian town none of us had heard of, a tiny place on the Tennessee side of the North Carolina/Tennessee border some miles from Pigeon Forge. A lot has been made in recent times about the plight of the Appalachian "hillbilly," but as with so many things that rise to the level of hype, you shouldn't believe everything you read. The Whitman family was poor, yes. They were not, however, toothless or uneducated. None of them played a banjo—or any stringed instrument, or, for that matter, any instrument at all. They weren't Bible-thumping patriots. None of them were addicted to drugs.

Brad's father was and is a mechanic. When Brad was a boy, Rick Whitman was employed at what was then called Goldrush Junction, a puny theme park that became Silver Dollar City that became Dollywood right about the time Brad was in high school. People in those parts think highly of Dolly Parton for taking the park up several notches and improving lots of other things in the process.

When the water park portion of Dollywood opened, Rick Whitman found himself assigned to work exclusively on the flume rides. Water parks in that part of the country are seasonal attractions. So, come fall and winter, Rick Whitman had a lot of time on his hands. Mechanics with a lot of time on their hands often take things apart, fix things, and build things. Rick Whitman most liked to build. He had two boys who needed to be kept out of trouble over those months when money was tight and their mother, Katie, was at work all day selling tires. So what he built were big, complicated, multipart projects that required the boys' help: a wind-powered grain mill that also produced electrical power; portable networked solar collectors he could take with him when the family moved (which was too often, as they were ever at the whim of one landlord or other); a 1942 Chevrolet G506 truck from parts he and the boys collected over a year's time.

Thus Brad learned *planning*. A person got an idea in his head—didn't matter what kind—and then set about making a plan. What's the first step? What has to happen next? And then what? For Brad, this idea-to-goal flowchart first manifested as grades good enough for admission to a college electrical engineering program. Then, early in his first semester, he got the idea that bored though he was, he could tough it out, get the degree, and go back home to start a company with his dad. They'd do custom design-build work in every electrical-mechanical area they could dream up: corporate and home audio and video systems and security; specialty machines like the mill his dad had built; conveyor systems, storage systems... There were more than plenty of opportunities for hardworking, resourceful men. If his brother preferred a life of drinking and chasing girls and making milk shakes at Dollywood, as it appeared he did, well, that was his prerogative.

We admire hard workers. We admire the determination it takes to start from nowhere and go far. Brad's father had some of that, but he wasn't as ambitious as his older son. When Brad came home from college that first (and only) year he was enrolled, he was full of plans for this company they'd start—only to have his dad tell him, "You know, if I was thirty years younger and wanted to hustle as much as I'd have to for what you're thinking, I'd sure want to get on board. Thanks, son. But that's not my speed. I like what I got and what I do already."

Brad was disappointed. He was angry. He'd put a lot of store in that plan. He went back to school after the break, and the fact was, his heart wasn't in it anymore. He could not make himself suffer through that *stupid* composition class. So be it. Moving on. New plan.

We didn't know, couldn't know, what all Brad was capable of. We have to say unreservedly and in unison that regardless of whose side we found ourselves on when the unraveling started, if even one of us had been privy to how Brad's mind worked, we would have stepped in and at least given Julia a heads-up. We would have seen the situation so differently.

Here we have no choice but to be trite and say, "Hindsight is twenty-twenty," and "What's done is done," and continue with our story because it's in the telling of a tragedy that we sow the seeds— we hope—of prevention of future sorrows.

33

"I'm off to the park to run," Juniper called to her mom up the back stairway. She was dressed for the activity and for the heat: sports bra, high-tech moisture-wicking tank top and shorts, her trail-running shoes. This was not the look she would have chosen for what was her true intention today. Funny how you could form something up in your imagination and then have the real thing, when it happened, turn out so differently.

But she was missing her other usual must-have for running: her phone. She said, "I think maybe I left my phone at work this morning, so will you check with Brad to see if it's there? I bet it fell out of my bag, under the desk."

"I don't like you going out there without your phone," Julia replied from the laundry room, it sounded like, or maybe Lily's room. "Take Grandma's."

"I'll be fine. There are always people around." This wasn't true. Today there would be, though. One particular person, and she needn't worry about him.

"Take it, I don't mind," said Lottie from the guest suite, down a short hallway from where Juniper was standing.

"Okay, thanks," she said, then called to Julia, "I'm taking Grandma's."

"See you at supper, then."

Juniper went into Lottie's room and retrieved the phone, yelling to Julia, "No, I have to work until close tonight. I told you. I'm going straight from the park."

"What about a shower? After your run?"

Juniper, at the back door again, tried not to sound impatient. "I won't have time. I'll towel off, don't worry—I sweat at work anyway."

"Okay then," Julia replied, and then Juniper was out the door into the garage and moving for her car, eager to get out of there before her mother found some new reason to hold her up.

Her hand shook a little as she started the engine and put the car into gear. She wasn't going to go for a run, and her shift at the grocery store didn't start until seven. She was going to meet Xavier in the park at a cabin she knew of, one of many that were available but rarely in use, as far as she'd seen in her runs out there. It was his turn to bring food, and he said he'd have all the other supplies, too. All she had to do was show up.

And try to relax.

She absolutely wanted this, despite the nagging voice in her head that insisted what she was about to do violated the vow she'd made to God and her parents and could ruin her ability to love her future husband with a clear conscience and clear mind, no memories of intimacies with other men to confuse or spoil her feelings about sex with the man she'd marry. That voice was a holdover, a stowaway from a different time and a different her.

Still, she argued with it, thinking, what if Zay was that man? Then it wouldn't be a problem at all, would it?

Did she really think she'd *marry* him?

Maybe. Eventually. There was no rush or anything.

What if they broke up, though? Would she, if they had sex (and of course they'd have sex, she was not going to wimp out), really have failed herself and failed God and all the rest of it? Would she really be ruined for all future relationships? She used to believe this without question. Now it seemed like propaganda—powerful propaganda it was, too, given how it still rattled around in her brain even as she rejected it.

She thought, *Hey, my mother wasn't ruined. She'd had* a child from another man *and that still hadn't prevented her from finding her Mr. Right.* Whether or not Brad was truly "right" for Julia was a matter Juniper, skeptical though she'd become, had no authority to judge.

Here was a question she'd considered at some length: At New Hope she'd been taught that premarital sex was more than just a bad idea, it was sinful. In God's eyes, though, what was the difference between having sex with someone you loved before you were married, and having sex with someone you loved after you were married? If you undertook the act in a genuine state of mind and heart, if it was done in *love,* didn't that make it a pure act? God knew her heart.

Another question: Why did the church treat sex like a commodity—like the *only* commodity and in fact the only thing of any real value young women had to offer their future mates? In all those youth group meetings she'd attended, never once did anyone assert that young *men* who had premarital sex cheapened themselves. Boys and men might get "confused" by lust and its satisfaction, the kids were told. They might make some questionable choices in their confusion. Never, though, were they considered to be at risk of diminishing their value to future prospective spouses.

As Pepper had put it during one of their many discussions, "That's absolutely the patriarchy talking, and I will not let you continue to be a part of it." Juniper got it then, and she really got it now, what with Brad behaving like she was more or less his property, or if not that exactly, one more object of lust.

When Xavier suggested the time might be right for them to go further than they'd done so far (a *lot* of kissing and touching and pressing themselves together), that maybe they should go where both of their bodies were eager to go, she'd agreed. So that's what they were going to do. Or as Pepper had put it, "Just get it over with and you'll see it's all fine. Also: "Seriously, just *get it over with*. The first time usually sucks, and you can't get to the second time until you've got the first out of the way."

Pepper was practical like that.

When Juniper pulled into the park's visitor center lot, Xavier was waiting beside his car.

She rolled down her window. "Sorry to make you wait. Again."

He shook his head. "Nah, I was early."

"Do you want to ride with me or follow?"

"I'll follow you—I've got all the stuff in my trunk."

He came closer to the window, leaned in and kissed her. Then, gazing at her intently with those captivating eyes of his, he said, "There is totally no pressure."

Her stomach did a little flip. "No, I know."

"Okay."

"You, either," she said.

"Thanks."

Xavier returned to his car and Juniper led the way deep into the park, past the lot she usually parked in and down a short service road that ended near the cabin she'd suggested for this date. She was going to go through with it, today, while they had the chance.

Pepper's "just get it over with" message had arisen from a conversation we referred to earlier in the story, on that morning at Blakely when Pepper told Juniper she had big news. She and her boyfriend, Michael, had "done it," and it was embarrassing and didn't feel great, but it went all right. And now they'd done it three more times since, with better results. She'd said "condoms are not terrible, although they smell funny, and Michael says it feels like how wearing gloves in science lab feels—you have most of the sensation of touching things but not all of it. Don't worry, though," she'd assured Juniper, "he's all for them if it means we get to keep doing it. Zay will be, too."

Pepper loved Michael. Pepper had sex with him. Pepper did not feel like she'd ruined herself or disappointed the Lord. She wasn't pregnant. She hadn't caught any disease. She was glad to have done it (and had done it again). It could be as simple as this for Juniper, too. It could be. She wanted it to be. It would be.

And if the experience of making love the first time wasn't anything close to the hot movie sex in, say, *Fifty Shades of Grey* (she'd seen it at Pepper's), and was instead embarrassing and a little painful and just kind of sucky in general, at least she would have done it here in this beautiful forest on this gorgeous day with Xavier Alston-Holt, and therefore it would be a win.

When they were at the cabin, Xavier opened his trunk and took out a folded blanket and a guitar in its soft case and a backpack in which he'd stowed the food that would be their dinner. "It's pretty basic," he said. "Cheese, salami, bread, tomatoes, and this." He held up a paper bag in which there was a bottle. "White wine. We don't have to drink it. I just thought it might . . ."

"Relax us. Or me," she said, knowing he'd already lost his virginity. He'd told her about the two girls and how he'd been relieved to do it and end the mystique, but how he'd also felt weird and empty afterward. Today would be different.

Xavier said, "Not just you."

"Yeah? Well, it was thoughtful just the same."

"And illegal."

She said, "Pretty sure the cops aren't coming around carding people here."

"No, but the park ranger might. I think it's illegal to bring alcohol here regardless."

"We'll just have to keep the bottle out of sight."

They went into the cabin. It was a small structure made of brown-painted logs, cool inside, and dim. A cricket chirped in one corner. Juniper, who carried the guitar, set it down carefully. Xavier put the blanket and pack on the planked floor. "It's nice in here."

"I guess people bring cots and sleeping bags and camp stoves, all that stuff. I'd like to do some camping. Hike some of the Appalachian Trail, maybe. Go out west—the real West, I mean. Rockies. Grand Canyon. Zion. Anywhere. Everywhere. The Alps—"

"You'd have to go *w-a-a-y* west to get to the Alps."

"I think my car could make it across the Pacific," Juniper deadpanned. "Don't you?"

"Actually it might."

Xavier twisted the cap off the wine bottle and took a swig, then laughed. "Classy, right?"

"Here," Juniper said, reaching for the bottle. "One must *sip* wine, like so," she said, then took several tiny sips while looking at him over the bottle.

"Noted," he said.

She wiped her mouth. "It tastes awful."

"I know, right?"

"Play me a song?" she asked, and he obliged.

The song he chose was delicate and soulful, something Spanish, she thought. It sounded Spanish. Exotic, warm. He held his guitar as if holding a lover. *This,* Juniper thought. This was why she loved him. This and his poise and his intelligence. His big heart. You couldn't play this song this way unless your heart was double-size.

When he finished, she said, "Wow."

"Yeah?" He gave his famous smile.

"You're going to be a superstar," she said. "Hey, there's a trail just past the parking lot that leads down to the river. It's maybe a mile long, not bad. I thought we could go for a little hike, you know, before we eat."

"Yeah, let's."

"And we'll bring this." She raised the bottle.

"Sure—just let me lock up the guitar."

"I'm guessing it was expensive."

He said, "I saved for a year to buy it."

"I never used to have money for anything—like, I was one of the kids getting free lunch at school. And then after Mom married Brad, she just gave me everything I wanted, basically. Not that I asked for much, I guess because I was used to there being no money. When I asked them to help me buy a car, I was thinking something like yours and I'd pay them back." She waited while he put the guitar in the trunk. "I think what I'm saying is, I admire your self-discipline. I hope I have it when I need it."

Once they were on the winding root- and rock-covered trail, Juniper said, "Keep a lookout for deer. I've seen fox, too. Oh, and you know the big woodpeckers?"

"Pileated," Xavier said.

"Right," she said, pleased that he knew. "They're out here."

"Used to be we had a pair that came to our yard, back before so much new construction was going on in the neighborhood. Never see 'em now. It's partly habitat loss, but also they're shy birds. They don't like all the commotion of saws and nail guns and trucks."

Juniper nodded. "When I was little I spent a lot of time outside in the country. I didn't know the names of most of the birds and frogs and bugs, so I gave them made-up names."

"For example?"

"Nothing very original. Cardinals were 'scarlets,' and blue jays were 'screechers.' Oh, this one isn't too bad: I called great blue herons 'birdy long-legs.'"

"I like it."

When they reached the riverbank, they climbed down to a stand of boulders and sat on one, looking out at the water as it flowed past. Neither of them spoke for a while, nor did they do more than sit close together, arms touching. The wine went down more easily. Juniper felt herself begin to relax.

Xavier laid back and put his arms behind his head. He closed his eyes. "I should do this more. It's nice, right? To get away from everything?"

Juniper looked at him. How beautiful he was. How well formed. She'd thought this the first time she'd seen him and felt it even more acutely now. The novelty of his being biracial was long past. She didn't even notice it anymore, or not as something exotic, anyway, only as one trait among many that made him who he was.

She said, "What are you thinking about?"

"Actually, I was remembering this time my mom took me to

Lansing to visit my grandparents," he said, eyes still closed. "The bird thing reminded me. I was, like, six? First trip on an airplane since my dad died—I didn't remember that one. Anyway, we were outside with Mama Ginny—that's my mom's mom—in this community garden. They lived in a neighborhood called Fabulous Acres. Mama Ginny still does. *Fabulous Acres,* like it's filled with Hollywood mansions or something, when really it's all these run-down houses and duplexes.

"The garden was this little fenced-in spot where some of the folks planted tomatoes and zucchinis and whatnot. It was weeding day, and Mama Ginny and my mom and me, we went out with pails. I worked for a while, not paying them much attention. They talked, talked, talked, and me being six, I didn't care what they were saying. I did like the sound of their voices, though. Mama Ginny's is high and sweet, Mom's is lower, solid. Then I got to where I was tired of pulling weeds, so I was sitting in a patch of sweet peas watching the butterflies and bees and these sparrows and finches that were hopping around. It was sunny. Not too hot. I saw a red-winged blackbird. A caterpillar crawled onto my shoe and I watched it try to figure out what crazy thing had gotten in its way to the next stem or whatever. I'd just started guitar lessons before the trip, so I was thinking I could write a song for the caterpillar and play it on the guitar.

"Eventually the ladies came to pull me out of the pea plants. Mom was like, 'I'm sorry, baby, you must be bored to tears,' and we went back to the house, washed up, all that. But I wasn't bored. It was a best day, you know? I still think of it like that."

Juniper thought, *I love him.* But she didn't say it. Too soon? Too much? How were you supposed to know when a thing was all right? Every move felt like a risk, a step taken along a narrow cliffside path with your back pressed to the wall for safety.

They stayed at the river for a while, talking, touching, kissing, until Juniper said, "I'm hungry."

"Same." They headed up the trail and Xavier told her, "Prepare to be impressed by my excellent offerings—" and then he started laughing.

"What?"

"I just realized how that might sound, what with our plan and all . . ."

"Oh." Juniper laughed, and blushed. "Yeah. Conceited!"

They reached the cabin and went inside, spread the blanket, settled onto it. Xavier unrolled a piece of transparent plastic. "Portable cutting board from the dollar store."

"My mom bought a cutting board made out of wood and marble. It weighs, like, twenty pounds. It's gorgeous. *Not* so portable."

"Probably cost more than a buck, too."

"Probably two bucks."

He laid out the bread and tomato, unwrapped the cheese and salami. "Got my employee discount on this. It's supposed to be some of our best stuff." From his pack he took a Buck knife and opened it up, showed it to her. "My uncle Kyle sent this to me as a graduation gift. I don't know what he thinks San Francisco is like, but I doubt I'll use it much unless I'm eating a *lot* of salami and cheese." He set about slicing it up.

"So . . . I talked to my Blakely counselor," Juniper said. "I can graduate early."

Xavier stopped slicing. "For real?"

She nodded. "I can fit all my remaining required courses into first semester. I'll be done in December! It's so great—six more months and then I'm out of there, out of my house, all of it. I don't have the money stuff completely figured out yet. I'm hoping my mom will front me some."

"I could help."

"You'll have enough to pay for as it is."

"If my mom wins the lawsuit, though . . ."

Juniper said, "Let's hope for that."

Soon they'd eaten all the cheese and tomato, plus most of the bread and sausage. Juniper washed down her food with the remaining wine. She felt loose, almost giddy—no wonder alcohol was called *liquid courage.*

Now sufficiently emboldened, she put the leftover food into

Xavier's pack and pushed the remaining paraphernalia out of their way, then lay down on the blanket, pulling him down beside her.

"I'm not so nervous anymore," she said. "You?"

"Still nervous."

Juniper kissed him, then looked into his eyes. "I'm really glad we're doing this."

"So am I."

34

We've shown that Brad was an opportunist—a trait that up to now had served him well. He was convinced that he never would have gotten so far in life if he was the sort who, upon seeing a chance to act and possibly gain, dithered instead. Why should this day and the opportunity it presented to him be any different? The following got under way at right about the same time the kids were down at the river.

────────────

"Sorry to bother you at work," Julia said when Brad answered her call.

"No trouble, I just finished a meeting. What's up?"

"Juniper thinks she left her phone there this morning. Will you have a look?"

"Sure, hang on."

Brad left the meeting room and went into the dispatch office, now occupied by his other part-timer, Gail. "Hey, just seeing if Juniper's phone is in here anywhere. She thinks it must've fallen out of her bag—under the desk, probably."

Gail scanned the desk's surface, then scooted back in her chair and had a look around the floor. "Here it is," she said, pulling it from beneath the desk. She handed it to him.

"Terrific, thanks."

Brad said to Julia, "Got it."

"Oh, good. She went off to run at the park and I made her take Mom's phone just in case. Kids think they're invulnerable."

"Can't blame her. We were the same. Hey," Brad said, an idea coming to him. "What's the plan for supper tonight?"

"Lily has a pizza party, so it'll be just you, me, and Mom. I'm thinking leftovers, if that's all right."

"I'm gonna beg off, then, if it's all the same to you, and go get some wings with Jimmy if he's free."

"Sure. You all have fun," Julia said. Her voice was flat.

Probably annoyed at being left alone with Lottie, he thought. He said, "Yep, thanks. See you later."

He ended the call and then opened the tracker app that showed him where, exactly, Juniper's Land Rover was at any given moment.

35

Every meaningful story has to have a crisis, and now here we stand on the precipice of this one's. We were not, a single one of us, prepared for what was ahead. We were distracted by Valerie's lawsuit and its merits. We were debating what to do about it—if anything could be done. We were divided in our views. (But this is not the division we mentioned at the start of our story. That's still to come.)

Was the love that Juniper and Xavier felt for each other real? The skeptics among us scoff. The romantics among us say yes, absolutely, who could have any doubt? Look at them, so measured and conscientious with their plan, so responsible, so devoted to each other's well-being. Anyway, how can we know for absolute certain when love is real unless it's been tested by time?

What matters is whether Juniper and Xavier believed wholeheartedly that their love was real.

What matters is that Brad believed his love for Juniper, inappropriate and complicated though it might be, was real, and that Juniper would, with his encouragement, soon confess she felt the same way toward him.

PART III

PART III

36

Brad left the Hub and started for the state park. He would do a good deed by returning Juniper's phone to her. No, she didn't *need* it, strictly speaking. Lottie's flip phone would do in an emergency. She would want it, though. She'd be glad to have it. She'd be grateful, think, *What a thoughtful guy.* Yes, indeed. Always looking out for her, taking care of her, going out of his way to do a favor she wouldn't have asked for, considerate as she was.

She'd be sweat-slick from her run, tired out and radiant.

He only wanted to look at her. Talk with her without Lily's interruptions, without Lottie's running commentary, without Julia's watchful jealousy due to Juniper's favoring him the way she did. He wouldn't lay a hand on her today.

Winding his way through the state park's access roads, he enjoyed the deep green light of the forest. He enjoyed the sight of trees in every direction, a reminder of when he was younger and living in the dense woods. He enjoyed the feeling of anticipation, the thought of how surprised and even excited she'd be to see him waiting for her when she finished her run. She might already be done. He might find her standing beside her pretty Land Rover flushed and damp, stretching those fine legs . . .

He didn't recognize the car that was parked next to hers. Nor was he concerned about whose it might be. Lots of people came out here to hike and run and ride their mountain bikes. They came to fish. To meditate. All of that. Juniper wasn't in sight. He'd hang out here and wait for her.

The nearby cabin wasn't apparent to him at first, tucked away as it was behind a stand of dense trees. He sat on her bumper with his phone in hand, scrolled through Twitter, checked his email and baseball scores—and then a sound got his attention. He glanced up, noticed the cabin, and went down the gravel path to have a look.

The door was not quite latched. He pushed it open, heard a gasp.

Juniper on the floor, her face turned his way, her expression one of terror.

The neighbor boy on top of her, naked.

It happened all at once: Brad moving toward them as they bucked apart, Brad grabbing Xavier by the hair, everyone yelling, Juniper curling into a ball, crying, Brad growling, "Get the hell out of here, you dirty little bastard, or I swear I'll kill you, don't think I won't," and flinging Xavier away from him, Xavier coming back at him, shoving him hard, Brad stumbling, then reaching for Xavier, getting his arm around the boy's neck: "This really how you want to die?," tightening his arm and then thrusting him away, Xavier grabbing his clothes, his pack, rushing out.

Juniper crying, crying, sobbing now, pulling the blanket up around her.

A knife clattered onto the floor.

Brad heard the Honda's engine start, heard the crush of gravel under its tires as Xavier sped off.

"It's all right now," Brad said, squatting down next to Juniper.

"It'll never be all right," she said.

Juniper didn't *know*, and yet she knew.

Alone with Brad, still wrapped in the blanket, Juniper trembled visibly. He wanted to take her in his arms, undo what had been done.

Innocent.

Damaged.

He said, "Tell me what happened. Did he follow you here?"

"What?" she said, "No, it wasn't like that."

"Why didn't you call me? Or call the police."

"The police? We're friends," she said.

Brad leveled his gaze on her and tried to keep his voice level, too. "You're *friends*. Okay."

"More, I guess."

"Are you dating him?" His voice rose despite himself.

"I . . ."

Brad stood up, reset his ball cap—and remembered the knife, which remained there on the floor just behind where Juniper sat.

"Juni, tell me the truth: Was it voluntary?"

She nodded.

"Really? Did he know about your purity vow?"

Another nod.

"Was this, today, the first time?"

"Yes."

Brad scanned the cabin. "What about—did he use protection?"

Juniper nodded again.

He thought for a moment. "Looks to me like he betrayed your trust, forced himself on you even knowing you'd made that vow," Brad said. "Made it hard for you to say no."

"No, it's on me. I could've said I didn't want to, but I didn't."

"You were scared of him."

"No," Juniper said.

"He's intimidating, no question. Tall, black. Big guy. Any girl would be afraid."

"*No.* It's not a big deal, okay? I just want to go home."

Brad took out his phone to take some pictures of the scene: Juniper, tearstained and huddled there, pitiful. The Buck knife.

She shielded her face. "What are you doing?"

"Documenting. In case that little shit gives you any more trouble."

"Don't ever show those to anyone."

"Don't you worry, I'm not going to let anything bad happen to you. Here now, I'll step outside and you get dressed, okay?"

While he waited, his mind turned the incident over and around, assessing and reassessing. So, all right, she'd lost her virginity, maybe on purpose, maybe not. Whatever had gone on here, one thing was sure: His little fantasy of being her first was ruined. It was a damn shame for her and for him both. They could've shared something meaningful. Once in a lifetime. A beautiful thing made all the more precious for its having been secret and singular.

Whereas that boy was nobody. Forgettable. Which didn't mean Brad was leaving him in the clear, though. *Nosirree.* He had an idea about how he might use this crisis to real advantage, if he played all the angles right. It was all about using leverage. Leverage, and influence. When you knew people in high places, you could work those relationships, ask for favors, get things done.

That boy took something that should have been his, and the boy's mother was trying to rob him, too, and for that they were going to pay.

───────────────

Xavier had pulled his boxers on outside the cabin and then left in that near-naked state, driving half a mile or so from the site before parking in a secluded picnic spot to finish getting dressed. The expression *his blood boiled* fit the way he was feeling as he pushed his arms into his T-shirt, his legs into his shorts. Steam rose from his ears. Combustion felt possible.

Phone in hand, he breathed heavily, trying to decide: call the cops, or no?

Call and tell them what, exactly?

I was having sex with my girlfriend when her stepdad showed up and we got into a fight. I think he could be dangerous. She might be in danger.

Did he really think Juniper was in danger? No. He really just wanted the cops to think Brad was dangerous and rough him up the way Brad had just done to him.

If he called the cops and the cops came out, what would they find? They'd find Brad Whitman, Whitman HVAC, local celebrity, wealthy white man, angered protector of his virginal stepdaughter. They'd question him: *What happened here, sir? You were protecting your stepdaughter, the virgin who'd made a chastity vow? What, the guy with her was black? And you didn't take him down? That's commendable self-restraint. Good job, sir! We'll put you in for a medal.*

And of course they'd have to talk with Xavier, too, take his statement. *He roughed you up? Well, what did you expect would happen? Man's protecting his white underage daughter. Okay, stepdaughter. You're lucky it wasn't worse. Think if he'd had a gun. Or a rope.*

Xavier set his phone on the seat next to him and pressed his head to the steering wheel. He stretched his arms out, put his hands on the dashboard and gripped it. What now? What now? He wanted to wait for Juniper. He wanted to be able to call her, hear her voice, reassure her and himself. Too bad for him. From now until she got away from Brad Whitman, that son of a bitch would keep her locked down, captive. Xavier could see it all: She'd be made to quit her job at the store, never left alone outside the house, never allowed to drive anywhere on her own.

Six weeks from now, he'd be gone to San Francisco, no chance to see her before he left. Six *months* between now and when she would finish school—assuming she was allowed to do what she'd planned. Likely her parents would coordinate with Blakely to stop that, too. Can't allow a girl to have a mind of her own. Can't let her make her own decisions, god forbid.

Tears flooded Xavier's eyes and he cried like he hadn't done since he was a little boy. Big, choking sobs that made him feel stupid but also slightly better, if only for the release.

Go home, he told himself, feeling the urge to have a guitar in his hands and let it be his outlet for anxiety, his companion and counselor, as it had been many times before. Would it work as well today? He doubted it. What else, though, could he do?

He started the car and drove out of the park, missing by only forty seconds the police cruiser on its way in.

37

"All right, Miss Whitman, why don't you sit down here and we'll try to wrap this up quickly. We just have a few questions, really—just need you to confirm what Mr. Whitman told us about what happened."

Juniper, who'd been seated at a picnic table outside the cabin while Brad was in the parking area giving his statement to the police, felt tears pressing hard and hot behind her eyes. She wanted to get away from here. She wanted to find Xavier. He must hate her right now for getting him into this. He hadn't wanted to get romantically involved with her or anyone, smarter not to, why had she been so determined to change his mind? She was in love with him, that's why, and more in love every day, and now, thanks to Brad, he was going to wish he'd never met her. Hate her, even. The humiliation was just about unbearable for her, and must be at least as bad for him.

"All right," she told the cop. "Go ahead."

"Mr. Whitman said that when he arrived here planning to return your missing cell phone, you were inside the cabin on the floor, and the man was on top of you and you were both naked. Is that correct?"

Mortified, she stared at her feet. Running shoes. Run. Off like a gazelle, into the forest, down the trails. Would they find her? They would find her.

She said, "Yes."

"When the man saw Mr. Whitman, he got up and went after Mr. Whitman, and there was an altercation."

Juniper glanced at Brad. "Xavier," she said. "His name is Xavier."

"We understand. He went after Mr. Whitman and the two of them fought. Is that correct?"

"He didn't . . . I mean, I think Brad attacked *him*. Everything was happening at once—"

"I'm sure you were very upset."

"I was."

"He pushed Mr. Whitman and Mr. Whitman attempted to defend both himself and you—"

"Not me. I was sitting on the floor. I wasn't in the fight."

"Did you feel that you might be in danger?"

"Well, Brad was really angry, but I didn't think he'd hurt *me*."

"Would you say that the other man was angry as well?"

"*Why* do you keep calling him 'the man'? His name is Xavier."

"Keeping it simple, that's all."

"It was really upsetting, okay?" Her voice sounded squeaky.

"We can take a break, if you want a minute to collect yourself."

"What? No, let's get this over with."

"All right. There was a wine bottle in the cabin. Were you drinking?"

"I had some, yeah."

"Have you had alcohol before today?"

"Not really."

"And was the man drinking as well?"

"A little."

"Who brought the wine?"

Juniper hesitated. "He did."

"Was it his idea to bring it?"

She nodded.

The officer made a note. "So, is it a fact that vaginal penetration occurred?"

Juniper reddened all at once. Her ears burned. "Yes."

"With a condom?"

She nodded.

"Did the man ask for your consent?"

"What, like—"

"Did he—"

"I could have said no, and I didn't." She wanted to really emphasize this. "It *wasn't* rape."

"How much had you had to drink at this point?"

"I don't know. I was really nervous, so . . ."

"Scared, too?"

"Well, I was a virgin. So yeah, a little, I guess."

"Mr. Whitman says the man wanted to date you, is that correct?"

"Yes, we were dating. Look, I'm fine. Really. This was a bad situation, but now I'm fine."

The officer made more notes. Then, "Is there anything else you'd like to tell us?"

"No, I just want to go home."

"I understand. But given what went on here"—and at this point the officer waved Brad over—"we'll need to have a doctor take a quick look at you and make sure you're not injured."

"I'm *not*," Juniper said.

Brad put his hand on her shoulder. "Honey, we should cooperate. They know what they're doing."

The officer said, "It won't take long. Your dad will be checked out, too."

"He's not my dad," she said, and reluctantly went to her car, to follow and be followed to the hospital, where she would be able to show them once and for all, she thought, that what happened here had all been a misunderstanding, a surprise, an overreaction.

She'd clear it up, and then try to mitigate the damage with Xavier.

A mistaken supposition, as it turned out.

In the hospital, an attendant put Juniper into an exam room alone and told her to wait there. A nurse would be in soon to talk with her.

"Can I use the restroom?"

"Not just yet," said the attendant. "She'll need to collect some samples from you."

"But—"

"It won't be long."

"Can I call my mom?"

"Just as soon as you're done here."

Left alone, Juniper sat in a chair beside the wall and stared at a diagram of the human circulatory system, then at the plastic box for discarded needles, the little sink, the stainless-steel tray holding tubes and slides.

She should not be here. This day should not have gone like this. Maybe she'd been stupid to think there would be no consequences for letting herself be swayed by feelings, by desire, instead of what she'd been taught, what she'd once believed was true. Reverend Matthews had warned her and the other girls. He'd told them how seductive those feelings could be. She'd rejected all of that, rationalized her way right out of it, and look where it had gotten her.

Or maybe it was all Brad's fault.

Juniper wrapped her arms around herself. This exam room was cold. Where was the nurse?

It was easy to blame Brad for ruining it, for overreacting . . . but given what she knew about him, how else *would* he react? She should have told her mom about the kiss. She should have done everything differently. This was all her fault.

The wall clock's second hand ticked loudly. Cold air shushed in through the vent. Her heartbeat thrummed in her ears. Where was Xavier now?

Finally, a kindly white woman, middle-aged and with a manner like you'd use with a spooked horse, came into the room, introduced herself, and sat down in the chair beside Juniper's.

"Sounds like you had a bad day, sweetie."

Juniper started crying.

"Hey now," said the nurse, whose name was Ms. Sheridan. She put her hand on Juniper's back. "You're safe now. We're going to take care of you."

"It's my fault."

"No, it absolutely is not your fault."

"I never should have agreed to it."

"But *did* you, really?"

Juniper looked up at her. "What do you mean?"

"According to your report, the whole situation was engineered by the suspect in order to get you to have sex when you were strongly opposed to it—when you'd made a vow not to."

"What? I never said that. He didn't make me do any of it."

"You think so, but it's all there between the lines. This 'date,' it was his idea, right?"

"I . . ."

Juniper tried to think back; *had* it been his idea? Yes. But so what if it had?

Ms. Sheridan continued, "He brought everything, made it seem like you'd have this sweet little romantic encounter."

"Yes, but still, I agreed to it."

"He brought alcohol and encouraged you to drink it."

"I *wanted* to have some. I was really nervous."

"As he knew you would be. Alcohol or drugs are classic tools for this kind of criminal. Look at Bill Cosby and all those women who thought they wanted to be with him, but not like *that*. These men charm you bit by bit, and then next thing you know, they're on you taking what they wanted all along."

Juniper frowned. "I don't think Xavier's like that."

"That's why it works: because you don't see the truth. I'll bet he's a really intelligent guy, right?"

"Yes," Juniper said hesitantly. The woman was so confident, same as the police had been. She was making Juniper feel less sure of herself, of her sense of the events, her perception of their relationship. Juniper said, "He graduated at the top of his class."

"There you go. Smart guys like him, they look for innocent girls like you who can be manipulated, and then they rape you."

"Rape?" Juniper shook her head. "I keep telling you all, that's not what happened. I could have said no."

"Are you sure he would have stopped?"

"I . . ." Juniper paused. "Yes. I mean, I *think* so."

"Tell me about the knife."

"He needed it for the food."

"Food that he deliberately chose so that he'd have an excuse to display that knife. He's a smooth one, but believe me, I have seen it all. None of these tricks are new."

Tricks.

Ms. Sheridan must have been reading Juniper's expression. Self-doubt. Mistrust. Confusion. She said, "Listen, sweetie, nobody likes to think they can be fooled. It's natural that you want to resist believing it. It is a fact that *two-thirds* of rape victims don't initially think they've been raped. Those of us who know how these men think, though, can see through them like glass. His behavior is slick and calculated and *not your fault*. You are a victim."

She went on, "I'm sure this afternoon was upsetting for a lot of reasons, but the good thing is that he won't be able to take advantage of you anymore. Now, let's take care of a few forms, then we'll do your physical exam and get you on your way."

The physical exam was yet another humiliation: After Juniper went to give urine and blood samples, she returned to the exam room and another nurse came in to stand as witness while the now-naked Juniper, draped in flimsy paper coverings, submitted to a scalp-to-toe examination that included oral and vaginal and anal swabbing and photographs of her undraped body front and back. When Juniper thought about it later, *this* was what felt like a violation.

Throughout it all, Juniper considered Ms. Sheridan's assertions, comparing them against her recollections of every encounter between herself and Xavier up to today and today especially. *Could* he have been fooling her all along? Was she that gullible, that ignorant? Had he seen her the way Meghan and Kathi did—Juni*pure*, the princess? The gullible Christian freak? Look at her, she got played by the first boy who'd ever really tried.

Was it true?

The adults were all saying it was true, and what did she know?

She knew Xavier.

Didn't she?

38

Valerie was in her living room with a book in hand. Xavier, upset and unwilling to divulge why, was in his bedroom playing guitar. Whatever was going on, thought Valerie, it had to be something with Juniper Whitman. Even so, Valerie held her tongue, reminded herself once again that she needed to let him *do* and *feel* and *be* without her input or interference. Treat him with the same respect she accorded her undergraduates—even the freshmen who sometimes looked as if they needed hygiene interventions. Electing to stop showering daily was apparently a form of celebrating one's independence from home.

The knock on her front door came as a surprise, but not as big a surprise as the sight that greeted her when she opened it: two uniformed police officers who stood there, tense and serious, each with a hand resting on his service revolver's grip. A second car was pulling into the driveway.

A big surprise that was no surprise at all.

If you are a black person in the United States, you live each day with the knowledge that this scene or one very much like it may be in your future. You needn't have done anything illegal or have broken any rule. You might be browsing dresses in a high-end clothing store. You might be enjoying a sunny day at your neighborhood pool, or grilling hot dogs at a lakeside barbecue pit. Maybe you're a black firefighter in uniform making building inspections. One of two black guys waiting for a friend in a coffee shop. Among a group of black women playing a slow golf game. A black man moving into a just-leased apartment, or moving out of one you'd lived in for years. You could be an excellent black student who got into *Yale,* for crying out loud, and fell asleep on the sofa in your own dorm's lounge. Maybe you're a black boy playing with an Airsoft or BB gun, same as lots of white kids do. And next thing you know, patrol cars are showing up, lights flashing. *You have done nothing wrong,* and yet you're facing one or two or five or a dozen men like the ones now standing on Valerie Alston-Holt's front stoop, and your heart tries to leap out of your chest as if attempting to free itself, to get the hell out before some hothead gets twitchy and draws a gun.

Sometimes you get shot. Sometimes they leave you lying in your pooling blood and you die.

At her door, Valerie gripped the knob and said, "How can I help you, Officers?"

"We're looking for Xavier Alston-Holt."

"Because?"

"Is Xavier Alston-Holt in the residence?"

No. No, no, no, no, no, no, no.

She said, "May I ask what the problem is?"

He displayed an arrest warrant. "We have reason to believe he was involved in the commission of a felony. Is he or is he not in the residence?"

Valerie forced herself to say, "Yes." Possibly all they wanted was to question him.

Right.

She added, "Do you want to step inside?"

The officer who'd been speaking nodded to the other, an apparent signal for him to go to the back of the house and monitor any other exits. Two more officers were exiting their patrol car.

"No. Send him out. I'll wait here."

Valerie was sweating as she went to Xavier's room and knocked on the door. She felt the dampness in her armpits, along her back, her forehead, her palms.

What has he done?

Has he done anything?

Where was the trapdoor into the escape tunnel?

Right now it made no difference to Valerie what this was about. She'd been alive for forty-eight years, almost half of those as a black woman in the South. Whatever this was, it was going to be worse for him than it'd be if his mother had been white.

Escape tunnel. Why hadn't she dug one? Because that would have presumed this day would arrive and she had naively believed it couldn't, not for him, not for them.

The music stopped. Xavier said, "Yeah, what?"

See Xavier in Valerie's mind's eye at this moment: He's eleven years old, it's the end of fifth grade and his music teacher has arranged a recital. His first serious growth spurt is under way, so it seems that all he does is eat and yet he's still gangly, a bronze cricket, curls drooping over his forehead as he leans over his Epiphone (he is so proud of that guitar, bought with money he made mowing the neighbors' lawns) and begins to play.

Her voice was shaking. "The police are here for you. What's this about?"

But there was no time for him to explain much. Xavier preceded her out of the room, saying, "It's got to be some bullshit with Brad Whitman," and she said, "I'll call a lawyer, don't say *anything,* don't get upset, do *not* get upset. Do you understand, do you hear me?" and then he was being handcuffed. He was being led to a police cruiser. He was locked inside of it. He was gone.

39

An hour or so earlier, Juniper had arrived home and gone straight upstairs before Julia laid eyes on her, locking herself in her bedroom and telling Julia when she knocked, "I'm not talking to anyone. Leave me alone."

Then Brad had arrived. He was on the phone and went straight into his den, mouthing *Later* and then shutting and locking his door. Julia could not hear him well enough to make out his conversation or decipher who was on the call.

Now she returned to the guest suite, where she and Lottie had been watching TV before all this commotion. *Magnum P.I.* with Tom Selleck, Lottie's dream man in her dream location. Both Julia and Lottie were eating cheese puffs from the bag.

"What in the world is going on?" Lottie asked Julia.

"I have no idea, except that Juniper seems to be in some kind of trouble. Nobody will talk to me. Brad's on the phone."

"Didn't Juniper say she was working tonight?"

"She did." And Brad had said he was going out for wings with Jimmy. "Maybe Brad caught her in a lie? I mean, why else would she be acting so hostile?"

"That girl, a liar?" said Lottie. "Hardly."

Julia looked at her. "Really, Mom, how would you know?"

"What, because I ain't been here but a couple weeks? Makes no matter. I *know* people. I don't have to live with them years on end to know. I think there's boy trouble behind this. Got her heart broken or something."

"She's not involved with any boys."

"Now, that's where you're wrong."

"You just said she's not a liar. Well, if she has a boyfriend, that means she's been lying."

"Not telling's different from lying."

"I think this is all nonsense, but whatever you say."

"What's your better theory?"

"I told you, I think she lied—*not* about a boy. I'd know if my own daughter was messing around. My guess is she went out joyriding in that stupid new car of hers."

"You're suspicious minded because when you were her age, you didn't hardly speak that you weren't lying about something. She ain't you. She's nothing like you."

"No, you're right. She's too polite to say something like this to *her* mother: shut up, all right? You're not helping."

And so they waited, faces turned toward the television. Julia wasn't seeing the program, though. She was seeing Juniper on a day when she, Julia, had been late to pick her up from after-school care because she'd gone out for a quick drink with a man who'd been a customer earlier that day at the Hot Nuts kiosk where she worked in the mall. The "quick" drink had been slower than she realized, and then suddenly it was seven o'clock and she rushed across town to Juniper's school, guilty, guilty. Juniper was the last kid left in the classroom, just her and the openly hostile teenager whose job it was to tend her. Juniper, eight years old, hurt and angry and silent.

"I'm so sorry, sweetie. Mommy had car trouble."

. . . you didn't hardly speak that you weren't lying about something.

Julia heard Brad's tread on the back stairs.

"Okay, ladies," he said a moment later, joining her and Lottie. He shut the door behind him. "I'm sure you're wondering what's up. Thanks for being so patient."

Lottie said, "Did we have a choice?"

"I guess you didn't." He gave a tight smile and sat down on the edge of Lottie's bed. "I had to work out a couple of things, get a few ducks lined up so I could help our girl. Now, what I'm going to tell you is going to be shocking and upsetting, so let me preface it by telling you that Juniper is going to be all right. As you saw, she got herself home without a problem, and there's nothing the matter with her that some time won't fix."

Julia's mind spun, attempting to measure this information against her supposition. "Was she in an accident, then?"

"Nothing like that," Brad said.

Lottie said, "Someone did her wrong."

"Well, now, that's astute of you, Lottie."

Lottie turned to Julia. "What'd I tell you?"

"There's a boy involved?"

Brad said, "There is. So, okay, to give you a little backstory— bear with me, now. It turns out that the boy behind us, Xavier, has been more or less stalking Juni, trying to get her to go out with him. She didn't say as much, but I've been piecing it all together."

"From what?" Julia said.

Brad held up a hand. "I said bear with me. Anyway, she's such a nice kid—as we all know; she tried to put him off, but she didn't try very hard. She didn't want to be seen as 'mean' or difficult, you know how girls are. So she said she'd date him. It hasn't been going on for very long."

He paused, took a deep breath, put his palms together, then continued, "Okay, so today she had just got to the park for her run and he showed up acting like they were going to have a little picnic and hang out. She says she'd told him she would. He brought wine, and she didn't want to make him mad by refusing to drink it. They were in a cabin. He'd set it up like a real seduction scene—wine, blanket, food. And—now, don't overreact here—he had a large knife, and he kept it where she could see it and she knew if she didn't do whatever he wanted, he might cut or stab her. He might kill her."

"Jesus God almighty!" Lottie said, voicing Julia's silent response.

"Thing is, she's terrified of him still. We—the police have already questioned her, and we couldn't get her to admit to it, but it's plain."

Julia said, "How did *you* get involved with all of this?"

"I'm getting to that part. So you remember you called and asked me to look for her phone. Well, I thought I would just drop it off to her on my way to meet up with Jimmy. Figured she'd want to have it—you know how teens are about their phones. I walked in on them. If only I'd been five minutes earlier—"

Julia said, "Did he . . . ?"

Brad nodded. "She went along with it, meek as a lamb, you know, that knife laying there where he could reach it if she fought him. She *says*, 'I could have said no, but I didn't.' Well, Christ, of course she didn't! We need to make sure she understands we do not blame her a bit."

Julia was on her feet and moving for the door.

"Leave her be," Brad said, catching her arm. "For at least a little while longer. She's been through a lot and needs time to lick her wounds."

"She needs her mother," said Julia, even as she remembered how she hadn't sought comfort or counsel from Lottie in the aftermath of her own rape. That was different. She'd wanted to protect Lottie—hadn't she? Or had she been too ashamed to tell?

Brad said, "Seems to me *she* doesn't think so."

"You don't have the first idea about anything where that child is concerned."

"She's not a child, I know that."

"Stop it, you two," Lottie said. "I'm trying to get clear on what happened. You found them . . . in the act?"

"I did. There's more to all of this—if you'll sit and listen, Julia, you'll see why I want you to wait."

She perched.

"I opened the door, saw them there, and as soon as the boy saw me, he came charging after me. Lucky he didn't think to grab the knife first—I gave him too much of a surprise, I'm sure. He got a few good licks in, but I managed to run him off. Told him I'd kill him and I believe I would have, if he'd stuck around. But then I got my head about me and called 911."

He continued, "We went to have her examined. She's . . . I want to be delicate, here . . . she was not seriously wounded by the act, and there's pretty much no risk of pregnancy. They told her it was smart of her to cooperate, under the circumstances. Better to be alive and get justice."

Julia was horrified and she was livid. She said, "Why didn't you call me?"

"Nothing you could do, so why complicate things? I knew you'd see her before long."

"I need to talk with her."

"You *will,* just hold on a minute. Now, one other thing the policewoman and the nurse both told me was that a lot of rape victims have trouble admitting they were raped. Some are scared of repercussions. Some feel like what happened was their own fault. Some deny the crime because they reject the idea of being a victim. Some don't consider date rape actual rape. We can expect some or all of these to be true with Juni. She kept saying, 'It wasn't rape. I planned it,' which is maybe all of that at once. But trust me: I saw her. She was *terrified.* She was trembling afterward and crying like I've not seen her do ever. That's a girl who's had a trauma, the authorities who checked her out agreed."

He turned to Julia. "So here's what you need to do: After you see her, get yourself and the girls packed up with the essentials, and when that's set, you all will go on out to Mom and Dad's place—they're happy to keep the girls for three, four weeks, no problem. And I just talked with Tony, too—"

"Who's that?" Lottie asked.

"The district attorney. He's a friend of mine. I asked him to make the situation a priority. The boy will be in custody *tonight.*"

"Good!" Lottie said. "Nice to see justice working, for once."

Brad said, "Yes indeed. So, anyway, as I was saying. Things are gonna be a little . . . *noisy* here, for a time, once the news gets hold of this, and I want you all clear of the commotion."

Julia, her head aswim with outrage and anger and concern for Juniper's well-being, was ready to put his plan into action. "You'll pick up Lily from the pizza party?"

Brad said, "Yep, and then let's aim for you getting on the road by sunrise."

"That early?"

He nodded. "I don't know for a fact, but my guess is there'll be news trucks on the block by nine A.M. Before you ask," he added, "no, they don't have Juniper's name and they won't get it, since she's a minor. And the assault part with me'll be kept out of the news for now. Nobody in the media will know the assault charge particulars until later. It'll all be on the boy."

"Thank God for that, anyway," Julia said. "Juniper's anonymity, I mean. She's been through enough." She paused for a moment, then said, "I should have known that boy would be trouble for her. From the minute we met him I thought, he's way too smooth, too confident. Damn him."

She wasn't thinking about how easily Brad had engineered the situation; it was so much easier to demonize the black boy.

———————————

Julia was sick about this. Her daughter had made a vow, after all, and from everything Julia had seen, she took that vow seriously— and now look what that rotten, selfish boy had done to her.

Lottie, too, believed Brad's interpretation one hundred percent.

And when the details came out later bit by bit, the story passed along house to house and person by person as with a bucket brigade, a few of us thought that interpretation could be true.

Juniper, meantime, was *not* convinced. Ignorant of the unfolding plan for Xavier's immediate arrest, hopeful that when he was questioned he'd prove to the authorities he was exactly the person she believed him to be, and deprived of computer and phone, she was desperate to communicate with him, so she did what she'd been doing: She wrote to him. When Lily got home a little later that evening, Juniper sent her running out into the backyard, through the gate, under the dying tree, and out to Xavier's car, with the note in a plastic bag to stick under his wiper blade or wherever she could reach.

Swear not to tell, she said to Lily.

I swear.

Juniper couldn't stand the thought that Xavier might be sitting at home hating her for not standing up to Brad, for letting Brad run him off, for her not finding him the first possible moment upon her return. He'd see the note in the morning or, if not that early, soon. Whenever he got in his car again.

Three news trucks were on Valerie Alston-Holt's street at 8:15 the next day. The reporters stationed themselves at the curb and prepared to give breathless reports of the alleged situation while they waited for Valerie to answer her phone (*as if*) or to come outside and make a statement (*not*), and meantime wondered why Xavier Alston-Holt, the black man whose mother was suing the city, its favorite HVAC company owner, and a prominent residential developer would—allegedly—rape an underage white girl, when every account they'd been able to dig up so far painted him as solid, a top student, a talented musician with a promising future. Were there other terrible acts he might have been hiding all this time?

Whatever the case, the public would be relieved to hear that he was off the streets for the time being. They would be glad to know that the city's parents of young (white) girls had nothing to fear from him, at least for now.

Valerie's door opened.

She came outside.

She walked to her car.

She got inside and drove away.

Ms. Alston-Holt refused to speak to the media was the first response reported, Valerie's rigid silence creating a hole that filled in fast with words like *hostile* and *haughty* and *uncooperative* because, as we all know, the news media is a monster perpetually hungry for red meat.

And this lede, from the highest-rated news station's top-of-the-hour broadcast:

Breaking news this morning: A local black man is accused of the assault and rape of an underage white girl . . .

Really, that's all it takes.

40

And speaking of ravenous institutions:

The criminal justice system is designed for efficiency (of a kind), not comfort. When being booked you are officially presumed innocent and yet at the same time treated as though you're the mass murderer the cops have been after for months. There's no eye contact. There's no conversation. The processing rooms are as blank and sterile and cold as the employees and the guards who process you. And when we say *process,* we mean you come out at the other end of booking feeling as ground up as yesterday's cows when they exit the slaughter-house.

Mug shot.

Fingerprinting.

DNA swab.

Surrender of all clothing and accessories.

Full body search, cavities included.

Orange jumpsuit, in your size if they've got it.

Then an interview. Questions, lots of them. A cooperative type will want badly to answer, to give his side of things, to point out the mistakes that have been made, are being made. A cooperative type, when he hears, "All right, son. Why don't you tell us what happened?," will feel desperate to clear it all up.

Xavier, shaking with rage, forced himself to respond politely to the minimum number of questions possible. He gave his name, his health status, his preference to say nothing else until after he'd seen his attorney. In return, he got smirks and derisive remarks about how much nicer it would be for both of them if he'd be more forthcoming. "Why the hostility, son, if you've got a clean conscience?"

And then if it's a felony you've been arrested for, as was the case for Xavier, you are eventually herded into a blank, cold, not-as-sterile-as-you'd-like-it-to-be community cell—a too-small-for-so-many-bunks chamber full of many other frightened or hostile men, men who smell like fear and anger and the gases that result from eating jail food when your stomach is already in revolt.

Here you wait for arraignment—two days, usually, though Xavier would wait three. Three days of stewing in silence, trying to work out how and why what happened at the cabin had resulted in *this*.

No sleep to speak of. One brief and terrible phone call to his mother, who assured him she'd find someone who could help. Her tight, anguished voice. His recollection of her warnings. He'd heeded every one of them until this summer. Until Juniper.

Well, Jesus, how could he heed that one? He couldn't.

We've all seen enough cop shows to have a sense of what life is like inside a county jail. And if you've read a John Grisham or Jodi Picoult novel, you've been to court. This story isn't a police procedural. It's not a legal thriller. Is it a cautionary tale? We think it is—but we wish it weren't.

Xavier had been in jail for nine hours when a mealy skinhead type sidled up to his bunk just before breakfast call and said, "What a pretty little nigger you are. Whoo, boy! You get to the big house, they will have a *time* with you."

Nigger. Pretty. A *time*.

Xavier managed to wait until the cell had cleared before he

vomited into a stainless-steel toilet bowl, the sight and odor of which made him vomit again.

He had been in jail for sixty-three hours when he was pulled from the holding cell and taken to a room with two chairs and a table and told, "Wait here."

"Is it my lawyer?" he asked the guard.

No reply. Why? Was it really so difficult or somehow wrong to show some humanity? Or did spending all day every workday in the company of nameless, faceless men in orange jumpsuits, an endless parade of angry or fearful or angry *and* fearful men, dehumanize you after a while? Or did the county deliberately put these automatons in the job so that on the occasion when some inmate lost control they could respond quickly with brute force, no need to waste even a second taking into account why the man might have cracked? Xavier had just spent sixty-one post-booking hours, give or take, amid those angry, fearful men; he was one of them; he could understand, now that he thought about it, how no person of sensitivity could last long in here, whether guard or inmate.

A guard, though, could quit.

The door opened and a trim, youngish black man in a navy blue suit came in. He had a lineup buzz cut, very clean. He set a valise on the table and took the chair opposite Xavier. "Carl Harrington," he said, extending his hand. "Your mother has retained me to represent you."

Xavier shook his hand. A black lawyer for a black defendant. It had to be a deliberate choice. She must know what she's doing, he thought. Or maybe Harrington was the only one she felt they could afford. Or the only one who'd take the job.

How old was this guy? Early thirties? He couldn't have been in practice very long. Did it matter? Xavier hoped it didn't. This should be a simple case, right? Clear up the misunderstanding, get him out of here, end of story.

Harrington said, "I've had a little time to look over the police report, and I won't sugarcoat it: We've got a serious challenge on our hands."

Fuck.

"I can tell you everything that happened," Xavier said. "I didn't rape her."

"Even if so, the eyewitness account is going to be a difficult hurdle."

Even *if*?

Xavier's voice rose as he said, "You don't believe me? Then get out and tell my mother to find—"

"Whoa, brother. Slow down. Let's keep our head here. All I'm saying is that Brad Whitman as an eyewitness and assault victim carries a lot of weight. People love him. They trust him. That thing he does where he looks straight into the camera and says, 'You are my favorite customer and that's a fact'? It's cheesy but it works."

"Whatever he said happened, he lied. He's—I don't know, I guess he thinks that since Juniper made that vow to stay a virgin, she had to be forced. But she wasn't! She . . . we . . ."

Xavier pressed his hands to his face for a moment, took a couple of breaths.

Then he said, "We've been going out. We *planned* to, you know, have sex."

Have sex. It sounded as sterile and cold as this room. They hadn't planned to *have sex*, they'd planned to make love together—though neither of them had used those words, either, or any words. They hadn't needed to. They'd both known it was the next step, a culmination of their desire for each other. At work they'd stood together in the parking lot, hidden from sight, kissing, yearning for more. He'd said, "Maybe we could think about doing . . . better than this. More. You know." And she'd said, "Yeah. I'm thinking, maybe, you know, we could go out to the park?" And he'd said, "I'll bring all the supplies. Including protection, if that's how it goes." Red-faced, she'd said, "Okay, good."

Now Harrington told him, "They have the girl's statement, too."

Had she changed her mind?

"And she said I didn't rape her, right?"

"Let me see the actual language, here . . . She said, 'It wasn't rape. I could have stopped him, but I didn't.'"

"*Exactly*. So why am I even in here?"

"Physical evidence. Eyewitness account. Assault accusation. Whitman provided some photographs that show a *very* distressed young woman along with a large knife left at the scene—"

"You aren't serious, right? She was *very distressed* because Whitman walked in on us! We— I sliced salami and cheese! I'm supposed to use a butter knife?"

"I understand your frustration, but I have to be plain, here. The DA's got a case. The simplest, cleanest way out for you—and where my fees are concerned, cheapest, but that isn't why I'm saying this—is to let me try to negotiate a lesser charge. I'm thinking we could ask for second-degree rape and get them to drop the assault. Then it's a Class C instead of B1. Makes a big difference in sentencing."

"Hold up," said Xavier. "*Way out?* That's not a way out, that's me going to prison. I'm *not guilty,* okay? Not of any degree of anything. Why would I say I am?"

Harrington leaned forward, his fingertips pressed together. "You are a black man accused of raping an underage white girl. If you put yourself in front of a jury, you've got twelve strangers who'll be literally sitting in judgment of you while the prosecution busts their ass to show how to that white girl that knife equaled a threat of death unless she cooperated with you. Some of those jurors will be women. Some of them will be white. White fathers of teenage girls, if the prosecution can manage it." He leaned back. "You want your fate in their hands?"

"Juniper isn't going to say she felt threatened. Jesus Christ. I can't even believe I'm sitting here having this conversation."

Harrington said, "Okay. Let's say that all of this is just some big misunderstanding, as your mother described it to me when we spoke. The sex was consensual. You have an explanation for the knife, et cetera—"

"It's *true.*"

"Let me be the devil's advocate for you here: Miss Whitman doesn't have to testify. In fact, if I was the DA, I wouldn't even have her in the courtroom."

"The supposed victim doesn't testify? That's fucked up. Can't you make her? She'd tell the truth."

"The prosecution will assert that she's afraid of you, or that her mental state is unreliable due to the trauma. They've got angles, trust me."

Xavier was trying to get his mind around this insane situation. He said, "Then . . . Then if they think she wouldn't help her own case—which no way is *her* case to start with—"

"What do *you* think happened, then? How did your romantic interlude turn into a rape charge? I want your operating theory."

"Her stepdad's pissed is all it is. He's mad that my mom is suing him, and he thinks I ruined his perfect little girl."

Harrington said, "And believe me, he'll say so in court."

"And I'll say what's true. And you get Juniper to somehow back it up. My mom, too. She knows we're dating. I don't see how Whitman can get away with this bullshit, once people see what he's doing."

"The dating thing is no help—they're asserting it's date rape."

Harrington went on: "Let me lay this out for you more specifically: If you go to trial and the jury likes solid-citizen Whitman and his story better than big black you and yours—because that's what it'd come down to—you are looking at a prison sentence of twenty-five years, minimum. *Twenty-five years*, my friend. Could be double that. Could be life, if Tony Evans persuades a judge that you're an aspiring murderer who just got interrupted. I *want* to think that won't happen. Still, it's a genuine risk. Judges have a lot of latitude with sentencing. Plead down, we should be able to get you, say, nine plus parole. And the sex offender registry. That part's unavoidable, I'm sorry to say."

Xavier felt like his head might explode. "Yes, it is avoidable, damn it! I'm innocent and I can prove it!"

Harrington was calm as Gandhi. "How? How can you *prove* it?"

"That's what *you're* supposed to be the expert on. I give you the facts and you prove them in court. That's what we're paying you for!"

"And I will fight for you with every tool I've got, if that's the route you choose," Harrington said. "Look, I can't blame you for your outrage or your naiveté. In your place, I'd be saying all the same things. But defense attorneys are not, unfortunately, the magicians you see on TV."

"I shouldn't need magic. Just good representation. Just a chance to show how it's not what Whitman made it look like."

"Good representation is me helping you navigate this realistically and getting you the best outcome possible. I don't want to see you locked up till you're fifty, or worse."

Xavier leaned over and put his forehead against the table. The surface was gray from a distance but speckled up close. Grains of sand. He breathed in . . . breathed out . . . in . . . out, and then, head still down, he said, "Do I have to decide what to do right now?"

"No. We'll get you arraigned and, I hope, out on bond, and then we can talk some more."

"Okay."

Harrington laid his hand on Xavier's back. "I know it's hard, but try to let go of that righteousness and think practically. A lot of brothers are dead because they were righteous when they needed to be smart."

"Sure." Xavier spoke to the tabletop. "How much is bond?"

"Let's see what the judge has to say on that."

———————————

Much shuffling of paperwork while Xavier stood, with wrists and ankles shackled, before the court. A sea of indifferent faces—save for one, his mother's. Xavier glanced at her but couldn't hold her gaze or he'd lose his shit right then and there. He did have some pride.

The judge was a middle-aged white woman wearing blue earrings shaped like fish.

The attorneys identified themselves for the record. The charges were read: first-degree rape, kidnapping, assault.

Kidnapping? Xavier thought in alarm. He looked at Harrington. *What the actual fuck?*

More conversation he couldn't make out. Then, "Mr. Harrington, how does your client wish to plead?"

"The defendant pleads not guilty."

"So entered. Proceeding on to the defendant's request for bail . . ."

Some back-and-forth between the judge and the clerks. Everyone acting like this was no more important than ordering a fast-food hamburger. Ketchup? Yes, but no pickles. Onion. Mustard. Add cheese?

Finally the judge said, "Very good. I'm setting one hundred fifty thousand on the rape charge, seventy-five for the kidnapping, twenty-five for the assault. Bail is set at two hundred fifty thousand dollars."

Xavier looked at Harrington again. Harrington was not looking at him.

The guards led him out of the courtroom. Harrington joined him in the corridor and told the guards, "Let us have a minute?"

A quarter of a million dollars was outrageous, but Xavier's first remark was "What is this kidnapping bullshit?"

"Apparently the DA had a closer look and thinks there's maybe enough evidence, so he tacked it on. It's a strategy to raise the stakes, elevate the case for maximum media attention. Makes you look like a dangerous criminal." He shook his head in disgust. "He really is gunning for this one."

Xavier had an odd ringing in his ears from the blood rushing to his head, his face. *Gunning for this one.*

"And two hundred and fifty thousand? Where am I supposed to come up with that?" He couldn't do it. He'd have to rot here for as long as it took to get on the schedule for a trial. And possibly longer. Possibly always.

Harrington said, "You don't have to raise all of it. We'll get a bail bondsman to front it. You pay ten percent."

Valerie had joined them in the corridor. She said, "Twenty-five thousand dollars."

"Correct," Harrington told her.

"But then we get it back after the trial, right?"

The lawyer shook his head. "No. Straight-up bail you'd get back if you paid it yourself. Most of it, anyway. If you have to use a bondsman, the ten percent is their fee for fronting the rest of it."

She said, "So if I happen to have a quarter mill laying around, I lose nothing. But if I'm one of the ninety-nine percent who don't, I forfeit twenty-five grand. *That's* a fair system."

"I wish it were." He turned toward Xavier. "Now you're getting a view of what's real—which leads me to my next question: Have you thought any more about considering a plea deal? You don't have to commit yet; I can raise the question with the DA informally, feel him out."

"No." He turned to his mother. "I've got maybe five thousand in my savings. If you can help me get the rest, I'll pay you back."

"I'll handle it."

"I'm really sorry for this trouble, Mama." His voice cracked. "I can't wait to get out of here."

"I know, sweetheart," she said. "Me, too."

The guards were already tugging him toward the doors that led back to the jail.

"We'll talk soon," Harrington called.

41

Predictably, Esther, who'd raised so much ire at the *Lolita* book club meeting, said of Juniper at the club's next meeting—in Ellen's house, without Valerie, "She never should've gone to the woods with him. You do not go out into the woods unless you mean for something to happen."

Predictably, Belinda replied, "Xavier's the one who should've known better."

Ellen said, "You *aren't* saying he raped her."

"No, I'm saying—"

"He absolutely did," Kelli interrupted.

"No offense," said Ellen, "but are you maybe saying that because you're white and he's not?"

Kelli said, "Are you defending him because Valerie is your close friend? Me, I'm saying he raped her, because she made a purity vow and she took it seriously. You all remember. We heard about it that night they had their housewarming. I remember seeing Xavier there. He was looking at Juniper like a hawk looks at a rabbit."

"Give me a break," said Ellen. "I've known Xavier since he was born. It's obvious Juniper lured him there to trap him as revenge against Valerie suing Brad."

Belinda said, "And this is what I'm saying: He should've known better than to get tangled up with her."

Esther said, "Hank had a vision about this—"

"What?" said Belinda. "A *vision*?"

"Dying people can see things we can't see. He said he saw a fresh grave."

"Whose?"

"I asked him. I said, 'Is it yours?' But he didn't think so."

Ellen said, "That's not helpful at all, Esther. It probably has nothing to do with this."

"He said it did."

"What did he say *exactly*?"

"He said none of this would be happening if Tom hadn't died like he did. He said, 'Then Xavier wouldn't hate white folks.'"

Ellen said, "Xavier doesn't hate white folks! For God's sake."

Belinda said, "Maybe the grave is Tom's and he's trying to speak to us through Hank."

Esther, who so often had the final word whether we agreed with it or not, said, "Maybe we should quit arguing about this and discuss the book."

42

"All right," said Carl Harrington, just before Xavier's release on bond. "Here's how this goes. No travel beyond state lines. Do not fail to show up for your next court appearance or they'll put you back in without bond. Don't break any laws—don't even get so much as a parking ticket or they'll haul you in. Also, a restraining order is in place. Do *not* under any circumstances attempt to see or contact Brad Whitman or his stepdaughter. And stay at least fifty feet from their property at all times."

"That's impossible. Our yards connect."

Harrington said, "You get me, though. Don't fuck up in any way. I'm going to talk to the prosecutor, feel him out. Then you and I will talk some more."

Talking, talking, so much talking, Xavier thought while he changed into his street clothes, and nobody getting anything done, nobody solving the problem. What was it to any of them? A job, that's it, nothing more. A job. His *life* was their nine-to-five.

Dressed now in the same clothes he'd worn to the park that terrible day, Xavier left the jail and got into Valerie's car. He asked her as they drove away, "Where did you get the money?"

"Don't worry about that. What's important is you're out."

Out. Outside. Fresh air. Sunshine. Humidity. Leaves. Cars. McDonald's. Car wash. Bike shop. Krispy Kreme. Playground. Park. Cafe. Bookstore.

He said, "You took my savings, though, right?"

"I didn't want to, but . . ."

"So you're broke, too."

She said, "I don't care about that. You are far more important to me than money."

"How much is Harrington charging?"

"I had to pay him a ten-thousand-dollar retainer."

"So . . . that's already thirty-five grand this has cost us. Christ. Will the ten cover me through a trial?"

She didn't reply.

"Mom?"

"Probably not. But like I said, I don't care about the money. I borrowed against the house, so we're fine."

"Sure. *Fine.*"

"Harrington is a good attorney."

"How so? He wants me to make a plea deal. I can do that for free."

"He's exploring all the angles, that's all."

Xavier felt tears rise yet again. "I can't go to prison, Mama."

"You won't," she said, but he knew she had no more confidence in that than he did.

They drove for a time in silence. Then Xavier said, "I'm going to call and see if I can get some extra hours at work."

"*Please* don't worry about the money. It's as much my fault as yours."

"*Mine?* You think I'm a rapist?"

"No—no! I just meant it's obvious Brad Whitman's trying to get back at me for suing him."

"So he tries to send *me* to prison?"

"I didn't give him enough credit for cleverness. The surest way to put a knife in me is by harming you."

She started crying. Xavier did, too, silently, tears of rage and frustration and sorrow. Growing from this, though, was an even stronger determination for justice. Somehow he'd see it done.

―――――

Later that evening, Xavier's manager said over the phone, "Listen, I know this is a difficult situation, but we can't have reporters taking up space in the parking lot and scaring off customers. Also, frankly, we have to err on the side of caution, where our female employees' safety and well-being is concerned. Not that we believe it at all, but . . . You understand. We hope everything gets resolved in your favor. Good luck."

―――――

In the mail two days later came a letter that read:

> Dear Mr. Alston-Holt,
>   Due to recent events that have come to our attention, we regret we must rescind our offer of enrollment and financial aid for the coming academic year. We wish you the best.

―――――

The local news trucks and reporters had now been joined by others from farther away.

43

With Julia, Lottie, and the girls away, every night after work, once the sun was down, Brad Whitman sat out back under his covered porch looking past the swimming pool, past the fence, past the dying oak tree, and smiled with contentment. Over there, Valerie Alston-Holt fretted over her son's fate and regretted tangling with old Brad Whitman, he'd bet on it. Over there, Xavier Alston-Holt was brooding but also learning a lesson about what he was and was not entitled to. Out west, at Brad's folks' house, Juniper was thanking her lucky stars that Brad had arrived when he did and saved her from even one second more with that bastard son of a woman who was nothing but an opportunist who couldn't land herself an honest man.

All right, no, he conceded, Juniper wasn't thanking her lucky stars. He knew better. That was him just wishing she'd see it his way. She was still upset and confused about how she could have been fooled so badly. Which was still Brad's official position on the situation, even as he was pretty sure the boy hadn't raped her. Probably hadn't coerced her, either—no more than any boy ever did any girl, anyway. Girls, women, they sometimes needed a little push, a little persuasion. Permission to do what you could tell they wanted to do, as he'd realized was the case with Juniper toward him. Could be she thought he was out of reach, so she'd turned her frustrated attention toward a black boy. Or she was trying to get Brad to pay better attention to her. Hard to say for sure.

He blamed himself, a little. He hadn't watched her closely enough, assuming—fool that he could sometimes be—that her moony behavior was all about him. To be fair, he thought, it *had* been all about him until they'd moved and she'd gotten lured away by that slick operator over there. How did he know Xavier was slick? Black musicians always had a few girls on a string at any given time, the same way black athletes did—everybody knew that. Maybe it was a cultural thing. He'd envied those guys so much back when he couldn't get a girl to look at him twice. He envied Xavier now—for being young, for getting to be the one who took Juniper to that cabin.

In truth, for all that Xavier had derailed (at least for now) Brad's plan where Juniper was concerned, he'd also done him a favor. He'd created for Brad the opportunity to strong-arm Valerie and get her to back off, drop the lawsuit, and Brad rarely walked away from a good opportunity. Now all the pieces were in place for a great big happily ever after, or nearly. In all probability, Juniper was now out of reach for him. But at least he'd come off as the hero once everything shook out. All he had to do was pull the trigger.

But just for fun, he'd let the boy and his mother twist in the wind for another couple of days, and then he'd start wrapping this thing up for good.

44

With Xavier home but silent, and Valerie silent, and the Oak Knoll neighbors reluctant to go on the record with public declarations for or against any of the parties involved, the news reporters cleared out for the time being. Maybe there would be a trial, at which time the reporters would flap back to the tree limbs like the vultures they were and hope to find a carcass.

For now, though, things seemed quiet. Decent folks had no awareness of all the rumbling that was going on in back-channel media, those dark spaces that are so comfortable for good ol' boys with deep prejudice and hair-trigger tempers and vigilante mind-sets. Plans were being made. People were mobilizing from a garage not far from Oak Knoll, to make sure the rapist got what was coming to him, since they couldn't depend on the law to get this kind of thing right.

Having sequestered himself in the house for a week, Xavier finally ventured out one late afternoon with no clear destination in mind. He might drive over to Dashawn's house and hang out, pretend he still had a life; Dashawn and Joseph both had been bugging him to "leave

his cave." There'd been no word from Harrington on the DA's incli-
nations toward a plea deal. Not that Xavier wanted to cut a deal; he
just wanted to know where he stood. The silence bugged him; did
the DA want him to go down so badly that he wouldn't even consider
some kind of compromise? Valerie said she thought the silence was
nothing more than the slow turning of the law's wheels; his fate was
nobody's priority but his, after all. The DA and Harrington would
get to it eventually.

Eventually.

Eventually he would be a pathetic loser whose friends had all
gone away for school while he awaited trial—it pretty much *had* to
be a trial, or he'd never see his name cleared.

Eventually might be months or a year or two. He'd been reading about cases that took forever to unwind. Cases where young
black men got fucked over because they made bad plea deals. Well,
that wasn't going to be him.

Maybe, though, Harrington would come back with something
that made both him and the DA happy. A misdemeanor charge, say,
for fighting with Whitman. Some community service requirement,
maybe, and a promise to stay away from Juniper (which he'd keep,
since it had become obvious from her and Pepper's total silence that
she had cut him loose). If there was something reasonable to consider, he'd consider it. He wasn't stupid.

If not, a trial. Put him in front of a jury, let him say his piece. He
wasn't just some random black perp, a thug from the 'hood. He was
half white (not that it should matter). National Honor Society. Let-
tered in concert band and orchestra. Scholarship to a prestigious private college. No record. An honest face. They'd have to respect all of
that. Right?

Doubtful.

But possible.

But unlikely. He'd read the stats. Black men (and if you, biracial
boy, aren't totally white, you are for every intent and purpose black)
were more likely to be wrongly convicted and to serve longer sen-
tences than whites. Separate those stats into North versus South and

the numbers were grimmer still. People could debate the causes and conclusions all day long; the numbers, though, didn't lie. Harrington was not lying, either: If Xavier went to trial, he was basically fucked.

All of this was on his mind while he walked down the driveway to where his car was parked at the curb. He wasn't paying attention to the sound of a large motor revving, the short chirp of wheels against pavement. Only when the pickup truck that had made these noises was coming up behind him did he notice and turn his head to look—not in alarm, just meaning to ensure that he had room to open his car door while the truck passed.

In the pickup's bed was a white man who leaned over the side. He had an object in his hands—a pole? Xavier didn't have enough time to identify the object, and he didn't have enough time to avoid it, either. The man yelled, "Take this, rapist nigger!" and swung while the truck came alongside Xavier, hitting him not (*thank God*, Valerie said later) in the head but on the hand he'd raised in defense as he ducked. He fell against his car *hard*. Then the driver raced off. Xavier, in the explosion of pain, thought he heard whooping and laughter.

He said so to the police a short while later, before letting Valerie take him to the ER. The cops listened to his statement without sympathy, saying they'd look for a gray truck but there were lots of them and maybe he should've gotten a license plate number and it'd be smart to stay inside if he didn't want more trouble. Then Valerie said this was *horrifying*, didn't they understand, this was a good neighborhood, damn it, this kind of thing doesn't happen here. Xavier barely heard them; his left hand, even as he kept it in a bowl of ice water, was swollen so badly that it had lost all of its features. It was a balloon hand, a cartoon hand, a hand with fingers that wouldn't function. Xavier was, temporarily, too stunned to cry.

There are nineteen bones in the human hand. Seven of Xavier's were shattered. His tendons were subluxated and dislocated and, in three spots, split. The ER doctor, a black man who unlike Xavier had managed to never get on the bad side of a sociopath and have his life derailed, reported the damage and said, "You're lucky, my friend.

It could have gone so much worse for you." The orthopedic surgeon, a white guy whose manner could have used a sugarcoat, said, "Professional guitar? *Huh-uh.* I don't care who you see for the surgery, none of us can work miracles."

45

But all right, maybe, just maybe, Xavier's luck was changing:

Two days later, Wilson Everly told Valerie by telephone, "You're going to want to sit down for this."

She was standing in her kitchen, looking out the window at her tree. "What now?"

"I just got off the line with Whitman's attorney. They'd like to offer you the opportunity to get your son's charges dismissed in return for dropping your suit."

Valerie was jolted. "Wait, what? I drop *my* case and somehow Zay goes free?"

"That's what they posit. It's clearly an attempt at extortion—"

"Do it."

"I understand your eagerness. But they don't have that authority, exactly. The DA is the only one who can dismiss the charges."

"So what are you saying? You think it's a trick? I drop the suit and then the joke's on me?"

"No . . . No, I would have to guess that Brad Whitman has already cleared this with the DA, and that's given him the confidence to leverage the situation in his favor. May have been his plan all along. If so, we could report it—"

"And then try to prove all of that mess while Zay's case continues?" She was gripping the phone so tightly she thought it might snap in two. She said, "No. I don't care if it's extortion. Make it happen."

"Ms. Alston-Holt, to say that this offends my sensibilities as a law-abiding attorney—"

"Damn it, I don't care! Figure it out *after* Xavier's cleared."

Everly said, "All right, I understand, and I don't want to prevent a good outcome for him. We can say yes conditionally, and then we proceed only after I somehow get confirmation on the criminal case. I don't like it," he reiterated. "It's like some backroom spy deal."

Valerie, though, was doubled over now, holding herself, practically in tears. "Who cares? *Do it.* Put an end to this nightmare."

"Yes, ma'am. And please give your son my best. I can only begin to imagine what he's been through."

"Thank you," Valerie said hoarsely, her voice almost stolen by her body's response to his words.

After the call, she collected herself and went to Xavier's room. His guitars stood in a row while he lay on his bed, his left hand in a fully immobilizing splint while he awaited the surgery that might restore function in the range of forty percent. It had taken all her skills to keep Zay calm, persuade him that the doctors didn't always know, that with physical therapy and time, he might regain full function. She didn't believe it but she needed him to believe it at least for the time being.

His headphones lay on the bed beside him. His phone was on the floor—dropped by accident or on purpose? She didn't ask. She hadn't asked him much of anything since the drive-by incident, hoping that time and pain meds and kindness would be all he needed to get past the worst of it. The idea that she could now bring him news of his deliverance made her almost giddy.

"I just got a bizarre phone call," she said, and then proceeded to explain in as calm a manner as possible what Everly had told her. Then she said, "It's a really promising development—and also proof that Brad Whitman is a nasty excuse for a human being. He jacks you up, causes you no end of trouble, and now he wants to be your savior."

Xavier said, "Fuck him. The damage is already done."

He meant his scholarship, his job, his reputation, his hand, his career. And probably Juniper, too. Juniper, who'd made no effort to see or contact him or set things right.

Valerie said, "That's not true. You're not in prison. You won't go to prison."

"I won't go to college, either. I won't have a profession. Probably won't even be able to get a new job."

"Honey, the charges will be dropped."

"The arrest record won't."

"We can work on getting it expunged."

"And can we undo all the news stories, too? And the neighbors avoiding me or looking at me like I'm dirt, or being afraid of me? Can we stop rednecks from trying to kill me?"

His words made her want to cry. Still, she had to be positive and upbeat, set an example for him to not only see but feel and follow.

She said, "After a time, all of that will fade."

He turned his head away to face the wall. "How much time?" he said dully. "And what am I supposed to do until then?"

"Come on, Zay. It's all going to get better now."

"Is it going to save the tree? No. Will I ever play guitar again? No. Is it going to bring Juniper back?" There it was, out loud. He said, "No, it's not."

Valerie started to say, "Why would you even want her—" and then stopped herself. "I'm sorry. This has all been stupid and wrong and I know you're hurting in every way. Speaking of: Did you take your four o'clock pill?"

He shook his head.

"I'll get it for you, and some apple juice. That'll be a start."

He turned his face toward her. "Yeah, all right. Thanks. I need to get over myself. It is good news—for me anyway."

"Everything that's good for you is good for me, too. I can plant another tree, right? But you're my only son."

"Hey," Xavier said as she started for the door. He was moving himself into a sitting position. "Could you hand me my phone? I'll call Harrington and tell him what's up."

Valerie couldn't suppress her relieved smile as she picked up the phone from the floor and handed it to him. "I expect Mr. Everly will contact him, but I know he'll be glad to hear from you, too."

Brad was in the Maserati driving home from work, rain beating down, when he finally reached his friend by telephone. "Hey, Tony, you know how much I appreciate you going to bat so strong on that rape thing for me. I just about couldn't see straight, I was so shook up."

"Glad to help a friend when I can," Tony said.

"Good, right. So here's what I need from you now. I'm working out a deal that'll get me completely out of that mess with the mother's dying tree. I just need you to drop the charges on the boy. I think he's learned his lesson, don't you?"

"Drop the charges, you say?"

"Yeah. Not really necessary to go further. Date rape—is that really even a thing? I was all hot about it at first, sure. But Juniper's doing fine now. She's having a little time away with her mama and grandparents. It's all good. The boy got a scare and some real consequences, too—he's burnt, there's no doubt about that."

Rainwater sluiced over the car's hood and along the side windows. The windshield wipers slid cleanly back and forth across the polished glass. He was a man in a Maserati ad, captain of industry, captain of his universe. Not captain; king.

"That boy assaulted you," Tony said. "He threatened Juniper with a terrifying knife, got her drunk, dragged her into a dark cabin—he needs to either plead to something reasonable or face a jury."

Brad, still feeling the confidence of his plan, said, "Now, take your DA hat off for a minute and see this. If you spring him, you save Kevin and me and the city a half-million dollars, and that's not counting legal fees."

There was silence for a moment, and Brad glanced at the car's display screen, thinking the call had dropped. Nope.

Then Tony said, "How did I get to be district attorney?"

Brad downshifted to take a corner, saying, "What do you mean, how? You were a damn good prosecutor and just as good a schmoozer. The voters love you."

"That's right. Now consider: I have a black man accused of the kidnapping and rape of an upstanding underage white Christian girl—a virgin, no less. The public sees this man as a threat to every other young white girl out there. I let him walk, I get all manner of hell rained down on me."

"No—see, you just say new evidence has come to light and it *wasn't him,* he's not the one, and you won't hold an innocent man a minute longer. Blacks will love you for that. I'll make a statement saying I was mistaken in identifying him."

"But you weren't, right? You aren't trying to tell me you made any part of this up. Because if you think you can—"

"Hell no, I'd never do you like that—but if *I'm* not interested in seeing him punished any further, you—"

"I like you, Brad," Tony said. "You don't cheat at golf. You contributed to my campaign. We've had some laughs together. You're a solid citizen. But you *do not* get to use my office to play chess with that woman who's suing you or with anybody else. Am I being clear? I am not your pawn."

"Jesus, of course not. I only thought that since we're pals—"

"The police brought me your complaint, I evaluated it—quickly, just as you asked me to—and based on the information, I brought charges. I still believe those charges are appropriate, and I'll get a lot of credit from the *right* people by putting this one in the 'win' column. You're going to have to resolve your lawsuit some other way."

"Yeah, okay, sure," Brad said. "No problem. Thanks."

When the call was done, he swung around another corner and

headed back to the highway to put the car through its paces, work out his frustration, see if he couldn't find another way to skin this damned cat. Goddamn Tony. See if he'd contribute to his next reelection campaign. Old Brad Whitman did not appreciate being made to look a fool.

46

The bad news came to Xavier from Carl Harrington.

Xavier was sitting at the kitchen table looking up potential colleges he might yet be able to attend and texting with Valerie about her weekend plans. She and Chris were supposed to be going to his daughter's wedding in Chicago tomorrow and making a little vacation of it, but now, as she was at the mall doing last-minute dress shopping, she was vacillating.

This is dumb. I should just cancel.

Canceling would be dumb. He typed slowly, using just his index finger. *I'll be fine.*

I hate all these dresses.

Just pick one.

Are you sure you can manage that splint?

I can skip showers until you get home.

That last was a joke. He could manage the splint. He could manage whatever was needed because now (he thought) the end of the nightmare was imminent. He wouldn't have said his future looked bright; he'd lost far too much for that. There was, however, some possibility of light where before there'd been the threat of none.

This, just as his phone rang.

—We want to stop the story here. We want to yell, *Don't answer the phone, Xavier,* the way you do when you're watching a horror flick. Don't investigate that noise coming from the basement; no good can come of it. Run.

But they always investigate the noise. They always answer the phone. It's as if it's fated. People can't go against their own natures; if they could, they wouldn't have gotten into the messes they're in, right?

(Wrong.)

"Hey, Carl," Xavier said, answering. "What's up?"

"I don't have room in my schedule to see you until tomorrow, so apologies for doing this by phone, but it can't wait: I checked in with the DA's office and Whitman didn't come through. I don't know if it was a bullshit promise to start with, or he spoke too soon, or the DA changed his mind, or what. I couldn't get a straight answer. Doesn't matter. We're back where we were."

Xavier's heart stalled, turned to stone, dropped into his stomach. "How could he even make the offer unless he—"

"Don't waste your brainpower on that. Do what you need to do to make a decision on pleading down, if possible, or standing trial, because if we're going to trial, I've got to start preparing."

No.

Xavier was in a well. Black. Dark. Deep. Cold. The walls were close around him, squeezing him, pressing the breath from his body.

"Did you hear me?" Harrington said.

Pleading? *No.* No. If you plead guilty when you're not, you're giving away every piece of you that matters. Pride. Integrity. You're *giving away* your freedom. Just handing it over as if it means nothing to you, like they deserve it, like you're fine with wearing chains as if you're a dangerous animal. Fine living behind steel bars, sharing your ten-by-ten with a man you don't know and wouldn't want to. Fine with the criminal record that will ride your back for the rest of your life, if they ever let you out. You plead guilty when you're not, you're saying, *Here, take my self-respect because I'll never be able to use it again.* Plead guilty when you're innocent and you've let wrong win the battle against right.

No.

Trial? Black men never prevail against odds like these. A trial would be futility made into spectacle. It would mean weeks of sleeplessness, of being nerve-sick every day, of having hope and dread churn in his stomach (and his mom's) while the DA gave press conferences full of verbal winks on how you had to make an example of "boys like Xavier" because "date rape" was "a national crisis." It was thousands and thousands of dollars spent for him to sit in a courtroom being scrutinized and vilified, having lies told and truths ignored, being dissected alive for the entertainment of rich white men who a few decades earlier would've gotten their thrills from watching him swing.

No.

"Xavier?" said Carl Harrington.

"Yeah. Yeah, I heard you."

"Your prelim is Tuesday. I need your answer Monday morning, latest."

Xavier made his mouth move again. "Understood."

"I'm on the run right now. Can you call Everly? Sorry about this, my friend."

"Sure."

"We'll sort it out."

Xavier pressed end.

─────────

We declare our right on this earth to be a man, to be a human being, to be respected as a human being, to be given the rights of a human being in this society, on this earth, in this day, which we intend to bring into existence by any means necessary, said Malcolm X.

Xavier closed the book and slid it back into its place on his bookshelf. He went to his computer and opened a bookmarked YouTube page.

We all, regardless of the color of our skin, are bound by a moral duty to demand equal and just treatment for all women and men under the law. When the structures of law fail us, we are morally bound to use every tool at our disposal to ensure that the injustice is not allowed to stand, said Tom Holt-Alston.

───────────────

When Valerie arrived home, Xavier was again sitting at the kitchen table. He hadn't called Everly, and he pretended Harrington hadn't called him. He'd had time to think about things. He wasn't going to need Harrington anymore.

He said to his mother, "Hey, so you found a dress?"

She set a shopping bag on the table. "Yes, but I really think it'd be better if—"

"You've had this trip planned for months," Xavier said. "*Go.* You don't need to stay home and babysit me."

"What will you do all weekend?"

"Read. Watch stuff. Same as if you're home. So just go, okay? You hovering over me every second's getting old."

"Zay—"

"It's insulting, if you want to know the truth. I'm not a four-year-old."

"You're right," she said. "I'm sorry. I've been your mom for eighteen years, so, you know, it isn't easy to turn off that switch. But you're right. I'll go with Chris. I'll have a nice time. You'll be fine here. And I'll be home again Monday night. All good."

Xavier nodded as if he were satisfied. He was not, but he would be if he could hold on to his convictions with the strength shown by so many men and women before him, his parents included. He could see only one route now to the kind of satisfaction he required.

47

Being stuck under the family microscope the way Juniper had been these past couple of weeks had worn her down to barely a nub of herself. She was eating little, sleeping less. What was going on with Xavier? How had things gone with the police questioning him? Had he gotten her note? Had he tried to reach her—or was he determined never to bother with her again? She imagined him telling himself, *Forget her, she's nothing but trouble.* She imagined him being glad to be rid of her.

The adults (including Julia and Lottie, who'd stayed two weeks but now had to get back for Lottie's doctor appointments) had been strict with her, denying access to any telephone and keeping watch over her activities. What were they so afraid of? Did they think she was going to plan a secret escape with Zay, the two of them sneaking off to, what, Montana or someplace where they could disappear into the hinterland, never to be seen again?

As if.

If only.

No one would tell her anything except how good it was for her to be out here in nature, to get away from all the stresses at home. Hiking. Fresh air. Waterfalls. Birds. Bears. "You've been through a lot. You need R&R." Except her mother saying, once, "Don't talk to me about love. He doesn't really love you, he *used* you, Juni. Whatever comes his way, he deserves it."

So she'd had to resort to deception. Wireless internet wasn't even an option out here, the house being tucked into a valley eight miles from anything that resembled civilization. They did have dial-up on the old desktop computer in the nook off the kitchen, though, so in the middle of one night near the end of the first week, Juniper snuck downstairs to try to get online, but she'd been unable to get past the password screen and was locked out. When she came down for breakfast that next morning, she got lectures from everyone—on respecting others' property, on being deceitful, on needing to accept hard truths about Xavier and herself. They all just wanted what was best for her, couldn't she see that?

"What's best is if you all will just tell me how Xavier is!"

"Tell her," Lily said from the table where she was eating Froot Loops from the box.

"He's fine," Julia told her. "Home, going about his business."

"*Mom*. Is he in trouble, though?"

"The legal system is doing its job."

"Which means what?"

Lily said, "Yeah, what?"

"Honey," their grandfather said to Juniper, "it's hard to accept that there are rotten people in the world who're willing to mistreat others for their own gain. We understand how you must be feeling. It's an ugly truth. We wish we could've protected you from that."

"We *can* protect you from making it worse for yourself," said Julia. "We *are* protecting you."

"So this gathering is just one giant lovefest for me and my well-being," Juniper said. "Great."

"I love you," said Lily.

Julia began, "You'll thank us one—"

"Save it," Juniper had said, exiting the kitchen through the back door.

Today, though, she was going to get a break.

"You're sure you won't go with us to Dollywood?" asked Katie Whitman, Juniper's grandmother, on this, the first morning after Julia and Lottie had returned home. "We're going to the water park. Lily would love it if you'll come."

"No, thanks," said Juniper. She'd already been there once this visit, and she wanted some time to herself. The sole benefit of being here was that she got to spend her time outdoors in the woods and fields.

Katie said, "What will you do with your day?"

"The usual, I guess. Help Grandpa if he needs it. Go for a hike. I still haven't found that wild violet I saw in my guidebook."

"He's got a dentist appointment this afternoon—root canal, poor guy. You'll have to go with him, you know."

"That's fine," Juniper said, though she thought it was ridiculous. And then she thought of something else. "It's no problem at all. I can read while he's in there."

"All right. Well, there's still some macaroni salad, and I bought the grape soda pop you like."

"Thanks."

Katie looked at her with sympathy. "Hang in there, girl. Everything will be back to normal before much longer."

"Sure," Juniper said.

Normal was the last thing she wanted now.

"You'll be all right, waiting?" her grandfather asked her when his name was called. Juniper held up the book she'd brought. He said, "Good. This shouldn't be too long. Hour and a half, maybe."

She sat with her book, letting maybe five minutes pass, then got up and told the receptionist, "I need to use the bathroom." She'd pressed her hand to her belly and fixed her expression into one of discomfort.

"Sure, hon. Out that door and around the corner, in the hallway on the right. You need anything?"

Juniper smiled pitifully. "No, thanks. Probably just something I ate."

She went out the office door and out the main door, to the street. The library was just up the road, a quick walk to the place where she would finally be able to get some information.

Inside the library, she found an available computer terminal and sat down, searched for "Xavier Alston-Holt"—and blanched at the results.

She clicked and read, clicked and read, the stomach pain real, now . . .

Arrest on assault, kidnapping, and rape. And the court of public opinion already had him tried, convicted, and ready to be hanged.

He'd been assaulted, for real. "A prank," the news story said. Perpetrators still at large, but the public should not fear other random attacks.

Tony Evans, the DA, was quoted as saying, "The state will do everything in its power for the young lady who was victimized to ensure that justice is served."

A photo of Xavier at his bond hearing: the too-small orange jumpsuit. The shackles. The expression of weary terror. He faced twenty-five years in prison, maybe more. Lifetime sex-offender status.

Juniper stared at the screen. No wonder they'd kept her on lockdown. They all wanted him in prison. Brad, her mother, Lottie, the Whitman grandparents—*all* of them. They thought he was scum and she was, what? A precious little doll, an angel, *Junipure*. No way that she, in her pure state, could see what a player Xavier was. They'd better protect her from her own soft nature, keep her isolated. Possibly they were planning to leave her there for as long as it took to get Xavier locked away. They were so invested in their wishful thinking that they'd let him go to prison for *decades*.

"That can't be happening," she murmured, stunned.

A woman at the terminal beside her said, "What's that? Yours slow, too? We need those Google fibers here. I pay taxes."

"Sure," Juniper replied, thinking of what to do next. After a minute, she looked up a phone number and wrote it down, then went back to the front desk. "Is there a telephone I could use?"

The librarian gave her a skeptical look. "You don't have a phone?"

"It's broken. Please, this is an emergency."

"A 911 emergency?" he asked, reaching for a telephone nearby.

Juniper shook her head. "Not like that. A good friend is in serious trouble and I need to alert someone."

"Ah. In here," he said, leading Juniper to a small glass-fronted office, then left her there, closing the door as he went.

Her hands shook as she dialed the DA's office. When a clerk answered, she said, "May I please speak with Mr. Evans? My name is Juniper Whitman. He knows me. This is urgent."

"Miss Whitman, I'm sorry, Mr. Evans isn't available just now and will be in court all afternoon today. Can I take your number and have him return your call tomorrow?"

"Where is he? Can I reach his cell phone?"

"No, as I said, he'll be in court—"

"But where is he *now*? Maybe he can talk for just a second? I can't have him call me back, I won't have a phone after, like, three minutes from now. I'm not even kidding. This is an emergency."

"Let me put you on hold for a moment, all right?"

A moment was a minute, was two minutes. She doodled in the margins of the desk blotter, a calendar framed with local ads. From the information desk, the librarian glanced at Juniper with raised eyebrows. She mouthed, *It's okay,* and gave a reassuring half-smile.

"Juniper?" A voice came on the line. "Tony Evans. What's happening? Are you all right?"

In a rapid burst, she said, "You have to stop this, all this stuff about Xavier, the charges. It's not true. He didn't kidnap me or rape me, okay? I told everyone that's not how it was, but obviously you all don't believe me. I mean, okay, he and Brad did get into a fight, but it wasn't anything big, Brad didn't get hurt. I wasn't raped. Not even date rape. It was consensual, one hundred percent. You need to let him go, all right?"

"Hey, hey, slow down, now. You sound really upset."

"I am! This is all wrong. I just found out—it's, like, *way* out of control. I thought when *I said* it wasn't rape, nothing bad would—"

"Did Brad put you up to this?"

"What? No. I haven't even seen him since—"

"Brad didn't offer you something to get you to make this call? A little incentive? Trip to Paris, maybe? All the girls want to go there nowadays. Small price for him to pay for saving a hundred grand."

Juniper frowned in confusion. "I don't even understand what you're talking about. An incentive? How—?"

"The defendant, then. He's gotten to you and is pressuring or threatening you. Are you in danger right now?"

"*No*, I'm fine—"

"This sounds a lot like Brad's handiwork, I'm not gonna lie— and if so, you should just tell me now. You won't be in any trouble, I promise you. I'll make sure of that."

"Brad has nothing to do with me calling you. I'm saying Zay is innocent, okay? *I'm* saying it. Me, the supposed victim, am saying it to you directly."

"Oh, I hear you just fine. What I'm trying to get clear on is *why* you're saying it."

"And I just told you! He's innocent."

"All right, let's back up a minute," Tony said. "You just decide today that you need to all of a sudden call me up to declare that boy innocent of everything, and you want me to accept that you're doing this of your own accord."

"*Yes*."

"And you aren't in any danger right now."

"No, none. I would have called you sooner but I didn't know—I mean, nobody told me anything. So now you can let him go, okay?"

"You have not been offered an incentive, nor have you been threatened with harm, from anyone."

"That's right, yes, my God. *Now* will you drop the charges?"

"So, all right, Juniper, I'm skeptical, but let's say for the sake of argument that this is genuine on your part. Here's the situation: You're a seventeen-year-old girl who experienced a trauma. That event was witnessed by your stepdad, who intervened to stop it, and—"

"No, see, that's what I'm trying to say—"

"Hold on, let me finish. Whatever is motivating you today—and right now I'm going to take you at your word that you haven't been coerced—the situation remains just the same as it was the day of your report, and it's the duty of the state to address it. I don't mean to be condescending when I say this, but you're still a child, a minor in the eyes of the law. There are good reasons why minors can't vote; your view is myopic—it can't be otherwise, that's not your fault. And I'm saying it's myopic now, with this. Whereas me, I've been dealing with bad guys for longer than you've been alive.

"See, Brad wants me to work *his* angle, and you want me to make all this trouble go away—well, I understand it's unpleasant and you're concerned about Mr. Seemingly Nice Guy, but when you get some perspective, you'll see that you don't want him doing this same thing to other girls, nor do I."

The paternalistic tone grated, but Juniper, thinking she had some measure of power, said, "All due respect, Mr. Evans, you have it completely wrong, and I'm not going to be any part of this, no one can force me to—and without me, you don't have a case."

"Now, see, that's not so. You being contrary actually lends weight to my theory, is what it does. I believe I'm right about all of this, and I'll be able to demonstrate it to a jury. As I told Brad: I'm working from the evidence, and I'm going to do the job the citizens have elected me to do."

Juniper wanted to scream. How incredibly smug he was. How righteous.

In tears, she said, "I'm not some idiot child who doesn't know her own mind. *I* was the one who was in the relationship. *I* know whether I was being manipulated. Xavier didn't do anything wrong."

"Then he's got nothing to fear from a jury and I'll have to eat a big plate of crow. You see, sweetheart? Come on, now, don't cry. That's how justice is enacted in our country. If he chooses to stand trial, he'll get a fair hearing based on the evidence and the laws of the land.

"Now, I'll be glad to put you in touch with a counselor who can help you with this difficult situation—I'll have my assistant give your mother a call. I'm sorry to say I have to run. Will you be okay? Do you need help right now? I can get someone else on the line—"

"No," Juniper said. She slammed down the phone and was about to leave the office when she remembered an ad on the desk blotter: Tim's Taxi. She considered for a moment, then called the number.

When she hung up the phone and stood to leave, she saw a small crowd had gathered at the desk and were watching her with concern. Apparently she'd been loud. She left the little office, saying, "Sorry, I'm fine, nobody worry about me," and was out of the building quickly, heading not for the dentist's office but to the corner, where she'd get a taxi to Knoxville, for the nearest Greyhound depot. She might not have her phone or her car or the aid of one single person who could or would help, but she had the credit card her mother had long ago given her to use in case of emergency, and that was a start. She was desperate to see Xavier. She was going home.

The taxi driver said he could get her to Knoxville, but if her plan was to get a bus, she was out of luck today. "Next one's to-morrow, around six-thirty A.M."

"Seriously?" Juniper closed her eyes for a moment, collecting herself. Then she said, "Fine. A hotel near the depot, then."

When she arrived there later and checked in, she used the room phone to make the necessary call to her mother, who first thing jumped on her for the worry she'd caused her grandparents and how inconsiderate it was of her to leave that way and how she'd better turn right around and go back—

"But, okay," Juniper said, cutting Julia off, "just *listen* for a minute, will you?" She related her conversation with Tony Evans, then said, "Whatever you think of Xavier, never mind that for now.

Brad did something shady—I don't know what, exactly, but maybe you can find out?"

Juniper was still trying to piece it together: Brad showing up at the park; his reaction when he caught them; his insistence on involving the police and then getting her out of town . . . and now Tony Evans thought Brad wanted her to intervene on his behalf? Which had to mean that Brad saw some big advantage for himself in getting the charges dropped. Possibly this had been his long game from the minute he found them.

"Wait," Juniper said. "I think . . . See if he'll tell you this. I think he wanted to bargain with Xavier's mom somehow. Since she's suing him."

Julia said, "How would that even work?"

"I don't know. But I bet he meant to get her to drop the lawsuit in return for doing this huge 'favor' for her, since Tony's his friend and all."

Brad trying to be a hero, when he was the one who'd caused all the trouble.

She wished he had succeeded.

"I can't imagine . . ." Julia began. "I'll talk to him. But go back to your grandparents while I sort it out."

"No, I won't."

"Juniper, I know you're upset, but I don't want you traveling by yourself on a bus—"

"Too bad. I'm done letting you all *handle* me. Every one of you is a racist. You're willing to let an innocent person go to prison. Why should I listen to any of you?"

Julia didn't reply right away. Juniper waited, and when her mother spoke again, she said, "It's not that I'm a racist. I'm a mom. Until you've had—"

Juniper hung up.

With this telephone at hand, she could now call Pepper. She could call Xavier, too. Except she didn't know their phone numbers, and even if she'd known Xavier's, she would have called it only to learn that the number he'd had was no longer in service.

Tomorrow. Tomorrow she would make the hours-long trip home and then tell her mother everything—how Brad, with his kiss and his lust, had betrayed both Julia and her. How no matter what Brad said or did—or Julia, either, or Tony Evans, or anyone—she was going to go public with her side of the story, so Julia had better prepare herself.

Juniper would get Pepper to help—in fact, she'd go downstairs to the hotel's business center right now and email Pepper using their school accounts, get her on the job right away. They could use social media to bypass adults completely, get the word out, put some pressure on Tony Evans that way. Would it work? It had to have *some* effect, right?

Tomorrow she'd be able to see Xavier.

Tomorrow was so far away.

She found the business center, composed the email, told Pepper to call her at the hotel if she saw the message in time; bought yogurt and a bag of chips and a bottle of chocolate milk, plus trail mix for tomorrow's ride. Then, exhausted and heartsick, she returned to her room, showered, and burrowed under the sheets to sleep for ten restless hours, her dreams a mélange of stillborn actions and thwarted efforts and a Sunday school performance in which she was onstage getting ready to sing and she wet herself in front of everyone.

It was Rosa Morton, the octogenarian who lived next door to the Whitmans, who told us the Whitmans argued that evening. She'd been outside in the backyard watering her potted tomato plants, since the storms that had threatened all day failed to deliver more than a few fat raindrops. The Whitmans were in their garage, where Brad was busy waxing that flashy car of his. "I'd been talking with him about it not ten minutes earlier," Rosa said. "How he likes to do the waxing himself when he has time—he made a joke about taking care of a car with the same loving care every woman deserves."

Rosa couldn't hear everything he and Julia said to each other over the music Brad was playing out there, but she knew they were getting into it about *something*.

Well, it happens that Julia Whitman, who didn't yet know the full extent of Brad's deceptions, understood enough to know she wasn't pleased about her husband playing games with her daughter's welfare, his trying to take advantage of the situation so that he could create leverage over Valerie Alston-Holt. She wasn't sure what to think anymore about Xavier; maybe he wasn't the "slick operator" they'd been so sure he had to be.

Maybe it was Brad who was slick. Maybe *she* was the one who'd been manipulated.

Even as the thought flitted into Julia's brain, she pushed it out, rejected it. Brad couldn't be as bad as that, because if he was that sort of person, what did that make her?

48

At the same time Juniper had been on the phone with Julia, Xavier was walking around in a former cigar warehouse. The building now held long rows of booths fronted by tables on which every manner of firearm and blade was displayed like candy for the paranoid home-owner, for the protectionist homesteader, for the violence junkie who liked to collect and pretend. Reasonable people buy weapons, too; we understand that. These shows, though, don't tend to attract the ordinary weekend hunter or the individual who's looking for ba-sic effective self-protection and is willing to do the necessary hoop-jumping and training to be a safe and responsible gun owner. Some of the people who go to gun shows are angry. Some of them feel hopeless. They feel powerless, helpless, and are looking to fix what-ever broke them. Some have a fire in their belly, a mission to fulfill.

Xavier, who was not exactly afraid to be here but not exactly confident either, walked the aisles musing on his plans for more than twenty minutes. He knew he had to do this, this way, now, or he might never get another chance. Still, now that he was here, he felt nervous and out of place. Conspicuous.

Finally he approached a table and asked the young man stationed there, "So how does this work if I want to buy a gun from you?"

"Handgun or long gun?" said the man, who wasn't much older than Xavier.

"There's a difference? Not in the guns. Obviously. In how it works to buy one."

The man seemed to be trying not to smirk. He said, "You want a handgun, I need to see a permit and ID."

"But not for the other?" Xavier said, and the man nodded. "Okay, then I'm looking for one of those."

"Well, you're looking right at 'em."

With his good hand, Xavier picked up a smallish rifle. "How much for this one?"

"This one here? This is a Ruger Mini-14, semiauto. It can take a twenty- or a five-round magazine, though why you'd want only five when you can have twenty is a question with no sensible answer. But if you're looking for more than twenty, I've got its cousin here—"

"No, twenty's fine. How much?"

"One-fifty." The man squinted at him. "Hey, did I see you on the news?"

Xavier's pulse spiked. "The news?" he said as casually as he could manage. "For what?"

"Like . . . I don't know, you rescued a drowning kid or something? But obviously not, or you'd be like, 'Yeah, you saw me.'"

"Yeah, no. Must've been someone who looks like me. You said one-fifty. Does that cover ammo, too?"

"No, that's an add-on. How much you want?"

"One . . . box?"

"One box of .223 Remingtons. You got it."

"Credit card okay?"

"Money's money."

Xavier didn't ask for instructions on how to load or shoot the thing. That's what the internet was for.

49

Brad left his big, gleaming white house at his usual time, backing the Maserati from the garage and pulling onto the street while the sun was still well below the tree line.

The engine purred politely while he eased through the neighborhood. Early as it was, there was no traffic on the surface roads and only a little on the highway. This gave him the chance to run through the gears. He enjoyed the engine's growl, simultaneously dangerous and controlled. Same as him, he liked to think.

Though now and then he was thwarted, sure. That was the nature of risk. For example, Tony had set him back and made him look bad to his own attorney and Valerie Alston-Holt's and the boy's, too; they must all now figure him for some kind of fool. The game wasn't over yet, though. He was still looking for another angle. He'd form a new strategy. He always did.

As for Julia's being pissed at him—well, that was collateral fallout. In truth, he was surprised she'd gone along with his story as easily and for as long as she had. She would calm down once Juniper got home. The misadventure would be good for their mother-daughter bonding, and before long the whole thing would blow over. Julia knew not to bite too hard the hand that fed her.

This was surely what Brad was thinking about while he backed into his spot at Whitman HVAC and got out of his car. He was ever all about the game he was playing. How to get his way this time. How to have his way always.

He didn't notice the young man parked across the street.

Imagine Xavier standing there, sighting the rifle over the roof of his old Honda, using the roof to help him keep the gun steady. His splinted left hand is screaming at him. His right index finger is on the trigger. His eye is at the sight. He's watching Brad open the Maserati's glossy door, sees him begin to climb out.

He's not happy about being here. There is no joy in this. He's in a corner, though, and Brad Whitman is the guy who pushed him there, who set him up against a system that has its mind made up and only pretends to presume innocence.

Young men who are innocent of the crime for which they're sent to prison are an especially cursed subset. They're too young to be jaded and toughened by life. They have no skills for survival inside, where their prison mates are actual criminals. They lose their faith in authority figures. They lose their faith. They have been bludgeoned by unfairness and are left cowed by the beating. They get no respect from the hardened men, who want them to stop whining about their innocence, who disrespect them for not being man enough to have done the thing they didn't do. So, then, if you're going to go to prison, go for a reason.

Xavier isn't going to go to prison, though. He's thought this through—of course he has, or he wouldn't be standing here, finger poised on the cold steel trigger, with the terrified confidence of a new soldier. Even guilty, he wouldn't survive incarceration. The small, shared cell where there's no privacy for anything, not even thought. The inability to play music—this as much as anything would kill him, is already killing him, in spirit if not in fact.

The absence of true darkness in which to have restful sleep. The absence of silence. The constant barrage of coarse conversation.

The body odors. The cleanser odors. The inability to eat when you feel like it, to prepare your own food, to have a snack, to go out for tacos. The inability to go *anywhere,* to hang out with friends, to watch the sun rise or set. The sameness of it all. The pointless labor of laundering clothes or mopping floors or washing dishes for years and years and years on end—pointless not because it doesn't need to be done, but because there is nothing to be gained in doing it the way there would be if that was his work on the outside, if after doing the work he got to go home to a girl he loves.

He has no hope of that. As far as he can see, Juniper has cut her losses. The situation for her is ugly, he knows that. He doesn't expect her to stick her neck out for him beyond what she's already done. There are consequences she might not feel capable of facing.

Though he wishes she would, even if it wouldn't change anything.

But even if she does still love him, what good would he ever be to her? He's no good to anybody now, not even himself.

Xavier aims the rifle.

The first shot hits the Maserati, shattering the windshield. The second hits the hood. The third hits Brad Whitman in the shoulder and spins him hard sideways. The fourth—a lucky shot, since the shooter has no training and is merely eyeing the scope and pulling the trigger hopefully—goes into Brad's back and straight through his aorta, piercing it precisely on its way through and out of his body.

At this time of morning in the industrial park, no one else is around. Various people who are some distance away hear the gunshots. None is close enough to fear for his or her safety. They hear the shots and wait. When there's no more noise, they go on with their morning activities, confident that whatever it was—even if gunshots—someone closer by will be managing the problem. No need to get involved.

Xavier watches Brad for several minutes to make sure he's done what he set out to do. His heartbeat thunders in his ears. There is the *planning to do,* and then there is the *doing,* and they are not so alike as he'd thought. The doing is so incredibly satisfying. So horribly wonderful. The noise in his ears is the rhythm of an orchestra performing the accompaniment to a beautiful, tragic aria, the song a lament on how it didn't have to happen this way and yet it had to happen this way.

When his success seems assured, Xavier puts the rifle in his trunk and gets into his car. He drives away at the prescribed speed limit while Brad lies beside the $160,000 sports car bleeding—but not as copiously as one might think, because when the heart's primary "out" line is punctured, the blood that the heart forces into that line in its last futile contractions pools in the chest cavity, where there's lots of space to hold it.

Is Brad Whitman dead at this point? Most likely, and if not, he certainly will be by the time his employee Brenda arrives at seven and finds him.

He may have a full minute, maybe more, of excruciating pain, along with the terrible realization that he's been outflanked somehow and this is his ignominious end. Xavier hopes so.

———————————————

But no, this was not what happened. As Xavier sat in his car watching Brad, he thought the whole plan through further, thought it *all the way* through, saw himself the way the news media would see him if he'd done it: just one more black rapist murderous thug doing what all those thugs do, right?

They wouldn't say, *Here was a young man who was pushed to the wall, a product of our institutional and cultural injustice who sought only to enact* real *justice where otherwise there would never be any.*

That was the fantasy he'd been nurturing, and if he executed Brad Whitman, all he'd be doing was creating the version of himself they all so badly wanted to believe was real. It wouldn't matter what his reasons were. It wouldn't matter that their actions had *created* him. All anyone would say, all anyone would hear, was *murderer.*

Which was what he would be.

He started the car and drove toward his other destination, while at the industrial park Brad continued into the building.

As Xavier pulled to a stop at an empty crossroads, an object at the base of his windshield caught his eye. A plastic bag stuffed into the top of his car hood, almost hidden by fallen pine straw. He got out, retrieved the bag, extracted a folded note.

Zay: I finally got home after the park and now my parents are making me leave for my grandparents' house in Tennessee. I don't have my phone or computer, so this note is all I can do. They're trying to convince me you manipulated me into everything and today was basically date rape. I just can't believe that's true. I don't want to believe it. I want to believe you love me even though you never actually said it. If you do, then just know that I love you too and somehow all this will just be a bad dream we'll put behind us. A story we'll tell each other while we drive our food truck to San Francisco, right? I love the Zay I saw, and I guess that's all I can say until I see you again.
    Juniper

Well, now. This explained a lot.

Juniper's words warmed Xavier while he drove at the prescribed speed limit the rest of the way to the state park, as planned. Those words gave him peace of mind, and strength. A measure of happiness, even. She loved him. She hadn't done him wrong.

The state park in early morning was alive with deer and birds and raccoons and fox, some of the creatures waking, some ending their watchful nights by climbing into dens or nests or by perching in shaded groves and tucking beak and eyes under- wing. Leaves dripped with the night's humidity, the droplets becoming falling diamonds where the sunlight caught them. It was a place of peace and beauty. There, now, was serenity.

Xavier drove in and parked in the same spot as he had the last time he'd been here. He swallowed a Vicodin, then took the rifle, his phone, and a notebook with him into the cabin and sat down on the floor where he and Juniper had spread the blanket that day.

Where had the blanket ended up? In Juniper's Land Rover? In the police evidence locker, with his knife and the wine bottle?

Evidence.

There had been a crime, all right.

The wooden floor was cool and worn smooth by so many years of visiting picnickers and campers. Xavier ran his hands over the wood and thought of how he and Juniper had sat here eating and laughing, both of them a little dazed by wine and anticipation.

He thought of how they'd believed they had all the answers to their future, that they'd needed only to let time pass and then they could access it.

He thought of how Juniper had pulled him down beside her. How nervous he'd been about making the experience a good one for her. How awkward but also sort of beautiful it had been as they'd fitted themselves together. How he'd looked into her eyes and felt . . . *everything*.

That moment. That was the one he was cementing in his mind.

50

The police officers found Xavier's note inside the cabin, along with directions on where they might look for his body. With the note was his phone. He'd turned off the phone's security to make it easy for Valerie to watch the video message he'd recorded, along with a short song he'd composed and recorded especially for her a month or so earlier, intending it for a montage he'd planned to give her right before leaving for San Francisco.

In his video message, recorded inside the cabin with sunlight from a window painting him in full color, he faced the camera and said, "All your heroes and mine, too, are people who one way or another sacrificed themselves for something important—some gave their lives, and not because they *wanted* to die, right? But because they couldn't live with things the way they were. That's me. There is no way out for me, Mama. No future that's worth living. Alive, I'm useless to everybody, including myself. Nothing to offer anybody. You get that, don't you?

"I know you'll be angry and upset and sad and freaked out, all of that. But after that, be proud of me for not giving in. Share this so that everyone knows how fucked up things are and how the wrong people have too much power and that's why this happened and it shouldn't happen to anyone ever again.

"Anyway, I love you so much." His eyes were teary here, and his voice cracked a little. "You are a great mom. I think—well, I hope, anyway—that we'll meet again up there in heaven. Not for a really long time, though, okay?

"Also: I'm not scared. It'll be a *relief*." He looked away for a moment.

"Dad's waiting for me, and I bet he'll be like, 'Hey, finally I get some time with my boy!'" Here Xavier smiled.

Then he said, "Last thing: Tell Juniper I love her, too. See you later," and ended the recording.

Also for Juniper was a haiku in a sealed envelope for Valerie to deliver whenever it could be put directly into Juniper's hands.

The rifle had gotten wedged between two boulders at the river's edge. His body was downstream a ways, thanks to the swift current. The coroner told Valerie they'd made a positive ID by his fingerprints, and recommended strongly that she not view his remains. She took that advice.

51

The day of the funeral came with summer's aggressive heat. A clear sky to start (Carolina blue). Humidity in the 70 percent range at one o'clock, when the graveside service was scheduled to begin. Clouds forming, as they are wont to do. Thunder later? Maybe. As we all got ready to go pay our respects, we knew we would perspire heavily in our black dresses and pants and suits. A small sacrifice. Tiny. You *should* be uncomfortable at a funeral like this one, that's what some of us were saying.

In one car en route to the cemetery, a debate got under way: Was Valerie some kind of bad-luck charm? She'd lost her husband, and now she'd lost her son. Should Chris Johnson be worried? (We might assert here that in this country only white men have even a shot at worry-free lives, and thus are the ones likely to say such a thing.)

In another car, no one said a word.

The public cemetery was vast. Rolling hills. Great huge oaks. At the grave site, a cerulean canopy offered shade for several rows of folding chairs. We all came out, driving slowly through the grounds, following one another and the signage. ALSTON-HOLT, and an arrow pointing the way toward where Tom, too, had been laid to rest. All, that is, except for Brad Whitman. Julia, chagrined by her own failures and missteps, disgusted by Brad, had stood in their living room with the girls looking on and told Brad that he didn't deserve to be a part of their lives and that they deserved better than him. She told him to pack his necessities and leave. Someone said they'd heard he went golfing while the funeral was under way; we hope that's not true but we don't doubt the possibility.

Having seen Pepper's viral video about what the DA and Brad had done to her friends (made before the horrible news got out), reporters with their cameramen were present, keeping a respectful distance for now.

Valerie and Chris sat underneath the canopy, along with the various members of their families. Tom's mother had made the trip. Her pale face stood out, there beneath the canopy, reminded us and those reporters, too, that Xavier hadn't been all one thing.

The murmuring started, alerting folks who hadn't noticed yet that Juniper and Julia Whitman were walking up now, and what would Valerie think of that? By this time everyone knew that Juniper was the girl involved, the one who'd allegedly been raped. We didn't know yet the ins and outs of her involvement.

Juniper walked over to Valerie and Valerie stood. Had they spoken before now? Juniper's eyes were on the ground. Her shoulders shook. Valerie put one hand on Juniper and wiped her own eyes with the other. They spoke briefly, and then Juniper went to stand with Julia.

When the crowd was more or less as large as it would become (several hundred, white, black, strangers, friends, activists, everything), the minister, a stately woman with gray dreadlocks and wrinkled deep-brown skin, stepped up onto a painted wooden platform and faced the assembled crowd.

She called out, "Welcome, everyone. We'll start here."

We'll start here.

They were just words, the same way this story is just words. Words, though, are how we humans have been communicating with one another almost since time before time. What has more meaning to humankind than words? Without a call to action, change rarely occurs.

Start here, please, in communion with one another despite our differences, recognizing that without *start* there is no *end.*

Epilogue

One of Julia Whitman's first actions upon hearing Juniper's account of the uninvited kiss was to put the portrait from the Purity Ball into the trash. Stuffed it in, frame and all. Their wedding pictures went next.

Julia had always liked the idea of living in Colorado, someplace in the mountains or with a mountain view. Lottie said it'd be easier to breathe without so much humidity, so after Julia's attorney had tended to the marital separation and custody agreement, Julia hired a mover and took a house in Lakewood, a Denver suburb, for Lottie, Lily, and herself. There in Lakewood, she signed up for yoga-teacher training, hoping she would learn both to access and guide others' connection to inner peace and confidence. Strength. Balance. Flexibility. Atonement, too, was something she would work on. It was a process.

Brad had to give her more than half of his net worth—and in order to do so, was forced to borrow against his assets, a loan he had difficulty repaying after word got out. A lot fewer people wanted to do business with Whitman HVAC, no surprise. He'd have to sell pretty much everything. Bankruptcy and a change of venue would wipe his slate clean, he figured. As with weeds, it's hard to keep men like him down for long.

———————

After some very dark days in which Juniper considered following Xavier's example, she realized that no, she needed to follow his *intentions,* and elected to finish school at Westover in Connecticut, a boarding school that she thought would give her the jumping-off point she needed for the new plans she'd made for her future. Come fall, she'll begin her college program to study sociology and poli sci at Columbia.

Her eight months of being removed from her former life have almost made it seem as if none of last year's events could possibly have happened. As if Xavier was a figment from a dream. As if Brad was a figure from some Aeschylus tale they'd read in English class.

She attends church now and then, more as a seeker than a believer. Skepticism is, she feels, appropriate. She calls home—that is, the new Colorado home—once a week. Lily has begun telling knock-knock jokes again. That's progress.

Xavier *is* a figment from her dreams. She's sees him often. They talk. He plays songs for her. His haiku is taped to her dorm room mirror.

Juniper is thinking of Valerie today. Maybe, soon, she'll call her and tell her about the program, about the courses she'll be taking, about her ultimate goal of becoming a defense attorney and then a DA. Maybe she'll tell Valerie the story Xavier told her, about the time he and Valerie went to visit her mother, how it was a best day. Maybe she'll tell her about the dreams.

Maybe Valerie will take the call.

———————

Valerie found a farmhouse for rent in central Virginia and moved into it in August of last year, entrusting Ellen and a Realtor with the sale of her house. She was in that farmhouse on the wooden front porch the day the couple moved into her Oak Knoll house, and she was out walking a winding country road with Chris on the day the tree service arrived to dismantle the great old oak.

Come December she had bought the house and nineteen acres of land, a lot of it pasture. Over the winter, she read and she wrote and she put logs on a fire and she drank bourbon and she adopted a dog, a mixed breed with strong Catahoula leopard features. She named the dog Grace.

On a raw late February day, Valerie walked down the long gravel drive to her mailbox. The heavy sky spit snow and light icy rain. She opened the box and found just one envelope, from Wilson Everly, Esquire.

> I am honoring my promise to act on your behalf and leave you be until I hear from you—save for this note, which I undertake in order to inform you that we've made a deposit to the account whose information you provided when we filed suit. The case concluded last month, with KDC and Whitman agreeing to pay a total of $335,000 plus your fees and expenses.
>
> I hope time has laid its consoling hands upon you. You are in our prayers.

With Grace at her feet, Valerie laid out big white sheets of craft paper and drew a map of the pasture over which the house looked, a wide, long, descending field of grasses that had gone from green to gold and now to brown but would be green again. Here in this pasture she would plant one oak tree for each year of Xavier's life.

And now spring has arrived, and with it, a team of UVA students who have volunteered to dig and plant. On this brisk sunny morning comes the truck with the trees themselves, tall and straight and ready, the way Xavier had been.